D1257964

WAR PAINT AND ROUGE

Novels by ROBERT W. CHAMBERS

WAR PAINT AND ROUGE

GITANA
THE RAKE AND THE HUSSY
THE PAINTED MINX
THE SUN HAWK
THE DRUMS OF AULONE
THE MAN THEY HANGED
THE MYSTERY LADY
THE GIRL IN GOLDEN RAYS
AMERICA
THE HI-JACKERS
ERIS
THE TALKERS
THE FLAMING JEWEL
THE SLAYER OF SOULS
IN SECRET
THE LITTLE RED FOOT
THE CRIMSON TIDE
THE LAUGHING GIRL
THE RESTLESS SEX
BARBARIANS
THE DARK STAR
THE GIRL PHILIPPA
WHO GOES THERE!
ATHALIE
THE BUSINESS OF LIFE
THE GAY REBELLION
THE STREETS OF ASCALON
THE COMMON LAW
THE FIGHTING CHANCE
THE YOUNGER SET
THE DANGER MARK
THE FIRING LINE
JAPONETTE
QUICK ACTION
THE ADVENTURES OF A MODEST MAN
ANNE'S BRIDGE

THE HAPPY PARROT
THE ROGUE'S MOON
BETWEEN FRIENDS
THE BETTER MAN
POLICE!!!
SOME LADIES IN HASTE
THE TREE OF HEAVEN
THE TRACER OF LOST PERSONS
THE HIDDEN CHILDREN
THE MOONLIT WAY
CARDIGAN
THE RECKONING
THE MAID-AT-ARMS
AILSA PAIGE
SPECIAL MESSENGER
THE HAUNTS OF MEN
LORRAINE
MAIDS OF PARADISE
ASHES OF EMPIRE
THE RED REPUBLIC
BLUE-BIRD WEATHER
A YOUNG MAN IN A HURRY
THE GREEN MOUSE
IOLE
THE MYSTERY OF CHOICE
THE CAMBRIC MASK
THE MAKER OF MOONS
THE KING IN YELLOW
IN SEARCH OF THE UNKNOWN
THE CONSPIRATORS
A KING AND A FEW DUKES
IN THE QUARTER
OUTSIDERS

WAR PAINT AND ROUGE

By Robert W. Chambers

D. APPLETON AND COMPANY

NEW YORK ✳ LONDON ✳ MCMXXXI

Dedicated to my
old friend
SIR GILBERT PARKER
who could have done this job
much better than I have done it.

CONTENTS

CONTENTS

WAR PAINT AND ROUGE

CHAPTER I

THE PRETTY SAVAGE

IT was June in New York City, and it was on a hot
Sunday morning that the Commander-in-Chief wor-
shiped at St. Paul's, attended by his staff and the general officers of his expeditionary force.

After church, walking from St. Paul's Chapel down
Broadway and across by Bowling Green toward Whitehall, Mike Whelan continued to talk about the war, and
how sick he was of it already. And the war scarcely begun, which was to last seven years! But neither of us
knew that.

He told me that one of Hardy's tuppenny cruisers had
recently brought in a forty-five-gun French frigate loaded
with provisions, clothing, arms, one hundred and ten recruits for the Regiment Artois, two score peasant-
farmers and artisans, twenty women, and gold and silver
money to pay the garrisons at Quebec and Louisbourg.

"You can have a French woman for yourself if you
like, John Cardress," he added.

"What for?"

"Musha, what's any woman for? I know if you
don't!"

But I told him, drily, that I did not go below stairs for a
mistress, and that the enlisted regimental women allowed
to each company were no concern of mine, either in the
French service or in our own.

I added that I could do with an assistant gardener for

I

McGinnis's company. But that Dick Rogers' battalion was never around to eat the fruits of its own farming, so to employ a gardener seemed extravagant.

"Well," said Captain Whelan, "do what pleases you, John. I'm only telling you that Otway's regiment also lacks a gardener and an assistant to grow vegetables at Fort Edward, and there's two companies of the 35th and the Royal American battalion which lack their quota of enlisted women."

We walked on past the fort and out under the ramparts toward Whitehall where we saw the French frigate, *The Pretty Savage,* lying in the stream with her recruits still aboard her as prisoners. We could see them very plainly in their white uniforms faced with bright colour, wandering about the deck or leaning over the rail to gaze at the city of New York with a humorous philosophy entirely French.

But on the wharf, their bundles at their feet, and chatting amiably with our British sentries, stood a long line of French peasants, men and women, not at all disturbed by their predicament as captives.

The girls were coquetting and laughing with our idle soldiery who had come down to Whitehall to look them over.

"They're not so handsome," remarked Whelan, "but they're healthy wenches and well planted on their legs. . . . There's a good-looking young woman—the one with the blue kerchief and white collarette and apron. She'll wash your shirts and darn your stockings and keep you warm o' nights."

In a low voice I bade him go to the devil. He laughed and went over and spoke to the wench.

I noticed several of Webb's officers on the wharf, and one or two of Abercrombie's—Lieutenant John Montressor under orders for the North; Major Eyre, down from Albany—others on leave in New York.

John Montressor, a vain, impertinent young man who presumed upon his father's reputation, swaggered about selecting this man and that wench without consulting their wishes at all. Which, of course, was improper, they being civilian captives and not obliged to work at all unless they wished to.

There was considerable saucy talk among the women about "rosbiffs" and "goddams"—in other words, Englishmen—and one rather pretty girl stuck out the tip of her tongue at John Montressor, replying with the monosyllables "flut" and "zut" to his invitations to enlist in the expeditionary force or in Webb's.

Whelan was rather short with the young engineer. He went about with characteristic Irish sympathy and affability, inquiring among the French for those of good will who desired positions as farmers, gardeners, artisans, servants, or who preferred regimental enlistment as bonnes à tout faire to the battalions in any of the three armies now ready to begin this long deferred business of deciding once and forever whether America was to become entirely English or French, and remain so until the last trumpet cracked the world in half.

As I sauntered along the line of smiling, gossiping prisoners on the wharf where a brisk sea wind was blowing their kerchiefs, coiffes, skirts and blouses, my random glance met a pair of dark, intelligent eyes fixed upon me; and, as I halted involuntarily, a smile broke out over

3

the smooth sun-browned face of a young lad who stood clasping his bundle of clothing to his bosom as a woman clasps a baby.

His smile was irresistible. I smiled back and said in French:

"Well, mon garçon, you don't seem to worry over the pickle you're in."

He just stood and smiled at me, and I continued to smile back. He seemed to be about eleven or twelve years old, to judge from his height and features—smooth, clear, bright coloured as a girl with his black-fringed brown eyes and carmine mouth and not a bone showing in his slight, plump body.

He wore sea-jacket, knitted shirt, sailor's béret, farmer's blouse of blue linen, and a peasant's straw-stuffed sabots.

I said to him: "Why do you smile so gaily and persistently at me, my lad? Yours certainly is a friendly soul."

He said in a girlish voice which maturity had not yet cracked to change to a masculine and sonorous timbre:

"I scarcely know why I smile, my Captain. But as soon as I saw you—'Voici,' thought I, 'mon affair! Behold my destiny which arrives garbed in a strange green uniform and bottes sauvage!'"

"And why," said I, much amused, "should you suppose that the uniform of Major Bob Rogers' Rangers had anything to do with your destiny, my young friend?"

"God knows, sir. . . . But you have a kind blue eye, my captain."

I said: "What have you been, my boy—a mousse?—a sailors' lad? Or do you know the farm, the plow, the basse-cour better?"

"Ah!" cried the child, "I know best of all that his honour, my English captain, would never let me go to prison from fear of crueller treatment."

"Have I said that I mean to employ you? You seem very gay and over-confident."

"Ah, Monsieur, my confidence and gaiety are due to youth; so be pleased to pardon these hardy faults and take me for your servant—"

"I already have a soldier servant—"

The consternation in the brown eyes touched me.

"Come," said I, "you may be useful to me. You seem a nice, clean, wholesome lad, and honest and clever. What do you expect to do for a British—or rather for a Colonial officer?"

"Anything! Anything, my Captain!" said the lad earnestly. "Only for God's sake take me!"

"Yes, but what could you do for me?" I insisted, smiling.

"Everything!" he cried.

"Oh, can you do everything?"

"I can attempt everything."

I laughed at his wide-eyed eagerness.

He had taken off his blue cloth béret and stood with curly, dishevelled head bent and his cap clasped to his chest.

After a little, as I said nothing further: "Don't let them send me to prison," said the boy, "—I can't stand it! I can't go to prison—"

"But, my lad, there are plenty of other officers to take you if I don't—"

"I beg you, sir," he said in a voice almost a whisper, and I was surprised at the strained and tragic intensity

5

of his gaze, and saw his knuckles whiten as he clutched his cap.

"Very well," said I, "what's your name?"

"Sandi."

"Sandi? What kind of name is that?"

"God knows, my Captain. It's all I have."

"Well, Sandi—pick up your bundle then. I'll speak to Captain Whelan who is commissary of prisoners."

"Oh, am I to follow you, sir?"

"Well, yes. Fall out and sling your packet over your back—"

I turned to where Mike Whelan had been, but he was gone. However, I saw O'Rourke, his lieutenant, and beckoned him.

"Tell Captain Whelan," said I, "that I'm taking this boy, Sandi, for the New Yorkers' garden at Fort Edward. I'll see Captain Whelan at General Headquarters later."

Then, smilingly, I nodded to my new servant lad who instantly shouldered his bundle and fell into step at my heels. So I adjusted my sword, shoulder belt, and sash and, taking an absent-minded pinch of snuff, shoved the lacquered box into the pocket of my scarlet waistcoat and sauntered away up Bowling Green, amused at myself and wondering how I was to get my boy Sandi to Fort Edward if, as I expected, I sailed with my Lord Loudon to take the amazing fortress-city of Louisbourg.

So I and my new servant marched up Broadway to the Indian Queen Tavern where I had lodging; and into it and up the stairs we proceeded with gravity and every decorum, to my chambers.

"Sandi," said I, "are you hungry?"

The boy let fall his bundle and sat down breathlessly.

"Well, I'm damned," said I. "What sort of servant are you who sits down in his master's presence?"

"Oh," cried the lad in a panic, "I'm sorry, sir. I'm not a servant—just a poor lad—and unaccustomed to service with the great—"

"Well, sit down, Sandi," said I, laughing at his blushes and his fright; "I'm not cruel—and you look very hot and tired and dusty."

"Oh, my Captain, I am so very hot and thirsty," he ventured.

This was a fine way to break in a servant boy. I laughed as I rang for a cooling pot of chilled flip; and when it was fetched I, still laughing, poured it out and offered it.

"Don't you get tipsy, Sandi," said I as he eagerly grasped the mug with both hands and began to drain it.

I don't know why I thought it so funny. It was as though I had gone crazy and adopted this French peasant boy—this smiling, scared, eager youngster with his black-lashed brown eyes and his curly mop of clean hair.

"Now, listen, Sandi," said I. "I'm spoiling you. Don't think for a moment I'm going to permit you any such indulgences. You're going to work and keep your proper place. You'll serve, probably, as assistant gardener for Dick Rogers' battalion at Fort Edward."

"M-my Captain?"

"Well, what is it?"

"You will be at this fort—this Fort Edward? Yes?"

"I will not!"

"Oh, mon Dieu! Why do you send me there?" he cried in a desolate voice.

7

"Well, I don't need you. I don't want you around under foot—"

"My God, sir, I won't get under your feet—"

"Come," said I, "you're a little impertinent, my lad. It's none of your business where I send you. And if you don't want to go to Fort Edward you have only to say so and I'll send you back to *The Pretty Savage*—"

"Oh, no!—oh, please!—" the horror in the brown eyes was unmistakable.

"Well, then, Sandi, conduct properly and with dignity, decorum, and submission. What the devil!—you are a French prisoner taken by one of our ships of war—and I am trying to give you a pleasant place to work in and forget your troubles."

"Very well, my Captain," said the boy meekly.

I looked at the lad; his brown eyes met mine—irresistibly, and I smiled at him.

"I'm going to a council of war," said I, "so, while I'm gone, you take pipe clay and polish, and shine up my dress uniform, for I'll require it tonight."

"Yes, my Captain."

"In the meanwhile, you go down to the kitchen of the inn and say that Captain Cardress sent you, and that they are to give you a good dinner and a half pint of small beer to wash it down."

"Yes, sir. . . . Shall I continue to wear my wooden shoes?"

"Why not?"

"Only—everybody was laughing at us on Broadway, sir."

"Have you any leather shoes in your packet?"

"Yes, sir."

8

"Very well; put 'em on. And if you've anything more civilized and more English than béret and blouse, put 'em on and try to look like a gentleman's servant until you go north to Fort Edward.

"After that," said I, "it won't make any difference what you look like."

That evening, in my chambers, smoking a long pipe and reading the New York *Mercury,* with a mug of chilled flip at my elbow, I chanced to look up to discover Sandi's eyes fixed intently on mine.

I don't know why, but it seemed like the gaze of an impertinent dog that meant to trick me.

CHAPTER II

THE MOON FLOWER SAILS

THE delay was maddening to me and to almost all the officers and men. But the summer heat in New York was merely making his lordship drowsy.

A council of war had been called for two o'clock. This matter of the Admiral was becoming serious.

The room in which we met was hot and stuffy and smelled of wine. It was Lord Loudon's dining-room.

Officer after officer, being called upon in turn, offered stupid or bored opinions.

His lordship's wine-heavy eyes sought the window and wandered vacantly up Wall Street to where, at its junction with Broadway, one of the newly arrived regiments was passing.

He didn't know which regiment. He didn't care. Neither the distant drone of their fifes and drums, nor the nearer buzz of his purple-jowled colonels offering valueless military opinions concerning the military situation, aroused him from increasing lethargy.

A violent desire to take a nap began to obsess him. He was tired. He was weary of everything—of America, of Pitt, of his fellow Scot, Vice-Admiral Holburne whose ships had not yet arrived. He was weary of this council of war and the commonplace people who composed it—colonels, brigadiers, engineers, aides-de-camp. He was weary of his King.

John Campbell, Earl of Loudon, had listened to his

officers as long as he was able; and he knew that if he tried to listen any longer he'd fall asleep.

I've forgotten which brigadier was talking when the Scotch peer yawned fearfully, blinked at the speaker, shook himself in his gorgeous military plumage like a big scarlet and gold feathered bird.

Then he picked up a walnut, gravely cracked and ate it, slowly swallowed another glass of Madeira.

"Gentlemen," said he thickly, "here's the whole cursed business in a pickled walnut shell; and you may take it or leave it—for there's no good talking about it any further.

"Here's the question: is America to remain English or French? English, of course. But the French own most of it. How are we to get rid o' them? By continuing our petty fighting? By making petite guerre? By nipping at Crown Point, nibbling at Ticonderoga, pulling frightful faces and shouting booh! at them in Montreal?"

Some of the giddy young staff officers were laughing, but the Commander-in-Chief gave them an owlish look.

"The way to rid North America of the French," said he, with the dissipated dignity which characterized him, "is to take that big French fortress-city which for fifty years has terrorized this continent. It is an incredible thing that such a walled, moated, and monstrous menace as Louisbourg should exist in the Western World. It is foreign to this land, it is barbaric, medieval! It belongs among the great fortress-cities of Europe, not in North America.

"Quebec was a warning to us. We should have stormed it and pulled it down long ago!

"Now, in addition, we've this formidable business of

Louisbourg on our hands—to be attended to before we can attend to Quebec and New Orleans.

"That's all very well. But here is the trouble. Here am I in this sultry, sweltering city of New York. Here are you, gentlemen. And here is my army—six or seven thousand of the best regular troops in the world—waiting in this broiling June weather to go aboard transports and sail for Halifax and Louisbourg!

"But where is the British Admiral and his warships, who has been ordered to New York to escort and protect our helpless soldiers in their transports?

"Where the devil are his battleships and frigates?" repeated Lord Loudon irritably. "He isn't here! He ought to be here. There are three French battle-squadrons cruising off Louisbourg, waiting to sink us. What's Vice Admiral Holburne going to do about them?

"I've told His Majesty and His Majesty's Prime Minister, Mr. Pitt, that I am going to take Louisbourg. Instead of our pitiable annual attempt upon Crown Point and Ticonderoga, I have chosen to attack France in America at her most tender and vital point, Louisbourg. It's my own idea. Mr. Pitt says it is his idea, also. Maybe. I scarcely expect any credit for it. That's not important.

"But if I and my army dawdle away the summer, marching up and down Broadway and waiting for Admiral Holburne, what is the King going to say to me? And what is Mr. Pitt going to *do* to me?

"Here's my quandary. And this was my question for your opinion: dare we risk embarking this army and attempting to land near Louisbourg with only Hardy's five little warships in the North River to escort us into Halifax?

"Or must we remain here until Holburne's tardy fleet arrives?"

He wiped his flushed face with his handkerchief and gave us an apoplectic look.

"The consensus of opinion," said he, "seems to be that we had better await the fleet.

"That, for the present, is my own opinion, gentlemen." He got to his feet, heavily. "Gentlemen, I thank you."

Colonel and Brigadier arose and, bowing to the Commander-in-Chief, shuffled away across the handsome dining-room and out of the door. As the line of gorgeous uniforms receded, buttons, epaulettes and swords glittering, and spurs a-clink on scores of polished boots, Lord Loudon, wearily bowing them out, said to me:

"Captain Cardress, be good enough to remain."

So I stood aside in the window niche to await his lordship's pleasure. And when the last glittering button and last scarlet coat-tail had disappeared, and the last tinkle of spurs had died away on the stairway, Lord Loudon closed the door and went and seated himself again by the window where I stood, and through which a faint, refreshing sea-wind from the bay had begun to blow, ruffling the crimson curtains.

He was polite enough to ask me to be seated and to have a glass of wine.

"Cardress," said he, "you're Scotch; so am I; so is Holburne. Yes, and so is Lord Whinnloch's son, Charles Follis. . . . And other damned Jacobites who have dodged the gallows. . . . Yes, there are all kinds of Scots—loyal and rebel. Hell, I suppose, is as full of Scots as Heaven is."

He cracked another walnut, and drank more Madeira. He always made me think of a big, red parrot cracking sunflower seeds.

"This is confidential," he said; "the King wants to catch Charles Follis and Lord Annandale's son, and hang 'em both!"

His Majesty, I believe, was not bloody-minded, but those Scottish rebels of noble blood, who had fought with Prince Charles Edward and who, escaping after the disaster to the Stuart cause, had entered France and the French service, to do England all the damage they could, were extremely obnoxious to the fiery little German King of England, George Second.

And what now particularly enraged him was that Lord Whinnloch's son, Charles Follis, commanded the Foreign Legion in the garrison of the Gibraltar of America, Louisbourg, the powerful French fortress-city on Isle Royal at the mouth of the St. Lawrence—a stronghold which his great minister, Pitt, considered the key to all French power in the Western World.

The King had said: "If Louisbourg falls, then Quebec falls; and New Orleans must follow. And that shall put an end to France in North America." Probably he had heard Pitt say it first. And Loudon had heard them both. However, all three were wrong.

Lord Loudon said to me: "General Webb has more aids and staff officers and specialists at his heels than he knows what to do with—such as you, a ranger-captain and interpreter; George Bartman, Engineer Captain; Harry Gordon, Engineer; Dick Rogers, Second in Com-

mand in Bob Rogers' Rangers and now on Webb's staff
—all those valuable and necessary people," he repeated
with heavy brutality, "wasted on a congenital coward like
Daniel Webb—" He gave me a look which said, "Tell
Webb what I called him, for all I care!"—then he swallowed the remainder of the Madeira.

"That's neither here nor there," said he. "This is what
counts; the King wants to catch that Culloden man
Charles Follis. If I take Louisbourg, Follis, knowing
what awaits him, is not going to surrender himself to
an English army when Louisbourg capitulates. Do you
understand, Cardress?"

"Yes, my Lord; he'll cut and run."

Loudon said: "The King *wants* him. If I don't take
Louisbourg the King will deprive me of command and
send me back to England. If I *do* take Louisbourg and
Charles Follis escapes, the King won't like me. Which
will end my fortunes. You follow me, Captain Cardress?"

"Yes, General."

"Cardress, have you ever been in Louisbourg?"

"No, sir."

"Who has taken over your company of Rangers in
your absence?"

"I first had Captain Grant's old company. Then I had
McGinnis's New Yorkers. After General Webb took me
as staff-captain interpreter, McGinnis took over his New
York Rangers and, together with Captain Dick Rogers,
and Captains Hobbs and Spikeman, formed the corps of
Rangers under Bob Rogers which today is operating
from Fort Edward."

"Well," said Lord Loudon sullenly, "I don't care what

Webb thinks; I'm going to employ you on special duty. And what I want you to do is to send spies into Louisbourg to watch Charles Follis, and the Chevalier Johnstone—that's Lord Annandale's rascally heir!—and all such Jacobites, and to send me news of what is happening in that huge citadel full of traitors and Frenchmen.

"And," he added, banging his red, puffy hand on the table, "I want you and your spies to see to it that neither Follis nor Johnstone escape if we take the city—and that nobody from outside shall get wind of what you are about, or creep into Louisbourg and warn Follis and Johnstone that the King means to catch 'em and hang 'em like the dirty Jacobite dogs they are."

"Yes, sir."

"I'm told," said he, "that Lord Whinnloch's French relatives are trying to get a spy into Louisbourg to warn Follis and Johnstone that England means to have Louisbourg and the King means to hang them."

"Well, sir," said I, "isn't it the business of the Admiral to stop such attempts?"

"Dammy, so it is. But where is this same Admiral? And, after all—in confidence—between you and me, Cardress, who in hell is this Vice Admiral Holburne? I never heard of him before. Who is he? And why doesn't he come? If he doesn't," added his lordship, ominously, "I'll get this kind of letter from Pitt:

" 'My Lord: I am with concern to acquaint your Lordship that the King has judged proper that your Lordship should return to England.'

"Yes, that's the sort of letter I'll get if this vanishing Admiral doesn't quit playing the Flying Dutchman and sail into New York harbour!"

He got to his feet with a kindly gesture of dismissal.

"I won't complain," said he, "if our invisible Admiral only keeps that mischievous relative of Charles Follis out of Louisbourg. Did you ever hear of her, Cardress —Mademoiselle d'Auvray?"

"No, sir."

"Well, our King hates her and so does Pompadour who is really the governing power in France. She helped the Stuart Prince out of Scotland, which is why King George hates her. She laughed at what the King of Prussia said about Pompadour, and refused a place in the Marquise's entourage—demoiselle d'atours—or something similar. By God, if it hadn't been that the French army was full of rebel renegade Scotch and Irish, and if it hadn't been that she was kin to Charles Follis, La Pompadour would have had a lettre-de-cachet ready for Gayette d'Auvray long ago!"

"Sir," said I, "do you tell me that this young woman is likely to try to get into Louisbourg and warn the city that we are preparing to ruin it?"

"That's what Pitt writes," said Loudon sulkily. "How can I help it? It's that invisible Admiral's fault if this young and mischievous woman ever gets into Louisbourg.

"I'm not afraid of their Governor and Commandant, the Chevalier Augustin Drucour, or of their Grand Marquis, or of their three admirals. No! But that renegade Scot, the Chevalier Johnstone, and Charles Follis, if warned in time, will organize and fight with the cleverness and fury of cornered rats. And might even contrive to save the city!"

"Do you think so, my Lord?"

17

"How do I know? Who can foresee what a Scot will do? Whoever yet really understood either a Scot or a woman?"

"Are you not Scottish, my lord?" I asked, smiling.

"That," said he with a crafty look at me, "is why I fear two Scots in a trap and a female Scot on her way to teach 'em how to get out of it!"

"Is this lady—this relative of Charles Follis—actually on her way to Louisbourg?" I asked.

"Mr. Cardress," said he, "Mr. Pitt maintains a thousand spies in Paris. All report Mademoiselle d'Auvray missing. From London I have the news, and am warned to stop her on land or sea and keep her out of Canada or Louisiana, and, above everything, bar her from the great fortress-city of Louisbourg. Because Mr. Pitt thinks that her mere presence there would be worth a brigade of regulars to the garrison—which God knows would make it invulnerable, as there are five thousand troops there already!"

I did not know what to say. He rang, and bade a servant to open another bottle of Madeira. He was moderately tight already.

"If I get my hands on that mischievous d'Auvray slut," said he, "I'll send her back to that painted harlot Pompadour, who'll lock her up in the Bastille for the rest of her meddlesome existence! . . . All right, Cardress; you need not remain."

I rose, took my cocked hat and sword from a servant, stood at attention.

"G'bye," croaked Loudon, waving one hand and slopping wine across his waistcoat.

18

I left him muttering and swearing while a servant strove to cleanse his neckcloth and waistcoat of the mess.

That night, while asleep in my lodgings in the Indian Queen Tavern, there came young Montressor, that self-righteous busybody, to hammer on my door, and himself hand me written orders from the Commander-in-Chief—who never was too tipsy to make blunders.

I read the order in bed by candle light.

"What's all this, John?" said I.

"You're not to go to Louisbourg with his Lordship," said he in his precise, affected voice.

"I can read that much," said I, "but what's all this about returning to Ford Edward?"

"That's what you're to do, Cardress. There's a sloop going up the river on the flood about two o'clock this morning. Get your servants and your baggage aboard. You read what his Lordship says—that there will be special orders for you aboard *The Moon Flower,* packet for Albany?"

"Very well," said I, disgusted, "—only I'm sorry I've got to go back to Webb." Also, I became instantly sorry I had said as much to this smug, favour-currying busybody; and was glad he had orders to go to Halifax, for I feared his wasp tongue as much as I detested General Webb.

He went away down the corridor. I looked at my watch. I hadn't so very much time to get aboard *The Moon Flower* which lay in the stream off Trinity Church.

So I gave the velvet bell-cord a hearty pull, and presently, to a sleepy, frowsy servant carrying a candle—"Go and wake my new servant lad Sandi," said I, "and find

19

Joyce, my soldier servant, and tell 'em to pack up and get my baggage and theirs aboard the Albany packet-sloop, *The Moon Flower,* within an hour:"

He went away, yawning, and I got into my shoes, stockings and breeches, and was trying to tie my queue-ribbon by the light of a guttering candle, when there came a knock at the door and Sandi thrust his smooth young muzzle around the partly open door.

"My Captain," said the excited lad in his pretty French, "if your honour is quite dressed I will come in and pack your valises—"

"What the devil is it to you whether I am dressed or naked?" said I. "Come in and put away all these articles. Is your own bundle ready?"

"Yes, sir—"

"Where is Joyce?"

"Joyce has gone for a hackney coach, sir."

"Very well; tie my queue-ribbon. Here!—don't get that powder all over my shoulders! Now hand me my waistcoat and coat. . . . That's right! Look for a clean handkerchief—in that other valise. . . . Thank you, Sandi—"

I took hat, sword, military cloak, and turned around to look at my new servant boy, who, though apparently half dead for sleep, gave me a dauntless and smiling look and naïvely showed me his new suit of clothes.

"Where did you get those clothes? They are very sober and decent and suitable for a servant lad," said I, much pleased.

"I had them of a tailoress in Paris, sir, for grand ten-ure—habit de fête—"

"Well chosen, Sandi. Now pack up my camp chest and valises so that Joyce and you can carry them to the hackney coach. And be polite to Joyce. He's a crusty veteran—one of George Washington's and Braddock's soldiers."

The boy knelt down and opened my valises, and was so deft and swift with my effects, and packed the valises and military chest so swiftly and so neatly that I remained watching him in admiration—only I said nothing, not wishing to spoil this willing lad with easy praise.

Joyce, trim, snug, black-gartered, pipe-clayed, came when the baggage was locked—a big, sour-faced soldier in his green regimentals; and between him and Sandi, all three of us, and all our impedimenta were stowed aboard the hackney coach, and we were soon on our way to the river, the horses going at a gallop.

"Well, Joyce," said I, "are you glad you're not sailing with the Commander-in-Chief for Halifax?"

"Sure, your honour, 'tis the same to a poor sodjer where they shoot him—whether on land or sea—or through the head or the behind—"

"You old grumbler," said I, laughing, "I'm asking you whether you're not glad to go back to dry land and Fort Edward."

"And Gin'ral Webb, sor?"

"You know," said I, "that Colonel Montressor would have you flogged for such impertinence. . . . Only that I happen to know you as a brave man, and really devoted to my service, I'd send you to the guard-house, Joyce."

"Wanst," said Joyce, "your honour said to us that you'd never say 'Go!' to us, but 'Come on!' So—if it's the garrd-house—am I to 'go,' sorr—"

"You'd see me there first," said I, laughing, "—is that it—you saucy Irishman? Joyce, you're spoiled, and a bad example for our polite little French lad Sandi—"

"Wisha, then, sorr, that lad is no Frinchy but a raw Scotty or some other dom thing—"

"What?"

"He is that, sorr. Lave him shpit his French like anny other cat, but he can talk Sassenach, too. Your honour, ast him can he?"

I looked at the boy in the gloom of the lurching lanterns:

"Do you understand English, Sandi?"

"Yes, my Captain."

"Well, why the devil didn't you say so? You're an impudent youngster!"

The lad, not at all abashed, looked at me gaily—indeed, his brown eyes fairly laughed at me.

"After all," said he, in English, "my Captain did not deign to inquire concerning my accomplishments. And is a gentleman's servant to vaunt himself under his gentleman's nose?"

I looked at Sandi in amazement and displeasure. His English was as bold and as pretty as his French.

"Are you a French lad?" said I coldly.

"Partly of French blood, sir."

"English, too?"

"Sir, I am partly Scotch by blood, partly French."

I said nothing more. The hackney coach turned south, in front of Trinity Church, and we got out on a little dock and into a rocking jolly-boat.

In the lantern-lit darkness I heard Joyce grumbling at Sandi:

"Ouch, ye Frinch spalpeen! Will you keep your buckled shoes off my shins? Wirra the day his honour found ye! Luk at me gaiter-buttons where the big feet of ye has scraped me shins—"

"Well, then, I'll have to hang my feet overboard—"

"Do so—and g'wan after them!—you girl-faced, girl-fisted, knock-kneed—"

"That will do, Joyce," said I. And, to Sandi: "What the devil possesses you to torment Joyce? Keep still! Stop your wriggling. Balance and trim the boat, I tell you, or we'll all be in the North River before you know it!"

I added, bitterly: "Has ever any man possessed such a pair of unmannerly, impertinent servants! Very well; I'm going to turn you both into the regimental garden at Fort Edward—you can rely on that—both of you!"

In the starry darkness I could scarcely see Sandi's shadowy features. But, somehow, I felt that he was laughing at me.

Then the sloop-packet, *The Moon Flower,* hailed us: "Boat ahoy!" And presently we came up under her lee quarter and, looking up, saw her riding lights against the stars and the glow from a lantern stabbing the glassy river deep with jagged golden javelins.

When I got to the deck I went below to look at my quarters. The tide already was making.

A boatswain came with a packet for me. It was my sealed instructions from his lordship.

I sat down on the edge of my bunk and read them by the vague gleam of the hanging lamp overhead:

Headquarters, New York,

SIR: June 17th, 1757.

As Vice-Admiral Holburne has not yet appeared in New York waters with his battle fleet, although expected early in March, the Commander-in-Chief, realizing the importance of sending trustworthy agents into the French fortress-city of Louisbourg on Isle Royale, instructs you to detail such men as you believe capable of this delicate mission, and to send them secretly, and by stealth and strategy, into the fortress-town by way of Fort Edward, Carillon, Crown Point, and the Richelieu, as soon as possible.

These secret agents are to keep you informed of events in the city until Lord Loudon with his army, and Vice-Admiral Holburne with his fleet, can properly lay siege to and blockade the fortress-city.

These agents, also, are to use every endeavour to keep under constant surveillance the officers of the Foreign Legion now serving in Louisbourg, so that when the city surrenders to the English arms these traitors shall not escape their just fate—in particular, the renegade Scotch officers, Lieutenant the Chevalier Johnstone, heir to Lord Annandale the Scottish peer; and Major the Honourable Charles Follis, only son and heir to the Earl of Whinnloch.

These Jacobite gentlemen are not at present alarmed, and know nothing of his Majesty's determination to make an example of them as a warning to all rebels and traitors and Stuart pretenders to the crown. Therefore, your spies, secret envoys and agents are to take particular care not to alarm these traitors, or the Governor and garrison and inhabitants of Louisbourg, or allow them to suspect that preparations are far advanced to accomplish the ruin of the city and the punishment of such traitors to England as shall be discovered when the city is surrendered.

GEO: BARTMAN,
Captⁿ.

24

I read the document with disrelish. I did not care for the mission. As for punishing the Scottish gentlemen who had fought against us for Scotland and Bonnie Prince Charlie, and now again were to fight us in behalf of France and painted Pompadour—well, had they not been sufficiently punished already? No, I had no relish for reprisals and revenge, and thought it small business for a King to treasure animosity and blood malice. No, that was not kingly to gloat over a few poor severed heads stuck up over Temple Bar—

"Come in," said I, as a tapping at my cabin door interrupted my train of thought.

Sandi came in, hat in hand, shyly, yet smiling, and asked if he might sleep on a chair in my cabin, as Joyce had promised to give him a taste of his belt buckle if he came into the forecastle again.

"Very well," said I. "You can't leave Joyce alone and he can't leave you alone, so you can hoe potatoes and hill corn together at Fort Edward, and I'll find somebody whom I can trust and who will treat me with consideration."

He thanked me meekly.

"There's a bunk there—across from mine. Get into it, if you like," said I, crossly. And, fishing out my tobacco pouch, pipe, flint and tinder, I went on deck to smoke and watch the sloop get under way.

Tide and wind favouring, we were off and flying up the Hudson with the white caps chasing us like a horde of white waterhounds.

I smoked and gazed at moon and stars, and at the widespread, foamy pack following us, until the deck became too wet for pipe and comfort.

As I went below and entered my cabin I heard a slight, piping voice like a cat-bird singing under its breath—and so discreetly and low that I scarce distinguished the treasonable words—

> *"The regiments of France cry Vive le Roi!*
> *—Carignan, Navarre, and Gatinois,*
> *From Seine to Marne,*
> *From Rhône to Loire,*
> *Artois, Béarn,*
> *Guienne, La Sarre,—*
> *Regiments Bourgogne and Bourbonnais,*
> *Regiments Touraine and Soissonais,—*
> *The regiments of France cry Vive le Rois!*
> *—Deux Ponts, Saintonge, and Agenois!"*

Walking into the lamp-lit cabin, I saw my new page, Sandi, in his bed and singing away with a heavenly smile on his saucy face of an urchin. However, at sight of me he looked embarrassed and stopped his singing.

"Well," said I, "what kind of gamin's gutter-song do you call that?"

The boy made a perfunctory scramble as though to get out of bed and stand respectfully at attention, but I bade him turn over and go to sleep. Besides, I suspected he didn't really mean to get up.

While I undressed he politely turned his back on me until I blew out the candle in the ship's lantern and got into my bunk in the pitching, tossing, rolling cabin of *The Moon Flower,* bound for Albany, Half-Moon, Saratoga, and Fort Edward where, unless rumour lied, the White Coats were becoming as thick as white butterflies in a meadow, and the painted savages of the Canadas were painting the poor, scalpless heads of our soldiers with thickly dripping scarlet.

"Sandi," I called in the darkness, "are you awake?"

"I am, your honour."

"You are to fetch me a bowl of chocolate by half past seven. If you don't you may expect a belt-flogging from Private Joyce of the Royal Americans. And I'll help him."

"Oh, my God," I heard him murmuring to himself, his voice brittle with laughter.

CHAPTER III

AS MAN TO MAN

THE boy, Sandi, was always at my heels and dog-
ging me on deck and below deck. It seemed as
though he were afraid of the crew, keeping clear of both
forecastle and galley, and of the sour-faced Joyce, too,
whose heavy hand was ever ready to fetch the lad a clout.

But Sandi proved too agile to be caught; his supple
body seemed but a single highly tempered spring under
its clear, smooth skin, and Joyce couldn't catch him to
administer punishment for misbehaviour.

I thought him an odd and rather cowardly lad to seem
so sturdy and straight, and yet was so faint hearted and
immature that his voice, still girlish, had not developed a
break or a crack in promise of approaching manhood.

And always he was skulking at my heels, sticking fearfully and closely to me so that finally I lost my temper
and fetched him a hearty slap across his plump buttocks:

"You get out from under foot," said I sharply. "What
the devil!—do you think you are a Scotch terrier? Keep
out o' my way, now. You're no good as page or servant
—no good to me, only a bother—and I don't know why I
ever took you into service at all—only you wheedled me
into it. What's the matter with you anyway? You're
one o' those pretty lads—that's the trouble. You're too
damned pretty—more resembling a girl and not like a
sturdy lad of your age! Can't you act more manly?"

"I'll try, sir," said he, fingering the edge of his béret.

28

"Well, for heaven's sake do try, then. What's a hearty clout or two from Private Joyce that you should be forever lurking at my heels and ready to dodge and run?"

"Joyce hurts when he hits, sir."

"Then be respectful to him. I'm disappointed in you, Sandi. I thought to make of you a useful, manly, plucky, body servant; but—" I shrugged—"I don't know what's the matter with you—and Joyce says you put on airs and are so damned delicate and private and exclusive that you're too good to eat and sleep and bathe and dress with the crew, and must run whining into my cabin if a hand grabs at you in sport."

There were aboard us, and quartered forward, some artillerymen—a draft of gunners for General Webb—and Joyce, in a rage, beat up two of them because they said that my page, Sandi, was no boy at all but a girl and my vigorous young mistress just sprouting into earliest womanhood.

"So I beat up thim gunners good, sorr," said Joyce, swinging his belt and looking about the deck for Sandi. "Wisha, then," said he, "an' I could catch that young lackadaisy scut I'd take some of the mincing out of him— I would so, and dom quick—"

That gave me rather an unpleasant sensation and I looked furtively and suspiciously at the boy when next he came into my cabin.

But, though he seemed in the face almost too pretty for a boy, nevertheless, there was about him nothing incompatible in regard to his evident and avowed condition as an unusually large, graceful, and agile lad of eleven or twelve.

Only I did think that his hands were devilish small and smooth, and not dirty enough for a healthy boy.

What those gunners said, of course, couldn't be. Nevertheless, I resolved not to have any effeminate lad about me or in my service, and I made up my mind to rid myself of Sandi when we arrived at the Fort.

In Albany the boy was full of curiosity, and running all over town, day and evening, snooping, gadding, and sniffing about like an impudent Scotch terrier, to make friends or try his busy impertinence on everybody.

Well, one thing was sure—he was no girl in disguise, with his flat chest, narrow hips and straight legs which showed no tendency to the female contour inside the knees. Only he was almost unpleasantly graceful.

General Webb had arrived in Albany with his staff— Major Morris, Captain Bartman, Mr. Adair, and Mr. Furnis. Colonel James Montressor was in town, also— on business of sending up ladders, chevaux-de-frise, mantelets, sand bags, tools to Fort William Henry and Fort Edward.

Albany was full of Webb's soldiers, and in great confusion, the streets crowded, no lodgings to be had, constant quarreling and no love lost between the New England troops and the New Yorkers and Regulars. Colonel Goff's New Hampshire infantry were still passing through, and I saw some of Captain Israel Putnam's men on their way up to Edward—a sullen lot of Puritans with their mean New England muzzles a-sniffing for sin among the Regulars who were more worthy to be called real men than the lank, fish-eyed bigots from Massachusetts Bay and Connecticut.

I saw Webb at the fort, and his were eyes that I did

not trust and a mouth to deny Christ—or so I thought—
for he had a wild, absent look, and Montressor told me
that he was obsessed by an insane horror of Indian war-
fare, and a terror of death by fire. Imagine sending
such a General into the Indian country! A fine general
officer, truly, to face Praying Indians and White Coats,
and their clever officers at Carillon—or Ticonderoga, as
we called it.

Well, it seemed as though half the world were going up
to Fort Edward and Saratoga—Regular regiments, Provincials, Rangers, Generals, staff officers, artillery, bat-
horses, cursing wagoners impressed by Loudon, scows,
bateaux, all travelling up to Edward and William Henry
where Otway's Regiment and the Royals already were
mustered, and the Rangers under Putnam—Bob Rogers
having been retained by my Lord Loudon to go with him
to take Louisbourg.

The road followed the west bank of Hudson's River
to old Saratoga, crossed here and ran thence to Edward.

So, as General Webb was going up, I went with him
and his staff, and had opportunity on the way up to show
him my orders from Lord Loudon.

I had never liked or trusted the sunken, timid eye
of Daniel Webb; I liked him and his scared eyes of a
homeless cat no better now; and what between him and
Loudon and General Lyman—whom I cared little about
—I could see no General officers in the field who seemed
in any way competent for this business of kicking the
French out of North America—only excepting Sir William Johnson with his rugged militia regiments and his
Iroquois Indians in their paint. Sir William seemed to
be a real man—with his grey eyes, grave or merry by

moments, and his ruddy hair and nearly six feet of muscular stature—a gallant man and a tried one who had seen the Hurons and the White Coats before and had defeated them in pitched battle.

On the 24th of June, about eleven in the morning, as we came into Saratoga, we met Captain Fletcher with a company of Regulars of Otway's and of Royals, and a Yankee Captain with three companies of Massachusetts troops, all come down to guard General Webb on his way up.

We arrived at Fort Edward that same afternoon. All guards turned out with rested arms, and, as we rode along the front of the 35th, Otway's men turned out with sidearms; a long ruffle was beaten on the drums, the piquet, with officers, advanced beyond the regiment's centre, and the officers in two lines advanced before the piquet.

All very fine. For myself I had rather have seen the tall figure of Sir William Johnson, in his red and blue uniform, riding out to salute us; and his Mohawks, and his Mohawk Valley Regiments drawn up to give us countenance.

Webb seemed anxious to know who I meant to detail to go into Louisbourg, but I hadn't made up my mind yet.

I don't know what it was about the Rangers—they did not seem very good scouts to me—even my own New York Company, while willing enough, lacked a cleverness that spies must possess.

We were an ignorant lot. Israel Putnam, who commanded the Rangers now, was both common and ignorant, though brave and fairly well versed in forest lore.

But I needed more than a forest runner to act for me

in Louisbourg, and was at my wit's ends to find anybody
capable of writing his name and reading it afterwards,
whom I dared trust to go upon so delicate a mission.

In all the six companies of Rangers—excepting a few
officers—I found no material in the ranks out of which to
make a single good spy. Massachusetts officers were
Captains West and Learned; Putnam and Safford had
the Connecticut men; Wall the Rhode Islanders, and Mc-
Ginnis and I the Yorkers. But, Lord!—I wouldn't have
picked a single officer or man for such fine and adroit
business as this mission required—though I sifted out
Burk's, Hartwell's, and Kerner's companies, and Taply's,
too. But found 'em culls.

I didn't know what to do. I asked Captain Bartman
for advice, but he had none to offer, saying that his chief
was so nervous about Sir William Johnson's Indians that
everybody had the twitters at Headquarters and could
think of nothing and attend to nothing properly.

The Mohawks from the Valley—Sir William's pet
painted devils—were forever prowling about Fort Edward
and the Island, and Webb had such a terror and antipa-
thy for any North American Indian that he couldn't endure the sight of their paint-smeared visages and issued
an order forbidding Indians to go into Fort Edward or
over to the Island where were our regimental vegetable
gardens, without a pass from him or from General Lyman; and also to keep away from regimental sutlers who
were not permitted to build hut or pitch tent, to sell their
goods, foods, and liquors unless our Adjutant Deputy
Quartermaster Lesley issued a permit.

I don't think I ever saw so timid a human being as
Dan'l Webb, the General whom Lord Loudon left here at

Edward to take care of the clever Marquis of Montcalm and eight thousand White Coats and Indians while he, Loudon, sailed to seize the city of Louisbourg.

Another matter worried Webb; on the Island were rattlesnakes, and he never would set his foot there to inspect the regimental gardens.

On the Island were barracks for the Ranger battalions, too; a brick yard and kilns, the King's Hospital, and some trenches and palisaded works.

I, however, being now detailed for special duty, had my own quarters, my own servants, my own food, and lived in a puncheon-floored hut on the east shore of the river. For the present I had no business to take me to the barracks of Major Rogers' men, or to our Souriquois scouts who, alone of all our Indians, were allowed to camp on the Island, where Webb offered a bounty of tuppence for every snake they slew.

Well, somehow or other I had to send a spy—two or three, in fact—into Louisbourg; and, if I couldn't find anybody suitable, felt that I had no other choice than to go myself. Yet hated it, because it seemed like work belonging to a hangman's assistant—and I had no stomach for it, and cared not a straw that the King desired to catch and hang two poor gentlemen whose only crime was a preference for Prince Charles Edward instead of for a little bouncing, vindictive German from Hanover.

That's the devil of being a soldier; no matter what you yourself are thinking, you go on and carry out your orders, even cruel ones.

Fort Edward was now becoming a considerable fortification. It lies in Kayaderoseras patent, New York province, just north and east of the junction of Fort Edward Creek and Hudson's River, where was Lydius's house—a square fort with bastions, curtains, ditch, officers' quarters on both sides of the main gate, barracks, stables, the northwest and southeast magazines—in fact, although only built two years since, and still not entirely finished, Fort Edward had become a regular and important fortification at the Great Carrying Place guarding the road to Fort William Henry more than nine miles away, at the south end of Lake Saint Sacrement. In other words, it was the key to the great highway which led from Quebec to New York through Lake Champlain and Hudson's River.

The barracks were comfortable—two stories high with outside stairs—the regular soldiers' barrack being known as the East Barrack, along the east curtain, the chimneys of which were built of field stone. The Provincials had the West Barrack, divided by the West Gate, where had been hospitals and which was built like the East Barrack.

Our officers' quarters were on both sides of the North Gate—a one-story building and another of two stories.

The casemates, also, were used for the men, but many regiments went into camp under tents—the filthy Connecticut infantry camping north of the northwest bastion, and the Rangers to the northwest along the cleared ground near the river. The ditch, fifteen feet deep, with its twelve feet of palisades, six feet in profile, was from twenty-five to fifty feet wide.

The several bastions varied much in size and outline, and were named Snoek or Creek Bastion in the southeast; Water Bastion to the southwest; Magazine Bastion and Royal Bastion to the northwest and northeast.

This fort, together with the Royal Block House and

other block houses across the river and the creek, was the base from which all operations against Crown Point and Carillon were to be initiated.

Well, this was the spot I had been inhabiting, when I went to New York, and it was here that I returned from New York late in June and took up my old quarters near the New York Rangers.

These were just south of the site for the new bridge to the Island, about 500 feet north of the Northwest Bastion which was still a-building. The bridge already could be crossed on a single plank.

Here I had a hut to myself near to the floored tents of the Yorkers, and here I settled, prepared to think out my plans and presently put them into execution.

The river here is swift and very shallow in summer—about two or three feet deep, running over shale; so our people could wade over to the vegetable gardens on the Island—and even cross the other branch and get to the western shore where the forest had been cleared and where several colonial regiments were encamped opposite the brick yard.

Now, no sooner had I got my baggage into my hut, and unpacked, when Colonel Montressor, very handsome in his scarlet regimentals, comes riding in to say that Webb's aide-de-camp required a return of all enlisted women in camp—not alone those who wash and mend, either. "And," says he, giving me an uncomfortable look, "I am told that officers' ladies—I mean the unmarried ones—are to be orally included in this return."

"Well, sir," said I, "what has that to do with me?"

"Sir," said he, turning red, "it is purely because of my

respect and friendship for you that I have permitted my-self the liberty of forewarning you, Captain Cardress—"

"But, my dear sir," said I hotly, "I have no woman, enlisted or otherwise, to report. Did anybody say I had?"

"Yes, sir," said he, embarrassed, "it is generally said you have fetched from New York a pretty wench dressed as a French sailor lad, and have taken her into your employment. It is none of my business, Captain Cardress, and if it's not true I ask your pardon for meddling."

It was kindly intended; we shook hands; he mounted and rode away to the Fort; I went down to the river and across on the single plank, to our New York regimental vegetable plantation where I saw the Souriquois hunting snakes.

Here presently I discovered two Mohawk Valley louts of our Ranger Company, hoeing and raking and sweating; and my poor little Sandi, red faced and wet with sweat, carrying water from the river to pour around the kitchen vegetables and fill the ditches which irrigated the field crops.

Out of the tail o' my eye I noticed other officers prowling around to inspect and keep a hungry eye upon their growing regimental gardens which now seemed extremely promising.

The boy, Sandi, with two buckets of water, was trudging along the rows of beets, lettuce, and carrots, soaking the green rows with river water, when I came into the New Yorkers' garden.

Sandi saw me and took off his small blue fisherman's cap respectfully, but I said nothing, only continued to watch him until he had finished his wetting down the

37

beets, and had gone back to the river shore for more water.

Thither I followed him and stood on the plank of the bridge as he, in his naked feet, waded out to refill his buckets.

When he had done so, and had set them both ashore, "Sandi," I said abruptly, "are you a boy or a girl?"

He turned scarlet under his sunburn, looking up at me out of wide, startled eyes.

"Oh, Lord, sir," said he in a confused and distressed way, "are you displeased with my services?"

"No, not very. But I ask you a plain question, and you shall answer it, for I'm damned if I know whether you're a slightly effeminate boy or a sturdy young girl in masquerade, and I'm not pleased that officers in this garrison gossip about you and me and say that ours is a romance, and that you dress as a lad for love of me, and are my mistress."

He gave me a shocked, breathless look. Then tears rushed into the lad's wide, staring eyes and overflowed his soft, dusty cheeks.

"S-sir," he stammered, "it is cruel to insult me who have not deserved such ill treatment—"

"Stop your snivelling. You're no lass but a lad, then. Is that it?"

A sob was my only answer.

"Very well; I make it a quarrel and a duel, then, with the next gentleman who attempts his pleasantries at my expense," said I wrathfully.

There was, nevertheless, something in the lad's dark, black-fringed eyes that I did not understand. Not that his eyes ever shrank from meeting mine. On the contrary they never avoided that encounter, and I was sometimes aware of a strain in the boy's gaze and smile, as though from the effort of sustaining my gaze.

"Come here, Sandi," said I, "and sit on this plank beside me."

"With your honour's permission——"

He set down his buckets, came slowly and seated himself on the plank, not very near me.

"Who are you, anyway?" I asked.

"I'm just a mousse——"

"Oh, no, not with those narrow hands which a little work here on the island has already blistered. Not with those small, naked feet of an aristocrat. So who are you, Sandi? Somebody's natural child? Some great person's, who abandons you? Or have you broken the French law and enlisted in the French Navy? Because you're no peasant lad or no petty shopkeeper. So what really are you?"

He shook his head either from bewilderment or obstinacy, I couldn't tell which, saying he was merely a poor lad from an orphanage at Passy.

"You weren't always an orphan, you know," said I drily. "Are you trying to tell me that all you can remember is a Passy orphanage?"

The lad sat with shapely feet hanging over the sunlit water, his narrow, work-scarred hands clasped between his knees, his curly head bent, staring at the river running swiftly underneath him.

"Come," said I, "answer me. I'm not going to keep a servant lad who can't account for himself any better than you can. . . . Besides, as you sit there, Sandi, you certainly do look like an extremely boyish girl. . . . And, by God, I believe you *are!*"

Sandi never stirred, only the smooth, tanned throat rippled once or twice as though swallowing.

"Sandi," said I, "you're hot, sweaty, dirty. Get off that plank, go to the bank, strip and take a bath in the river. . . . Do you hear what I say?"

"Yes, sir."

"Well, then?"

He gave me a strange, white look, then got down, waded to the opposite bank, and caught at his shirt with both hands as though to pluck it over his head.

And all the while I had been hearing a soldier shouting to somebody: "Look out, you fool! Have a care, you boy down there!—" And, of a sudden, I understood that he was shouting at Sandi. And then I saw the boy's bare legs were close to a banded rattlesnake.

Into the water I jumped in my spurred boots, and stepped between Sandi and the brown and yellow thing that lay in an S shaped loop on the shore, its stubby tail a misty blur as it rattled out Death's own alarm and warning.

Swish—slash! went my riding whip, and left the snake squirming and rattling feebly in the sand; and two Rhode Island soldiers came down the bank and finished the deadly little serpent with stones, and cut off its five rattles to sell to Sir William Johnson's Indians for medicine.

"Captain Cardress," said one of the soldiers, "these snakes usually travel in pairs, and the mate of this one will be soon hanging about here. It would be sensible, sir, if your servant lad put on his shoes and gaiters before he goes on with his garden work."

"Sandi," said I, "yonder squirms a very deadly creature which is unknown in France. So go you to the hut and put on your thickest stockings, leather leggins, and brogans before you come back to work in this place."

He looked almost stupidly at the dead and bloody snake which was still quivering and twisting on the sand.

Then, without any word at all, or even a look at me, but very white of face and with the eyes of a sick creature, the lad moved slowly away, wading across the river as though fatigued and weakened by the heat of that oppressive day in June.

He didn't return. I set it down to shock from fright. There seemed to be a nervous streak in the lad, in fact, something of cowardice, which was extremely unpleasant to notice.

As for what this youngster really was, I was not perfectly sure, even yet, though it seemed incredible that Sandi could be anything except a boy.

It was about five o'clock, and as General Webb had sent for me I went to my hut to change my boots, put on full uniform, gloves, and sword before reporting at Headquarters.

Sandi was in the kitchen, pale, silent, building a fire in the chimney place to heat a kettle of hot water.

"What are you about?" said I.

He said he preferred to bathe in warm water, with soap, and was heating a cauldron of water for that purpose.

"Very well," said I, "I'll be back in a moment to see that you get a good scrubbing."

"Very well, sir," said the lad, coolly, "shall I wait until you return, sir?"

I shook my head.

On my way to Webb, "Well," thought I, "there's no question about Sandi being the lad he says he is. But there's *something* wrong with him and I'm not going to keep an impish, girl-faced youngster in my household, who is believed by the whole army to be a girl."

All Webb wanted of me was to ask me to make a list of officers and soldiers, other than Rangers, who were willing to go on scout, and be relieved of all other duties. The weekly allowance for a person on scout duty was to be seven pounds of bread and five pounds, three ounces of pork. I said it was not enough, but Webb did not agree with me.

George Bartman said that a hundred men had been sent into the woods to cut sixteen foot fascines for saucissons, and were grumbling at their rations—saying the peas were full of weevils and the butter stank.

Webb didn't like this criticism of his commissariat, and changed the subject, insisting that Captain Bartman request all regiments to return to him as soon as possible the number of enlisted women, and their names and to which regiments they belonged.

"For," says he with an oath, "we are too near to the French Indians to doubt that they'll be after the long-haired scalps of our camp women, and if I can have my way with my Lord Loudon I'll clear every damned wo-man out of Fort Edward!"

As I say, Webb was obsessed by his fear of Indians, and the terror of them was always in his ratty mind, so that he even conceived it to be dangerous to permit the camp women to remain, lest their long tresses inspire and attract the French savages, and put them in mind of atrocities they might not perhaps otherwise remember to commit.

We officers who were, or had been, serving on Webb's staff were perfectly aware of his idiosyncrasies, and of the disgust he inspired in such warriors as Sir William Johnson who plainly said he was a coward and ought not to command British troops.

There were a number of other irritating and petty orders which the men found annoying—one particularly ridiculous one which forbade our soldiers to pitch pennies—and why, I never could learn, because there was plenty of card gambling going on.

The following day General Webb and his staff went up to Fort William Henry after noon dinner, where Colonel Munro commanded, who had some sixteen hundred dependable men, and a number of guns which could not be depended upon.

I think Webb went up to look at Munro and his troops and his defective cannon, moved by the same morbid impulse that fascinates a mob which gathers to gaze upon a doomed man before his execution.

George Bartman said to me that the Scotch Colonel and his garrison never could withstand an assault of determined White Coats and Indians through a breach prepared by the French artillery.

"Damnation, then," said I, "why doesn't Webb either reinforce Munro or withdraw him?"

Nobody knew.

It was a hot, sunny day in the woods. After Webb and his officers had ridden off toward Fort William

Henry, I walked slowly back toward my hut. Always my mind was occupied by the problem, how to get two or three good spies into Louisbourg before my Lord Loudon arrived to besiege and assault that powerful place.

The heat had become depressing. Everything seemed to wear a gloomy aspect to me. I knew our General was timid, perhaps a coward, and of doubtful value to England or to America; I had no great confidence in Lord Loudon, nor in the phantom Vice Admiral whom I dubbed the Flying Scot, and who never yet had appeared to mortal eyes in North America. All kinds of minor matters irritated me, too; there were no men in the Rangers to be relied upon as spies, or fit to be sent into Louisbourg; all our soldiers had become dissatisfied and sulky because forbidden to pitch pennies; one of Captain Taply's men, playing ball, fell dead o' the extreme heat; a soldier of the Royal Americans, having deserted, had just been caught, courtmartialed, and was to be executed; discipline everywhere was bad; there was a soldier shot off his gun accidentally and shot a man in the next tent, through the body, who never spoke more words than these, "I am a dead man, the Lord have mercy on me."

So, feeling hot, and low in my mind, I walked toward my hut, and presently heard a commotion — yelling, splashing, jeering laughter down under the river bank.

Looking over the bank I saw that some loitering soldiers of the Massachusetts Ranger battalion, who had been fishing, had seized hold of my boy, Sandi, and were threatening to strip him naked and throw him into the river. They shouted:

"Which are you, lad or lass? If you're a girl you'll

scream! If you're a witch you'll swim! In with you, if you won't talk!"

My lad was fighting them in silence and with a swift and deadly fury that made me proud.

But just as I raised my voice sharply, bidding the New Englanders drop their horse-play or take a heavy flogging apiece, they ripped the last rag from poor Sandi who fell with a splash into the crystalline flood amid shrieks of indecent laughter.

But these mirth-convulsed New England yokels did not see me coming before they felt the knife-like cut of my riding lash. Then, roaring lustily, they ran for their own lines, scuttling rat-like through the shallows, across the island and out of sight beyond the willows near the brick-kilns and stockade north of the Rangers' barracks.

The red sunset in my eyes made a blinding glitter over the rapid river. In it, clothed only in the dazzling rosy light, stood a naked girl, knee deep, covering her face with dripping, desperate fingers—

CHAPTER IV

AS MAN TO GIRL

I HAD finished my supper of hasty pudding. Joyce and Sandi, also, had supped; Joyce, with a warrant for rations, had taken his rusty camp lantern and gone over to the Island, in company with other soldiers from every mess in the 35th and 62nd regiments, to draw fresh vegetables against the morrow, from the regimental gardens.

So Sandi and I were left alone in my brush hut. The hour for reckoning had arrived.

Sandi, watching me with a sort of bashful defiance, sat on the kitchen chopping block.

I was seated in an arm chair made of ashen staves, by Joyce. A candle burned on the camp table between us.

When I had loaded a new churchwarden pipe and had set it alight by the candle flame, I replaced the candle, leaned back in my chair and told Sandi that I was ready to listen to what she had to say.

But Sandi, it appeared, had nothing to say. Through the shamed colour in her face she seemed to be desperately striving to endure my hostile gaze with a courage I could not but notice.

"Very well," said I; "here is your case, then. Some of Captain West's Rangers, in their horse-play, stripped the clothes from a twelve-year boy who now turns out to be no boy at all but a well-grown girl of sixteen or more."

46

Sandi's face was surging in hot, rich colour, but she still forced her gaze to sustain mine.

"Just why you have been masquerading as a boy, I don't know," said I. "All I know is that you lied to me there on the Whitehall dock in New York."

"Yes, sir, I did lie to you," she admitted in that blind, smiling sort of way.

"Why did you pretend to be a boy?"

"I was afraid of what English sailors and marines might do to women prisoners."

"Did they mistreat them?"

"No, sir."

"Then why did you continue to deceive me?"

"A boy has better chances in adversity than a girl has."

"You're a bold and hardy young one," said I, "——coming into my cabin and invading the intimate privacy of a man's quarters!"

Tide after tide of scarlet ran riot over her face, but the faint smile remained fixed like a grimace, and her eyes seemed actually sightless as though the punishment mine dealt them was blinding them.

"Listen to me, young woman," said I. "You don't look like a harlot though you seem as hardened and insensible to delicacy as any young wench in the stews. Nevertheless, I don't believe you to be a trollop."

She made no effort to speak.

"How old are you?"

"Eighteen," she whispered.

"From your impertinent assurance, you might be three times that age. . . . What is your name?"

"Alessandine. Or, Sandi."

"Alessandine—what?"

47

"That is all, sir."

"What are you—a grisette who have no surname?"

"Nothing worse, sir."

"I am wondering," said I, "whether you know that a French spy came to our outposts last night and tried to bribe a sentry."

Her face remained expressionless.

"Not that I suppose you to be a spy," said I. "But General Webb has ordered a return of the number of enlisted women and their names, belonging to the different regiments, to be given in as soon as possible to Captain Bartman."

I thought I saw a slight trace of fear in her eyes.

"What is to happen to me, sir?" she asked.

I shrugged: "You are not an enlisted woman, but I must report you."

"May I not enlist?"

"Yes—if you can find some soldier to marry you. . . . Or if you choose to enlist as—laundress, for instance—or as a camp follower of any sort."

She gave me a straight look, then her face burned again, and she lowered her confused eyes.

"You are trying to frighten me," she said.

"Don't think it, young woman. You're in a bad enough pickle to scare anybody."

"You say that because you are angry with me for my impertinence and deceit. If you were generous you would laugh at this adventure of mine—" She hesitated, looking at me in a kind of pleading and gay anxiety: "What will they do to me if I am not an enlisted woman?"

"Send you down to Albany and keep you there under police surveillance."

48

"In jail?"

"Under proper restraint. Yes, probably in the woman's prison."

The girl looked at me in real consternation.

She said: "There must be some way you can help me. I can't go to jail; it would kill me. There must be something you can do for me, Captain Cardress."

I gave her a grim look: "I could keep you from being sent away by saying to Bartman that you are my mistress—"

Her startled eyes flashed on mine like a pair of poniards.

"But," I continued, "I don't know why I should lie to him out of any generous consideration for you!"

She sat with lowered gaze, nervously pleating the hem of her blue fisherman's blouse. Presently, however, she lifted her head of tangled curls, with the old instinctive effort to meet with courage and sustain my eyes; but this time her own eyes fell, again, and she continued, for a while, aimlessly pleating her blouse's hem. Then her head slowly drooped lower, and presently she took it between both hands and rested so, all doubled up, a picture of most desolate woe.

After a long silence she said in a stifled voice: "Are those the only ways I can keep out of jail—by becoming a soldier's trull, or a camp prostitute, or your mistress?"

"I'm afraid so."

She said in the same faint, muffled voice, "Do you mean that I must actually become—become your mistress?"

"What damn nonsense," said I, exasperated. "I don't want a doxy, and I wouldn't pick you even if I did! You've been a nuisance ever since I was foolish enough to employ you. You are insolent to Joyce and impudent to me; you don't know how to work; you're of no use at all! And now, dammy, you suddenly turn into a kind of species of girl with your sun-tanned skin and curly hair and your shape of a saucy schoolboy—"

I got up angrily and began to march up and down the puncheon floor: "If it lay with me I'd send you into Carillon devilish quick. I'd be devilish glad to be rid of you. But Webb won't do it. I know him. He won't. . . . So there's nothing for me to do, I suppose, except to lie to Bartman about you, and endure you until I can decently be quit of you."

I scraped out my long pipe, grumbling to myself and giving her a malevolent glance every now and then.

"No," said I, "I wouldn't turn a sick kitten out doors; and I shan't turn you out. I'll not say a word to anybody about you unless those Massachusetts yokels of West's Company tell their brutal story. If they do, then I'll have to lie *to* Bartman."

"Will you be obliged to tell Captain Bartman that I am your tender and guilty friend, sir?"

"That's what I'll have to tell him—that you are my romantic and guilty sweetheart—douce amie—whatever sounds most respectable. . . . Maybe I won't have to tell him anything. . . . Now, do you get you into your bunk presently, and go to sleep, in God's name. I'm going to see what can be done about this business. I'm going to find out whether those dirty, psalm-whining Yankee yokels can set upon a servant of a New York officer with impunity."

I took my cocked hat from a peg, tucked my riding

whip under my left arm, and strode forth into the starry night.

West's Rangers were quartered on the Island and I soon came to their lousy barracks where a lank, big-nosed sergeant presently produced the three louts who had made up the fishing party which had bullied Sandi.

"Now, you damned, witch-killing Puritans," said I, "you ambushed and set upon my servant and threw him into the river! I saw you do it. And all I want you to remember is this, that if any of you ever dare tell of what you did—*you understand what I mean!*—I'll prefer charges that will cost each of you five hundred lashes—if you live through the flogging long enough to take the five hundredth stroke."

They were terribly frightened. They seemed a dirty lot—as dirty as that Connecticut regiment of ours that had to be warned in general orders to appear in shoes and stockings when turned out for parade!

I said to their sergeant: "You need not take any steps in this matter unless I carry it to Captain West. Then I'll let you kill these three Plymouth Rock saints."

Whether or not their sergeant liked taking orders from me I didn't know or care, but I suspected he'd not make any trouble for his own people to oblige me. Everybody knows that no two colonies in America ever liked each other.

So I went back to my brush hut, lifted the burning candle and glanced into the woodshed and kitchen where my servants slept. Joyce's bunk was empty. The girl looked up from her blanket and flashed a most enchanting smile at me in the wavering candle light.

"Am I to go to jail, sir?"

"I think not."

"Thank you, Captain Cardress," she said gaily.

I scowled at her: "Your gratitude would be more acceptably expressed in a pie," said I. "Female obligation," said I, "is most agreeably discharged by cookery—such as puddings, sauces, and syllabubs."

As I turned away, carrying my candle: "But," I added, "I don't suppose you know how to cook."

"You'll be surprised," said she with a little laugh that rang saucily in my ears as I closed the kitchen door.

CHAPTER V

SANDI

SMACK-BANG! The morning gun at Edward. Then, very far away, bang! The gun at Ann. Then, just distinguished and no more, the sullen boom from Fort William Henry, thirteen miles away.

I rolled over in my blanket and saw the oiled paper window-pane all golden with the rising sun, and heard robins loud and joyous, and the thrush's golden fluting at the forest's edge.

For a little while I lay, and even slipped back to the edge of sleep, so that already the dusky tide lapped over me a little. Then something aroused me again. Listening, I heard a rustle and stirring like a mouse in the woodshed, and presently saw Sandi. She had been to the river where it was plain she had been disporting her before the morning gun brought the sun.

Her hair was wet; she had swathed her body in her blanket; and now she came speeding swift, on velvet feet, casting at me an uncertain glance as she passed on into the woodshed.

Here, then, was a young servant girl who took baths!

I wondered whether there really was quality in Sandi. The girl looked it, but one never could tell. However, this love for water was anything except French. Even great ladies in France—yes, and in England—did damned little bathing. The peasantry did none at all. Nobility—and wild birds—alone bathed; and not many

53

of the nobility, either. The French King, they say, hated soap and water and used it only when in fear that he had contracted something contagious somewhere.

Well, I had my idea that this little servant maid in boy's dress was the victim of at least one parent of quality, if not of two. It seemed odd to me—as long as the King of France and nine-tenths of the ladies and gentlemen at his court were acknowledging their bastards —that nobody responsible for this pretty child's conception and birth had acknowledged her and provided for her. . . . A cursed funny thing, to be sure—unless, of course, she was some illegitimate Scottish brat whose guilty parent—or both—were too poor to acknowledge her and provide a dot for her to marry somebody her equal in Prince Charles Edward's shabby nobility.

I lay listening to the sounds from the woodshed— heard wood being split, flint scraped, kindlings spluttering, crackling, roaring into flame.

After a while I smelled a most appetizing odour of coffee and something delicious a-frying.

So I got up, washed and shaved in cold water, put on a banyan, turban, and moccasins, and went out into the woodshed. Sandi, hot and flushed from the fireplace, squatted like a child on limber haunches, before a pan of frying trout. She looked around at me with the gayest of grins.

"Sandi," said I, "you certainly have surprised me. Where did you get those brook trout?"

"I caught them," said she, lifting them out upon a beechen platter and laying the crisp, red-hot pork beside them.

Then she placed a pan of hot biscuit handy, a pot of

coffee, and a great dish of soupaan with fresh milk, butter, and some brown sugar scraped onto the blue paper from the cone which smelled like wild honey.

When she had waited upon me:

"Sandi," said I, "have you breakfasted?"

"Not yet, sir—" She filled her own tin plate, took her soupaan and a little pannikin of milk, and went and sat down on the chopping block.

She was so pretty and gay a thing that I was tempted to make her sit at table with me—but knew it would ruin discipline and very soon disclose her true sex to Joyce and to anybody else. Also, there was no telling what effect it would have on her—she might mistake the invitation as preliminary to inviting her to share my camp bed; and become presumptuous and intolerable. . . . One can't promote a servant materially and demote her morally and not regret it, no matter how pretty her face and body and ways. No; it was better in every sense that Sandi should eat by herself on the chopping block. And sleep by herself. . . . At least, as far as I was concerned. . . . I gave her an unpremeditated glance, then with the sour face of a Massachusetts Puritan I ate my hasty pudding. . . . By God, if she started any wench's tricks in my service I'd send her packing. . . . I'd have no other man taking the same liberties which I refused to myself.

I caught the girl's eye, and she gave me so heavenly and chaste a smile that I felt mean and ashamed that my vulgar mind should run on matters of which her own thoughts, so evidently, were virginal.

"Sandi, your cooking is extremely palatable. Where did you learn to flavour?"

"Ho!" cried she disdainfully, "this is not real cooking,

sir. This is nothing. Anybody could fry trout in pork and cornmeal. Wait until I make you a ragout, sir, or a soup or an omelette, or a paté— My God, Captain Cardress, wait until you taste my Truite à la Cardinal, or my Omelette Soufflée Diabolique, or Filet de Bœuf Charles Martel!

"Wait, sir—I'll go up Fort Creek and catch for you a basket full of little écrevisses which I saw there today! And then I shall make for you a bisque d'écrevisses à la Saint Antoine—oh, my Captain, it will tempt you far more madly than the dames sans culottes tempted that poor Saint Anthony to carnal pleasures."

She became prettily excited, and I was laughing as she ran off on her shapely fingers the lists of her culinary accomplishments, naming a score of dishes I never even had heard of.

"Where on earth," said I, "did you learn to prepare such fare? Only the rich and titled could have their tables garnished with luxuries such as you describe!"

She made a graceful gesture with body, shoulders, and hands: "Tenez, monsieur, j'ai pensé qu'il convenait, au moment, où nous sommes un peu géné ensemble, de faire mon possible pour vous être agreeable!"

That quaint Scotch-French made me laugh, yet charmed me, too.

"My dear Sandi," said I before I knew it—and too late to realize that one doesn't so address one's servant— "I don't believe you ever were turnspit to anybody's chef, and yet you must have lived in a great house, at some time, or you never would even know the names of these dishes you threaten me with so charmingly."

56

"Sir," said she, "God is my witness I do not mean either to threaten you or be charming!"

We both laughed at that.

"My Captain," said she, always using the French mode of address when speaking in English, "it would be useless to deny to you that I have known a little something of luxury and of ease and well being, having served a great lady—well, great in one sense, since she has great power and great riches—"

She smiled in reminiscence and looked down, linking and relinking her fingers.

"In what capacity, Sandi, did you serve her?"

"Oh, as a kind of maid. You may not believe me, sir, but the lady had more than three dresses for every day in the year!"

"You looked after those dresses?"

"Well—no. . . . I was invited to take some such position in her household. We call it dame d'atours."

"Demoiselle d'atours?"

"Something like that, I suppose, sir," she laughed, "—as I am what you call a demoiselle."

"Who was the lady?"

Her cheery smile altered. After a pause: "Captain Cardress, you never have kissed her hand," said Sandi, so sweetly, yet with such cool self-possession that the rebuke itself did not astonish me as greatly as did her amazing savoir faire and the astounding sophistication of this young thing in skirted boy's coat and snuffy breeches and stockings, who poured water upon our battalion garden to make carrots and cucumbers thrive.

I felt my face flush a little.

"Very well," said I, "—I don't mean to pry into your affairs."

"Even a servant is entitled to privacy—though nobody believes it," said she. . . . "Even a dog likes the seclusion of his kennel sometimes, and looks dubiously upon a beloved but invading master."

"You are amazingly philosophical."

"Monsieur Voltaire—if you know who I mean, sir, is even a more amazing philosopher than am I," said she.

Her eyes, which slanted up in the corners a little, her delicately tilted nose, her jeering, rosy mouth of a very rogue, all combined so impudently to flavour her impertinence that I laughed in spite of myself.

"You are very saucy," said I, "—and with an odd kind of insolence, too—as though your sarcasms were due to some superiority of birth as well as of mind. One would think you had to do with an inferior."

"Oh, sir, can you think it!" she cried in consternation —or in pretense of consternation which still seemed to have an ironical hint of roguery in it.

"Sandi," said I, "you have been, I believe, the confidential and personal maid of some great lady, and from her have learned a thousand little insolences and impertinences. Is it not so?"

"How can you say it, sir, of a young woman so poor, so uneducated, so entirely without wit! What have I done—"

"Well, you've done something to get yourself aboard a French ship, and be taken prisoner among a score of soldiers' women, penniless, and in boy's clothing!

"I can't guess what you've done—run away from your husband, for all I know—or fled the vengeance of a noble lover you deceived—or an angry wife; or you perhaps have barely managed to dodge a lettre-de-cachet and the Bastille.

"But whether you are running away from the King of France, or his painted Pompadour, or fleeing from lesser fry, nevertheless you are as clever as you can be, and full of resource, wit, and courage. . . . You bathe, also, and smell too damned sweet to be either a peasant or a bastard of the Blood Royal—those nasty French Bourbons, poxed and lousy and unwashed—"

"Well, I'm none of those!" she cried. "Mother of God, sir, if I wash my body and smell like a flower it is because I like to smell flowers when fresh washed by dew or rain!

"As for my wit, and what you are pleased to call my courage, you seem a kindly gentleman, an indulgent master, and a soldier with as innocent a heart as it is a stout one. . . . And, sir, in all France I have heard of only a few such pure and chivalrous chevaliers!—" and gave me a look almost devilish in its sparkling and malicious defiance, "—and, sir, one of these few is Prince Charles Edward Stuart!"

I burst out laughing. "Oho! So that's it! Since Bonnie Prince Charlie lacks a shirt-tail, you go without a chemise under your scant clothing!"

"Yes, sir," said she, calmly, "as naked as God made me. Hence the blouse of a mousse in which you discovered me!"

"It was you who discovered *me*, Sandi," said I, smiling. "Come, suppose you tell me, now, why you selected me as your vehicle for escape to freedom?"

The girl gave me an almost shameless look which most impertinently enlightened me.

"So you thought I looked kind hearted and stupid, and could easily be managed?" I asked.

"Oh, Captain Cardress!"

"What was your plan? To become my mistress?"

"No, sir."

"What, then? To make profitable acquaintance among the military quality in this army and so escape the hazards, pains, and poverty of an enlisted woman?"

She reddened. I was vastly annoyed at her and she with me.

She said, with the angry colour glowing in her face: "You have no true reason to speak lightly of me, Captain Cardress. Have I tried to seduce you? Or any other? Would you ever have learned my real sex if your filthy Yankee Rangers had not uncovered my naked body in the river?

"Where is there, then, any mystery in a frightened French girl putting on boy's clothing to save herself from the world's annoyance? Why is it very strange that I saw in you an English gentleman who seemed civilized in this accursed country of Yankee yokels and brutal British oafs? Why is it odd that my desperate eyes mutely begged your aid, and my trembling voice solicited employment—to save me from barrack and brothel or the starved dole flung at those for whom, in the world, the fortunate and powerful have found no place excepting the gutter or the stews?"

I looked at her in astonishment to hear such speech, and such calmly bitter choice of English word and phrase.

Here was quality! Here also was tragedy. But concerning either I knew no more than that both existed in the person of this boy-shaped young girl in boy's attire, whom I had taken from a French prize on Whitehall wharf one day, and having no intention of doing such a thing until I found that already I had done it.

"Sandi," said I, "would you like me to ask for a Court of Inquiry concerning you, where you could give every evidence in regard to your true identity, and offer satisfactory guarantees that, in case you were permitted to proceed to Canada, your liberation would not be in any way detrimental to the English cause?"

While I was speaking her face was changing oddly with every word I uttered.

And when I ended she came to me in silence and took hold of my sleeve with both hands; and stood looking up at me, deathly pale.

"What's the matter with you?" I asked.

"I want no court. I wish to remain with you."

"What for?"

"My God, sir, where else am I to go and be certain of kindness?"

"You mean you'd prefer to remain the servant of a British Provincial Officer who is not likely to annoy you, rather than to take your chances in Canada?"

She nodded; hung her curly head of a lad; and her slender, sun-tanned fingers wandering over and picking at the military gold lace on my sleeve.

I was touched. I liked the girl. Also, now, her preference flattered me. Besides, this young thing was a sweetly healthy creature to look upon, compared to the nasty, sickly army women and the painted strumpets who, excepting a few officers' ladies, were the only women at this post—although George Munro—I mean the Colonel commanding at William Henry—had respectable and agreeable looking women in his garrison.

I put my arm around Sandi. The odour of her was as fresh as a flower at sunrise.

"I like to see you around," said I. "It's like having lavender in one's linen. . . . You don't want to be my mistress, do you?"

She gave me a troubled look.

"Do you?" I repeated.

She shook her head slightly and picked at the gold lace on my sleeve.

"Very well," said I, laughing, "don't look so serious about it. All you have to do is to continue to go about in a smock and boy's breeches, and cook for me, and you'll not trouble my sleep."

She looked up then, with a breathless little smile; and I didn't intend to, but I kissed her full on the mouth.

That was silly of me. I don't know whether I was as white as she was—for I had my share of the shock—so unexpectedly hot and sweet the contact.

"I ought not to have done that," said I, "—being well enough off and content as I was. . . . Who'd have dreamed that there could be such troublesome heat and sweetness in a woman's kiss!"

She said in an odd, stiff way: "Have a care, or you are lost, sir; and likely to carry me with you into hell."

Her deathly pallor faded; and the blood was heating my own face, too.

She stammered about God being cruel to a young girl on her bed of folly, and that the world of men was even crueller.

SANDI

"Why do you cry out," said I, "who stand in no peril from me?"

"Sir," said she, "my sentiments both bewilder and confuse me. Seduced, I could hate you; neglected, I might by turns detest you and entertain for you a perilous tenderness which invites and yields. . . . You had better let me alone until I know what truly is in my mind concerning you and your kiss."

"I think so, too. . . . I never have intended to annoy you."

"It's not annoyance. And it is the more dangerous for that reason."

Her emotional confusion and lack of virginal resentment; her inborn honesty, troubled me. The sweet indecision of her mind indicated no lack of sophistication. She seemed to know quite well what raised the wind and what the dust cloud hid; and what was impulse, and whither passion might lead it.

"Have you never loved a man, Sandi?" I asked.

"Not with—sinful abandon, sir."

"You've never yet had a real lover?"

"Yes; but never have been his real mistress." She laughed uncertainly, then scowled at me.

"You didn't love him," said I.

"Not enough, I suppose. . . . I don't know of what stuff love is made. . . . There was more of it in your kiss than ever I have known before—"

"More of love?"

"Inclination for it. . . . I don't think we'd better kiss again for quite a long time."

"Why?"

"Not that I am cold. . . . Could it remain this way,

sir—that if I wish for your kiss I'll venture to make my inclination known to you?"

I began to laugh. Such honesty was more seductive than the subtlest art—or so it seemed to me—and the very innocence of it made me laugh to hear and see it.

Sandi, looking at me under rumpled curls, smiled uncertainly. She said: "We'll not play at mistress and lover—or at love or any such games—if you please."

"No," said I, "there's mischief in it, and we'll let it alone."

"I hope you will have no regrets, sir."

"I shall have none other than those devil-inspired ones which assail a man when he has taken no advantage of opportunity."

"Sir," said she, "do you believe that I am an opportunity?"

"I fear so," said I.

We both laughed gaily and with all our hearts.

CHAPTER VI

SONG OF THE SOURIQUOIS

I HEARD the Souriquois singing at dawn. Inter-threaded with bird melody and the golden wash of water over shale, their monotonous, nasal melody seemed to blend naturally with the noises of a waking world at daybreak. Excepting for these sounds, such a pale, misty stillness possessed the forest that the splash of feeding trout in Fort Creek was sharply audible above the ripple of the running water.

Nothing in God's celestial paradise above, it seems to me, could be more beautiful than this northern forest world of ours in spring and early summer.

What choir of cherubim could vie with the hermit thrush's chorus? What perfume in paradise could be more heavenly than arbutus scent? Where hath God in His own aerial domain created such witchery of beauty, such angelic grace, such awesome grandeur as in His living tapestry of forest, lake, and peak which our great river drains?

I got up, tied a towel around me, opened the door and looked into the woodshed-kitchen.

The girl was fast asleep under her blanket, her head with its crisp curls cradled upon an arm crooked beneath it.

Joyce, who slept and messed with the Yorkers at their barracks, had not yet appeared.

65

All was dusky and still, with the mountain chill in the air.

So I took my towel and went down to the foggy river where I bathed me; and saw the sentinels at the barrier, pacing their posts, and heard the cocks crowing on the Island.

It was not until I had heated a tin of water and had shaved and dressed that the morning gun banged to salute the hoisted flag, and the garrison of Fort Edward awoke again to see a painted sky glowing behind the forest where the entangled sun was seeking his misty way to his happy hunting grounds on high.

Drum-beat and fifing, roll call and mess call, bugles musically eloquent, fragrant smoke from kitchens, appetizing odours of baked johnnycake and frying meat, the timed cadence of guard relief, of details, patrols; music of some regiment marching out; far volleys, single target shots, or the rattling racket of a company cleaning its pieces—all these familiar noises greeted the rising glitter of the sun. Later came a scraping of mattocks and shovels on unfinished parapets, and the din of two score New York carpenters busy with unfinished barracks.

Sandi, fresh as a flower in her boy's smock and breeches, her tangled curls tied in a short queue, yawning, humorous, her veiled glance hinting of impertinence, fetched me my hasty pudding or soupaan, with a jug of milk and a crust warm from the baking.

She washed some wild strawberries which Joyce had fetched, and these I had, too.

"Why were the Souriquois scouts singing, Joyce?" I inquired.

"Lieutenant Colings, with the Souriquois and a scout

66

of twenty-two, are ordered to lie on the mountains west of South Bay, and lie there three days, sir. The Souriquois scouts have been greasing and painting themselves, and singing their whining song since before sun-up."

When I had finished my breakfast I told Sandi to wear stout leggins and boots when working on the Island, and to beware of rattlesnakes where rocks were, or dense, uncleared brush.

There was a general court martial of the line to sit at eight o'clock, to try such prisoners as should be brought before it. I was a member—my commission being in the Royals—and Colonel Young was President and Captain Woodall Judge Advocate.

But General Webb adjourned it and sent for me to come to him instantly in his quarters. Which I did; and found him red and agitated over a silly tale told by one of our British regulars who, at dawn this morning, being on piquet across the barrier and close to a hard ridge running easterly from the fort where there is a swamp to the north, caught a glimpse of what, in the uncertain light, he took to be a huge humming bird.

When he had glimpsed and heard three more of them, the fifth hit a tree by which he was standing.

It was a feathered arrow, and it stood quivering in the bark.

"Here it is, Captain Cardress," said Webb in an anxious voice. "I suppose, in the absence of Sir William Johnson, that you are better qualified than any other to tell me what kind of arrow this may be."

"Why," said I, taking it from him, "it is an Indian war arrow, made and fired, no doubt, by the Ottawas."

"Is it poisoned, sir?" he asked quickly.

"Oh, no, General; the Ottawas don't do that."

"What do you suppose it indicates?" he demanded nervously.

"Why, sir," I replied, smiling, "it indicates that the French employ Ottawas—which we already knew—and it warns us that their warrior-Marquis and his White Coats are moving up the lakes to have a closer look at us."

"To attack this post?"

"Well, either this or Fort William Henry, sir."

"Damnation," said he spitefully, "I wish Lord Loudon would get about his business of Louisbourg more smartly. He has eight thousand men. He has skinned the valley. He ought to be before Louisbourg now. And, if he were, we'd have no murderous Marquis of Montcalm with his White Coats and his filthy Indians skulking at our back door to scalp us in our beds!"

He was such a poltroon that he made no concealment of his peculiar terrors concerning Indians.

I had nothing further to say to him. He asked me what I was doing about getting spies into Louisbourg. I said it still remained a problem to be solved; and that, other material lacking, I would make the attempt myself.

"Have a care," cried Webb, aghast at the idea, "they hang all spies, you know. Let the enlisted men do that sort of dirty work. I don't want it said that any of my officers were hanged by the neck."

I did not know what to say to this preposterous General, Dan'l Webb, so, when presently dismissed, went to see Colonel Montressor with a bad taste in my mouth.

Although father of that little ass, Lieutenant John, Colonel Montressor was a gallant officer and an excellent engineer—No. 2 in the British Army.

He told me that the stores and the mail from Albany had come in very heavily guarded, late last night, and that in future all piquets and local covering parties were to parade with twenty-four rounds.

"There's no doubt," said he, "the French are on the move. Their spies are trying to tamper with our piquets; their Indians are hanging about for scalps; and our Mohawks have brought in a French prisoner from the Regiment Artois, whom they caught last week near Crown Point."

"I didn't know it," said I.

"Oh, yes, it's true. I saw the lad. No doubt, as staff-captain interpreter, you'll be ordered to examine him."

As I took my leave of the Colonel, and went out of the fort, I heard the drums of the Connecticut Regiment. Presently they appeared on the parade, to be inspected by Lyman. And I smiled as I noticed that their trousers had been washed and they wore their shoes and stockings under their spatterdashes—the dirty pups!

I went up the river a piece to see the Souriquois in their camp. They were making ready to go to South Bay. They are a decent lot. I always liked the Souriquois, and had them once under my command during Sir William's fight at St. Sacrement, after the death of the grand old man of the Mohawks.

Well, as I walked into their camp where their women were cooking and their children playing ball, I was recognized and greeted merrily by warriors, women and children all a-grin.

"I heard you bark-eating foresters singing before sunrise," said I, shaking hands with a dozen brawny, painted warriors who came, one by one, to say with a grunt that they were glad to see me.

They showed me the peeled and painted post in which their war hatchets were still sticking, and before which their chief sorcerer, Jahaiac, wearing all his gaudy regalia and a huge wildcat's mask, was laying out the contents of his otterskin medicine bag and his turtle-shell rattle.

He heard me, looked around over his shoulder, and called out to me in a bantering voice that he remembered my uniform but that my face had altered beyond his recollection. Thrusting out a sinewy hand in welcome, he repeated that my feet had forgotten the Souriquois trail.

"You still make magic?" I asked laughingly, squatting down beside him. "Have the Souriquois become so cautious that they dare not take an Ottawa by the scalplock until you play tunes on your rattle?"

He gave me a funny, humorous look as though to say, "You always see through me, but maybe you don't see *everything* inside of me."

He said, with a smug smirk: "Brother, precaution is necessary because we Souriquois, as you know, are not a numerous people. The Ottawas and the Praying Indians from Caughnawaga might do to us what the Iroquois did to the Cat People—the Eries—and to the great nation of the Andastes. The sun casts their shadows no more."

"My brother is right," said I gravely. "I made a jest, as you know. It is entirely proper to examine into the future before attempting such an enterprise."

He looked at me uncertainly, but, seeing that I had become serious:

"We sang a great many songs before sunrise," said he; "every warrior selected for this scout sang his own song and struck the post. . . . Perhaps we boasted. A full belly laughs and lies, brother."

"Who gave you your red wampum?" I inquired curiously.

"Sir William. He sent us a bundle of little red sticks and a great red belt. We took what he sent, although the Abenaquis warned us to kick any red belt around our council fire."

"Naturally. . . . I wish I were in my paint," said I, "and going with you."

I was sorry I said it, for they set up a clamour for me to lead them until Gayfeather, their war-chief, made them stop their noise.

He had a bit of broken glass for a mirror, and sat cross-legged at his lodge door, painting himself while his pretty wife roached his hair and braided the scalp-lock.

"Brother," said he, "have you examined the French soldier whom the Mohawks have brought in from Crown Point?"

"No," said I, "why do you ask, Saquahayac?"

The Indian gave me a shrewd look: "He did not seem very anxious to escape, this White Coat—or so it seemed to us of the Souriquois."

"What is that you say?"

"I say, brother, that this French soldier in his white uniform did not seem very eager to get away from the Mohawk scouts. I was there. I saw the Mohawks chasing him. He could have escaped. He ran up a hill where aspens grew. The beaver had felled many trees

71

to slide them down to the dam below. This Frenchman stumbled over one of these pointed stumps. . . . *And did not get up.* But he was neither exhausted nor injured."

I nodded.

Then the Souriquois warrior stood up in his fluttering feathers and naked paint, and touched my breast with his finger-tip.

"Brother, tell General Webb not to trust any French deserters, for they will desert again from the English ranks and carry to Montcalm sufficient information to ruin everybody.

"Brother, if Lord Loudon is a great chief, why is he not already in Louisbourg?

"He waits in New York for his Admiral. But he will not come, this Admiral. Lord Loudon will not go to Louisbourg."

"Why do you think so?"

"Because Montcalm is a greater chief than Lord Loudon, and he wishes to fight the war here on these two lakes, and not in the north before Louisbourg."

"Yes, perhaps. But why should we oblige Montcalm?"

"No, *he* obliges *you*, brother! He has had his way with you already," said the Souriquois with slight contempt. "Look, brother; use your eyes! What do you see at Carillon? Eight thousand White Coats and Indians. Now look northward. What does my brother see on the Royal Island? Nothing except the great fortress-city where life continues as calmly as it passes in Quebec and Montreal."

"Saquahayac," said I, "here is a secret for you alone:

I wish to get into this damned Louisbourg. I have no-body to send who is fit to go upon such a mission. So I must go myself.

"What I wish you to do is to guide me as far as the last outpost of your people. Will you do it?"

"When, brother?"

"When you return from this useless scout. I will ask Sir William Johnson's permission to employ you and arrange for your compensation with him."

The Souriquois smiled: "We are a poor people, brother; the Mohawks and Oneidas and Senecas are rich in comparison. Nevertheless, neither my brother, John Cardress, nor my father, Sir William Johnson, need pay me to perform this act for my captain-brother. You are my *friend*. You may give what you choose, or give noth-ing except your friendship. Your Souriquois brothers will take you safely wherever you desire to go."

Lieutenant Colings came up in his Indian forest dress. He said that a Major of Sir William's Palatine Regiment and George Croghan, had designated me to interrogate the French soldier fetched in by the Mohawks.

I asked Colings what he, his scout, and the Souriquois were going to do at South Bay, and he said, "Nothing more than try to count the White Coats for General Webb."

He spoke with a slight sneer as though without respect for our commanding officer.

"I wish," said I in his ear, "that either Sir William or General Lyman led us. Or even Loudon."

He said, "God help Fort William Henry and Colonel Munro when Montcalm marches. . . . I don't want to be

73

forced into that fortress—I can tell you that! The Souriquois feel the same way, and Saquahayac told me that if Webb ordered the Souriquois into William Henry they'd go, but they'd go in death-paint and wood-ashes, every warrior singing his death song. . . . And, by God, I would feel like reciting the prayers for the dying as I marched at the head of my men, if Webb ever orders me into that damned and doomed fort!"

We stood gloomily watching the Souriquois at their battle toilet. They were not tall Indians, but they were built squarely and powerfully—and, as they sat or stood about, naked except for the flap, painting their hides or being painted, oiled, roached, or head-shaven, they had a wild, forest-animal look—like a herd of panthers— which neither the Mohawks nor Oneidas had, and seemed as untamed and dangerous as the pagan Ottawas who, I think, are the most degraded, ferocious, and utterly untamable of all Indians I ever have encountered.

Colings impatiently spoke to Saquahayac, urging haste; but nobody—not even Sir William Johnson—nor God himself—could hurry any Indian. Colings knew it as well as I did—as well as the Souriquois trackers themselves knew it.

A lean, muscular Indian who had painted his belly a poisonous yellow, and his shaven head scarlet—his name, in the Souriquois dialect, meaning Woodpecker—started a sonorous nasal chanting as he wrenched his hatchet from the scarlet war-post and began to strut around it and tap-tap it with the pick end of his polished war-axe.

In English his bragging chant meant something like this—

74

SONG OF THE SOURIQUOIS

"I am the Woodpecker,
My head is red,—
The head is redder still
Which I peck with my bill!
I am the Woodpecker,
I scalp my dead!

"Now wolf and bear
May feed their fill!
Where my dead lie with hairless head,
Mine's not the only skull that's red!"

A very young warrior who yet wore two eagle-feathers
sagging low from his scalp-lock, stepped swiftly to the
post and wrenched from it his war-hatchet.

His name was the Fire-Lighter. He threw himself
into violent pantomime, chanting as he acted in terrible
earnest the words of what he sang:

"I am a young fighter;
When I strike, my enemy screams!
I am the Fire-Lighter!
I see flames in my dreams!
I know how to torment a prisoner to death
By fire in a thousand ways!

I watch his heart and I watch his breath,
While he lives and shrieks three days!—
Three days of skinning alive,
While his eyes run down his cheeks—
The Fire-Lighter makes him thrive
At the stake where he gasps and reeks!"

75

They all chanted:

> *"Let the Praying Indians flee;*
> *Let the Black-Robes weep!*
> *From under the Great Tree*
> *Our polished hatchets leap;*
> *Hark to the war-birds' cry,*
> *The Iron birds on high,*
> *Ha wa sahsay! Koué!*
> *Let the Ottawa Nation die!"*

Saquahayac, terribly excited, jerked his war-axe from the partly shattered painted post:

> *"I am Saquahayac!*
> *The Ottawas call me a rogue!*
> *I am Saquahayac!*
> *My clan is the Togue;*
> *As I swim to the Horicon from Michilimacinac,*
> *Neither Muskelonge nor Cousin Bad-eye dare attack!*
> *Nor the great Tiger-pike of the North!*
> *Be ashamed, O Caughnawagas! Dare to come forth!*
> *They run to their Black-Robe Priest,*
> *The renegade Iroquois!*
> *While the Togue and the Seagull feast*
> *With the clans of the Souriquois!"*

All the Souriquois scouts, now, were strutting, stamping, posturing, chanting around the post.

I said to Colings: "They'll be ready by noon, I think. Good luck to you!"

He gave me his hand and a sombre look:

"I have not been a very good man," said he, "and I pray God will not punish me by letting me be driven into Fort William Henry."

I went back to the guard-house within the lines of the Valley regiments, and there saw the French soldier of the Regiment Artois who, I understood, had offered to desert his colors and enlist in our Indian department.

He was well but conspicuously uniformed—although his white coat and breeches were no more conspicuous to an enemy rifleman than our scarlet and buff and white.

He was a cheerful young man, and well mannered, and sprang to attention when I entered his prison. I couldn't help smiling at him, so young, eager, alive he seemed with all that energy, vitality, and humour which is more Gallic than Celtic, perhaps, yet seems born of both.

"Instead of interrogating you," said I in French, "suppose, to save time, you tell me all about yourself and your business."

"Well, then, sir," said he in English, "to save your valuable time, sir, I am the soldier Paul Lebel, 5th Company, Regiment Artois, and was on scout with the Abenaquis when taken by your Mohawks near a beaver pond."

"All that I know, Private Lebel; now tell me something of interest that I don't know."

"Very good, sir. Monsieur de Montcalm's army numbers about eight thousand—"

"I know that! I know all about his infantry, artillery, scouts, and Indians. What I wish to know is, what are his intentions?"

The young man was very voluble. Of course he explained he was merely a private soldier in the Regiment Artois, and he was not in the confidence of his General. Here he laughed and showed his very white teeth —but, as well as he could make out, the Marquis, on reconnaisance, had found Forts William Henry, Edward, and Ann too strong for him. Also, it was said that General Lord Loudon had out-manœuvred him, and he was compelled to fall back and try to help in the defense of Louisbourg which was threatened by a huge British fleet as well as by Lord Loudon's army of regulars, now preparing to march aboard their transports.

"Oh," said I, "has Vice Admiral Holburne arrived in New York?"

"That, Captain, is what is being talked about in the French army. And it is said that Monsieur de Montcalm must renounce his plans against these forts—"

"*Why?* Are there no French battleships off Louisbourg?"

He gave me a guileless look and shook his head: "No, sir, I hear that there are no French warships near Louisbourg."

"So that's why General the Marquis of Montcalm's army is about to withdraw from these forts—and from this campaign? To sail for Louisbourg?"

"Yes, sir."

"And you tell me that the attempt upon Fort William Henry is to be abandoned, and that your army is to retreat, also, from Carillon—or Ticonderoga—because there is no French naval force at Isle Royale to give battle to Admiral Holburne?"

"Yes, sir, I assert it to be a fact."

He was so pitifully young, so handsome, so gallant, so full of misdirected courage, and so terribly easy to see through—so utterly at my mercy—that my heart revolted at what must happen to this gallant boy in his white uniform—and, my God!—traces of pearl powder and pomatum on his beautifully dressed hair of an aristocrat!

The sudden thought of him strangling to death on a military gallows sickened me. At the same instant I realized that I could save him from such a death if I accused him of espionage *while he still wore the uniform of France!*

If I gave him time to discard that uniform this charming boy was as certainly dead as though the drums were rolling and he hung choking in the hollow square at a waxed rope's end.

Something he noticed in my gloomy gaze may have averted him of approaching trouble, for a very slight flush mounted to his cheeks and he looked at me intently.

"Suppose," said I, "I should tell you that three powerful squadrons of French warships have arrived before Louisbourg?"

He sustained my gaze admirably, as he denied it.

"Suppose," said I, "that I tell you, further, that this Vice Admiral of ours has not yet appeared in New York waters; and that your General knows quite well that Lord Loudon does not dare embark his army unprotected."

The young man said politely that the most recent information was positive.

"Yes, it is," said I. "And here it is—part of it just fetched in by our scouts sent out from Halifax! There are three squadrons of French ships at Louisbourg, and the names of your admirals and the names of their ships, and even the rating of each ship, are known."

I pulled from my pocket a paper, gave him a cold, hard look, and read aloud:

" 'Admiral Du Revest with four ships of the line; Admiral De Beauffremont with four ships of the line; Admiral Du Bois de la Motte with nine of the line and two frigates.' . . . Come, soldier, is this true or is it a lie?

"Did you never hear of these tall ships?" And I read off the alarming list of them aloud:

"Le Formidable,	80 guns
Le Tonnant,	80 guns
Le Duc de Bourgogne,	80 guns
Le Defenseur,	74 guns
Le Héros,	74 guns
Le Diadème,	74 guns
L'Hector,	74 guns
Le Glorieux,	74 guns
Le Dauphin Royal,	70 guns
Le Superbe,	70 guns
Le Bizarre,	64 guns
L'Achille,	64 guns
L'Eveillé,	64 guns
Le Vaillant,	64 guns
L'Inflexible,	64 guns
Le Bellequeux,	64 guns
Le Sage,	64 guns
Le Célèbre,	64 guns
L'Abenaskise,	38 guns
La Brune,	30 guns
La Fleur de Lys,	30 guns

La Comette,	30 guns
La Fortune,	30 guns
L'Hermione,	26 guns"

I finished reading, folded the document, gave the young man a terrible look which, I must say, he sustained with courage, although there was now a fixedness to his expression betraying strain and effort.

I said:

"What the devil is all this nonsense you have been telling me about your Marquis and his army?"

"I have told you only facts, my Captain," he replied steadily. He was a brave youth, God knows.

"You wear the uniform and facings of the French regulars, don't you?"

"Yes, Captain."

"Of the Regiment Artois?"

"Yes, sir."

"Your regiment is yonder at Carillon with General the Marquis of Montcalm?"

"Yes, Captain."

"And you were out on special scout duty with the Abenaquis when captured?"

"Yes, sir."

"And now you are willing to desert your colours and take service in our army—under our flag?"

"Yes, Captain."

"That is why you give me all this information about your army?"

"Yes, sir."

"Where is the Regiment Bourgogne?"

"It, also, is at Carillon, sir."

"And Boishébert and his forest runners and Indians
—is he also here?"

"Yes, sir."

"Young man," said I, "you lie. You are a French
spy. You have determined to get into our camps for information. You deliberately permitted our Mohawks
to catch you. You pretend, now, to wish to enlist in our
Indian department.

"Everything you have told me is a lie. The ships I
have named, and their guns, crew, admirals, all are at
this instant in Gabarus Bay off Louisbourg, ready to attack our transports and drown the entire English army
of eight thousand men under General Lord Loudon."

He gave me a calm, colourless look, but his smooth,
tense, boyish throat jerked in a kind of spasm as though
the rope already scraped it.

"More than that," said I, "your Regiment Artois, four
hundred and thirty-seven strong, is part of the Louisbourg garrison. If you came from it on special duty
with the French Indians, you have come all the way from
Louisbourg.

"And I'll tell you, also, while I'm on the subject, that
the Regiment Bourgogne, also, is at Louisbourg—five
hundred and thirty-six strong. Two hundred and sixty
coureurs-de-bois and Indians under Boishébert are at
Louisbourg. Also, four of the marine battalions of two
hundred men each. . . . If I count in the Foreign
Legion—in which I do not doubt you really are an
officer disguised as a private in the regulars—and if I
count, also, artillery, Quebec troops, and volunteers from
your fleet, it will give you more than three thousand
garrison for Louisbourg. Add the eight thousand of

Montcalm—and a battle-fleet of twenty-four ships more powerful than Holburne's—well, young man, figure out the problem for yourself.

"I'll tell you the answer if you like; it's this: your clever, fighting Marquis and eight thousand regulars and Indians are going to invest and assault these forts just as soon as a few such spies as you report conditions. . . . And, as for me, I know damned well that my Lord Loudon ought to be at this instant, instead of playing Sister Ann at New York to Holburne's cloud of dust on the horizon.

"And this I shall report; and I shall advise all coureurs-express to stop Lord Loudon and fetch him back here in haste. And—though you never will live to know it, much less carry word of it to your clever Marquis—unless my General is crazy, upon his arrival here he will march instantly on Carillon, and forever purge these two English lakes of the French rat's nest so long infesting them!"

The young man's face had become deathly drawn and white under his mask of tan.

"Soldier Lebel, you are a spy. Confess it," said I.

But he denied it in a hoarse, unsteady voice.

"I tell you to admit it. And, further, I advise you to confess the details of the plot which sent you here from Louisbourg. And if there be other French spies in this camp, and if you will reveal their identity, the military court which tries you will take that into consideration as a mitigation in rendering a verdict."

He shook his head but said nothing. Whether fear actually closed his throat, or whether a determination to die without betraying those who accompanied him, if any, or those who sent him, stiffened his courage, I do not know.

It had made me sick enough to discover his design. He was so young—so lively, intelligent, humorous, so good-looking. I was thankful that I had spared him a gallows death. I had no doubt at all that this pretended private soldier, Lebel, of the Regiment Artois, was actually an aristocrat and a commissioned officer in the Foreign Legion under Charles Follis and the Chevalier Johnstone, where many a sprig of English, Irish, and Scottish nobility served France in the ranks, through sheer hatred of the dumpy little German King of England.

"Private Paul Lebel," said I, "you may believe that I am sorry indeed to see you under these circumstances. You have not learned to lie well. It is plain to me that deceit is not natural to a nature so frank and young and—courageous.

"And if I, casually, and unskilled in such matters, have had no difficulty in detecting your real purpose, it will not take a military court very long to come to a conclusion concerning your business at Fort Edward."

I made him a slight gesture of adieu; he gave me, under the blinding shock of discovery, the officer's salute—attempting to disguise it the same instant in his dire confusion.

It was too painful for me—anything that smelled of legal murder and the hangman—and I was glad to step into the outer air and sunshine after instructing the sergeant of the guard to use every caution in securing this young man pending orders from Headquarters.

As I came out upon the parade, through the sallyport

and across the drawbridge, I heard my name spoken, and, turning, saw Sandi at my heels.

"Where the devil did you come from?" I demanded, displeased to find the girl loitering under foot when I was engaged in so delicate and vital a business as had taken me to the guard-house.

"They told me," said she, innocently, "that you were examining a French deserter in the Yorkers' old guard-house; so, thinking it might prove amusing, I sat down on the settle to listen——"

"Oh, that's what you did!" said I, sharply. "Well, have you overheard what I have been saying to this same French deserter?"

"It bored me."

"Answer me. Did you hear what was said?"

She shrugged her shoulders. "Do you suppose, sir, that all this military chatter means anything to me?"

"I'm wondering," said I, giving her a sharp look, "just how safe it is to have you in this garrison."

"You do honour to my head in which you pretend to suspect a brain," said she gaily. . . . "What of interest did you learn from this little French soldier?"

"I learned," said I, "that probably he is a French spy sent here from Louisbourg and instructed to desert and enlist with us. I don't suppose they'll hang him—he being still in his own uniform. . . . As for you, you mind your business and keep away from him, and don't loiter around this guard-house, either. Why aren't you on the Island at the morning distribution?"

"I brought full rations of onions and carrots to the Yorkers' barracks; and Lieutenant Colings told me to find

85

Joyce and tell him to say to you that the Souriquois had
eaten up a week's rations in two meals, and were clamoring for meat and corn and tobacco before starting with
the Scout for South Bay. Their sorcerer, who wears
the head of a great cat, refuses to interfere until he can
have a magic talk with you. I saw him. He is eating
soupaan."

"Very well. I have drawn some material and I wish
you to make me a rifle-shirt. Can you sew?"

"Better than I can kiss, sir."

I began to laugh: "Did that old fraud of a witch doctor
say he wanted a magic talk with me, Sandi?"

"Yes, sir. He says that you are a better witch doctor
than any lousy old shaman in Canada."

At that I laughed again, realizing that the old scoundrel
meant to wheedle extra rations out of me before his people
started, and knowing well enough that Sir William Johnson would not countenance it, but relying on my intimate
friendship for and knowledge concerning his rather unknown and misunderstood Indians of the Souriquois Nation—or, rather, Tribe. And I think that only Sir
William and George Croghan and I really understood
these strange people and their strange beliefs, supersti-
tions, clans—their friendships and their hatreds. For
they are, after all, the simplest, least artful of all savages,
—more naïve, more credulous, less suspicious than their
masters, the Iroquois, yet, if understood and treated
kindly, brave, reliable in important emergencies; but otherwise, children and governed by all the fears, impulses,
passions, and friendships which govern children.

So, motioning Sandi to walk beside me, I went out

onto the grand parade outside, and crossed it toward the outlying lodges of the Souriquois scouts.

As I approached I could hear the lugubrious song of the Souriquois; the drumming, rattling, and squalling of their old witch doctor flourishing his turtle rattle full of shot:

"Hai! Hai!" he shouted:

> *"We Souriquois are few,*
> *Few as panthers compared to hares;*
> *What shall we do*
> *To escape the Ottawa snares?*
> *A world of weasels, rabbits, and moles,*
> *Of jays and squirrels draw about us—*
> *Miami, Abenaqui creep from their holes—*
> *Prairie Pagans and Caughnawagas flout us;*
> *What shall we Souriquois Panthers do,*
> *O clans of the togue, the snipe, and the shrew?*
> *In song they call us the Mouse-Folk—*
> *The timid and bark-fed;*
> *What will they sing when our*
> *Panthers' claws rip the hair*
> *From their heads?*
> >   *Hai! Hai!*
> *The red-dripping hair, sticky and*
> *Hot from their heads!—"*

I saw a bored lieutenant of the Indian department, standing near his horse and watching them—one of the Palatine officers from the company of Mounted Rangers.

"For God's sake, sir," said I, "tell Colonel Croghan it's not worth while to haggle over rations; and that I take the responsibility of sending the Souriquois scouts of Colings on their way toward South Bay!"

"Very well, sir," said the Valley officer, saluting and climbing disgustedly into his saddle.

He went off toward the Grand Parade at a stiff gallop on his bony, New England plug which some thieving Connecticut horse-dealer had sold to the Mounted Rangers.

I turned around to speak to Sandi.

"Where the devil," said I, "is that boy?"

I hunted for Sandi all over the Island, throughout the fort, parade, outer works, and every block house.

There was no hotter, dustier, madder man at Edward than I, who had drawn enough Osnabrig for shirting and Indian breeches, and enough tow-cloth for leggings and hunting shirt—being unable to endure the summer heat any longer clad in regimentals, or the buckskin Indian dress of the Yorkers.

Something, some odd intuition, turned my steps toward the guard-house. And there, outside the barred cell of this Frenchman, upon the settle, sat Sandi, an Indian basket and napkin upon her lap—and it was perfectly plain she had fetched food for the prisoner who, doubtless, was now a-munching.

I was so enraged that I remained speechless at sight of her.

She gave me an innocent and pitiful look: "The poor young man," she cooed, "—so I made him a bowl of lemonade and fried him a little fish. . . . There is no harm in that, is there, sir?" she added, her eyes widening as the signs of my wrath became more visible.

I approached her, my chest heaving, my eyes narrowing, and a prey to such a fury that I could have flogged her.

All I could utter was: "Did I tell you to keep away from this guard-house, and to mind your business?"

"Yes, sir, but I only—"

"You go home," said I, hoarsely, "and pack up your duds, because I'm done with you and out you go!"

CHAPTER VII

CAMP-WENCH

WHEN I came into my quarters Sandi, sitting on the chopping block, looked up at me fearfully.

She had been shredding parsley, carrots, and scallions for soup, a beechen bowl upon her knees. I could see that the graceless youngster was scared.

"If you were a real boy," said I, "instead of the sly young jade you are, I'd flog you well for your meddling with that French spy!" And I went to her and gave her a shake: "You are to understand," said I, "that your damned impertinence is a serious business. You are French—so is yonder prisoner who is under suspicion of espionage. And I don't doubt he came here to spy on us. Have you no sense, then, to invite suspicion concerning yourself?"

"You don't think I am a spy, do you?" she whimpered. Her tears fell slowly among the chopped vegetables.

"No, I don't. But I don't know, either, how treacherous you might prove to be if an opportunity occurs. . . . What did you talk about to that French soldier? Did he ask any questions about this fort and garrison?"

"No, sir."

"Did you give him any improper information regarding conditions here?"

"No, sir."

"What did he say?"

"I asked him if he was hungry and he said he was. So

I told him I had some soup for him, and he was very grateful and said so."

"Did he tell you he was going to face a court martial?"

She stared at me so stupidly that I did not repeat the question. I said:

"That fellow came here to let himself be made prisoner in order to enlist with us and then desert to the enemy with all the information he could pick up. He let our Mohawks catch him. Do you understand?"

She merely gazed at me.

"Sandi," said I, "you're neither dumb nor brainless. You know well enough what I'm talking about. You knew perfectly well that it was improper for you to approach that French prisoner. What your idea was—and maybe still is—I don't know and I don't care, now. Because I don't trust you. I consider you both mischievous and sly, and I think that you might even turn spy and informer and betray me and everybody else in this camp if you had a chance to do so.

"So I'm going to get rid of you."

She had become very pale, but she said nothing at all; not a word.

"You can make up your mind," said I, "what you'd prefer to do. I will, if you wish, write a letter to the General commanding at Albany, and give it in charge of our Wagon-Master, requesting a position for you as maid in some genteel private family. Or, if you prefer it, you may go to New York again with a letter to my friend, Captain Whelan, asking him to recommend you as maid servant to some respectable family in the city."

After a silence in which her dark eyes were fixed upon me with melancholy and reproach:

"Come," said I, "which do you choose? For you shan't stay here; I'm damned if you shall!"

She shivered a little:

"P-please forgive me, Captain Cardress—" she stammered.

"No, I won't. I was a fool ever to let you come here with me. The more I see of you the more I begin to realize how clever and how dangerous a young one you may be."

"I—dangerous, sir?" she repeated with a sobbing break in her voice.

"How do I know you're not? I don't know anything about you. I took you off *The Pretty Savage,* a French prize full of recruits for the Regiment Artois, camp women, military stores. You turned out to be no lad at all but a young woman already mature and evidently of good birth and education.

"And here you are in a British camp—a French subject, patriotic, clever, capable, and almost in touch with a numerically superior French army. . . . I'd be culpable to let you remain where you could do us a harm if chance permitted."

Her tears flowed unrestrained: "Do you think I would do you a harm?" she wailed.

"Perhaps you wouldn't wish to harm me, personally, but if you had a chance to do a service to France at England's expense, why, I'm devilish sure you'd do it and thank God for the opportunity."

She gazed miserably into the bowl of vegetables, gulped down a sob, fell to shredding another carrot with trembling fingers.

"How can you have the heart to send me away?" said

she, "when all I do all day long is to sit here and try to please you by my cooking?"

"I don't want to send you away, Sandi, but I'm afraid to keep you."

"You—you seemed to like me—enough—to kiss."

"I like you enough still."

"You don't. You wished to flog me. You were all white in the face when you came in, and your riding-whip swishing and cutting your boot-tops—"

"I was furious, of course—"

"Because I gave a bowl of broth to a poor young man—"

"Damnation, he is no poor young man, but a cursed fellow who comes here to ruin us!—a treacherous, tricky, insinuating, lying Frenchman!"

"Have you no sense, Sandi? Yonder," said I, sweeping my riding-whip in a half circle, "are eight thousand French soldiers and Indians! They're all around us in these woods. They're everywhere, I tell you. I have no doubt at all that within listening distance of a loud haloo a hundred French scouts and naked Ottawas are lying hid to spy upon this post and cut off and murder any who strays alone!"

Sandi, her tears still falling like the last rare drops after a June shower, washed the vegetables, took the lid off the kettle and, enveloped in steam, peeped forlornly into the boiling depths of it where a chunk of butcher's meat stewed.

I watched her seasoning the savoury mess—a slender, lonely, pathetic young thing—and already I was a little ashamed of my anger, of the treatment I had meted out to her, and of my suspicion concerning this youngster who really seemed to be as much of a child as she was a woman.

Well, she was destined to be somebody's camp-wench—fated to scrub, iron, mend, cook for some subaltern—maybe even for somebody from field or staff. Somebody was going to take her anyway. She might make a comely officer's lady in proper clothing. . . . However, perhaps she would begin and end as a soldier's camp-wench.

She covered the iron pot with the lid, raked up the fire which needed mending, turned wearily away to collect more chips, and stumbled directly into my arms. They closed on her, and her two hands took hold of my arms above the elbows. Then she hid her face against me.

Nothing was said. Her fresh, fragrant, and impudent little muzzle bored hard into my shoulder until her features were well hidden. Her hands still rested on both my arms which encircled her; her fingers clutched my sleeves.

"Are you minded to betray me, Sandi?" I asked.

She shook her partly buried head, violently.

"Will you mind your own business in future if I forgive you?"

Her head, with its mess of disordered curls, nodded as violently as it could.

"Will you keep away from all jails, prisoners, guard-houses, and police cells?"

More vigorous nods and a tighter grip of her fingers on my arms.

"You don't want me to be disgraced, do you? Perhaps even courtmartialed?"

It seemed that she did not, emphatically.

I said: "I don't blame you, Sandi, for being patriotic. If you are French you can not help loving France and wishing well to her soldiers. I understand all that. You would be a poor and miserable creature unless you did love your country. But you are not a soldier of France, and there is no reason why you should actively concern yourself in a war which is really just beginning, and which promises to be a long and terrible struggle between your native land and mine."

After a silence she lifted her flushed face from its burrow between my chest and left arm-pit, and looked up at me.

It almost startled me to see what a really lovely little thing she was. At the same time I was aware of a glint of mischief in her tear-wet eyes, and of an air of charming impertinence in her closely held, supple body.

I gave her a little hug, then kissed her impudent, tilted nose. Her wet eyes laughed in mine though her lips still trembled.

"Always," said I, "you get the better of me, Sandi; and now seem to be amused at so easy a conquest. You *ought* to be spanked!"

"I, sir?"

"Yes, *you*! You always are slyly laughing at me, even when you seem hurt and tearful—"

"Oh, Lord, sir, I must be a very comedienne to pull such faces as you describe."

I took her mischievous, rosy face between both hands, and saw the wild-rose colour deepen and her eyes take on that confused, veiled, embarrassed look, yet still sustaining the gaze of mine.

So I kissed her lips—and the kiss, a lingering one, be-

95

came gradually an embrace, until the odd, fragrant warmth of it grew into a melting heat that left her breathless, clutching both my arms with convulsive fingers. Her dark eyes grew misty and she gave me a lovely, blind look.

I wanted more of her; and for a moment her soft, lithe limbs yielded; then her whole body stiffened and she strained away from me and leaned against the woodshed door, breathing fast and brokenly, her bruised lips edged with a frightened smile.

Of course, after it was too late, I realized I had made a fool of myself—a pretty conclusion to a determination to send this young woman to Albany or New York, to be rid of what might prove a danger to my country and myself.

What was in my mind now—to make this highly intelligent young French-Scotch woman my mistress? And perhaps have her betray me daily to any spy the enemy might already have managed to lodge among the soldiers of this garrison of Fort Edward?

I wished to God I had not taken any liberties with her. I wished it bitterly. For there was something—a fresh and passionate sweetness to this young thing's mouth that I could not lightly forget. . . . Not easily. . . . I already knew that. . . . It was something in the mere touch of her, too—in the subtle odour of her smooth, cool skin—in the contact with the rounded body of her under her clothing—

Hang it all!—

I turned and went toward my room in an unseeing, unsteady sort of way. What the devil was all this about, anyway?

Noon dinner call was beaten on the drums of one regiment after another all about us, from Island to creek, while I sat there collecting my disordered thoughts and frowning out of the hinged window with its oiled paper pane now swinging open to the July breeze.

Presently, tip-toe, and with lowered head, came Sandi to fetch my dinner and place it upon my camp table before me.

"I don't wish to eat," said I. "Eat, if you like."

"As far as I am concerned," said she, "what we did has given me an appetite."

Catching my sombre eye, she laughed outright, and her laughter said very plainly to me, "Good Lord, sir, what ails you then, to scowl upon the world when you have but just enjoyed the clinging pleasure of a pair of not unwilling lips!"

"Sandi," said I, smiling at her, "how, I wonder, would you seem in woman's dress?"

"It is whispered, sir," she said demurely, "that I am not unpleasing to the eye when charmingly attired."

"Sandi!"

The girl came to attention.

"At orders, my Captain!" she said with a saucy salute.

"One would think," said I, "that you had been bred to arms and drilled by the King of Prussia himself. . . . Sandi I think you had better wear patch and powder and lip-red and a silken gown with panniers!"

"Oh, Lord, sir, that would reveal me to the world as a woman and your mistress—to my everlasting ruin and unhappiness."

"Do you think it would destroy you to be known as my sweetheart?"

She seated herself on the chopping block, with her bowl of soup, and began to eat it with a big pewter spoon. When she had finished she set aside the bowl and took her plate of meat and bread.

I always gave her a glass of my wine when she dined, and now I filled for her a large glass of claret and set it beside her plate of meat and vegetables, on her own rough little table.

"Lord," said she, "I don't see how you, a fine gentleman, can endure to kiss a greasy, common slut of a servant maid!"

"Good heavens, of whom are you speaking?" said I, "—for you are always as fresh and sweet as a rose in the rain!"

"Nevertheless, how can you kiss and fondle a common camp-wench?"

"I seemed to endure it with courage and resignation," said I. "And you are as much a camp-wench as am I a dirty, rum-soaked sutler!"

She laughed at that and sipped her claret, saying that it made her feel as though she were in France again. Then: "I am not to be sent away to Albany?" she inquired, guilelessly, "am I, sir?"

"No. . . . If you betray me they'll cashier me. No, I want you to remain."

"With *you?*"

"With me, Sandi—"

"Remain with you as your boy, Sandi, sir? Or—"

"Which shall it be, Sandi?"

"I don't know. . . . Do you feel as though you might possibly fall in love with me, sir?"

"And if I did?"

"Well, my Captain, then it would be high time for me to wonder whether I am capable of reciprocating your passion."

"And if you are?" I asked.

"Mon dieu, Monsieur—" she shrugged her pretty shoulders—"what else would there be for me to do except to love you?"

"In every way?"

"God knows, sir."

"What would happen to you now, if I told you I was going away? Would you care very much?"

She had finished her dinner. She took a basin out of doors—soap, orris, and a towel; and cleansed her hands, her face; her mouth and teeth with a birch twig made into a brush.

When she was done she turned and came slowly over to where I stood a-lighting of my long clay pipe.

"Are you going away, sir?" she asked gravely.

"Yes. Why?"

"Will you take me?"

"I can't, Sandi."

"You could, sir. I can go everywhere you go if you will dress me in forest dress, and properly as for a man's journey."

"You have no idea where I am going, you poor child."

"I have, though."

"What!" said I sharply; "how can you guess that?"

"Good heavens, sir, it's no secret in this camp that you have tried in vain to discover some proper persons to send into Louisbourg; and that, finding none, you must go yourself!"

"Damnation!" said I, angrily, "I might have known

that in such a silly camp as this, and under such a damned incompetent General as Dan'l Webb, every decency of military conduct and professional decorum would be ignored and abused! Who is to teach the Provincials and discipline the Regulars unless the Commanding General sets proper example? A post takes its character from the officer who commands it. And, by God, I'm not so cursedly surprised that news of my private, professional, and confidential mission to Louisbourg is become common camp gossip!"

She said, demurely, that she never could suppose I was so profane in my speech, whose lips held such fatal seduction when they kissed.

"Well," said I, "it would make the Pope himself swear to have to do with such a General and such troops as these! Their gabble and gossip may cost me my life," said I. "I may hang by the neck one day, on account of their idle chatter in this God damned camp!"

"For goodness sake, sir—"

"Yes, for God's sake, too!" I interrupted in a fury; "I am a fool to remain in this fort under so asinine a commander! Only that my Lord Loudon trusts me, I'd resign my commission today! Why, what a jackass am I to remain and undertake so perilous a mission when, as you say, everybody in camp knows all about it—even you do—and so, no doubt, does that French prisoner, too! And am I expected, in spite of all this bad faith—all this indiscipline, all this gossip among Provincial rank and file, and indiscreet tattle in officers' quarters—am I supposed to pay it no attention, but go about my duty where now, no doubt, I shall be seized and hanged as soon as I appear?"

For half an hour in glowering silence I sat and smoked my long clay and scowled at Sandi where she moved about her petty domestic duties.

She seemed very grave and boyish and very, very young as my sullen gaze followed her movements from water-butt to wood-pile, from fireplace to wash-tub—always swift, slim, graceful—confident of bearing, and with small head held high and gallantly, and eyes that glanced askance at me in veiled curiosity, or rested demurely on me, but with a hidden sparkle betraying the unquenched gaiety of a Gallic heart.

So after a while I got up and went over and took Sandi into my arms, saying that as long as she thought our lips had conspired against our peace of mind, our minds had better determine what was to be done about chastening them.

The indescribable freshness and fragrance of her mouth! It was like crushing spring flowers against one's lips. What senses I had were already sadly addled by her youthful and unexpected ardour as both her arms tightened around my neck and she pressed me to her with a flash of passion that set my blood afire.

I thought that it was my loud and heavy pulses throbbing, beating in my ears like muffled drums; but it really was the rolling drums, and I realized it as their loud alarm burst heavily from the fort; and through the terrific, sullen outcrash we heard the bugles of the regulars wildly warning all to be on guard; and then came the deafening bang! of a gun from the parapet.

The enemy at last was among us!

I gave Sandi one last impassioned smack and bade her

run to the fort; then seizing my sword and a pistol, and clapping on my laced hat, I hastened over to the Yorkers company of the Rangers, where already a buck-skinned line of tall, wiry, fur-capped fellows was falling in, the men slinging bullet pouch and powder horn and buckling on war-hatchet and heavy knife, while calling off.

"What's the matter, McGinnis?" I asked as I ran up beside their captain.

"Well, I'll be damned if I know then," said McGinnis, "—only the drums and the gun—you heard 'em yourself —and yonder go Putnam's Rangers running like hell-hounds from the Island—"

"Ti-yi-ki-yi-hi-yi!" yelled the buck-skinned Rangers of Israel Putnam as they came crowding and scrambling across the shallow water, wading it like a rush of stamped-ing deer as the water boiled along their flanks.

I saw the squat, battered, sun-scorched face and figure of Israel Putnam, now, and called to him: "What has happened, Captain? Where do you want the Yorkers to go in?"

He said he didn't know what the alarm was about— thought probably it was a false alarm from some timid soldier who had seen our Mohawks or Souriquois in their naked paint, outlying on the road to Saratoga.

Webb, handsomely mounted, followed by Bartman, came riding over to speak to us. Webb was deathly pale, and sweating under his gold-laced cocked hat.

Putnam was blunt and short with him:

"By God," said he, "I wish there was reason for all this tooting and drumming, but I fear it is some cowardly fellow frightened by our savages who are out toward

Saratoga. . . . The trouble is, General," he added in his loud, coarse way, "there are too many God-damned cowards in Fort Edward!"

His manner, attitude, language were outrageous. Webb looked at him without a word. Bartman, red in the face, could scarce restrain himself at such disrespect. But Webb seemed dazed and said nothing—merely turned his horse as though unconscious of what he was about, and rode slowly across the grand parade toward the drawbridge.

A few moments later some mounted Rangers from Colonel Munro galloped in to report the alarm to be a false one, and that our Indians from South Bay, taking the war path with Sir William's Valley scouts, had frightened some raw levies from New England, who had run bawling into the Royal Block House.

"That's all very well," said Israel Putnam loudly, "but I'm none too damned certain that it wasn't French Indians they saw."

However, he dismissed his men and went away swearing.

I said to McGinnis: "I think Captain Putnam is right. Anybody ought to be able to tell our Iroquois and Souriquois Indians from the French savages. Dismiss your Yorkers and let us go over to the Royal Block House and question these militia levies."

But when we arrived we could make no sense out of their incoherent stories, and it was impossible to determine whether they really had seen Montcalm's Indians or merely the Six Nation savages of Sir William Johnson, or our Souriquois.

I told McGinnis that, whether ordered or not, I'd take

a few platoons of his Yorkers and push out toward William Henry early in the morning.

But he said that I must wait until after our troop beat for guard mounting, as General Webb desired to inspect the ceremony in person.

So I went back to quarters where, presently, came Sandi, and there we supped and discussed the false alarm.

"Nevertheless," said I, "always run for the Fort when you hear the alarm beat. Do you understand, Sandi?"

She said she did. She seemed tired and subdued—not in spirits—and I told her to leave the dishes for Joyce and get her to her bed and rest.

At that she gave me a glimmer of the loveliest smile I ever saw on human features, and, taking a candle, went to her bunk, closing and bolting the woodshed door behind her.

Which showed how much confidence she had in me; and I smiled to myself, and then, dismissing the matter from my mind, lighted my long pipe and walked across to the Yorkers' barracks to have a serious and secret talk with Captain McGinnis.

For the situation of our army at this post and at Fort William Henry, Fort Ann, and Fort Miller, under so incompetent a commanding General as Webb, had begun to worry me very deeply. And I made up my mind that I would not be caught inside any of our forts, and there besieged by White Coats and Ottawas—nor let Sandi be so trapped, either—because I knew that neither William Henry nor Edward could long hold out against a regular siege with artillery, and that surrender meant massacre because Montcalm never could control his savages.

CHAPTER VIII

PETITE GUERRE

ON the next day, which was very sultry, it being now the middle of July, General Webb personally examined the French deserter, Lebel, assisted by George Croghan and myself; but came to no conclusion and decided to re-examine the prisoner before ordering him to face a military court.

That day General Webb, who seemed sick and very nervous, requested me to do staff duty; and so I guided Captain Nelson and a detail of one hundred and fifty men to work on the very bad road between Edward and Saratoga; and returned late at night, too weary to eat, or even to speak to Sandi.

Ours was a very sickly army. Every day there were deaths from diseases.

On the 19th, Mr. Lesley and I instructed the several quartermasters to see that in future all graves were dug and the dead buried within the limits of the new burying ground, instead of every battalion planting its dead wherever it pleased—even in our vegetable garden.

I then went with Colonel Montressor to measure the heights east of the Fort William Henry road and found that Webb's easily aroused fears were well founded this time, and that it really was forty odd feet higher than the Fort.

When we reported this to Webb he was extremely uneasy, and I saw his bloodless face sweating so that the hair-powder caked on his hair.

The next day I was obliged to look upon a tragic and revolting spectacle—a wretched soldier of the Royal Americans who had deserted, was shot at eight o'clock, a-sitting on his own coffin.

Sandi heard the doleful and smothered drums beating a dead march, but I made her keep away from the Island and the parade and made her promise me to close door and window-shutters so she might neither see nor hear the musketry.

As I came back, sad and nervous and out o' temper with the world, some dirty and jaded horsemen came limping in, all over mud, many of them wearing bloody bandages, who gave a sullen account that their leader, Lieutenant Dormit, had been killed at South Bay where they had had a brush with French scouts.

They had not fetched in his body, and I told them they might be ashamed of themselves.

When Webb heard this he seemed much cast down. And very soon Captain Learned, whose scout had gone out six days before, came in to report the northern forest swarming with French savages, and coureurs-de-bois at Carillon.

Webb had no orders to give; didn't seem to know what to do or say, and always upon his pallid face was stamped a kind of horror—death by torture being the perpetual terror of this timid man who could not endure the presence of any savage.

As he had nothing to say to me, I took General Lyman's orders which were sensible and clear, and he arranged that the forts at Saratoga and Stillwater were to be relieved by a detachment from the line of the entire army, parading on the grand parade at five o'clock in the morning, with teams to carry tents and luggage and extra ammunition.

General Lyman kept me very busy all day; and again, at night, I was too tired to eat my supper, and though Sandi set my soupaan and syrup at my elbow, I could not touch it—and so drank a little brandy and water and went to bed with scarce a civil word to her. I think Webb's conduct really was worrying me into an illness. Besides, there was no news of General Lord Loudon, and I did not know whether he was going to attempt Louisbourg or not.

Sandi seemed timid and silent in face of my evident physical fatigue and mental depression. She had the tact and common sense of her nation, which forbade her to press upon me either food or attention unless invited.

Her cool silence was pleasant after the hot, dusty noise of the parade and casemates, and the stench of unwashed, sweating men and horses, camp-smoke, latrine, and scorched and stinking food.

The troops for Saratoga marched out at six the next morning. I did not see General Webb although I reported for orders. The engineer officer, Gordon, said he was indisposed, having had a disturbing letter from Colonel Munro.

For some reason or other General Lyman reduced a sergeant in Fitch's Company, which caused a lot of grumbling among rank and file.

About noon dinner time General Webb sent me word that he'd examine the French prisoner, Lebel, again. Then he sent word he wouldn't. Not knowing what to

do, I idled away the day awaiting his pleasure and missing my dinner, until finally I learned that Webb had
gone to bed with a headache.

Until midnight I wrote orders and letters for General Lyman at his headquarters, and then we talked together until after one o'clock.

I have no quarrel with General Lyman though I do
not like New Englanders as a rule. But Lyman was an
officer of sense and courage. It is not true that he showed
cowardice when Marin attacked. He took over the command from Webb, who they say was scared nearly to
death, and he did what was proper. I wish to God he
had been in command at Edward when the White Coats
came to William Henry!—but my pen is outrunning my
narrative in this journal which I am now rewriting and
assembling—for, like almost every other officer in our
army, I have kept a diary of sorts, although why I do
it is not very clear to me.

Still, in a vague way, I used sometimes to think of
marriage, of a home, and of children who might perhaps be entertained by such a journal written by one who
saw the White Coats in battle at Saint Sacrement—that
same and peaceful pond which now we call Lake George!

Well, the July heat awoke me before sunrise next morning. I found a pot of chocolate awaiting me, but did
not see Sandi. So went out in my banyan and bare feet
to bathe and cool me, and found even the river mist
cooler than my quarters.

It was quite dark yet, the fog obscuring the water,
and as I floundered into it I stumbled over somebody who
was swimming—or trying to—and knew instantly, from
the soft cry of consternation, that it was Sandi. We

both rolled over each other in the water, and then I staggered to my feet, lifting her up, half strangled, coughing,
spitting water, and all wet and naked.

In the dark o' the mist, I was ass enough to kiss
her; and she fetched me such a box on the ear that it
almost stunned me, and yet another swift clout on the
other ear that made my head spin and ring again. Then,
with a slippery flip and spatter, she wriggled free of me
and into the water and away, with a skip, hop, and a
splash, and up the bank and gone before I could collect
my senses.

The red ball of the sun was rising in the fog before
I came into my quarters, dripping wet in my gorgeous
silken banyan, and saw Sandi in her boy's dress, red,
vexed, but apprehensive in her unquiet glances and in
every movement as she set my soupaan, syrup, milk, and
bread upon my camp table, and retired on tip-toe.

Still eying me with lively uncertainty, she seated herself and began her own breakfast; and to see that she
really was scared, as well as madded, made me suddenly
laugh outright.

Which relieved her visibly and she smiled a grim little
smile but asked no pardon for clouting me.

"Since when," said I, "have you practiced boxing the
ears of gentlemen who employ you?"

She turned scarlet at that, but made no answer at first.
Then, as I was still laughing:

"I am sorry," she said, flushed and sulkily, "but that
was a shameless business to kiss me naked like that!"

"I'm sorry, too," said I. "Did I hurt you when we
rolled over in the dark?"

"My pride was hurt. I don't know why you should make nothing of a girl with whom you have not lain, and who may be chaste for all you know."

"I didn't know you were there in the river, Sandi. I didn't see you when I jumped in."

"I thought it was done a-purpose."

"Lord, no! I wouldn't do such a thing to you, Sandi!"

"Because," said she, "even if we had been lovers, it was not seemly—not decent. . . . I'm sorry, however, that I boxed your ears, sir."

"That was the proper spirit," said I. "But Lord, how my head buzzed! Those were no love-pats, Sandi."

She looked at me as though still scared and apprehensive, and the rosy shame still staining her throat and cheeks. Then suddenly she laughed a little.

"If cleanliness be godliness," says she, "oh, heaven, sir, what perils and adventures by flood and dark do you and I encounter in our holy zeal for clean skins!"

"Sandi," said I, "you have a self-possession in difficult situations, and a refusal to be vulgarly concerned, which is supposed to be a quality of only the sophisticated and nobly born."

Her bright gaze and brilliant colour, the effortless charm of her bearing—of her every movement—even in her pewter-buttoned jacket, linsey smalls and woollen hose—had already begun to claim my admiring attention and stir my slumbering curiosity again. For here was a young girl with every exterior grace, and the acquired manner of the better classes—that is, I mean, what is called quality. And yet she was servant to me in my quarters, and seemingly not greatly disturbed by any danger to her chastity as long as all procedure was en regle and conformed to the polite rules, usages, and manners of a respectable and formal seduction.

But this Jupiter-Poseidon, river-god roughness, though Olympian and classical was no more than plain and vulgar rape to her, and it was very evident she had no mind for it nor any intention of countenancing or enduring it.

"You are quite right," said I, "I ought not to have kissed you, and I got what I deserved. I bear no malice, do you?"

"No, sir—not if you don't."

"Well, then, I don't. . . . You are very sweet, Sandi, and I would not have you think that I make little of you."

"And I would not have you think that I make little of *you,* sir, just because I boxed your ears," said she with her adorably impudent nose up-tilted.

She started to pass by me; I extended my arms; she shrugged, gave me a veiled, indescribably defiant look, then altered her course and walked straight into my opened arms which closed on her.

And, there entrapped, something so utterly unexpected happened that at the moment I could neither account for it nor even understand it. For, holding her in my arms, a sudden passionate curiosity concerning her seized me, and I looked deep into her brown eyes which did not avoid me and sustained my gaze in their lovely, veiled way.

And there and then, her bewitching eyes did me a harm that I felt as perfectly as though a sharp arrow had pierced my body; and I knew I had been injured, but had no thought of the wound's depth and if it might be mortal. How could a man's mind suspect such things when his little maid servant was in his arms—a poor young thing in a brush hut, dressed in linsey-woolsey like a lad, and her slim fingers catching desperately at my shoulders, and her lips, slightly parted, responsive, joining warmly to mine with a half-checked sob—

Suddenly came a noisy outbreak of drums from the Yorkers' barracks as our troop beat for guard mounting.

The next instant, through the rumbling drums, I heard a gunshot, then another; then a loud, irregular rattle of musketry. I heard a man's hoarse voice bawling:

"For God's sake, turn out! The savages are scalping our carpenters in the lumber yard!"

Still confused with the swift passion of our close embrace, I tore my lips from hers. Her loosened arms fell from my neck, releasing me. The next instant we were on our feet and she had reached the doorway at a single bound.

"The French are here!" she cried. "Oh, God!"

I fastened my Ranger-officers' war-belt, with its swinging knife and hatchet, slung over my shoulders my powder horn and beaded bullet-bag, and, seizing my long rifle, primed and loaded it.

Sandi stood gazing at me with a strange gleam in her brown eyes, like the sun sparkling on a forest brook.

"The French are here!" she cried again, with that strange light transfiguring her features till they seemed all golden and afire.

"Go to the Fort," said I, passing one arm around her body. "Stay in the casemates where no arrows or bullets can fall." I drew her to the door: "Now, go!" I said.

"Yes—" She seemed to have lost her head for an instant—not from fear—for as she passed through the hut door she turned and caught me around the neck and kissed me fiercely.

I said: "I love you, Sandi—"

"Yes—but it is *real love* with me, John Cardress. And some day you won't believe it! . . . Oh, God, I thought it a sacrifice to love you, and I know now it is no martyrdom—"

She hugged and kissed me as though crazed, and the violence bruised our mouths. Then she tore free of me and ran for the Fort, dodging among galloping officers and mounted Rangers, and avoiding the herd of onrushing Provincials who came bellowing and bravely, but without any order or purpose.

I saw Lieutenant Humphrey who called out to me that the French Regulars and Ottawa Indians had fallen upon our carpenters and a working party of eighty men who had been getting out timber from the woods.

He said that Learned's covering company and the piquet was already engaged with the enemy.

And all the time our camp, fort, and outworks were in a terrible uproar, nobody seeming to know what to do. Colonel Montressor and General Lyman went galloping and bucketing about with a number of bewildered staff officers; Webb remained invisible. Then there came a roar as Israel Putnam's Rangers came running from their barracks on the Island, passed the Fort; and I saw McGinnis and the Yorkers crossing the river, and ran to join them.

There is a ridge of hard land running for a third of a mile easterly from the Fort. It is fringed on the northern side by a swamp, and on the south, where the brook turns north, by Fort Creek and by stretches of marshy forest where are the only great trees left standing near the Fort.

And here there was hell to pay; our poor carpenters were running from the fierce and painted pagan Ottawas who, crazed at the sight of their first bloody scalps taken, were rushing about like maddened wildcats, chasing everybody with horrid yelps and screams so that, in the dusk of the woods, they seemed like very devils, demons, and goblins of the fiery pit itself.

And all this was going on within eighty rods of Fort Edward, and Webb never gave an order or offered to send any aid.

Well, all I saw of that vicious fight was when Israel Putnam went into action with his Rangers and ran bang into nearly half a regiment of white-coated French Regulars.

Putnam yelled across the smoke to Captains West and Learned that he'd take care of the White Coats if they and McGinnis and myself with the New York Rangers would stop the Indians.

I shouted back that we would do so; but soon discovered hundreds of French savages in front of us who, checked, had taken to the big pines, and there squatted and fired upon us, their big-bore trade guns knocking our men flat and making frightful wounds.

The piquet under Captain Litler, of the Connecticut Regiment, was standing them off very gallantly, and so was the covering party.

We, also, had taken to trees, and there we lurked and fired whenever we could see a savage, but there were hundreds of these fierce, howling wolves in the woods, and they grew bolder and came at us suddenly in long cat-leaps, swinging their polished war-axes, and crashed into our men in single combat. And I saw Lieutenant Titcomb run away and desert his men.

West, in his high-pitched nasal voice, yelled to me: "The gol-darned French catamounts have gone crazy, I guess. Tell your men to shoot at their bellies and blow their guts out!"

There were, in front of our lines, a dozen or more of our poor fellows lying dead and mangled in the mud or on the forest floor. All of them had been butchered and scalped.

"Davy!" I called across to Lieutenant Humphrey of the line guard, "tell Captain Putnam that we are ready to charge if he is!" But Putnam presently sent back word to me that we had too heavy a force in front of us and that as yet no relief had come out from the Fort excepting a single battalion led by General Lyman.

Somewhere, just ahead of us in the forest, a small body of British Regulars had been holding out under overwhelming odds. But now our men, creeping forward and firing from tree to tree, filtered through and came into contact with them. I saw Captain Litler shaking hands with their officer who was expressing his thanks very calmly—even smiling.

My old company, the New York Rangers—men from the Mohawk Valley who had a sad acquaintance with Indians—began to trot forward like fierce hounds on a blood-trail; and the dirty Ottawas and Wyandottes seemed to know they had men to deal with who meant to destroy them, for they began to leave their trees and bushes and gullies and retreat northward through the morass.

Suddenly their musketry died away; a feathery whispering filled the forest; and through the drifting smoke a flight of arrows came whistling among us. Our Rangers were struck in the body, the limbs, the face; men ran away screaming with pain or staggered about plucking at the barbed war shafts buried in their bodies.

Some sank down dead in the ferns, with scarlet winged arrows piercing mouth and eye and brain. And still the red-winged Wyandotte war-arrows shrilled through the woods until, no doubt, their gaudy quivers were empty.

Lieutenant Humphrey got his hands on one of the ferocious Ottawa archers who had just driven an arrow clean through the horse of a mounted Ranger. The Ottawa's knife was out instantly, but I hit him a crack with the flat of my war-axe, and, while Humphrey held him, our riflemen shot him to death—being obliged to shoot him four times, so tenacious was this burly devil of life; and snarled and clawed and spat like a mangled tree-cat to the very last.

I saw an oiled and naked Abenaqui warrior painted like a rattlesnake with yellowish belly and brown and black blotches; and he was scalping one of our carpenters, and in such a savage hurry about it that, having his gun in one hand and his knife in t'other, he seized the loosened scalp in his teeth and tore it from the dead skull.

My bullet hit him with such a smack that it knocked him flat in the mud, but it seemed as though nothing could kill these demons, for he was up with a splash and spatter like a wounded wild duck, and as he ran his broken arm flapped horridly. One of our riflemen took careful aim and knocked him over with a long shot; but you must know that this mutilated and hell-born creature got up again and limped on, howling, and, like many a wounded creature of the wild, got clean away.

Everywhere among the clumps of swamp-weed, swale-grass, and ferns lay our wretched workmen, stone dead and scalped, their bare, bleeding skulls shockingly visible in the sombre forest light.

Distantly, now and then, I got glimpses of white uniforms where, in an ocean of gushing, whirling smoke, Israel Putnam's Rangers were firing upon the French Regulars.

Now, on my right, I heard Captain West swearing and cursing and damning; and:

"Dammy!" cries he, "yonder come their cursed Praying Indians with their bloody hatchets fresh blessed by the French Jesuits! By God," cries he, "if anybody will follow me we'll catch them with our hands and skin them all alive!"

With that a Caughnawaga chief, magnificent in his yellow paint, and wearing a scapular and church medal over his oil-smeared chest, threw his war-axe and hit one of our men full in the face, splitting it in two from brow to teeth.

Then the woods rang with the most terrific uproar that man can utter—the hellish, hysterical, falsetto war-whoop of the Huron-Iroquois, which seems like the hell-born tumult of yelling devils and tortured souls, and like nothing else.

But the mere sight of these reeking mission demons was too much for McGinnis and his men, who broke into a murderous rush for them, whining with excitement.

I fired and hit an Abenaqui warrior. Almost instantly I saw a renegade Wyandotte in the act of hurling his war-axe at me. The aim was bad and the hatchet hit a poor devil of the Connecticut Regiment, who screamed and pitched forward, spouting brains and blood all over the ground. And straight at him leaped the ferocious Wyandotte to take his scalp.

It was the most impudent business I ever beheld; and I dropped my rifle and caught the painted Wyandotte by his beaded war-belt, giving him such a jerk that I pulled him off his feet which flew up and, giving me a hearty kick in the chest, knocked me flat.

The next instant he and I were at death grips. Wrestling with that filthy white and yellow painted warrior who stank horribly, and whose naked body was so oiled and painted from his shaven head to his ankle-moccasin, I found no place to hang on to except his war-belt and his braided and plumed scalp-lock.

I couldn't seem to do anything with him except to grasp his wrist and, for a while, avert death from his high-swung, poised, and polished hatchet.

Then McGinnis, seeing my extreme peril, came over and passed his knife through the Wyandotte, slashing deeply and ripping upward from his navel, so that he disemboweled the wretch under my very nose, and I had enough to do to escape that dreadful crimson cataract that splashed everything as he fell wallowing.

That was a filthy fight. Rangers whom I do not choose to name ripped and tore the scalps loose from dying Ottawas and, panting and reeking from the dreadful struggle, tied these nasty trophies to their war-belts.

I saw one of our men skin the leg of a dead Wyandotte—"to get me a razor strop," said he.

Another Ranger, drunk with fighting, his eyes bloodshot and his rifle-shirt wet with blood, showed me scalps he had taken from the war-belt of a dead Abenaqui, saying they were the scalps of white people. But I knew better because there were nits in the hairs—a certain sign that the scalp is Indian—for many of them are lousy—only the Jesuits keep the Praying Indians pretty clean.

Well, I think the fight lasted no more than an hour before the French bugles sounded a retreat and their Regulars drew off. The enemy Indians retreated, also, slowly, sullenly, a dangerous pack, ready to turn and fly at us if pressed too hard.

We had only about two hundred and fifty Rangers to follow them. God only knows why the Fort left us without support.

I had started with McGinnis to follow the retiring Wyandottes when Captain Bartman rode up in vast excitement, calling to me by name, and saying that Captain West would take my place in the pursuit and that General Lyman desired my instant attendance.

So I went back to the Fort where I saw General Lyman in full uniform, very much disgusted, and desirous that I write for him, at once, the following order to be issued at once to the army:

The artillery to send a field piece to the Fort immediately, which is to be mounted on the north-east bastion where the flagstaff is placed.

In case it be necessary to turn out the lines, a cannon will be immediately fired on the bastion and a flag hoisted, upon which every regiment is to turn out at the head of their encampments, and to divide along the intrenchments as far as their tents extend.

In case of any firing in the woods the piquet is immediately to advance and support the party attacked.

The Rangers, likewise, are to turn out, officers at the head of their companies, and are to march with the first advanced piquet. . . .

Upon firing of the alarm gun . . . the 35th Regiment is to send a company, the 60th Regiment three companies, the Independents one company into the Fort.

(Signed) LYMAN.

I wrote all this at his dictation, my hand very clumsy and still unsteady from excitement and exertion.

Nobody had seen Webb. Lyman, red and vexed, and his handsome uniform torn and smutty from powder and swamp-mud, said to me that it was mortifying to discover how unprepared our regiments had been for such a surprise attack, and that had Montcalm's army assailed us instead of a war party of only five or six hundred, we had been dead men or prisoners, every woman's son of us.

I said nothing. It was Webb's business. Where he was at this crisis nobody seemed to know. I asked his aide-de-camp, George Bartman, where Webb was and why Lyman was in command; but he only turned red and made me no reply. Whether he was ill, or drunk, or had merely swooned from fright, I never knew. And I never knew why the conduct of this poltroon was whitewashed by our dumpy little German King.

On my way to my quarters I stopped in the casemates to look for Sandi, and, not seeing her, made inquiry concerning my servant lad.

Nobody semed to recollect seeing Sandi in the casemates.

While I was still seeking her, the artillery ordered out by General Lyman passed us, with a clash of chains and harness, and heavy bumping of gun-carriage and caisson across the parade.

The gunner officer in command called out to me from his saddle that the French prisoner in the Yorkers' guardhouse was gone.

"What's that you say?" I cried.

"What I tell you is true," repeated the gun lieutenant, "—your prisoner is gone! Captain McGinnis sends you the message, sir."

I went over to the guard-house. The cells were empty. In the excitement of the French attack—so poor was British and Provincial discipline under Webb—no barrack guard had been left to look out for either quarters or prisoners.

McGinnis, mad as a bantam game-cock, pointed out the broken lock.

"Somebody from the outside let out that prisoner," said he. "D'ye see, Cardress? Here—it's plain enough. Some man took a bar and ripped off bolt and lock. Which shows us, b'God, that there's another spy in camp —if he hasn't run off to his friends."

Whose fault it might be I did not care to say. The Frenchman, Lebel, was gone, anyway. Probably, when freed, he had managed to join his white-coated friends during the shameful panic and uproar both at Fort Edward and in the outlying works and fortified camps.

Well, he was gone clean away in all probability. Nevertheless, McGinnis sent out a scout to comb the surrounding bush, and to notify the pursuing battalion under Putnam and West.

Not being able to discover where General Webb really was, I reported the matter to Captain Bartman and to Major Fletcher in actual command of Fort Edward.

Then, very weary, perplexed, and chagrined, I went back to my quarters in the bush hut, to which I had no doubt that Sandi had, by this time, returned.

I was very tired; I'd had no dinner; it was past supper time now, and the sun low over the forest.

I saw no smoke from our brick chimney; however, that might indicate preparation for a hot supper.

Puzzled, apprehensive, I went in. There was nobody there.

But I saw on my camp table a sheet of ruled paper torn out of my book of accounts; and, upon it, scratched hastily with an unmended and badly inked quill, I read:

MY CAPTAIN:

You are a soldier; duty and honour come first; and inclination and pleasure last—if a broken heart be inclined for pleasure.

Sir—I am French! I came to America upon a mission. To fulfill it I would gladly offer my life.

You know, sir, that my ship, *La Belle Sauvage,* was taken. In my desperation, and disguised as a lad, I saw you, and begged you to take me into your service. It was my only chance to escape and to fulfill my mission and my duty.

Sir—whatever you think of what you will stigmatize as my treachery, I pray you to remember in your anger that you, too, under like circumstances, would have done what I am about to do.

Sir—as for our love making, I let it go on, willing to use any wile to allay your suspicions which might enable me to remain here and in your employment until the moment for escape arrived.

It has arrived. I must go. I take with me the soldier of the Regiment Artois, known to you as Lebel.

You won't believe that you have made a lasting and tender impression upon my heart. But it is true. You won't deign even ever to think of me again save with scorn.

Alas!

Now, sir, I go, with the soldier Lebel, to Captain Marin who is attacking this post; and, with the help of God's Holy Mother, I shall fulfill my mission.

And, so that you may not suffer from chagrin or believe yourself degraded because you have caressed and been betrayed by a servant—well, sir—you need not have blushed for yourself even had you offered me marriage. . . . And I pray that God, and this news, may reconcile you to think less angrily of one who never yet has had husband or lover, but who, in happier times, might have seen both of these in you, John Cardress.

Adieu—

SANDI.

CHAPTER IX

THE COWARD

WHEN I had read the letter left for me by the perfidious Sandi, and had recovered from my astonishment, I was the maddest man in the Province of New York.

I was madder still when I began to find out how much I missed that gay little parcel of impudence—that treacherous baggage in boy's clothes.

I missed her careless, cheery, active coming and going. I missed her mischievous way of looking at me and speaking to me, always alert to see how much I'd endure. I missed her beguiling smile, her engaging bashfulness, her humorous impertinences, her childish rudeness. I missed her lissome, boyish figure—the nameless charm of her nearness. I missed her. wind-tanned, healthy skin, her disordered curls clustering around sun-brown, carmine tinted cheeks, and the slender amber column of her throat and neck.

Hell and fury!—it seemed incredible how I could so painfully and so passionately regret the lying, ungrateful little hussy—

But I already began to realize that it would be a very, very long while ere I could forget the fresh, cool sweetness of her mouth—or the scented fire of it in its checked sob of passion—

Hell's hobgoblins and yellow devils! The more I thought of her the more I missed her. I could no more rid me of this loneliness that, at night, rode me like a hag, than I could strangle in my throat the sighing and broken breath that unconsciously was my wakeful tribute to this wicked wench.

I missed her! Hell-bats and hell-cats!—here was a pretty affair—to inflame a man's heart and utterly involve it before he knew that it was mortally engaged. And then to betray him!

Anger, passion, heart-hunger, loneliness, concern for the double-faced jade's welfare, fear lest she come to a harm all alone among those accursed French!—

Devil-dam and bedlam!—she was French herself! And, from her hint, a youngster of consequence and quality—and of the titled world—or so it would appear.

And if my heart quickened and my blood raced, and all the strength and fire and beauty of a lover's passion had invaded and possessed me when I held her in my arms and she pressed me closer between hers—at that deafening, dazzling, dizzying instant when the cowardly outburst of frightened British drums robbed us of our magic moment, of the moment which never, never could come again, at that blinding instant of unconsummated passion she was as surely mine as though my soldier's blanket had been the swansdown of our wedding quilt, and the bunk in my brush hut had been a damask-curtained wedding bed, silent and scented, looming in the golden gloom of some vast and noble house suitable for a maid of consequence and quality whose boyish nickname was Sandi.

That was the way my nights were spent—rambling interminably on and on—now feeling the bitter taste of chagrin, or the sting of anger, or the dull and wearying pains of desire and regret—

Insomnia—a thing out of hell—which, before I knew Sandi, I never had known—came now to enrage and exhaust me, torturing my brain, my tired muscles, my unrested nerves, my aching bones, my lonely, lonely heart.

At night it painted pictures of this young sorceress for me—bright, laughing, vivid against the dark—this wicked witch—ethereal, immortal in her rainbow hues of paradise!

It filled the tiny chambers of my sleepless brain with vague, wakeful little voices out of which grew suddenly and sweetly *her* voice—to the very life, softly startling, heart-breaking, lovely beyond words—

It set my pulses leaping and filled me, drowned me in a perfume—the lost odour of *her!*—the fresh, flower-like scent of her mouth and throat and breasts—

Hag-hounds and hurricanes! How long was this hellish torture to continue? Was I actually in love then—because this vixen, Sandi, had suddenly turned into a demoiselle of quality under my stupid nose?

Had I loved her any less when I thought her of lesser breed? Love? Oho! Was that really the word then?

And what, in the name of the filthy, pig-footed fiend, had been my intention concerning this lonely little jade in her blouse and béret and her linsey-woolsey breeches?

Was it even to make her my mistress in respectable and proper fashion? Was it not, rather, to engage in a casual and careless encounter—because nothing better had offered?—an amourette en passant—of which I was a little ashamed?

Well, then, I was well punished already. Outrageous
Fortune had spitted me on her arrow when in the
very odour of flagrancy! Now I could get no rest. This
youngster's tormenting face was ever taking graceful
shape and colour before me; her voice was ever soft in
my tortured ears; the memory of her sweetness—the
touch of her hands, of her body, her lips—all, all came
to obsess me, exquisite as dreams; or came as ghostly,
lonely, miserable imaginings in the dead of night to
hurt me, torture me, teach me that when love is love
it will not be jested with—no, not even if one fails to
recognize it under its lesser guises!

And so I could not sleep by night or find rest by day
for ceaseless thought of Sandi.

Nevertheless, there was enough trouble afoot to keep
any soldier busy and even alarmed; and except for this
constant anxiety and excitement I think I'd have fallen
ill from the amazing violence of my desire for Sandi.

But already, around Fort Edward, and around the
lonely garrison of Fort William Henry, the terrors of
this French and Indian war were closing in like black
storm-clouds edging a white and furious surf of mounting seas.

I told General Lyman that my servant had released
the prisoner, Lebel, and that both had escaped to the
French. He remarked that it made damned little difference, now, because general hell had broken loose in the
forests which swarmed with White Coats and were all
a-crawl with savages.

"Also," said he, "General Lord Loudon has missed his
mark, in my opinion, and it's too late for him or for that

flying Dutchman, Holburne, to do any harm to Louisbourg."

I asked him respectfully what I was to think in that case, and how interpret my orders to enter Louisbourg.

"Well, then, Cardress," said he with a wry face, "you have your orders from him who also gives me mine, and I see nothing for you to do except to obey them. Do you?"

"No, sir," said I, reddening with resentment.

"Did your orders hinge upon any contingency, Captain Cardress?"

"No, sir."

"Very well, sir," said General Lyman, "I have no doubt that you will conduct properly and as becomes an officer and gentleman."

Which meant that I had no choice except to stick my head into the hangman's noose merely because an incompetent General had ordered me to do so.

Very well, then; I'd go to Louisbourg, and hang there if that was to be my destiny—a victim to the cowardice, incompetency, and stupidity of a British Vice Admiral and two Major Generals.

Well, I made my preparations to travel and awaited opportunity to get away.

Suddenly, one after another, the French began to deliver their terrific strokes until their blows fairly rained on this British army of ours crouching here in the forests of Northern New York, bewildering the rank and file, discouraging staff and line, and utterly terrifying the poltroon in supreme command.

Matters began almost immediately following the flight of the wretched Sandi.

On the 24th of July, the day following this attack on our poor workmen in the woods close to the eastern bastion of Fort Edward, our Rangers returned in safety from their pursuit; and everybody considered it only an episode of the petite guerre which, it seemed, their supposedly clever and capable Marquis of Montcalm had decided to begin.

A few of us did not think so—Captains Whelan, West, Humphrey, and I. But we were of inferior rank and nobody listened to us excepting Colonel Croghan.

Now, it was an odd thing to happen—yet only a part of the general demoralization under the incompetent leadership of Webb—for the celebrated battalion of Rangers made famous by Bob Rogers, now with Lord Loudon, began to sulk and malinger and show gross insubordination and unwillingness to do scout duty. And Israel Putnam could do nothing with them, and so they complained to Major Fletcher that their pay and food were not commensurate with their dangerous services. So Fletcher promised them three dollars a month bonus apiece, and half a pint of rum a day—which mortified me and so angered me that I would have nothing to say to our Yorkers, who looked mean and ashamed when they saluted me, I bidding them to go to hell and take their disgraced colours with them.

Which insubordination of our white scouts was the reason that Webb believed the forest was now clear of French and Indians, and that they all had gone back to Carillon.

So he, never doubting his personal safety, took Colonel Montressor, Captain Bartman, a numerous suite, and a battalion of Rangers; and on the 25th July he rode across Half Way Brook to call on Colonel Munro, commanding at Fort William Henry, leaving Lyman and Fletcher at Edward.

On the 28th, Lyman ordered all the boatmen, sailors, and ship's carpenters in camp to march to Fort William Henry—I don't know why, to this day. All that afternoon various battalions of our garrison were at target practice, and the racket frightened the garrison of the small outlying forts, which sent in runners to inquire the reason. Another example of wretched discipline and incompetency.

The next day Captain West came in from his scout. He told me that, at South Bay, they had found the remains of poor Lieutenant Dormit with his head, arms, legs cut off, and his body butchered.

General Webb came in from Fort William Henry with Montressor, Humphrey, Bartman, Gordon, and Captain Gallup and Ensign Minor of Lyman's staff. With them was Israel Putnam with two hundred Rangers.

Webb looked deathly pale as he rode into the Fort, and Captain Gallup whispered to me that the reports of Munro's scouts had scared him badly and that he was ordering detachments of the 35th Regulars and the 2nd Battalion Royal Americans, with their baggage, to William Henry. With them he meant to send, also, two four-gun batteries of light artillery and the Independent Regiment.

I can not describe the strange sense of uncertainty, distrust, and of sullen indifference which invaded the troops in garrison at Fort Edward.

All seemed to be affected by the general incompetence

of the commanding general and the suspicion that they were likely to be sacrificed by the ignorance and stupidity of high command.

In the midst of this came a court martial to try a lieutenant of the Massachusetts Regiment for shamefully quitting his post during the recent skirmish east of our fort.

News of it made the garrison gloomy.

Early in the morning the artillery, the 60th Regiment, and some companies of the Independent marched for William Henry—with other troops under commands of Colonels Fry and Young.

I had spent a wretched night of anguish, and awoke sick and astonished that my passion for this young creature had already so miserably undone me. For there seemed in her a witch's magic which I had sucked from her breath and which, once breathed, I never again could be free of or ever again let her alone in my thoughts.

I was nearly ready to start for the north, and only awaiting word from McGinnis that the trails were clear, when, late that night, I heard a courier gallop into the Fort, and, going out with a watch lantern to hear the news, learned that Montcalm and eight thousand White Coats, Indians, and Canadians had landed near Fort William Henry just as our last wagon went in, the horses lashed to a gallop.

McGinnis said that the enemy occupied both sides of the road between our fort and William Henry.

I said to Captain McGinnis—and cared not who heard me—that it was a damned shame not to reinforce Munro properly. Montressor, hearing me, gave me an odd look but offered no reprimand.

All our piquets that night were trebled and our battalions slept on their arms.

As for me, I got no sleep until after midnight.

It was before five o'clock on the morning of August 3rd that we, at Edward, were aware that the siege of Fort William Henry had finally begun. We heard the report of the first cannon from that threatened and lonely fortress—a heavy, ominous sound rolling southward over the forest and through the fog of early morning. Boom-boom! Boom!—three or four shots a minute for a time, then a dull report every ten minutes or more.

At ten o'clock the firing stopped. At two in the afternoon it increased and became a sustained and rolling thunder until six.

McGinnis came to me with an account that West's scouts had taken a French deserter from the Royal Rousillon Regiment, who asserted that the Marquis of Montcalm had four thousand regulars and nearly five thousand savages at William Henry, besides artillery and scouts.

I said I thought it was a damn lie; and I went over and examined the Royal Deux Ponts soldier—for that turned out to be his regiment—a German—who insisted that what he had stated was gospel-true.

Anyway, it seemed certain that Fort William Henry was now invested; and that unless Webb went to his rescue the brave old Scotchman, Colonel George Munro, must either capitulate to superior numbers or fight and die amid the battered ruins of his fort, leaving his soldiers' bones to the flames and their women and little children to the tomahawks of the Ottawas and Wyandottes.

Those were terrible and trying hours in the early Aug-

ust weather. Days were horribly hot, nights chilly and
white with fog; and through the long, sunny August
hours the cannonading at Fort William Henry never
ceased its ghostly boom-booming, hour after hour, throbbing, rumbling, dying away as the wind shifted, then
suddenly loud again from the northern wilderness, boom-
boom-boom!—

Our scouts took another prisoner, a Lieutenant of Canadian marine infantry, who claimed that Montcalm had
eleven thousand men on the lake.

At midnight I was summoned to the commanding General. He was so frightened that his voice shook as he
dictated to Captain Bartman and to me letters to Lieutenant Governor DeLancey, admitting that he was going
to abandon Munro to the fortunes of war, and begging
for militia for Fort Edward.

"There has been a continual fire of cannon and small
arms from daybreak till almost sunset," he wrote; . . .
"and we have some fears it can not have turned out in
our favour.

"We are . . . in no condition to assist them. . . . Let
us have all the reinforcements you possibly can, as the
fate of this colony [of New York] depends upon it!
Excuse the hurry I write in!"

I was ashamed to copy such a letter, and I saw Bartman was very red in the face.

The next day he wrote more letters. He was one of
those letter-writing generals.

He even wrote three letters to poor Munro, saying
that he didn't think it "prudent" to help the wretched
garrison at William Henry to escape the war-hatchets of
nearly five thousand savages in their battle paint!

He wrote that he "thought it proper" to inform Munro that he need expect no help; and suggested that the latter "make the best terms" possible for a surrender, adding that the bearer was a sergeant of the Connecticut regiment, and "if he is happy enough to get in [into William Henry], will bring advices from you" to Fort Edward.

The reason for this particular outburst of poltroonery I did not understand until Bartman showed me privately a letter from Munro, fetched in by a scout—a brief, touching note merely saying that he was attacked suddenly by a great body of French and Indians, that the Marquis of Montcalm had summoned him to surrender, and that he had refused.

All day long on August 5th the cannonading continued. I offered to go out with a scout from the Yorkers, but was refused.

Webb seemed ill with fear. He had called a council of war, I was told, for eleven o'clock, at his house in the Fort, to give opinions of the situation and whether Fort Edward should not be evacuated and the army retreat to Albany.

I could scarcely believe this was true, but Colonel Montressor assured me that it was a question whether we should not abandon Fort Edward.

The officers present at the council were Webb, Lyman, Major Fletcher, Colonel Glazier, Colonel Angel, Captain Ord, Colonel Montressor, and Captain Gordon. Before it had been decided whether to leave a garrison at Edward and retreat, Webb broke up the conference in a nervous manner, bidding the several commanding officers to keep their men ready to retreat at a moment's notice.

Captains Putnam, Humphrey, McGinnis, and I went

to Lyman and asked permission to march to William
Henry with our Rangers and any other troops who volunteered. We were refused.

On the 6th the cannonading was terrific from five in
the morning until eight at night.

About nine o'clock I heard cheering from the New
York Regiment, and, in the battle-lantern's glare, I saw
Sir William Johnson and his mounted militia and In-
dians ride into the Fort. I was devilish glad to see him.

Lord Howe, also, arrived from Massachusetts—a well-
beloved officer and admired by regular and provincial
alike for his manliness, modesty, and sense.

I was happy indeed to know of the arrival of Sir William, and I lost no time the next morning in presenting
myself at his tent, to do myself the honour of waiting
on him.

Webb hated him, and the wise, brave, and gay baronet
detested and disdained Dan Webb, and always had
thought him an incompetent and a poltroon since he first
knew him as a Colonel of British Regulars.

Well, I talked with Sir William about my mission to
Louisbourg, and he very pertinently asked me what use
I could be to my Lord Loudon and to our phantom Vice
Admiral if they were not going to attempt the siege of
that great fortress-city of Isle Royale.

"Sir," said I, "no man cares to be hanged by the neck
because a testy German King wishes to catch and hang
a runaway Scotchman in the enemy's service. Yet, what
choice have I, Sir William? His gracious Majesty orders
Lord Loudon to send a spy into Louisbourg to watch the
Chevalier Johnstone, Lord Annandale's heir; and to keep
an eye on the Honourable Charles Follis, Lord Whinn-

loch's only boy, lest they escape the capitulation and get away before his Majesty the King of England can have them courtmartialed and hanged!

"And my Lord Loudon has ordered me to go. And now it seems that there is to be no siege of this great fortress by sea and land. And still, though it can do no service to King, General or Admiral, I have no choice other than to go into this fortified city of mystery, merely because subordinates have no option but to obey any order given by authority."

Sir William Johnson was a handsome man, grey eyed, with a glint of red in his dark hair—a finely moulded man, being nearly six feet in his riding boots. He limped a little still, from the wound he got when he got his baronetcy a-fighting the Baron Dieskau and his French White Coats at St. Sacrement in '55.

Always I had considered him a great man—one of the great leaders and empire-builders of our times, who was, also, Indian Superintendent for North America and the only man in the New World absolutely trusted by the Indians, because he never had deceived them.

He was, also, a great land-owner and a great colonizer; a man of infinite honour, of vast wisdom, a lover of mankind and a keen judge of men.

These are not the only reasons why I came to consult Sir William in my perplexity regarding Louisbourg, and how best I might attempt to enter it.

There was another reason; Sir William Johnson was a nephew of Admiral Sir Peter Warren who, in conjunction with General Sir Jeffrey Amherst and Sir William Pepperrell, had taken the fortress of Louisbourg in '45, when it was small and weak as compared with the terrific strength of the fortress and the extent of the powerful walled city of today.

Sir Peter Warren loved Sir William, or Billy as he called him, who was his favourite nephew; and I was sure that he had told Sir William more concerning this mystery city of Louisbourg—about which we had heard so much—than most people in America had any knowledge of.

So I went to him, and he showed me in his quarters some very fine maps of the fortress, made by our British engineers while it was in our possession in 1745.

These maps, of course, were now more than ten years old, and it was generally understood that millions of money, since that time, had made of an already powerful French fortress a huge and formidable French walled city of several thousand people, magnificently fortified and armed and garrisoned by numerous regiments of regular troops as well as of Canadian auxiliaries, marine infantry, Indians, Rangers, and battalions of the famous Legion Etranger, or Foreign Legion, under such desperate young officers of the rebel Scottish army as the Chevalier Johnstone and the Honourable Charles Follis.

Well, Sir William and I, at his commodious camp table—and in company with one of his deputies, Colonel George Croghan, a most remarkable man—worked out the various routes by trail.

And after a long morning's work it was decided that my only chance of getting into Louisbourg was to go past Carillon and on up Lake Champlain until I came into touch with the voyageurs along the Richelieu. From there, speaking their tongue and wearing the buckskin dress of a French forest runner, I must find excuse to induce a fisherman or perhaps a naval vessel or transport, to carry me and my canoe down the St. Lawrence and into Gabarus Bay which dents the bleak, windy shores of that strange island on which stands Louisbourg—which island is called by us Cape Breton and by the French Isle Royale.

Well, the Albany and Schenectady militia were now arriving—nearly fifteen hundred of them—and I was happy to believe that this garrison would now march out and drive the pretty Marquis and his White Coats and Wyandottes back to their own cursed country.

In fact, our Rangers, already anticipating the advance to Munro's rescue, were being inspected by Captain Putnam who acted for Major Rogers as commanding the battalion, when McGinnis came in damning and swearing and saying that Webb refused to stir.

Astounded, we dismissed the men and I went to the Fort where Montressor told me that several times he had applied to Webb to know whether or not this Fort was to be defended, in order to pull down all outstanding obstructions; but Webb made no reply at all.

One of our scouts of twenty Rangers came in to acquaint us that the French were now throwing shells into Fort William Henry with considerable loss of life in the garrison.

When Sir William Johnson heard that he went to Webb and requested permission to march the Rangers, his own militia, and his Indians to Munro's rescue.

Webb nodded; but we had not been gone ten minutes when an express overtook us ordering Sir William to return.

It was the most shameful action I ever heard of, and I admit that the troops were very close to mutiny. It was terrible, with our heavy forces, to sit supine at Edward and listen to that deadly, unbroken roll of thunder in the north. The militia were fools. Those occupying the hill north of the Fort did no work but spent their time making rustic bowers. Not a trench dug!

That night, being the night of August 9th, I supped at one of the mess houses with Colonel Montressor and Sir William Johnson, and then went out to the hill where we beheld a pitiful sight in the northern sky above the forest—fiery signals of distress, begging for help, were flung up from Fort William Henry; and all the while the guns were pounding away, boom-boom-boom—without any interval at all.

Came to us on the dark hill an express from Munro, having got out of the fort and evaded the Indians; and this was the message of Munro—that his gunners had split most of the cannon; and that, unless General Webb could afford him relief, Fort William Henry must surrender.

It was now about ten o'clock. Not a cannon was to be heard from the northward, only the fiery signals of distress flamed up and died out in the northern skies.

About eight o'clock next morning the cannonading ceased abruptly.

I went to the Fort to learn what I could. A Captain Thaxter came in about ten o'clock, saying that one of his men had seen the French flag flying on Fort William Henry at eight o'clock this morning.

All that day there were terrible rumours around the

fort and camps, concerning the treatment of the prisoners by the French; but nothing certain could be learned as Webb, half dead with fear, kept us all under arms ready to retreat, abandon Fort Edward, and run for Albany at the first sign of a French advance.

Then, about eleven o'clock, our mounted scouts came galloping, and on their heels a rush of disorderly soldiery from Fort William Henry who had been in the outer trenches and who seemed terribly confused at the behaviour of the French Indians. These told us that, after the surrender, the Ottawas, Wyandottes, and Western Pagans, naked and in their battle paint, had suddenly attacked our unarmed soldiers and their women and children, and had begun an indiscriminate slaughter, robbing, murdering, and scalping all they encountered.

Then we began to hear of horrors which the French regulars could not prevent and which the Canadian irregulars permitted—they looking on while these screeching savages massacred the prisoners, even shoving aside their armed French guards to tomahawk, disembowel, and scalp them.

Fort Edward was in a horrid tumult; our soldiers had friends, relatives, even wives and children in Fort William Henry; and, as news of the massacre continued to arrive with every breathless batch of fugitives, there was very near to a panic in barracks, trenches, casemates, and camps, and much angry cursing of a commanding General who would let such things happen and never stir foot to assist the poor folk who were falling under the treacherous hatchets of the Wyandottes.

Some fugitives came in who gave an account that the

THE COWARD

French regulars were doing all they could to protect the prisoners.

Then there arrived soldiers of the colour guards, who fetched in their regimental colours; and some few officers came—Captain Cunningham, Lieutenant Collins, Ensign Portis, and others—all puzzled, perplexed, bewildered by the massacre, and furious because the French had not protected them after the surrender.

And as for this wretched coward, General Dan'l Webb, he did not lift a finger to help anybody. He had more than four thousand fresh troops arrive in answer to his call of distress to Governor DeLancey and the other Governors; he had Sir William Johnson's regiment, 1,600 strong; Colonel Hoffman's regiment, 900 strong; Whitney's, 650; and the battalions of DeKay, Ellison, Ashly, Nicholls, and Hardenburg—nearly 5,000 troops in all, not counting the garrison of Fort Edward and of the outlying fortifications and camps.

With these he could have saved Munro, driven the pretty Marquis headlong into Carillon, and cleared Lake George of the last Indian.

God knows what a miserable condition this army was in, how disreputable and demoralized it had become.

I saw a letter writ by Governor James DeLancey to Sir William Johnson, asking the reason for "the great and scandalous desertion of the militia of this province!" It made me sick with shame.

Sir William Johnson said: "What does he expect of militia placed under command of such a man as Dan'l Webb who is the only British general—nay, the only British officer of any rank—I ever heard of who was personally a coward!" And to Captain Philip Schuyler

141

he said that Webb was and is a coward and that nobody who ever served under him could fail to perceive it. "He was nearly beside himself with physical fear," said Sir William. "His army was in good spirits and anxious to fight. The General alone was panic stricken."

Nor would he do anything for the wretched fort, neither order our burial parties to care for the murdered dead, nor rescuers to bring in the wounded and those lost in the forest.

Not one thing did that man do except to order guns fired from our parapets to serve as guides to those who might be wandering in the woods.

Well, if Webb can sleep on his pillow o' night, thought I, then I should contrive to do it, too, for I have been betrayed only by a woman, and nevertheless I mourn her loss, but Webb has betrayed men, women, and children to a bloody grave, and shall mourn them in hell through all eternity.

CHAPTER X

WHO DIE IN VAIN

TWICE did the Marquis of Montcalm have to remind us that there still remained English prisoners and wounded and unburied dead at Fort William Henry. Twice did General Dan'l Webb, still a prey to terrors, send out armed escorts and burial parties to take over from a regiment with yellow facings—Deux Ponts, I believe—such of our people as they were guarding from the Praying Indians and Pagan Savages, and such of our dead as these same savages had not burned or cut into fragments too small to be discovered.

And one never would have discovered these shapeless lumps of decaying flesh in the undergrowth except for the tiny roaring of the swarm of green death-flies, or the heaving and settling of the dead tissue where orange-and-black burying beetles were at work.

I went out with a burial party of Yorkers—it being New York's tour of duty—and never have I seen so horrid a place as what once had been Fort William Henry.

As much of the fortification as could be burned the enemy had burned. The rest had become a loathsome plague spot upon the mangled face of nature.

The loud buzzing of millions of golden-green flies made a dreadful and unbroken requiem over our dead. They lay in every conceivable position and posture in the forest, in the shallow water of the lake shore, all over leeches; in patches of weeds and vegetables, and everywhere about the ruined fort from glacis to parapet, in the ditch, on the ramparts, in casemates and barracks, and on the shell-torn parade. *All* of them had been scalped and tumbled and dragged about or dumped together with the offal of the butchers, barrack swill, and filth from the latrines. The contents, also, of the military cemetery lay about in shocking condition. The corpses had not been buried deep and had been dug up by wolves, or by Wyandottes, Caughnawagas and Ottawa ghouls, to strip the rotting hair from the dead in order to claim scalp bounty.

Under an August sun the stench in the forest became almost unendurable, but our sickened fellows persisted doggedly, discovering here a baby which some brawny savage had swung by its little feet to knock its brains out against a tree; there a heap of women's clothing stiff with blackened blood, partly covering the poor, scalped corpse of wife or soldier's trull.

And here was a charred skeleton—all that remained of some pretty, wayward wench who had followed the drum to her terrible undoing. God knows that, amid these stark Adirondack solitudes, the beasts of prey were not as fierce as their blood-thirsty human brethren—white men and red.

A burial flag drooped above an espontoon planted on the steaming, stinking ruins of the fort; another fluttered limply above the bomb-battery of the recent besiegers—but the battery had been evacuated; the French gunners had embarked their mortars and field artillery and, while we were hunting up and burying our English dead, always we could see upon the lovely Lake Saint Sacrement the barges, batteaux, canoes, and sloops of General the Marquis of Montcalm's victorious army. Like gorged tigers they retired, satiated, heavy with slaughter, moving sullenly back to their lair at Carillon—too drunk with blood to make another effort toward Fort Edward or the Saratoga and Stillwater forts—which were all that in God's affrighted world barred them from Schenectady, Albany, Esopus, and the uneasy city of New York itself.

General Webb, knowing well in his cowardly soul of a damned man that his conduct would be questioned by a military court unless he employed influence to avert disgrace, started now to curry favour with his brigadiers and other officers of rank, against the day when they surely would all be summoned to England to testify against him.

But Munro, dazed by the catastrophe of William Henry, broken-hearted at his heartless betrayal, would have none of Webb; nor would Sir William Johnson; and it was fearfully whispered in the army that, rather than face the testimony of Colonel Munro, Dan'l Webb would see to it that the brave and unfortunate Scotch Colonel should never reach England alive.

I do not pretend that George Munro's sudden death could truthfully be attributed to his own General; but it was so rumoured; and Dan'l Webb did profit thereby when the grim order came recalling him to England for trial concerning his personal behaviour and military conduct during the dreadful days of the siege and fall of Fort William Henry.

The French and their Indians were still slowly and leisurely arriving at Carillon, stringing along by land and water, White Coats, Canadians, coureurs-de-bois, Indians.

No slightest demonstration toward Fort Edward had followed the reduction of William Henry. It really seemed as though the fighting on the lakes was about over for the year.

Then, as I came into Fort Edward from the Lake, I was met with information that my Lord Loudon had sailed with his army for Halifax; that the flying Scotchman, Vice Admiral Holburne, had appeared in American waters and had squared away for Isle Royale; and that I was instantly to make my attempt to enter Louisbourg, disguised as a forest runner, and carry out orders from Lord Loudon to the best of my ability.

There came to Sir William Johnson an Oneida runner from Schenectady, with despatches to him which contained a cipher letter for me from my Lord Loudon, written by Captain Bartman while at sea, and sent back to New York by despatch boat. Captain Croghan, having the key of that particular cipher, kindly de-coded it for me:

Captain John Cardress,
  Staff Scout Interpreter.
SIR:
  This God damned delay I can no longer endure! I have taken what few ships Hardy has here in New York Bay, and have sailed for Halifax on my way to Louisbourg.
  Therefore, you will get on to that same fortress without delay and, when inside, contrive to keep me informed, if possible.
  But I desire to repeat to you what is to be your particular function in Louisbourg: you are to keep your eye on that arch traitor Charles Follis, and on the Chevalier Johnstone,

and you are to see to it that when Louisbourg surrenders they shall be included in the surrender and shall not be allowed by the French authorities to slip away secretly and escape.

This is your principal mission in Louisbourg—to charge yourself with this responsibility, and see to it that Charles Follis and the Chevalier be secured and sent to London for proper and instant trial, where they shall inevitably suffer the punishment reserved for such Scottish villains as they— which is that they shall be hanged, their entrails drawn out of them while they are still alive, and their bodies cut into quarters.

Any failure on your part to execute his Majesty's particular orders in this business will lay you open to suspicion of disloyalty, and I do not doubt you will be obliged to explain your failure to a military court.

Therefore, I take it upon myself to add and subjoin another command: that, in the event of your inability to carry out his Majesty's orders regarding these same two Scottish traitors—that is, to see that they are secured and surrendered when the city and garrison are surrendered—then you are to take your pistol or sword, or other convenient weapon, and commit a summary justice upon these two Scottish wretches, making sure that they have ceased to live, rather than allow them to escape the rigour of the laws which they have violated and the anger of a justly offended King.

This is not a matter for your choice, sir; it is a Royal command, and therefore obligatory; and any failure on your part will, I assure you, prove very fatal to you.

Sir William Johnson should furnish you with proper scouts for your purpose. Use a Souriquois Indian if one can be obtained.

There is, also, a rumour that this Charles Follis has a female relative, or a mistress, or a light-o'-love of some sort, who has learned of his peril and who is on her way to Louisbourg to warn him not to let himself be caught within the walls if ever the city is besieged by the English.

I expect, however, that between Hardy and Holburne the ship she travels on will be stopped at sea and her mischief terminated. Therefore, upon receipt of this letter, sir, you will make all haste to depart upon your mission.

I am, sir, etc., etc.,

JOHN BARTMAN,

Captain and A. D. C.

I went at once to see Colonel Croghan and found him coming from the quarters of Sir William Johnson.

"What the devil," said I, "has this Charles Follis done, after all, that I should be set upon his tracks like a King's bloodhound!"

"He hasn't done anything yet," said Croghan, "but he has sworn to show no mercy to British prisoners, and he's warned us that he'll tie a bunch of English heads to every flag-pole, spire, and tree in Louisbourg, if we dare to land on Isle Royale!"

"Why, the dirty Scottish dog!" said I. "Where did you hear that, Colonel?"

"We have it from Paris, Captain, by despatch from our secret agents, that it is common boast and gossip there, and that ruddled hussy, Pompadour, brags of the bouquet of heads that Charles Follis hath promised to pluck in Louisbourg!

"And there," says he, "is your painted French slut! So you had best make sure of your two Scotch dogs, for I think she has bitten 'em both and all three are gone mad!"

"Who is the French harlot who you say is on her way to warn this treacherous Scotchman Charles Follis?"

"I understand," said Croghan, "she's his mistress or kinswoman—a duchess, they say—Duchess of something or other—"

CHAPTER XI

MAGIC

SIR WILLIAM JOHNSON gave me as warrior-guides a Canienga or Mohawk named Gawasa, the Snow Snake; Cioio, or Pretty Brook, a Wyandotte half-Huron; and an Algonquin called Ariaque—a renegade Nova Scotia Souriquois or Micmac—if really there be any particular difference between them.

There is no hurrying any Indian. Both cats and Indians take their own time. Three witch doctors from three Huron clans—the Deer, Hawk, and Snake—came out of a common and stinking witch-lodge, wearing their gaudiest regalia, and made strong medicine in order to prophesy properly regarding our prospective expedition I was heartily sick of their damned drumming before they had done with the Ga-no-io-o; but I will not assert that there was not a certain kind of melody in their singing which they timed to drum-beat and knee-rattle—the latter made of three rows of dry deer-hoofs and tied below the right knee.

The shaman of the so-called Yagontrunon, or Snake Clan—which I think was merely another name for the Souriquois Ogontena, or Eel Clan—had really a fine, melodiously wild voice. He wore a painted wooden mask indescribably hideous, it being carved to represent the degeneration of a human into a beast.

The Canienga sorcerer, called Gano or the Arrow, also sang a song called "Ga-go-an-da," or the Blow-gun; and the Snake Sorcerer played this air upon an instrument called the yaodawasta which had six finger holes like a flute; and, between them and the mouth-piece, is the whistle which makes six consecutive notes—the seventh of the octave being missing.

The handsome Wabeno of the Hawk Clan, wearing the mask of Atensi, kept time with a turtle-shell rattle full of flint-corn; and now and then the strange measure of the Ostoweygowa broke in, and now and then the sinister tempo of the Wasasseh, or war dance.

Well, they squalled and drummed and danced all day, and my three war-guides watched them respectfully and gravely as cats watch the fire on a winter's night.

I said in a rage to the Souriquois, Saquahayac: "I do not care a curse whether they find the omens good or bad! May the itch and the great pox seize me if I go not to the North this moonlight night, by God, whether the Hawk, the Deer, and the Snake follow me or go to roost each according to its kind!"

Saquahayac patted my shoulder. He was a pretty thing to behold, having across his face a wide band of bright green paint and a number of yellow and blue slashes under his eyes to make his beauty perfectly dazzling.

He wore scarlet leggings—the brilliant Giseha, and the moccasins ataquaoueh—the flaps wide opened, and dyed purple and embroidered with Siwan in fern forms and circles, and edged deeply with crimson and orange trade-beads. Except the gostowel, or ceremonial headdress, he was otherwise naked and his body was painted with symbols of which I could make nothing. but which meant serious things to him.

The sorcerer of the Yagontru, glaring behind his mask,

fixed his blazing black eyes on each of the warrior-guides
in turn while he sang to the notes of the flute, and the
timing of the yenchenohasta:

"Toka onenh,
  Onontio in white and silver
  Came to the Horicon,
  To the Lake of the Horicon!
  The Great Onontio!—
  Came against Corlaer!
  Came against the English!
  Came against the Long House!
      Continue to listen!
  Carillon was a hornet's nest:
  The hornets, red and white;
  They swarmed around Corlaer
  Stinging! Stinging!
  Neoni the English yielded
  As the Lenape—
  As the Lenni-Lenape
  Yielded to the Kannansioni
  In the Great Days that are no more!
  O Tharon!—Tharon—hiawathon!
  Rakatkatos! (He sees me!)
  O Tharon!—Tharon—hiawathon!
  Katarioseres! (I am going to war!)
  Etho kati onenh—
  Thus, then, now,
  Katatiase,
  I speak in favour of one
  Who wishes to go by stealth
  Into the Lodge of Onontio

Which is in the fortified village called Louisbourg,
And from there bring information to our brother Corlaer,
So that the English and
Those of the Long House
Shall know how to make
An end of Onontio forever!—"

And all the time while they were chanting their "Onenh
—haih—haih!" I was cursing the delay under my breath,
yet knew that God himself could not stir my Huron,
Iroquois and Souriquois scouts to action until these stubborn witch doctors got through with them and advised
them whether to go forward or to wait.

"Athonde! Iya-thondek!" they chanted, "—continue
to listen and to hear!"—while the turtle-rattler, in imita-
tion of the sachems of the Anawara, struck his rattle as
rapidly as three times within the second, chanting the
Karenna of the Asera Ketotanese—the wild hymn of the
Uplifted Hatchet.

"Oyah," they chanted, "now another thing we say *niare*
concerning *oyada* wyia—the handsome somebody—who
desires to strike Yonnondio with lifted hatchet—"

The Souriquois gave me an exalted look which I returned with a hideous scowl; and followed it with an oath,
bidding him get along with his damned medicine or I'd
get along without any further aid either from sorcerers
or scouts.

Finally this miserable business was terminated with the
solemn decision that though danger threatened their White
Captain Akahenyon, the Wary or Sly One—meaning myself—nevertheless the omens were pretty good. Therefore, the Snow Snake, Pretty Brook, and Ariaque, or Bad

Eye the Souriquois, as they now called him, might strip, oil, and paint themselves for war, and undertake with reasonable confidence the dangerous trail to the land of the Black Robes and the Praying Caughnawagas and Mission Indians of Saut St. Louis.

My Indian scouts liked me. "Akah," they called me in good-humoured but respectful abbreviation—which means "Our Wily One"—and, because I spoke their gabbling language and dialects, shading even the subtler intonations of the *a* sound, and substituting *y* for *k* when turning from the Mohawk guide to address the Wyandotte.

Also, because I held that God and the Iroquois Tharon, or Tharonhiawathan, were one and because I knew about the Huron's Atensi and Juskeha as well; and because, further, I understood their Karenna, could recite parts of the Great Rite, and repeat sonorously—

"—*Continue to listen, ye who established the Great League!*
Now, then, hearken, ye who were rulers!
This was the roll of you—
You who combined the work,
You who completed the work,
Kayanerenh—Kowa
The Great League!—"

And because I knew something of the others—the Rite of the Younger Nations—and unexpectedly I applied it to these three scouts:

"Yo o nen o nen ti eh o ya!— Now then, another thing **we** will say, we three brothers. . . . We came here of our own good will—came to your door that we might say this. . . . We will try to do you good!"

For these reasons, then, Gawasa, Cioio, and Ariaque listened in astonishment to whatever I had to say to them; and now, in particular, they were frightfully attentive to the solemn words I put into their mouths.

Then at last the Snow Snake said fearfully that he would be faithful to the death; and the Wyandotte, Pretty Brook, looked at me very seriously. The Souriquois knew nothing about all this, being a wild Algonquin, but he seemed awed by the attitude of his brother scouts.

I thought to myself, watching them painting their faces and bodies for war, that I had three very reliable guides and warriors on this perilous trail, and was thankful that, in idle hours, I had taken pains to learn a little about the language and customs of these red foresters of the north.

When they had oiled and painted themselves, and were stripped naked to the clout and ankle-moccasins, they carried each a blanket, rifle, ammunition, parched corn thickened with maple sugar, tobacco, war-axe, and knife.

I myself went light. I wore leather—a deer-skin hunting shirt, breeches, and moccasins made by an Oneida woman; and I carried in my pack spare ammunition, extra shirts and stockings, a little food, and not much else.

I had my own rifle which was reliable only because I knew every trick of the crosseyed old slut, and how she bore low and to the left nearly an eighth of an inch in thirty yards, not allowing for windage and a drifting bullet.

Our council fire, south of Fort Creek, burned redder and redder as daylight failed in the fading West.

"Get on with your war songs," said I impatiently to the Snow Snake, "for I mean to follow the full moon's path across the Horicon, and if you are still bragging and strutting when I start, you may follow me afoot or swim behind the Old Bad-eye the pickerel, for all I care."

"Patience, O Sly One," said the Snow Snake earnestly, "we three scouts have only our war songs to sing before Atensi, the White Witch, peeps at us and beckons us from behind the moon!"

He felt of the horned-owl's feathers in his scalp-lock, adjusted them, grasped his war-hatchet and trade rifle, and, stamping the earth like a stallion, sang his song in a nasal, whining voice:

"I am the Snow Snake!
I fly faster than moonlight.
Let the White Coats watch their lake,
For I shall cross it this night!
My hatchet is swift
As an arrow in its flight!
Where the iron birds drift
Screaming above the fight!

"—The iron birds, birds of War
Screeching above the dying—
I hear the wailing afar
Where the Ottawa women are crying,
And their fires burn cold and dim when the death yell
    breaks,
Where their scalped dead swim
With the eels in a hundred lakes!"

Instantly Pretty Brook the Wyandotte, with a horrible
laugh, began to imitate the Ottawa and Abenaqui wid-
owed squaws, sobbing, and screaming, and yelping:

"Koue—e—e! It is Cioio;
He is skinning our warriors' heads!
The Pretty Brook, Cioio,
Is running blood-red!
Let the Praying Indians take net and hook
And fish for our dead!
Koue—e—e! It is Cioio! Look!
Who has scalped my husband's head!
Now, by the fire glow,
The scalp he hoops and paints and braids the hair!
Let Black Robe and White Coat and the Ottawa dogs
*   beware!"*

Then the lean, slit-eyed, ferocious Souriquois ambled
up in his soiled war-finery, all bedaubed with greasy paint:

"I am a Souriquois Bear;
Little nephew to the Lenni-Lenapé.
My people are Delaware;
My tribe comes from the French Bay!
Algonquin my race,
Micmac my speech;
Between land and sea I take my place,
Being the child of each!
If my enemy swims in the sea,
Like a white-shark I swallow him!
If to the hills he'd flee,
Like a grey-wolf I follow him!

If into the sky he leaps,
Like a goshawk I claw him;
If into the rocks he creeps,
Like a ghost-bear I paw him!
His corpse to the crabs I cast;
His scalp I sell for rum;
Without weapon or food he dies at last,
And must starve in the Life to come!"

I was by this time so impatient and madded that when I spoke my voice was hoarse and unsteady with wrath.

"Now, God damn your painted hides," said I in a passion; "cover your fire and launch the canoe in the moon's path, or go back to your lodges to be mocked by your women and children!"

But they took their time and only laughed among themselves, saying: "Our Sly One is impatient and angry with us. We will have to show to Akahenyon, our elder brother, that our minds and hearts are as determined for war as are his own!"

They stank like March wolves in a den when at last, filling the long birch canoe, we embarked upon the black, transparent flood which the moon's spectral torch lighted in a long, sparkling pathway. The moon's path never seems entirely straight and perpendicular to the glowing, silver orb, but oddly bent a trifle to the left.

The Snow Snake spoke of it and said it was because nothing in this life is clear and straight, because the evil spirits delight in deceiving us. I suppose there is a real reason which Science understands.

Nearly all night we paddled; and before the first faint

pencilings of grey in the eastern heavens we landed, carried our canoe inland and concealed it; then, in single file, silent, cautious, bent on murder, we crept onward along the vast and endless line of the French watch-fires that lead along the lake where the great western war path traverses the unbroken wilderness to the Canadas.

CHAPTER XII

FOLLOWING THE DRUM

ON the second day the Snow Snake, who had been scouting far ahead with Cioio, came back to tell me that he had been in the French camp and that Montcalm had sung the war song again with the Ottawas and Hurons, and with the Western Pagans, but the ceremonies, which had lasted three days, had not yet been concluded, and it was uncertain whether the Western nations would continue on the war path if the English appeared before Louisbourg.

So, after all, the siege of Louisbourg was decided upon!

There seemed to be no longer any doubt of it. Lord Loudon, with the flower of the Hudson Valley troops, was on his way to Louisbourg. If Louisbourg fell, then Quebec and Montreal must follow. It was perfectly evident that their clever Marquis of Montcalm was now marching to face this expected storm, and had turned his back in contempt upon the coward whom he had first chased from Oswego and who, later, had basely abandoned the garrison of Fort William Henry to a murderous and merciless enemy.

There is a valley set between mountains, heavily wooded to the crests, about four miles long, and it lies between Lake Saint Sacrement and Lake Champlain. This, my Indians reported, was occupied by the French army, eight thousand strong, and a detachment of two thousand savages representing more than forty nations, tribes, and lesser subsidiaries which perhaps might be termed tribal clans but not national clans.

There were nearly a thousand Praying Indians—renegade Iroquois—under their French priests from the missions of two mountains, La Présentation, and Caughnawaga.

There were Wyandottes from Lorette; Abenaquis of the Missions St. Francis and Missisqui; Algonquins of Three Rivers; Souriquois of Acadia.

Here, also, were seven tribes of the Ottawa nation; there were Mississaguas and Ojibways from the Great Lakes; Sacs, Foxes, Winnibagos; mounted Miamis from the western prairies; and pagan Iowas.

My plan was simple. It was merely to carry my scout of four to the French Souriquois. By that road I could enter Louisbourg as a volunteer for the Regiment Etranger or Foreign Legion. There I could execute my mission and also keep track of those two Scottish soldiers of fortune, the Chevalier Johnstone and Charles Follis, whom the petty, tyrannical little Hanover-German, George II, King of England, wished to hang, draw, and quarter as soon as his army under his profane and peppery lordship, General Loudon, had taken the city of Louisbourg.

That was the plan. The French Souriquois would suspect nothing when they saw among our Indians one of their own nation from Ingonish. Truly, Sir William Johnson had cleverly selected my scout of three—Gawasa the Snow Snake, an Iroquois of the Mohawk Nation; Cioio, Pretty Brook, a Huron or Wyandotte; and Ariaque

the Ingonish Souriquois, called Bad Eye the Pickerel, but
for what reason I never learned.

Well, there was nothing to do except to go forward,
present ourselves, and brave scrutiny from French, Canadian, and savage alike.

About four o'clock in the afternoon, moving in single
file on the great western war trail which now had become a real wagon road, we came into contact with
White Coats—French Regulars of the battalions Béarn
and Royal Rousillon, under Bourlamaque.

A fat, jolly Frenchman of the Canadian brigade Courtmanche, stopped us and called an officer of the militia
battalion Saint-Ours, who in turn sent for the Jesuit,
Father Roubaud, St. Francis missionary.

When Father Roubaud came to look at us he had
with him Father Piquet, of the Caughnawaga Mission;
and these two, as they came toward us, gave us pleasant,
intelligent looks out of keen and clever eyes.

We stood in a little grove of white birches near the
lake shore, where sentinels of the Regiment Languedoc
kept a careless eye on us.

As the two priests advanced, the Snow Snake muttered aloud: "Now we shall deceive both Black Robe and
Onontio with our cunning."

And I heard the Wyandotte repeating: "Yonondio and
the Black Robes shall play with death and never know
it until death bites them in the dark!"

"Salute, Father," said I in French, taking off my
fur cap with its dangling coon-tail.

"Well, my son," said the lean, sun-scorched priest,
"what is this they tell me about volunteers for the French
service?"

"It is true, Father. I offer for the Foreign Legion, being of Scottish blood. I fetch my friends from the Mohawk and Sacandaga—the Snow Snake, Pretty Brook, and Bad Eye."

"Your name, Monsieur?"

"Ian Cardress, Father, of the Mohawk Valley, and lately a Militia Captain in the tenantry battalion the Colonel of which is Sir William Johnson."

The calm, level-eyed priest considered me pleasantly:

"It seems odd," said he, "that so many Scotch Highlanders of the true faith should remain loyal to Sir William Johnson. I think, my son, that you are the only Scot, so far, who has come to us from Johnstown where we ought to expect two hundred or more Catholic Scotchmen to help us wipe out their disgrace at Culloden!"

"Father, I don't know very much about Sir William's Scotch tenantry in the neighbourhood of Mount Johnson and the Valley. I am as well born as Sir William, as Sir Peter Warren, and can hold up my head with the Chevalier Johnstone and with Charles Follis. As for the Campbells and McDonalds of the Valley, let them bicker and quarrel as they may, nevertheless they stick together, and to the valley, being a thrifty folk and far too canny to risk their porridge for a chivalrous dream and a ragged prince and the forlorn hope of the Foreign Legion in Louisbourg!"

Father Roubaud spoke to the Snow Snake in the Mohawk dialect, who replied bluntly that he desired to fight the English but cared nothing about Two Mountains and Jesus Christ.

Father Picquet addressed himself pleasantly to Cioio; and that warrior, also, denied any interest in the Virgin

Mary and Lorette, saying coolly that his business was war and scalps, and that he had his own ideas concerning the Holder of Heaven.

The two priests smiled and exchanged glances, and I saw that they already considered the conversion of these two painted warriors a probability. Then they both looked curiously at the Souriquois, Bad Eye, whose paint-bedaubed features became as mild as the countenance of a purring cat, and who admitted a desire for religion, for Ingonish, and for the society of his fellow Souriquois whom he had been so foolish as to quit, persuaded by the blandishments of Colonel Croghan.

Father Roubaud, who possessed all the culture and charm and exquisite sophistication of his order and race, walked with me in pleasant conversation through a section of the vast French camp, where I saw Bourlamaque's regular batallions already marching down to their boats, and the Regiments Guienne and La Sarre forming to follow.

The priest named many officers to me as we walked leisurely along; and there I saw young Longueuil, and Lévis, and Bougainville, and the leader of all the Indians, Saint Luc; Marin who scared us at Edward; and those hardy, half-wild, forest-running officers and sprigs of nobility who commanded Canadian regulars, irregulars, and Indians, men such as Rigaud, Niverville, Hertel, Fleurimont, and Langlade who had married an Indian girl, and Sabrevois who hadn't married his.

Pennahoul, chief of the Ottawas, stared at me and at my Indians, and came striding over to inspect us.

"I smell English paint," said he. "Who," said he harshly, "is sending out these English Indian spies into the camp of Yonnondio!"

"—Which is a lie," said I, looking him in his face, "and it is not strange that a cannibal Ottawa can no longer smell the English, the Iroquois, and the Souriquois who are real men!"

Father Roubaud, turning very red, caught the Ottawa by his naked arm as he was pulling at his hatchet with a wild, panther light in his crazy eyes.

"I beg of you, sir—" he said to me who had unsheathed my own hatchet, meaning to stand no nonsense from any Wyandotte.

Pennahoul howled: "I have counted more moons than any Ottawa in the Canadas, but this white forest runner shows me no respect!"

"I'll show you the flat of my hatchet and let you bite it if you exhibit any more insolence to an officer," said I, sharply. "Tell that to this noisy, Macinac pagan chief, Father!"

I don't know what the Jesuit said to him, but he gave us a furious look and strode away toward a throng of his paint-smeared brethren who were gathering to listen to the French Commander-in-Chief, General the Marquis of Montcalm, who was to sing the war song.

As a matter of fact, Bougainville sang it at dusk, in the midst of two thousand painted, greased and stinking savages surrounding the fire circle.

There, in the torch-light, were crowded and packed the Mission Indians and the Western Pagans. And there, in white broadcloth uniforms—coats, waistcoats, and breeches faced and embroidered with pale blue, violet, yellow, green, and scarlet, and their cocked hats heavy with gold lace—stood the handsome Marquis of Montcalm, surrounded by his courtly, gorgeously uniformed

young officers—a gay, graceful and youthful company
in their laces, and hair-powder, and perfumed gloves
which smelled of Paris and Versailles a thousand leagues.

When I approached him the Marquis was talking to
Lévis about an oil mill which he owned in France.

Father Roubaud led me forward and presented me
to the Marquis whose thinly veiled distaste for a deserter
was scarcely veiled under obligatory politeness.

Half disdainfully he asked me a few questions which
I answered truthfully because he already knew everything
worth knowing about Fort Edward.

He said there was no objection to my enlisting in the
Foreign Legion; then, returning my bow with some stiff-
ness, he turned me over to that partizan killer of theirs,
Captain Corbière—the same who, on July 26th, had
ambushed Colonel Parker's command near Sabbath Day
Point, and whose Indians chased these wretched New
Jersey soldiers into the lake and speared nearly two hundred of them with their feathered lances, as though they
were spearing fish for salting.

Corbière seemed indifferent as to what I did or where
I went. He pointed out to me the camp of the French
sutlers, and also told me briefly where I might draw
rations for myself and my savages.

Marin, also, came up, and Corbière named me to him.
But it was plain that these French and Canadian officers
had little interest and less respect for deserters. With
the Chevalier Johnstone and Charles Follis, and the Scots
in the Foreign Legion, it was different. They never had
served George II in the armies of Loudon. But I had;
and no real man cares for the aroma which hangs around
a deserter as the stench clings to a skunk.

It isn't agreeable, even by one's enemies, to be classed in their minds among these latter animals.

Even that lousy Ottawa chief, Pennahoul, had scented treason—only that he alone seemed to guess where that treason really was, and whither it, already, had guided me and my three savages.

But now Bougainville, in full uniform, his white coat covered with gold arabesques and orders and a broad crimson sash crossing his jewelled breast to form a bow above his sword-knot, stepped forward toward the central council fire; and, on a long line of rude benches and camp chairs, the Marquis of Montcalm and his brilliant throng of young officers seated themselves.

The scene was amazing. I had very often assisted at councils of the Iroquois at Sir William Johnson's residence and elsewhere in the Mohawk and Sacandaga Valleys; and, with Colonel Croghan, Guy Johnson, Colonel John Butler, and others, had seen the Six Nations come from the Long House in all their fierce power and savage finery to listen to Sir William, to receive his belts for war or peace, to be praised or rebuked or warned; and, in turn, to reply with strings and belts through the mouths of their national chiefs and sachems, or through the sachems of the Six Nations in Federal Council assembled.

But never had I beheld so fierce and wild and weird a gathering as this, where the graces and elegancies and laces and perfumes of France were confronted by the paint and grease-smeared hordes of the West and of Quebec, Montreal, and Three Rivers, led by their missionary priests and by their naked, bedaubed chiefs with bodies oiled and heads shaved for battle.

The torches and the council fires painted the tree

trunks red, and sparkled among vast masses of pine
needles.

In two masses the savages squatted. The Marquis
and his officers sat at the head of this living corridor
of painted and stinking human creatures. They were
already gorged with food, having been stuffing themselves
all day and evening; and the kettles still steamed between
the lines, and dark, filthy Indian fingers still burrowed
into the kettles from time to time to drag out smoking
bits of chopped meat.

And now Bougainville, without a trace of latent humour
or of self-conscious awkwardness, walked out into the
firelight and, stamping the earth with his silver-spurred
heel, broke into a monotonous sing-song chant:

> *"Let us trample the English under our feet!*
> *Let us make of the Mohawks wild-cat meat!*
> *—Meat for the panther, wolf, and bear,*
> *Meat for the red-tail buzzards to tear!*
> *Meat for the bitch and cubs in her lair—*
> *The grey wolf, the vixen red,*
> *The carcajou in his stinking bed!*
> *Lift up your thirsty hatchets, you men of the North!*
> *Lift up your feathered lances and come forth,*
> *You men of the West—*
> *You with the bison crest!*
> *You of the Lakes!*
> *You Mountain Snakes!*
> *War! Let your dry hatchets drink deep;*
> *Death! Let the English and Iroquois women weep!"*

He offered a scarlet war-belt of wampum to whoever
would take it.

Then a Wyandotte chief sprang up and snatched it; lifted his war-axe and, passing down the lines, sang his war song and reseated himself, still singing.

Pennahoul sprang to his feet for the Ottawas, took the belt, sang venomously his war song; passed on. A wild looking renegade Oneida chief rose in behalf of the Mission Indians and seized the belt:

> *"The Master of Life,*
> *The Holder of Heaven,*
> *Calls to us to fight!*
> *I have questioned my knife*
> *And the Dancers Seven;*
> *They answer I am right!*
> *I love Jesus and Mary, too,*
> *I pray to them the same as you,*
> *But I hang a shirt and leggins on a pole*
> *And pray also to the Manitou to save my soul;*
> *If Onontio desires us to kill,*
> *Let the Nipissings also do his will!*
> *Let the lakes turn red with the English blood;*
> *Let Corlear bleed till the seas are a scarlet flood!"*

He stood a moment, offering the red belt.

Then an Iowa chief got up; but nobody—not even any western interpreter—could understand his language. However, it was plain that he wouldn't fight. He refused the belt. He told us in pantomime that he wanted to go home.

The Sacs and Foxes, painted a hellish crimson, yelled their battle songs, telling us they had enemies enough in the far west and meant to go home and fight them. They refused the belt.

Then into the fire circle rode some mounted Miamis and Winnibagos, magnificent in their paint, ornaments, war bonnets, glittering plastrons of Siwan, and handsome beaver fur blankets.

They carried lances; their full quivers rattled on their naked backs; their trade rifles rested across their horses' necks.

They were singing and gesticulating.

Nevertheless, in spite of all this noisy truculence and display, they also wanted to go home.

They were homesick, they said to Montcalm, and were extremely tired of looking at trees and mountains when the flat, treeless, grassy prairies were more to their taste.

They turned their painted and gaudily ornamented horses and rode away, still singing their wild, barbaric songs that nobody understood.

Then the handsome Marquis of Montcalm arose. He held a purple and silver chain-belt in his white gloved hand. It was a belt of the finest wampum, twenty rows deep.

He spoke in French, very slowly; and six interpreters, in turn, explained what he said to the nations, tribes, and tribe-clans. He said:

"*My children!* Onontio—or, as some call him, Yonondio—has now come to thank you for having joined in this praiseworthy business of driving the English away from the Holy Lake which rightfully belongs to the King of France. Now, forever, it shall remain the property of his victorious Majesty, Louis the Fifteenth.

"*Children!*

"As long as you remain united and in alliance with your father, Onontio, the English can not resist you!

"Listen attentively!

"The great King of France has sent me here to protect and defend his beloved children of the forest and the prairie. And, above all, he has charged me to make you happy and unconquerable by establishing among you the union which ought to prevail among the children of one father—the great Onontio!

"Now listen attentively!

"You who have taken my red war-belt, to you I show another belt to confirm what I tell you—this great chain-belt of six thousand beads of ancient Siwan! The union of these beads is the sign of your united strength! By it I bind you all together so that you who have taken my red war-belt shall remain in brotherly alliance until the English are driven from New France—chased away from Louisbourg with your war-arrows in their backs and your hatchets sticking in their heads!"

He held out the shining belt. Pennahoul took it.

"Brothers!

"Behold! A circle has been drawn about us by the great Onontio!

"Brothers!

"Let none of us step outside of it! For as long as we remain within it the Master of Life will help us in all our undertakings!

"Listen attentively!

"We Ottawas do not understand why you horse-riding Sacs, Foxes, Iowas, and Miamis of the West ride away on your horses.

"But we are not going to quarrel with you about it. Go in peace, therefore; and when you are riding in green grass so high that it covers your scalp-locks and your horses' ears, then, as you ride and sing your hunting songs, and loosen your arrows at those vast and shaggy beasts you call the buffalo, remember your Northern brethren of the Great Lakes; and how you went into battle side by side with the White Coats and the Ottawas!

"*Brothers!*

"Ride home in peace! But do not forget us if the English ever prove too strong, and you hear our cry for help!

"*Brothers!*

"I have finished!"

Then, in the flame-shot darkness, I saw the mounted pagans ride away toward the west.

Nobody paid any attention to me or my Indians.

I went to a sutler and bought what food we needed. Then, from the Indian Commissary attached to Rigaud's camp which was on the Mohawk Trail running west of Northwest Bay, I drew rations in addition.

This northwest Mohawk war trail, by which route Rigaud's two thousand savages and irregulars had marched on William Henry—there being too few bateaux to carry all—was now worn into a wide, rough wagon road. Along it, by turns, regular regiments and irregular battalions marched to give to other troops their turn in the bateaux.

Torches of fat pine, and camp-fires, too, glowed red and smoky all along it, lighting the road for those battalions which had not quite completed their étape by daylight.

While my Indians made our fire and began to cook our meat near a little trout brook that runs into Artillery Cove, I strolled to the edge of the rutty highway where the Regiment de La Reine was still passing—or, rather, where its baggage, bat-horses, wagons, beef-cattle, and its camp followers, women and children, were now plodding along northward toward the bivouac.

Military police signalled them forward and indicated their route to the tired, dishevelled, trudging women, old and young, some burdened with little children asleep in their arms, others bearing bundles of food and clothing, and all plodding along to the melancholy tap-tap-tap of a drum which, although against regulation, was humanely permitted by Montcalm, to aid and direct the poor, footsore stragglers.

As I stood beside the road, in the wavering torch glare, I don't know why, for the first instant, I was not very much surprised to see Sandi.

I had probably just been thinking of her; I often did. Then, suddenly, there she was, in the flesh, before my eyes, and so near I could have touched her.

As I say, for the first moment I did not seem to be very much surprised or disturbed. Then a shock went through me like a bullet, and a terrible confusion seized me so that I did not really know whether I had cried out or not.

She wore her dress of a French peasant girl and was seated astride a poor, bony old nag which a good-looking sous-officer of regulars was leading by the bridle.

Her slim legs hung down on either side of the nag's wizened ribs, so far, indeed, that her tucked up skirt revealed her naked thigh above the knee.

On her slim feet two sabots dangled and waggled with every lurching step of the horse.

I thought she was asleep where she sagged sleepily in

her saddle between a roll of bedding and another of camp blankets, and both her arms thrust into the handles of market baskets, buckets, and a thin, copper kettle, up to the very shoulders of her.

I do not believe I uttered a sound; at least nobody except Sandi heard or noticed it if I did—but *something* made her lift her head and turn it—for if ever silence called frantically to silence, it happened in that straining instant.

She looked directly into my face. A second or two passed before she knew me. Then such a look of terror! —such white astonishment and fear!

Baskets and kettles slipped and fell clashing and banging to the roadway, which made the poor old horse shy and caper.

The good-looking sous-officer of the Regiment de la Reine picked up these utensils with a gay inquiry as to how she was feeling, adding that their bivouac was not very far away.

So I stood there in the forest alongside of the rutted roadway, and saw Sandi, in the coarse garments of a regimental jade, frowsy, dirty, her skirt at her shameless knee, go lurching northward along the Mohawk war trail, on the back of a broken down nag that might indeed have served to carry Old Man Death himself.

Sandi! My Sandi! God help her! Following the drum like any other soldier's slut! . . . A little, vicious camp-wench, already enlisted to do anything, everything, or, possibly and honestly, nothing more sinister than washing and mending.

But if this little jade's business in the French camp **were** honest or otherwise, I had no means of knowing or surmising; and all I knew was that a great tumult reigned in my disordered senses at the mere sight of this sleepy, curly headed young thing with her dangling sabots and the under lip of a really lovely mouth almost sensual in its scarlet and sagging surprise.

CHAPTER XIII

UNDER THE MOON

CALM incredulity, then shock; then a swift flare of passion; then anger—these were the emotions which swept me as a tempest sweeps a tall young pine, stirring its very roots under the heaving earth which bedded them.

In the red shadows of the torch-light the scene seemed crude, raw, gaudy, unreal. The passing regiment with its single monotonous drum—dub-dub—rub-a-dub-*dub!* Dub-dub—rub-a-dub-*dub!* Dull sparkle of firelight on button, buckle, bayonet; shapes of tired folk bending under burdens; strangely exaggerated shapes of weary horses, their long, grotesque skulls and clattering, shambling skeletons horribly apparent under their caved-in contours—

Dub-dub—rub-a-dub-*dub!* Dub-dub—rub-a-dub-*dub!* And there, a-horse, jolted Sandi, her curls in her drowsy eyes, her full lips drooping apart, and her long, smooth legs hanging heavy with iron-banded sabots—

Regiment de la Reine, with its baggage and women. And, among its baggage and women, Sandi!

I and my three Indians built us a fire by the lake's edge and cooked and ate the rations I had drawn: beef, bacon, bread.

Scarcely anybody paid us any attention at all. Ten thousand victorious Frenchmen, Canadians, and savages

were unlikely to notice four more human beings. The
army was in no danger. No possible peril could threaten
these battalions from the poltroon at Fort Edward. It
was scarcely worth while mounting guard in this wilderness where the only war-whoop that insulted the troops
was the blood-cry of grey wolves.

So full my shocked and distracted mind with thoughts
of Sandi, of her situation, of my own condition and destination, that I ate without knowing what I was about,
my sullen eyes roving hither and thither, looking yet
seeming to see nothing; and, in my heart, dull fear and
anger, and the hurrying current of a dark, swift passion.

My Indians ate after the manner characterizing their
race and nations—Iroquois and Huron crunching and
bolting bone and sinew and flesh with the snap and gulp
of wolves; but, oddly, the Souriquois ate as daintily as
a raccoon at the river's edge—and I noticed it, yet did
not consider it until afterward.

I saw two or three Indians come near to our fire and
look at us—Abenaquis, by their paint and moccasins—
and they seemed sneering and unfriendly, saying something about those in war-paint and wearing the lock, who
made it convenient to feed fat after a battle in which they
had not shared.

"No," said I, "nor did we share in treachery and massacre, either; nor break Onontio's convention to murder
women and little children at Fort William Henry!"

The Abenaqui who had offended me demanded furiously what his nation had to do with that massacre.

"Why, you dirty yellow dog," said I, "it was the Praying Indians of your nation, from Panaouski, who started
that filthy business!"

Suddenly my temper slipped. I got to my feet and snatched a stick of firewood: "Get out of here or I'll cave in that rattlesnake face of yours!" I said in a fury. "Get up!" said I to my Indians, "and drive these carcajous away!"

The Abenaquis shrank back, turned and fled, astounded and dismayed by my fury, which was due, alas, to a mind suddenly thrown into unhappy disorder by the glimpse of a faithless girl who, God knows, should have been of little consequence to me.

But I could no more shut out from my mind that drooping, dishevelled figure with frowsy hair and dangling, sabot-shod feet, than I could tear that same mind out of the grey convolutions of the brain encasing it.

This vision that I had seen, daubed with gaudy firelight, dimmed by the red and rolling smoke of torches, passing through the infernal glow to the timing of a solitary drum—this strange and dream-like apparition so obsessed me that I could still feel the nervous disintegration of the shock—was angrily and helplessly aware of the disorder into which my senses had been thrown by this strange, unaccountable, and wayward jade.

My Indians made a bark hut for me, but they themselves lay in their blankets close to the fire.

Lap-slap—lap-slap! went the water along the shore as the thin, silvery waves came speeding and succeeding one another under the staring moon.

Everywhere in the moonlit dark hung a heavy smell of smoke, of sweating animals, of unwashed men. Everywhere, in the silver darkness, an unbroken, endless murmur waxed and waned in waves of sound ebbing and flowing through the depthless shadow of the forest. It came from subdued voices and whispers of women and men; the stirring and sighing of tired beasts of burden; the crackle of burning logs in a thousand fires; vague noises of wind-touched foliage, of lofty, swaying pines,— liquid whispering of the trout brook flowing into the Holy Lake through Artillery Cove.

In my blanket I lay sideways in my lean-to, looking out over the Horicon.

The Snow Snake and Pretty Brook slept; the Soriquois was awake and his partly closed, glittering eye encountered mine.

After a long while, not being able to put from me thoughts of this young jade, I got up and went down to the rocky lake shore.

The Souriquois rose and followed me.

"The mosquitos are troublesome," said I.

"What can sting like a man's thoughts?" said he calmly.

Startled, I turned to stare at this painted savage.

"Brother," said he, "I lie awake as you do. Memories of my own land and my own people sting me so that I can not sleep. . . . What sorrow keeps the Sly One awake?"

I made him no answer.

He pulled his blue blanket around him and looked out across Lac Saint Sacrement.

"The French call it the Holy Lake," said he, "and the English call it Lake George after their King. But it should be known by the name of those ancient people who dwelt here before the white men came—the Horicon."

I nodded. Presently I asked him about his own clan-tribe, the Souriquois of that wind-lashed coast to the northeast.

"They are Onontio's people," said he, "and wherever they are they call Onontio father."

"Then you can't go to Isle Royale with me," I remarked.

"No, Akah; for they would roast me at the stake and carve me to slivers as I roasted. . . . Yet, they are my own people. . . . There are no people like my own. Have you ever seen the Souriquois, Akah?"

"No."

"They are handsome and full of grace. None is fat. The young men and the young girls are so nearly of the same slim shape that when in their deeply fringed shirts and leggins with sea-green thrums, one can scarcely tell which is boy and which is maid. Only that the maidens have two belts—one passing under the breasts. . . . We are not bad people, Akah. We are very poor, and very often hungry. . . . The sea gives its fish as it chooses—not always—not every time to our lance and arrow and our hook of bone. Akah?"

"Yes?"

"I am a Souriquois of Isle Royale. I have seen Louis-bourg."

"Tell, then."

"That is a vast and fearful place of high towers and walls of massive stone—of thick bastions and many rows of cannon. A city of little streets, and full of store-houses and houses of wood. . . . And there are squares and convents and hospitals, and a palace—and barracks, magazines, markets— Akah?"

"Yes, I hear you, brother."

"A place of strong walls and of spires and chimneys.
. . . And, everywhere, cannon! And soldiers. Everywhere soldiers, on the walls, in barracks, upon towers,
marching across squares and parades, strolling along the
stony streets—everywhere White Coats and their officers
in blue and gold and red and gold; and their ladies in
furs and lace and silks. . . . My people are free to come
and go. Also, they may travel the roads or camp near
the fishing stations; and none shall mistreat the Souriquois. . . . There are French officers of noble birth who
have married maidens of my people."

"Yes," said I, "the French do that. . . . We make
friends with your warriors and sachems; the French
make friends with your women. We are not alike, the
English and French, you see."

"Akah?"

"I listen."

"Even their greatest Onontio—"

"Frontenac," said I. "Oh, yes, I know. . . . And
nearly every Governor, Intendant and Captain since the
great Count's day. Well—are your people the better for
it?"

He said: "If only the French were the stronger we
could love them better than we do the English."

"Yes, I understand. But long after your love for the
French has turned to weariness and indifference, you will
serve the English in alliance; and you will take hold of
your end of the great chain with both hands, and call
upon your sachems and chiefs and wise men to scour it
and brighten it!"

After a long pause:

"Akahenyon?"

"Yes?"

"It is true."

When at length there were no sounds at all from the sleeping camp, and the sustained, monotonous, lilting song of night insects had ceased, and no more rising fish splashed in the lake of molten silver, then I rolled over to the fire and unwound my blanket from my body and got up, cat-footed, and so to the road and northward.

As I walked, my hatchet slapped my right flank, my knife my left; and the night wind off the lake blew my hair across my eyes.

Scarce a sentinel hailed me, and then only in perfunctory fashion—gay, white-coated young fellows walking their posts with a song on their beardless lips which pouted like schoolboys' as the "Qui vive!" escaped like a laugh.

In their white cities of spotless tents the White Coats lay encamped, regiment beyond regiment, in the dazzling moonlight along the silver Horicon.

A lounging voyageur with an Indian girl, answering my low-voiced question, told me where the Regiment de la Reine had pitched its tents.

The sentinels, sympathetic always when a woman was concerned, paused in their swinging stride to point out the sutler's tent and the rude bivouac of the camp-women beyond.

I had no notion of how I was to discover this young woman. Everybody and everything seemed to be asleep —horses, camp-dogs, everything except a spangled cock which the moonlight excited and deceived and who kept on flapping his wings and crowing cock-a-doodle-do! from his perch high on an army wagon full of spars and sails.

I walked very slowly along the brush-huts, tents, sheds and wagons, and heard no sound except the cock-crow and the lap-lap of the lake water along the shore.

Then I was aware of a shadow moving across the hemlock shade where it was barred with moonlight—a shape that kept pace with me like a grey ghost of mist rising from some forest fen to join the spectres drifting along a sheeted shore.

"Sandi!" I called.

She came waist-deep through foggy ferns and down across deep mosses to the shore.

"My God, sir," she whispered, "what are you doing in this French camp?"

"You, also—what are you doing here?"—I could scarcely speak, so strangled was I by passion—by the emotional sense of her nearness.

"My poor friend," she whispered, "I am here where no harm can reach me. But you, they will hang if ever they discover who you are!"

She began to whimper, lifting her apron and hiding her eyes in it. I pulled it aside:

"Why did you deceive me and desert me?" I whispered hoarsely.

"Oh, Mother of God," she sobbed, "there are other things more important than being caressed by you! . . . There are matters other than my own seduction which demand my impassioned energies! Do you suppose that only men can hear the call of honour? I recognize that summons as well as you do, my rash young Captain. I am answering it; this is all!"

"Why did you steal, secretly, out of my life, Sandi?"

"I stole into it, sir. May I not steal out of it, too? All hearts are free even when the body serves—though you may not know it."

"Your heart?"

"Yes, my heart. . . . I have one, you know—though from the way you used me I don't think you believed I possessed a heart."

"I thought you cared for me—a little."

"Not a little; but greatly, sir—that's how you thought I cared for you. . . . Maybe I did. . . . But one may care superlatively for other than your highly desirable self!"

"Oh. . . . Then there *is* another?" said I, sick with the very thought.

"Yes, sir. . . . There is another."

"I see," said I in a cold, blind rage that throttled me.

"No, sir, you do not see. Nevertheless, there is another—nay, *two* others!"

"What!" said I, "do you pretend to hardy promiscuity, then?"

"I suppose you mean to ask if I am a soldier's trull? Do you think I am?"

"My God, I don't know what you are—seeing you here like any enlisted wench, and following the drum!"

"Yes," said she, "I follow the drum. . . . Into Louisbourg, sir. . . . And whether I lie innocent or with such as I choose to favour in the Regiment de la Reine, after all, sir, what is it to you?"

"You used the word 'love'—not so many days ago," said I.

"Yes? . . . Did you, also, sir?"

"Love?" I repeated, reddening.

"Yes. I remember hearing you mention it, my pretty Captain."

"Lying between your arms, Sandi, was there any need of speaking—even if your lips had not already closed mine? Was it necessary to tell you that I made love to you even while I was about it—"

"To make love and to pay your court are two different matters in the French language, sir. Neither require that you should *be* in love. Or that you should say so. . . . You are dishonest, my Captain; you *did* say so. . . . I don't remember whether *I* did or not," she added, looking down at her wool skirt and stockings and wooden shoes.

I said: "I treated you kindly. You betrayed me. You turned loose a prisoner of war for whom I was responsible. You yourself abandoned me, also."

"Yes, sir, I did do these things."

"Because you made little of me and held me in contempt—you treacherous little French-Scot!"

"And if I had died with pleasure every time you kissed me I would still have done what I did."

"Yes," said I bitterly, "because all the while your heart was otherwise engaged and you love somebody else better than you loved me!"

"Did I say I loved you, sir?"

"By God, you did! And you behaved as though you did—a-sighing and a-dying in my arms—"

"I sighed no more nor died any oftener than did you in *my* arms!" she retorted hotly.

She rose abruptly from the log where she had been sitting, standing straight and still and scornful as a

Gypsy princess in her soiled garments and wooden shoes. Then suddenly she began to laugh:

"What the devil torments you, sir? If you had had any sense when you were a-kissing me you must have known that I was not what I seemed. . . . Because I offered no barrier to your ardour. . . . My lips and arms made little resistance. . . . That ought to have taught you something! . . . Don't you know that it is the basely born who are noisy when mating! Gods interlace in silence. The love-bed of Olympus is as still as the heart of an opened rose."

She shook her cheeks free of her clustered curls, stepped toward me in the moon's white lustre, and laid her hands flat upon the breast of my hunting shirt:

"Had you been less than you are—why, sir, there were your pistols, loaded and within snatching reach.

"Had *I* been less than I am"—she shrugged her shoulders with a scornful smile, "—well, have you never heard a tumbled wench's giggling screech? The nobly born love and die in silence."

"In God's name, who are you, Sandi?" I burst out—and her cautioning, swift hand closed my lips:

"I am Sandi. . . . Do you imagine it was the pleasure of a promenade that brought me across the ocean to North America?"

"I realize that you must have some secret mission here," I admitted.

"A desperate one, sir. Does a gentlewoman brave the Atlantic in a dirty transport—and take menial service with an enemy captain—merely from caprice or a senseless desire for adventure? . . . Look at me, my poor friend—"

She stretched out her blue apron and ragged skirt impulsively, exhibiting her beggarly, half naked condition. Then, a gay devil of perversity seizing her, she spread her fingers, made her naked knees knock together, suddenly toed in, crossed her eyes, stuck out her tongue, and pulled a horrible face at me.

"A pretty thing—am I not?—to take into your arms and bed," said she, spinning around on the toe of one wooden shoe. "Look, sir! I am all legs like a spider!—" flinging herself into a spin again—"Mother of God, am I not a dainty creature for a lonely man to dream of and desire?"

My flushed embarrassment and surprise excited her to outright laughter which she instantly and violently arrested and stifled with both palms against her lips; and so stood looking at me over clutching fingers, slimly huddled there in her rags, one clinging knee resting within the curved hollow of its fellow, and always a gay devilry glittering in her eyes.

Now she seemed but a crazy young gallopin of a gutter gamine, and nothing other; and, only that I knew the contrary, I might have believed her to be the vicious little slut she looked, and as hardy and depraved.

"Is part of your mission to follow the drum like any camp-woman?" I demanded. "And who was the sergeant leading your nag?"

"You don't believe that of me, do you, my Captain?"

"Well, then, no. But where are you going in rags and all alone like any drab? Why did you abandon me and deceive me, Sandi—"

"You found the letter I left for you?"

"Yes—"

"Very well; I wrote it down that you would never believe me nor understand what I was doing. You see I am right." She came closer to me and took hold of the cape of my hunting shirt:

"If there were treachery in me, my poor young friend, I would betray you instantly. But I don't, you see. . . . Why do you come here to spy on this army?"

"Doubtless you have guessed," said I sullenly.

"Yes; you are for Louisbourg. . . . I don't know why though."

I remained silent.

She leaned a little against me, twisting, tying, and untwisting the deer-hide latchets at my throat.

"Don't go to Louisbourg," she murmured. "That is a perilous place for any Englishman."

I shrugged my shoulders in silence.

"Listen," she said, "do you wish to see me again when all these battles and sieges and wars are ended? Because, if you really do, I will write you a letter to the headquarters of my Lord Loudon as soon as it will be possible for us to meet again. Shall I?"

"Yes. . . . But—this may be a long war."

"Are you, by any happy chance, impatient to have it end on my account?"

"You know it, Sandi."

"Why? To make love to me, or make your court to me? Which? Both? . . . Oh, heaven, sir—if you please—the moonlight betrays what we are—about—"

With a deep sigh she wound her arms around my neck and touched her faintly breathing mouth to mine; and I felt the firm spring of her slight, young breast against me, and the beat of her hurrying heart beneath it.

"I'll promise," said she in her breathless, stammering way, "—that you need—you need not court me when you know me as I am, unless—unless you desire to. . . .Oh, Mother of God, this—this is a wild business we two are about—"

"Sandi, I do love you—"

"You *mean* to love me—if I'll let you!—that's what you mean to say and do!—and I'm but a young fool, my Captain—and destroyed—"

I kissed her.

"Oh, heaven," said she, "I don't know what we are about—"

"You know quite clearly what you're about, you calm and pretty minx!"

"No; I'm a little fool, my ruthless Captain—and seem to you too easily persuaded. . . . Ah, sang de Christus! that I should be so light minded that the first pretty fellow trusses me up! Listen, John Cardress—you show no gentleness. You show no mercy when you kiss me too far down below my throat! Well, then—God forgive us both—for you can see for yourself how un-formed I am— Nevertheless—here is my mouth—"

"Oh, Sandi—"

She pushed my head aside and held it so, listening:

"Hearken to the wolves—the *other* wolves—your brothers—on that dark mountain over there. . . . Oh, John Cardress! John Cardress!"

"Sandi!"

"Let me go! You have bruised my mouth and my neck and breast; and I don't care! . . . Lie still, then! . . . Where are you going, my passionate enemy, in your quilled and beaded moccasins and your gay deer-skin shirt? John Cardress—where are you going?"

Our lips touched, clung; but she would not have it, and demanded again of me whither I was bound.

"To serve my country on command. . . . And you, Sandi, where do you travel?"

"Parbleu! to serve mine!"

"Then, if you are, as you say, French and well born, you are with your own people and safe. Why then do you still play at camp-strumpet to the Regiment de la Reine and ride an old nag, astride in wooden shoon and naked knee?"

She made no answer.

"If," said I, unwinding her slender arms from me and holding her aloof to look into her darkly veiled eyes, "you are truly well born, what is your true name?"

"And if I told you," said she, "and if you named me aloud in this camp you would ruin me soul and body!"

"What is that you say?" I demanded incredulously.

"If I tell you who I am, you would be thinking, maybe, that I lie. And if by any chance you believed me, and if you told my name to our handsome Marquis, or to Vaudreuil, our bragging Governor, or to Bigot, the thieving Intendant, or to young Lévis, or to Courtmanche, or Saint Luc, Niverville, Fleurimont, Longueuil, Father Roubaud, or Bougainville, then God forgive you, for they would send me back to France and there I should lie in prison till these curls you kiss turn white as snow!"

"What do you mean, Sandi?"

"I tell you, do I not?—that if I tell you my name, and you betray it, and my quality, then I die—or my youth dies in me—behind the four battlements of the Bastille!"

I said: "And if you betray me, Sandi, then I agonize at an Indian fire while they slowly peel the roasted skin from me, having every care to keep me alive. . . . For as true as I kneel here on the moss beside you in this hour, the French will turn any captured spy over to their Ottawas and let them do their worst."

"Even," said she, "if you were a stranger to me, John Cardress, I would not betray you to your death."

"Nor I, you to a prison. Yet, I can not understand how you, a French subject, and well born, are in deadly terror of the French as well as your natural enemies the English; and yet travel fearlessly through both these hostile camps to fulfill some strange mission here in the wilderness of a land you never before have beheld."

She leaned nearer and framed my face with both her narrow little hands.

"I tell you this, John, and no more—that Pompadour harlot, who paints her sickly lips scarlet and who rules France, has a long arm which reaches from France even into this wild New World!

"Yes, and your damned Pitt, too!—your accursed Pitt of Hell!—his skinny arm reaches even into this wild forest, and beyond! And these two—either, or both of them!—would not hesitate to take hold of my throat and squeeze it to death, if they knew I was travelling through these woods toward my destination! . . . Look at my neck, John Cardress! Span it with your hands—thus! . . . You have kissed it, too, until it is bruised. . . . Well, this same little neck both Pompadour and Pitt would pinch to death if they could! And what do you think of that?"

"In God's name, Sandi, who are you and what is your mission in this hemisphere?"

She shook her head, refusing to reply. She was too young—too soft and lovely to be a real wanton; nor could I believe that she had come to this Continent, and into this wilderness, through fidelity to a husband or a lover. Or to join any man whose remembered arms were dearer to her than mine, whose caresses she more ardently desired, and to whom she had ever responded more passionately than to me. I don't know whether what was passing through my brain and hovering in my mind somehow and occultly was transmitted by a sensitive propinquity to her mind.

She said, with a forced laugh: "Well, sir, I've all but given myself to you. And so, doubtless, being a man, you suppose me any man's baggage, that all he need do is to pack up and carry me with him wherever he chooses—"

She sprang from the moss to her feet, stepped into her wooden shoes which, somehow, had slipped off.

"John," said she, "where are you going?"

"I can't tell you that, Sandi. Where are *you* going?"

"Ah," she exclaimed, laughing under her breath, "there speaks a man and tyrant. . . . Follow the Regiment de la Reine, John! If you desire to watch my moral conduct and learn my destination, follow the drum as I do! And maybe, some night, you will awake in the starlight to find me in your arms!"

She put aside my outstretched hand, lithely avoiding me:

"Close your eyes and open your mouth and follow the drum, John Cardress—and see what God will send you!"

CHAPTER XIV

SAVAGES

I COULDN'T rid my mind of her. I couldn't sleep.
I lay with eyes wide and restless in the lustrous moonlight. Her voice was in the liquid laughter of the little
brook; in the soft tone of the lake-tides sighing on reef
and silver sands. I saw her white body in the languid
mist-shapes drifting over a curling floor of fog. The
fragrance of the south wind was like her breath in my
face; like her narrow hand was the caress of the wind's
cool fingers ruffling my hair, lingering about my face
and neck—

The strangeness and charm of her stimulated me; the
mystery of her excited my mind to wakefulness and
torment.

Who was this young thing, then, whom our cruisers
had captured when they stopped the French transport,
The Pretty Savage, and made prisoners of crew and
passengers?

I saw her first as a cabin-boy—a mousse. She was
servant lad to me for weeks before I discovereed her to
be no boy at all but a young girl, and mature at that!

Into her arms I had drifted—God knows why and
how!—but her body and limbs inclined to mine as in-
tuitively as did mine to hers, and the heat of our joined
lips so melted and welded us into one that *her* heart
seemed to beat within *me* and stir *my* body with its every
throb.

193

Breath as sweet as scented meadows. . . . Lips that drew the very soul through the lips of him who kissed her!— Good God, what swift flame clothed me, mind and body, at faintest thought of her!—

I couldn't sleep. Stars waned, darkness faded; bang! —Montcalm's morning gun shattered everything—dream, starlight, the magic of the dawn! Then the sun surged and showed his colour in a flurry of fog, like a golden fish already swimming close to the world's outer edge. His dazzling and aureate back humped up higher above the flood of rose-flecked mist.

All the world of trees and rocks and water and fog and mountain peaks thrilled to the wild clangor of the French bugle calls; and the feathery thudding of the rolling drums was like the beating of a thousand wild cock-grouse in sylvan and viewless depths.

That marked the second day of our march northward. I did not see Sandi because the Regiment de la Reine took to the boats, and canoes, and bateaux—officers, men, women, and children—and I knew of it only when, far away across the water, a soldier pointed out to me a swarm of tiny boats on a bowline that swept into the northern haze and melted away like far floating gulls upon a sunset sea.

There was no such transportation for me and my Indians. But that happened so because of a shortage of craft, and not on account of any suspicion of us.

No; several thousand French and Canadian regulars and militia marched on that account. So did some of the Mission Indians, led by their priests, the Black Robes, stepping along sturdily through the forests.

Two hundred English prisoners had gone forward—
I think by the eastern war trail and by water—the Huron
blood-hounds and Ottawa hyenas who escorted them were
hurrying homeward to sell or slay their wretched captives.
The handsome, clever Marquis himself dared not attempt
to interfere with these hordes of wild-eyed warlocks who
drove their miserable captives with yells and blows and
a vast snarling that left the French troubled and watchful
and uneasy about their own security at night.

At times it was like moving in a vast, unreal night-
mare to traverse those spectral forests peopled by legions
of yelping devils in their paint, who hopped and danced
and ran along, light-footed as wolves, seeming in the
woodland dusk like swarms of demons heaved up and
vomited from hell itself.

A rank stench followed the Ottawas—those dirty,
pagan cannibals who stank like wolverines so that even
my own Indians, who were none too fragrant, noticed
it with disgusted scowls or jeers, flinging sly insults at
passing Ottawas which, for a day or two, they did not
actively resent.

But there came a day, near the Richelieu, where it
makes into the St. Lawrence, and where the widening
waters stretch westward toward La Chine, that my Mohawk, Gawasa, the Snow Snake, called to a hurrying
Ottawa, "Yes, hasten then, you corpse scalper, or your
goods will rot before Onontio in Montreal can buy
them!"

The Ottawa halted and turned an enraged visage toward us.

"Dog of a Mohawk!" he retorted, "your name tells

what filthy habits are yours and your people's, and yonder
at La Chine you proved it many years ago!"

"A lie!" shouted the Snow Snake, "it is Ocquari the
Bear who gave the Canienga the name of Mohawk. It is
the Ottawas who are cannibals!"

The Ottawa screamed his fury; other Ottawas came
up with menacing shouts and gestures, and very soon
there were a dozen of these wild-eyed pagans, with their
shaven heads, greased and painted hides, and in their
battle paint and stark naked excepting the beaded, embroidered clout-flap.

"What do you want?" said I harshly, walking out to
where they were gathered on the edge of an oozy thread
of water marking a morass full of icy springs along
which ran an immemorial runway made by wild game.

An Ottawa chief yelled at me and struck his painted
chest truculently.

At that I stepped swiftly forward and struck him
across the face with the flat of my open hand, so violently that he lost his balance and went slam! against
a tree.

"You filthy Ottawas," said I, "don't you dare be impudent to a white man! You are corpse diggers. You
dug up the dead at Fort William Henry and took scalps
which you were too cowardly to take in war. Clear out
of my way, you stinking carcajous, or I'll feed you the
edge of my war-axe!"

"Yes!" shouted my Wyandotte, "you dug up Dick
Rogers who died of smallpox, too, and took his scalp!
I saw you do it, and I laughed! And now only wait
a little! For that dead and scabby scalp will start a pox

among you Ottawas that will clean out your whole stinking nation as fire consumes a nest of maggots!"

Our insults and effrontery seemed to astound these wild warriors of the North; and, as for me, I intended to stand no nonsense from any French Indians, pagan or convert, for, since that affair at William Henry, such a loathing and contempt for them had overwhelmed me that it was as much as I could do to stay my hand when one of them passed too near to me.

What my Wyandotte had said about poor Dick Rogers' scalp was likely to be true. In fact, I heard a French regimental surgeon say that the Ottawas already had the smallpox, and that they had caught it doing their ghouls' work in the military cemetery at William Henry.

I now primed and cocked my rifle and let the long barrel fall into the hollow of my left arm, so that the muzzle bore directly upon the paint-daubed belly of a principal Ottawa war-chief.

"Move on!" said I harshly; "you Ottawas are as poisonous as rattlesnakes. Go burrow in the ground for scalps and give the pox to the moles and woodchucks, but get away from civilized folk or I'll splash your guts all over these junipers!"

The principal Ottawa chief was now portraying such a picture of flaming and concentrated fury as I never before have beheld save in the ferocious features and attitude of the great lynx when trapped.

Hell's own fire darted from his blazing eyes; he tried to say something but his voice was a cat's hiss, and he made a terrible gesture, screamed something at his warriors.

Instantly there was a terrific caterwauling; their naked

hatchets flashed; and with a final insult in their brandished guns they went bounding away into the darkening woods ahead of us.

"That was their war-cry, brother," said the Souriquois in a sober voice. "Already the Ottawa were our enemies. Now these people will set us a pretty ambush beyond earshot of the army."

"And if they do," said I, "for every Ottawa scalp you show me—and it must have nits and crown-whorl, *too!*—I will pay you at the market rate paid by Corlaer in Albany, and let you trim your sacks and quivers with the mangy hair beside!"

The Snow Snake, being a thrifty and enterprising Mohawk, was all for starting instantly on the heels of the vanished pagans.

"How far," said I sarcastically, "would you get away from this travelled trail before their axes were sticking in your stupid skull? Go, if you choose. But I tell you that in five minutes' time, and within thirty yards of where we stand, we shall discover a score of these Ottawa wolves tearing at your loosened scalp!"

For the forest swarmed with these murderous devils. My Indians knew it as well as I did. Anybody venturing to leave the rutty road—*anybody,* friend or foe, white or red—would be murdered as soon as out of sight; killed for the value of the beaded flap, for the greasy deer-skin shirt, for the hair that sprouted on the crown of his head—or for nothing other than the mere pleasure of the murder.

There was not an officer in the French army, or in the French Indian department, who did not detest and fear their ferocious allies—pagans and converts alike—

and only their priests could put up with and endure the cruelties, filth, and wickedness of the Praying Mission Indians and the lousy pagan beasts from the upper lakes.

As for me, I didn't care a damn one way or another. If these Ottawas wanted trouble, and if there was blood to be let, then I could let it as well as they. So I believed, anyway.

And I was in a sombre and ugly mood—still sore at heart and confused by pain and passion. And vicious with it—bewildered at the violence of my desire for this girl, Sandi, at my own loneliness for lack of her—and fierce with the emptiness of a heart that hurt me physically, as though it had been an empty and starving belly.

I said to the Souriquois: "Never take another threat or insult from any Ottawa, but slap your war-axe into his skull and give it a jerk so that his right eye looks into his left, and half his mouth yells at the other half!"

The Snow Snake laughed: "One day near the great carrying place," said he, "an Ottawa jested with me with his bow and arrow. . . . I caught him and struck him so hard that my hatchet's two points spanned his spine and his lower front teeth! That was a funny jest of mine!"

The Souriquois said seriously: "Let us catch us some Ottawas to make sport!"

"Yes," said the Wyandotte, "and I will show you how to play cat-owl with a prisoner. . . . It is this way— we take his head and keep on screwing it around until it comes off. Then we put it on again and tell him to go home and tell his friends about it!"

Yells of laughter greeted his exquisite humour. I did not suppose that this grotesque cruelty ever really had been practiced, but the Snow Snake assured me it had.

We camped near to a spring.

The Souriquois, Bad Eye, came to me late that evening and asked me whether I expected to have a fight with the Ottawas before we arrived in Canada. I said that I was certain they meant to play us some foul trick or other and that we would, doubtless, have to fight for our lives if ever they caught us away from the line of march.

He said in that case he'd put on his death-paint in order to be ready to die as a Souriquois warrior ought to.

"Also, Assan * our Captain, I have a little daughter in the transport of the Canadians, who has followed me from Fort Edward, and I would be glad if my Captain would send her on to Isle Royale in case the Ottawa slay me."

"Why did you bring a child?" I asked, vexed.

"She has no mother and neither aunt nor uncle. How could I leave her with the Iroquois?"

"Very well," said I, "I will ask the officers of the Canadian regulars to see that she goes to Isle Royale on the sloop that carries the foreign volunteers."

"Will my Captain-brother give her food for her journey?"

"Kaalato—certainly."

"And say a word to the captain of the ship?"

"O'hou! Yes."

"Ouliouni nijia—thank you, brother."

"Niga ouligen—that's all right, Bad Eye my brother. It is well, perhaps, to provide for evil hours beforehand.

* Assan, or Sa, in Souriquois means John.

That Ottawa—Aagei! He has a split tongue!— Niktou il noq!"

"Santu is my little daughter's name, Sa Captain," said the Souriquois, smilingly reassured. And he added naïvely: "If she by chance pleases my brother Assan, let him take her into his lodge to cook and mend and play the young wife at night."

"O' da! Menak! It is not my custom, brother."

"Talaak? My captain has had a wife for a month!"

"Tan?" I retorted sharply, "—when was it?"

"At Fort Edward in July—"

"Tan wen?" said I, angrily.

"Sandi! . . . Que Sandi!"

"No," said I, "neither wife—nor widow if I die under the Ottawa hatchets—mala! Tok! Menak quepeum!"

"Eli ouliak! It is well," said the Souriquois. . . . "Yet—tok—Santu, my little daughter, is Bouyniskoue— E! Kil outchit!—yes, for love of you Santu can be a real witch!"

"Lok! Am I Bouyn the Wizard, who requires a mate? O' da! No! Kisosoo! The sun shines pleasantly upon my lodge that needs no Osayana."

"Akaye!" said Bad Eye, smiling, "—Saba pili kisos. Let us await, nidokan, and see what your Kchi and your Alakys mean to do about it!"

I laughed, too: "Nidobo, my brother," said I, "neither my star nor my god nor the new moon ever will incline my heart and mind to an Indian wife—even for an hour."

We camped near to a Canadian regular battalion— Fleurimont's, if I recollect correctly. Anyway, there were Malicite Scouts connected with it, and some Micmacs; which troubled me for fear they might discover and question my Souriquois. So I made my Indians leave hut and fire and go on along the torch-lighted trail to where the battalion of Sabrevois lay—or so I supposed —and where a considerable stream poured through a shallow, wooded ravine which, we understood, lay at right angles to, and very near the Iroquois war-trail. Not at all, as we discovered at sunrise, when a scarlet winged war-arrow came whistling into our fire, upsetting a kettle which my Indians had stolen, made of tin and iron.

"Damnation!" said I, getting up in a fury, but an arrow ran along my ribs and hung twixt bone and skin like a sliver, and I jerked it out and took cover, soaked with blood.

The Snow Snake called to ask if I were badly hurt.

"No," said I, "but I'm sore as a mink with the mange! What cursed arrows are these, then?"

"Ottawa," replied the Wyandotte who had unslung his bow. He seemed to have two quivers full of arrows— one kind white feathered, the others feathered with black and yellow.

A storm of scarlet-winged Ottawa shafts came whizing. I called across to ask Pretty Brook what he meant to do with two kinds of war-arrows.

"Te-he!" he tittered, "—a Mississauga lay dead in the Horicon after the fort burned. I saw that he had greased his arrows with rattlesnake lard, so I took them."

"That's a dirty Mississauga trick," said I. "Are you going to use them?"

For answer he threw up the bow and pulled the arrow till the feathers brushed the pendant lobe of his right ear. Then the string clanged and almost instantly I saw a horribly painted Indian leap up from a thicket of ferns and start to run, an arrow wagging like a tail, just to the left of his haunch.

Clang! Whiz-z-z! Another arrow sped and struck the wretched, reeling creature full in the neck. Down he flopped, and lay scrabbling.

"Why?" inquired the Souriquois in surprise. "Was he not a dead warrior anyway?"

The Wyandotte replied, coolly, that he was not sure how powerful the Mississauga rattler's poison was, so he'd given the Ottawa a double dose.

I never before had seen poisoned arrows used; I'd merely heard that one or two tribes used them.

Well, the Wyandotte fired away all the venomous western arrows, and all of his own clean shafts. Then, apparently, the Ottawas seemed to think that we had no other weapons except knife and hatchet, for they burst out of the juniper and came springing and leaping forward; and seemed horribly surprised when our rifles roared in their very faces.

Down went two of them; the others—nearly twenty astonished warriors—turned in a panic and ran. After them bounded my excited Indians, utterly regardless of ambush, and of what they were about, having gone blood-mad.

In vain I shouted at them to beware of an ambush and return; but they paid no heed, and were raging and slashing and ripping at scalps in the ferns and junipers, and pulling poisoned arrows from their swollen and dying victims, with yells of laughter, when in all its fury and horror the Ottawa onset burst upon them.

There seemed absolutely no chance for us. The encircling woods swarmed with Ottawas, and their hatchets made a continual flash and glitter like sunlight on running water.

As I fired I saw the Snow Snake go down to his death, cloven by hatchets that sheared through his skull as though it had been cheese. Down went the Wyandotte, knifed and gralloched and scalped, while his yell of despair still echoed among the rocks.

The Souriquois and I turned tail and ran; and after us ran so many of the hideous, naked pagan devils that all the forest seemed moving about us.

That they meant to take us alive, for torture, was evident, for they did not fire upon us or throw their knives or hatchets until, suddenly, they realized that we were escaping them.

Already, ahead, I could see a streak of sunshine in the vast, green demi-light of the unbroken forest, where a road or a stream must run to let in the sun like that.

Toward it I fled like a scared devil out of the pit, chased by St. Michael. Then, and then only, they let fly their hatchets and knives and arrows, and a few bullets.

I heard one of these latter hit a soft, living body with a splashy smack!—and, looking around, saw my poor Souriquois in the act of falling—already dead on his two feet, and his brown skin an ashen pallour from brow to naked ankle.

That is all I had time to see before I sprang breathless into the great northern war-path, among Hertel's Canadian battalion trudging northward in their bedraggled uniforms, to the ghostly tap of a single, wheezy drum.

CHAPTER XV

WAITING

MY Indians were dead. Those who had done them to death were watching to serve me the same way; and, no doubt, would have done so except for two reasons—for one, I kept close to the Canadians; for the other, the Ottawas had the smallpox; there could be no doubt about it, or concerning the horrible manner in which they became infected.

So the Canadians gave them wide berth—drove them away at the muzzles of their muskets—until we reached St. John's.

Here were recruiting sergeants for various native battalions; and from here, I was told, I might reach the river with such voyageurs who had gathered to travel thither in company, for the purpose of self-protection.

Now this Canadian army, once separated from the French regulars, very quickly relapsed into its characteristic and careless habits of indiscipline and lazy good-humour, in spite of some of its officers who knew better.

Concerning their efficiency I could only judge by the treatment meted out to me; for they accepted my presence among them without question, made no inquiries whatever. Otherwise, they conducted like a gay, chattering, careless, swaggering parcel of good fellows who got drunk when God sent them the opportunity, and squeezed any acquiescent hand and kissed any receptive lips available.

At the mouth of the Richelieu, recruits, volunteers like myself, and the Canadian battalion destined for Isle Royale were sent into barracks or allowed to pitch tents or erect brush huts and await the arrival of some vessel destined for Louisbourg.

The remainder of the army had been directed across to Montreal, Three Rivers, and down to Quebec, and I saw nothing of them—indeed, I saw no White Coats at all excepting such battalions as were destined for Louisbourg.

I was sad at the swift and unnecessary destruction of my three poor Indians; yet realized that any warriors foolish enough to run headlong into an Ottawa ambuscade would have been no good to me upon Isle Royale.

For there, and on the mainland adjacent, lived the French Souriquois—the real and principal bulk of this clan-nation—who remained entirely loyal to France, and who very soon would have become suspicious of my lone Souriquois, my Iroquois, and my Huron.

I was sorry; I missed the Snow Snake, Pretty Brook, and my Souriquois friend, Bad Eye; but there could be no doubt that I was safer without these Indians and far more likely to succeed in my difficult mission alone.

But what never, never ceased from troubling and saddening me was my parting from Sandi; and the manner of it. Never again was I likely to see this strange youngster; never learn whether she was alive or dead; or how Fate had served her, whether fairly or foully.

And I had guessed pretty well by this time that the longing I now felt for her was love of some kind—genuine and real love—with all its amazing aches and characteristic miseries and pains.

No man who ever had kissed her lips and been kissed by them would ever again know rest and a tranquil heart. At least I thought so, and feared so. For I could not drive her from my mind and be rid of her, or have done with the memories that ever left my mind and body faintly burning. . . .

Hertel's battalion sailed, leaving Canadian regulars encamped along the Richelieu and the irregulars—coureurs-de-bois, voyageurs, militia, volunteers and Indians—wandering from one whitewashed village to another, irresolute, apprehensive, but usually docile and obedient to the Jesuit missionaries or parish priests.

In our little village of Sainte Anne de Sorel—a hamlet of a few farm-houses and a tiny white church—several Germans and Swedes and Hollanders, destined for the Western Legion in Louisbourg, were gathered. But I kept to myself in general, and made me a brush hut in the neighbouring woods in a sugar bush where, from the south shore, was a wonderful outlook over the St. Lawrence and Lake St. Peter.

Here, also, were the sturdy French Souriquois under a needy noble of some seedy Seignorie or other—a young man named d'Olier, poor and proud, and possessing only part of a shirt to his back.

The Souriquois had met their women here, who had come up from Isle Royale and Acadia, past the Saguenay and Quebec, to welcome their returning warriors and escort them back to their own terrain.

There was much singing, boasting, dancing, strutting, stamping, during the first few days. I went down to the Souriquois tribal fire to look on, once or twice, and there saw young d'Olier who proved to be both polite and agreeable, and made his Souriquois mistress patch my breeches for me.

From him I received my first shock when he told me that my Lord Loudon, fearing that the season was too far advanced, and that already the campaign had been rendered impossible by the outrageous delay of Vice Admiral Holburne, had left Halifax and was on his way to New York with his entire army of British regulars.

However, he added, British cruisers still haunted the mouth of the St. Lawrence.

This news almost stunned me. Yet, I did not feel at liberty to give up my attempt to enter Louisbourg merely because the Commander-in-Chief had postponed his operations.

Young d'Olier took it for granted—and I, also, was persuaded—that the attack on Louisbourg was certain to come next year.

Of course it might well happen that Lord Loudon would be recalled to England and replaced by a more energetic General—perhaps even by that strange looking and sickly young brigader, James Wolf, for example. In fact, I had no doubt that this year would see the last of his peppery, port-drinking Scottish lordship, as well as of that abject coward, Dan'l Webb.

Nevertheless, I had no choice other than to go on, learn what I could in Louisbourg, and keep an eye upon Charles Follis and the Chevalier Johnstone until such time as the city surrendered to an English General and an English Admiral. For, surrender it must, sooner or later, or else every English man, woman, and child in North America might as well be packing up to quit a continent destined to be French for all time.

D'Olier, lounging outside his tent and gossiping with me in the sunset light, spoke with quiet bitterness of the Souriquois who had taken Sir William Johnson's red belt and were serving with Webb at Ford Edward.

"The Souriquois," said he, "are peculiarly a French Indian. They are not red-skins. Their skin is not copper colour; it is brown. They don't readily mix with the red-skins, either. I don't see how Sir William's authority divided the Souriquois and caused a portion to betray the French cause."

I told him truthfully enough that Webb had only a dozen Souriquois scouts. "Always," said I, "some Indians of every nation turn renegade. For example, Sir William employs a few Wyandottes, and our clever Marquis has the Caughnawaga Iroquois."

"That is quite true," said the young fellow; "no Indian nation and no savage tribe declares unanimously for either France or England. . . . Neither do men of our colour. Look at our battalion of Foreign Volunteers at Louisbourg, with such Scots as Major Follis and Lieutenant the Chevalier Johnstone enlisting to fight with France against England and her colonies. And," said he, smiling cordially, "you yourself, sir, are a gracious example of a Scottish volunteer!"

"Sir," said I, "you can have no idea how detested is the King of England by those whose kin fell at Culloden."

"I can imagine," said he with sympathy. "I hope your ship escapes the English scout ships on watch at the mouth of the St. Lawrence."

We stood for a while in silence, looking out over the vast stretch of water called Lac Saint Pierre, which now was all stained with mauve and purple, crimson and scarlet, from the western blaze of the setting sun.

"God, how beautiful!" said d'Olier, under his breath. "Sir, I do not know France. I am lord of our Seignorie, and Canadian born; and I never have beheld the glory of Paris and of Versailles—never have seen a greater city than Quebec or a gayer Court than our Governor's.

"But, sir, however gorgeous may be the land, the city, the Court of my gracious King Louis XV, I do not believe there is as much majesty and heavenly beauty in all France as we see now before us amid this Canadian sunset; or as much brilliancy and glory, or as many gallant men and beautiful women as we may behold in Montreal, Quebec, and in that great dream city on Isle Royale, Louisbourg!"

Now in the intense stillness of approaching twilight I saw an osayana—a Souriquois girl—slim and shining as the sickle moon in her white Siwan, come out upon a rock and stand so, her hands upon her hips, looking into the glowing West.

And, in the purple forest's shadow, I saw a young man wearing a single eagle-feather and a beaded clout—and naked otherwise—come to the wood's edge and set his Indian flute to his lips.

This is what this lover played liked a golden linked thrush song threading the crimsoning glade:

Moderato

WAITING

CHAPTER XVI

SANTU

WELL, orders came; at last we were to embark for Louisbourg—I and the other foreign volunteers, and one battalion of Canadian regulars. It appeared that the Flying Scotchman, Vice Admiral Holburne, having recently arrived at a post where he had been due for half a year, was now reluctant to leave. We were, therefore, to take our chances of dodging the English cruisers at the river's vast and misty mouth. "Die resisting," was the order from Montreal. . . . Where Vaudreuil drank and feasted with his mistress on his knee.

The French regulars sailed comfortably for Montreal and Quebec. What did they care if we died resisting in Gabarus Bay?

Some took ship directly across to La Chine of bloody memory, after marching from St. John's; some continued to St. Peter's Lake and there went gaily aboard the fat transports and huge warships safely moored in midstream. We still awaited our fate.

Everybody and everything else went aboard the ships; troops, Indians, regimental wagons, animals, women, light artillery, siege pieces, sutlers, bat-horses, train-des-equipages. The whole forest was in an uproar for days with the noise of departure—shouts of command, drumming, fifing, cries of women, gabble of savages, sheep bleating, cattle lowing, cocks crowing, oxen bellowing in fear. There was an enormous dissonance of hammering, sawing, splashing; rattle and creak of winch and cordage; clank-clank of windlass and chain.

So, day after day, the ships filled, weighed anchor, hoisted sail and bore away for Montreal and Quebec.

A ship for Louisbourg was to be ready for us within twenty-four hours.

I said good-bye to the few acquaintances I had made, then lay down in my blanket, watching the flaming west.

Stars came out of it, pure as diamonds.

It was lonely ashore now; lonely on the river, too, where scarce a warship or transport or even a fisherman remained. Only a few riding lights glimmered over Saint Peter's Lake; scarce a camp-fire glowed ashore.

Against the sky I saw a solitary figure standing—a girl wearing the quali-bua-zi, or the caribou capote of a Souriquois.

It was Santu, the Osayana, slim as a river reed in her pointed hood and blue-grey fur cloak made of wild reindeer hide; and she stood with both arms opened and looked into the West as though praying.

I had seen her only once or twice after Bad Eye's death. She was all smeared with ashes and her hair masked her.

I had promised her she should have food and shelter as far as Isle Royale.

So she wept forty-eight hours for Bad Eye; then she washed her face, combed her hair, and seemed to forget her grief in the forest with a swaggering lieutenant of Canadian Militia. At least it seemed so until I saw him walk out of the woods and over to his company fire, swearing and stanching a badly mauled visage which looked as though a lynx had been busy with it, using its hind toes.

"That damned wildcat slut——" he began, amid shouts of laughter from brother officers; "oh, well; laugh, then! And you may have all the young Souriquois in the northland, messieurs. For me, the Souriquois exist no longer!"

Now, where I lay in the blaze of sunset, on the rocky river-bank, I had a picturesque view of this same Souriquois wildcat, outlined in fierce, nameless grace against the conflagration in the West.

Presently, turning to look down the glowing river, she espied me.

"Kuai!" said she with easy coquetry, "hello!"

"Kuai, Santu," said I, smiling. "What are you doing; praying to some manito for a safe voyage to Isle Royale?"

"O'hou. Yes." She added, "Kalaato nigia," which was more civil; but the gay effrontery of her eyes denied any racial or sexual submission.

"I thought," said I, "that you were a civilized Mission girl, Santu."

"Eim!" she nodded.

"How can that be when you pray to some pagan manito?"

"Elp kohi sazos," said the girl, tranquilly, "I also pray to Jesus and God. Some one of these three ought to be listening; don't you think so, Captain Azo?"— using the Abenaqui name for John with its impudently caressing and provocative inflection.

"Santu, toni wadosaan? Where do you come from,

214

anyway?" I asked, amused by her coquettish impertinence.

"You know, my elder brother Azo. It is *painted upon
wood* how we of the Lenni-Lenape chased the Tsalaki
from the turtle's back, and then went into the land of the
Snake—the Sinako and Mengoui."

"Fine language for a convert," said I, to tease her.

"Talaak—why?" she inquired, innocently.

"You speak of the earth as a turtle—"

"The world," said she, *"is* a huge turtle—and we all
live on its back. A turtle is a manito—"

"I thought you had become a communicant, Santu."

"Menak! No, but I shall be. Idech!" She took hold
of my hand and came close, whispering: "Kachkan—
speak lower so that the Black Robe with the Canadian
militia shall not hear us and scold me. . . . Shall we
go to my lodge and lie together and look at Pili Kisos
the new moon, which Niaski, whom you call your God,
has made so prettily to delight us all—pagan, Souriquois
and Christian alike?"

"Toni ait—where is it?"

"Mala—over there. Ouijahoui—come with me," she
whispered, her lips against my ear.

We walked together through the infernal crimson light
to a knoll set with silver birches and hemlock, or alnisedi,
where she had fashioned her an oddly woven and bird-
like nest.

"My clan," she said, "is the Hawk—the Seguanilha!
You see how well young hawks weave their nests!
Tok! Do you wish to mate with me? O'da? Talaak?"
But I only laughed.

There was a slender thread of smoke from the ashes

in front of this strange and pretty lodge. I laid upon
it a ball of dry moss and two sticks. The girl flung aside
her reindeer cape with its pointed hood and, dropping to
her knees, crouched low and blew a slight blaze into the
tinder. Then, rearing up but still on her limber knees:

"My elder brother," said she mischievously, "is like
all men; the sweetest part of a woman is her tongue—
ouilalo!—when it calls to him to eat!"

"You offer me dinner, Santu?"

"O'hou! Yes, I do!"

"Talaak?"

"Kil—" She laughed: "Well, then, guess if you don't
know already, my Bouyn Captain! Eli ouliak! The
trout are soft because it is October—it is Penibagos, the
time of falling leaves!"

Gossiping like a pretty-voiced little bird, partly to me,
partly to herself, this young Souriquois, kneeling by the
fire, swiftly and deftly prepared a meal, the technique of
which she never learned in a Souriquois lodge:

"Some little fish," she murmured, salting them, "—sis
namas iia; and oysters—mussels—alsaq'!—together they
make the soup—broth Kzobo! And now, on the coals,
nolkaiia—venison! Tell me, my magic brother—my
wizard Captain—is Kasko the heron better fed? Is
Kokokhas the owl? Or any siamo—any bird of prey?
Does Kakivis the sea-gull feed more juicily? Or old
Awasos the bear in blueberry time? Or even little Nana-
tasis the humming-bird—does she feed more sweetly than
my brother—my young sorcerer who has bewitched my
body, nhaga, and my eyes and brain and mouth—M'don!
. . . Losa ni!" she murmured, pointing to the warm

corner of the fire where a wolf skin lay. "Sit there, Azo my young shaman, for the air is like November— like Mzatanos—which is ice—and not like my heart which is like herbs seething with a sweet smell of samphire and cherry birch in the pleasant moon of Temezowas and Temaskikos—"

"Santu!"

"O'hou?"

"How old are you?"

"Nisinska—twenty!"

"Well, then, you talk like twenty little birds with twenty tongues! My God, what a garrulous girl!"

"Lok! I talk like rain!" she said, laughing.

"Menak! Like a river over shoals!"

"E! I *was* sibosis the little brook until I beheld my witch-captain! Now, over night, I am grown into Sibo the River—"

"Pel! Be silent and hold your tongue, little fool; thus!"

I drew her head back against me and covered her mouth with my hands.

"When," said she, "will you know in your heart whether you want to love me, nidokan?"

"I—don't know, nidobso."

"Saba? Tomorrow?"

"O'da."

"Siguaga? Next spring?"

Her head slipped back and across my left shoulder, and I was looking at the delicate brown throat and softly parted lips.

"You little pagan," said I, "what do you learn in your Mission, anyway?"

"To love."

"To love *God!*" I pointed out.

"Eli ouliak. And all His works. . . . Man is His work, also, my white sorcerer. . . . Look at Pili Kisos, the New Moon. . . . It is God's work; I love it. Look at Ki the World! God made it; and rested on the Seventh Day! E! Well, then, I love the world. All of it!—"

She picked up a bit of gravel and held it up in the firelight toward the crescent moon:

"Nothing is too humble for me to love," she said, "—not even Senis the pebble, made like a turtle-egg by Kohi, to please our manito. . . . My Captain?"

"E!"

"Love is like Gau—gikpesa the rain—falling by chance and drenching who happens to be abroad. Love is like a prayer—Seko—alasudma!—which is its own answer— merely another prayer—akaye! Alas! Aagei! Oh, woe!"

She looked up at me laughing, still on her knees, her head lying back across my shoulder.

"Tok!" she said, and pulled my face down against her lips.

Afterward we ate our kzbo.

In the silver river sands we washed our hands.

"Amalkan?" said I, "do you dance, Santu?"

"Amalkaye—I dance. I sing, also."

"Tach?"

"All the songs of the Souriquois! Even the witch songs:

SANTU

> *"N'pemego*
> *For love of you!*
> *N'pemego,*
> *Like gua esu!*
> *With the Wolf Malsem*
> *In the midnight dew,*
> *With Sagues the weasel, too,*
> *N'pemego*
> *Like a witch*
> *For love of you, O'hou!"*

"That is very strong medicine," I said with mock gravity.

"E!"

She sprang up and began to move like a tongue of flame in the fire. The light of the coals painted her face and shoulders scarlet. . . . And her budding breasts and belly.

> *"Aké-yu—*
> *Aké-yu*
> *Kach kan—*
> *Kach kan—*
> *M'don!*
> *N'haga*
> *Aage-i!*
> *Palliton!*
> *Alas!*
> *Alas!*
> *Speak softly—*
> *Speak softly,*
> *My mouth,*

My body,
Speak sadly
Of War!—"

Her beaded sporran fell, leaving her all brilliant and naked as a golden snake.

Suddenly she threw back her head; her eyes blazed; her scarlet lips parted in a cry:

"Sayewi talli—..
At first . . . an extended fog!
Then the wind blew!—
Wich—ouagan—"

It was the opening cry of that magic chant of the Lenape called the *Oualam Olum*—or Red Roll-Call: the mysterious recitative of the entire Algonquin Race, which not half a dozen white men ever had heard except perhaps a muttered fragment now and then, stifled on drunken lips. . . .

And here was this Souriquois girl singing it like a sturdy, fearless witch, her young voice husky, yet sweet, and as though awed by the solemn legend she chanted, which was the one and only utterance of a race whose origin remained a mystery.

"—War! War!" she chanted, swaying in the fire glare, like one of the golden flames—

Those of the North agreed,
Those of the South agreed,
To enjoy it—
To enjoy the war—
The coming war!
Over the water—the frozen sea—

SANTU

Over the wonderful slippery water—
Wul-el-emil ouchakupek!—
Over the stone-hard water of winter
They swarmed out of the Snows,
Over the Tidal Sea!
Warriors of old,
You were mighty in battle
When Beautiful Head was chief,
When you slaughtered the Sinak,—
The Seneca Snakes!—
You were mighty in battle
When White Owl was chief,
When Guard Keeper was chief,
And after him when Snow Bird was chief,
When White Beaver went East,
When Snow Bird went South, . . .
When Snow Father was chief,
When Big Owl was chief,
When White Bird was chief,
When White Fowl was chief,
When Wise Wolf knew how to make war,
When the Talligewi possessed the East,
When the Talega slew our chiefs,
All of you cried together: War! War!
. . . .

The Pipe-Bearer was chief,
White Lynx was chief in happy days,
Pretty-Blue-Bird was chief;
There was much fruit!
Little Cloud was chief,
Snow Hunter was chief, east of Talega!
A great land! . . .

A land without snakes,* a rich land, a pleasant land.
Red Arrow was chief,
Making wampum at the great sea!
The Painted Man was chief!
The Mengwe,
The Lynxes,
All trembled!
White-body was chief on the sea shore,
Peace Maker was chief, friendly to all,
He-Makes-Mistakes was chief,
Hurriedly coming.
At this time the White Man
First Appeared on the Eastern Sea!
White-Otter was chief,
White-Horn was chief;
He went to the Talega,
To the Hilini, . . .
Visiting all his children,
All his friends!
The Watcher was chief,
He looked toward the Sea.
Then, at this time, from North,
From South,
The Whites came.
They are peaceful;
They have great things,
Who Are They?

Now, slowly, her glistening body came to a quivering
immobility. Like a shining, wind-blown river reed she

* Enemies.

bowed, doubling her body to put on her little painted moccasins.

Then, as a pure, far young peak clothes itself with snow, Santu drew over her the silvery quali-bua-zi.

"I have told you who we Souriquois are," she said; "I have recited to you our history until the white skins first came to the land of the Lenape.

"Now teach me who you white skins really are and whether you are gentle or cruel to poor people who are few and weak and utterly alone."

"You know our history."

"Yes; you taught us to pray to God's Mother. Then you lay with us or killed us, as suited your fancy. And if we cried out, and if our hatchets sparkled—Koué!— anew spoke the great Manito—a manito to manitos . . . and to men. . . . Thou shalt not kill! Thou shalt not commit adultery!

"Then the Crooked Knives laughed—Wa-ya-yan! . . . "

She passed one arm around my neck: "Come," she said, "you are no Black Robe; you are Bouyn the Magician. Tell me the truth about this Jesus Christ Manito and whether it is true that he is the Tharon of the Mengwe and our own Manito of Manitos?"

"O'hou. He is your Manito, too."

"Oh. . . . Then it is true that Christ gave us fish and turtles and beasts and birds?"

"E!"

"Then it was He who made the flies and gnats—who caused the first motherhood?"

"O'hou!"

She embraced me with a joyous little shiver, her naked arm around my neck.

"O'hou! Listen then to what the Red Roll-Call—the Red Accounting—teaches us!" And, swaying gently, cross-legged, there with me upon the wolf-robe, she began the "Saiewi Talli"—which is older than the oldest thing beyond which man's memory has never run:

> "At first
> In that place
> Where on Earth
> Was an extended fog,
> The Great Manito was;
> —At first
> Forever lost in space,
> Everywhere
> The Great Manito was.
> .   .   .   .
> He made . . . land and sky;
> . . . The sun and moon and stars.
> Wind blew,
> Water flowed,
> Islands grew,
> Manito spoke anew:
> All creatures were friendly then,
> All gods kindly,
> Giving wives to men,
> Fetching food;
> All were cheerful,
> All had leisure,
> All thought in gladness—"

Her arm uncoiled from my neck and her dark eyes glittered:

SANTU

"—Then, very secretly,
A Sorcerer came to Earth,
Bringing the first evil—
Bringing wickedness,
Bringing quarreling and **unhappiness,**
Bringing storms, sickness,
Bringing death!"

"Santu?"

"E?"

"You are no pagan. That is scripture you have re-cited."

"Menak! That is older than Christian scripture. That is the Red Roll of the Lenape I have chanted for my white witch-brother!"

"Then you Algonquins need no conversion."

"None! Why, then do your Black Robes come to convert us? Why teach us about the ark and the flood? It all is in our Red Roll-Call—

"Linapi-ma
Tulapi-ma
Tulape-wi
Tapit a wi—"

She bent her head; her pointed hood covered it. Suddenly she looked up, laughed; the hood fell to her shoulders:

"Oh, my white Sorcerer," said she, "there is only one God, and He teaches only one lesson to all the world—"

She flung up her arms toward the crescent moon and

dropped back across my knees and lay there, flashing her tongue-tip at me—a pale gold and sinuous thing as graceful as that friendly, burnished little serpent that all the Northland knows so well.

CHAPTER XVII

THE MYSTERY

FORTUNE favoured our voyage to the castled city of the East—that strange and fabled place of which the whole world had heard but which so few ever had gazed upon.

Under clear skies, out of the West a great wind blew us, foaming, from St. Peter's Lake. We sped by Orleans Island like a hunting panther, bounding on between Bellechasse and L'Islet south of us, and Montmorency, Charlevoix, and the majestic Saguenay to the northward. And it was as though the roar of falling waters was ever in my ears, so accustomed had they become to the cataracts of Montmorency and the Saguenay, and the thunder of dark waters battering at Cape Eternity.

Like a sinister dream I carried the memory of the high battlements of Quebec, crouched upon its Rock; of the black cannon of Levis across the waters, their powder-fouled and gaping maws all grinning in a row. I saw the white crested eagles sheering the sky above Cape Trinity, and the first returning winter gulls below. Far to the southward, off from Halifax, an impotent English fleet was slowly beating homeward to New York, in the wake of the fat transports carrying my Lord Loudon and his regulars. And the shame of a wasted year.

Now, on the second week out, when we neared that vast sea set with islands as great as European kingdoms, I saw in the northern skies the white Labrador falcons hunting

227

southward; and, at night, the magic conflagration of Aurora painting the boreal vault with its phantom rainbow, and flirting flippant silver ribbons across the awful arctic pit.

Wild coasts and wilder seas; sea-birds, now, driving by in thick grey squalls like flying tarnished snow; incessantly, everywhere, the querulous clamour of gulls; and, high in the blue, a suspended stratum of frost, not moving, not thickly obscuring, but delicately veiling the vast window of the sky with silvered curtains.

It was near to sunset when I first saw Louisbourg across the fiery tinted water, low floating like a cloud city of fairy-tale.

Sunset turned its glowing battlements to vermilion and shell-pink, and struck tall spires and crenellated towers with burning lances of light.

Out of hundreds and hundreds of unreal little chimneys smoke rose and made a purple and orange edged tent afloat in air above the city, like a gigantic water-lily pad supported by a thousand little stems of chimney smoke.

Everywhere in the bay and straits lay the great French battleships, noticing us little as we came floundering on in a cloud of spray, disdaining our politeness, ignoring our drums and twitching flag—although it was the only national symbol of France which flew in bunting—and noticing not at all the futile pop-bang! of our forward carronade frantically saluting three Admirals and the Commandant of Place.

After all, who were we to hope for drums and fifes and clarions from some kindly Admiral's gilded poop, or the deference of a dancing flag or two, or the crack of a shot across the sunlit water?

No, we were only the old privateer, *Blanc-bec,* converted to homely transport use, and carrying a few seasick foreign volunteers and Indians and a careless company of Provincials.

Off of Pointe Blanche in Gabarus Bay, the Indians aboard were clearing their canoes on deck.

Santu came to me. She had not been sick. She was brown and healthy and gay, having bewitched every white man aboard us. She seemed full of the devil's own coquetry now, to see the younger warriors of the Souriquois in their ceremonial paint. They were already darting black looks at one another, in mute contention concerning possession of this wild young thing, and as to which canoe was to carry her to the lodges of the Souriquois nation.

"You go with the old Wampum-Keeper we picked up at Tadousac," said I, "and, when you are ashore, speak politely to the chief matron."

"E!"

I continued in a low voice: "Be a true child of your dead father! Bad Eye was a great chief. He is worthy of being bewailed. Bewail him. He is worthy of condolence. Mourn, then, according to your custom, and your people will condole with you."

"E!"

My voice became a whisper.

"Remember that you and I are loyal English subjects. Be secret, clever, cunning, fearless, faithful. . . . You know what is done to spies?"

"E!"

"So do I. God bless you, little sister, and save us both."

"So be it, my elder brother."

"Very well; go and mourn with your people. Go in the shaman's canoe."

She turned away without another word. We were off Cape Noir, and they were putting overboard all the Indian canoes in the infernal crimson glare of sunset.

Never, never have I seen so incredibly superb a sight.

Swinging in the golden and rosy fire of sunset, the fortress-city of Louisbourg dominated the Bay. In front of us were the fortifications on the Isle de l'Entrée—crenellated walls disclosing barrack roofs, and a flag flying over them. Beyond was the Batterie Royale, flanked by two battlemented towers.

Then, inland, but its ramparts bordering the sea between Point Rochefort and the Black Cape, rose the great walled fortress-city of Louisbourg in all its enchantment and legendary glory.

In front of us, piercing the air, was the arrow-like, cock-crowned spire of the great hospital, just to the left of the Princess Bastion. Beyond it, big guns in battery glistened on the Bastion de la Reine whose massive, lofty walls look out over the Black Cape.

Now, high in the sunset glow, dominating everything else, rose the beautiful domed tower of the barracks at the King's Bastion, from the middle of its vast slate roof from which dozens of chimneys sent thin coils of smoke into the smouldering evening sky. High above the tower flew the flag.

Here was the Château St. Louis, a stately edifice of hewn stone four stories high, the tall roof slated, the entrance being over a drawbridge, to the left of which is the King's Chapel, and on the right the donjons. On the south of the Citadel were the Governor's apartments.

To the right were the King's Storehouses; to the left Le Billard and the residence of Monsieur de Mezy with its beautiful peaked roof, dormers, iron balconies overlooking the quay. Far beyond, in a direct line, rose a sharp slate roof from the mass of roofs and chimneys. It was the magazine of the Dauphin's Bastion from which a gilded coat of arms sparkled in the setting sun.

All else was but an endless conglomeration of peaks and pointed roofs and myriad smoking chimney-pots just visible above the bastions and the city walls which encompassed the entire fortified place from Point Rochefort and the Black Cape to the superb gates beyond the Dauphin battery.

My God, what a fortress! And what a city!

And everywhere along the quays, docks, fishing wharves, were forests of masts of fishing vessels, coasting vessels, auxiliary war craft, and the spars of great ships warped in for loading or repairs. Beautiful! Formidable! Magnificent!

Crack-bang! Our silly carronade was saluting the eastward forts; and suddenly a vast cloud of white smoke obscured them and a thunderous cannon shot bade us mind our business and stop annoying the great fortress with incessant and noisy politeness.

And now, in the last embers of the kindling West, we came to an anchor.

Under our bow-chains it was already dusky. Somewhere down there a voyaguer was rowing in a cockleshell and singing of the hunter's moon and of wild rivers, of brotherhood, and of woman's love.

CHAPTER XVIII

THE STREET OF THE LITTLE BIRDS

I HAD been in Louisbourg a week, having agreeable and dignified lodgings in the house of a lady of noble lineage, Madame de Miré, widow of a Canadian officer who had fallen during the first siege.

There is—or was—a little stony street running north-west and south-west between the rue de Scutarie and the rue de France, on the north and south, and the rue Dauphine and rue de l'Estang on the west and east. It is called the rue des Petits Oiseaux—the Street of the Little Birds; and here I lodged in a house of some pretension, built of stone and half-timber construction; and convenient to all points of the town, the river, the water-front, wharves, docks, quays, and—most important—near to bake shops, pastry-cooks, and cafés—in fact, only a few squares from the Royal Bakeries, the pleasant odours of which never let me forget my three meals a day, and a supper, too, when God permitted.

I had a bed-chamber and another pleasant room to sit in, which had two casements glazed with diamond-shaped panes, and a shuttered peep-hole.

From it I could see, beyond the city wall and ramparts, the nid-de-pie, or stone watch tower called a "magpie's nest," on the Devil's Mount beyond the Miré Road; I could see the windy shore of Gabarus—or Carabus—Bay with its hurrying grey-blue waves and frothing rocks awash, and the wild foreland set with swampy vegetation except where golden moorlands came to the ocean's edge between vast blackish blocks of forest.

Now, when I came into Louisbourg I felt instantly and instinctively that here was a land of slack morality and lax discipline. One divines it—at least a soldier does, where, despite a brave and martial showing, the secret canker of private interest, dishonesty, and lack of principle in high places saps at the foundations of military strength.

I did not then know what was the trouble, but I knew that something must be the matter with a strong place, its commander, its officers and garrison, when a strange Englishman could come unmolested, almost unquestioned, into such a fortress and such a city, and go about freely and at leisure wherever it suited him to go.

All I said to a young officer of police, sent to my lodgings by the Town Major, was that I might wish to join the Foreign Legion if there was a commission to be had.

All the reply I got was a peevish one, and to the effect that there were no commissions lying around loose in Louisbourg; that if God himself wanted one there was not even an ensign's berth to be had at present; and that, however, if I desired to apply for something in the non-com ranks, I might collect my credentials and identification papers and present myself at the barracks of the Regiment Etranger in the Princess Bastion, between 10 A.M. and 4 P.M., Mondays and Thursdays excepting fête days.

Which extraordinary reception took a weight from my mind, and the ever-fringing shadow of a gallows death from my heart.

However, I knew that I had better lose no time in showing myself everywhere where authority might perhaps hunt for me unless I appeared voluntarily.

So first I went to call upon Captain, the Honourable Charles Follis; and learned he had gone to sea for a short cruise with the French Admiral.

The young officer of artillery who told me this winked at me and remarked that they'd have a gay old time aboard a flagship which was already celebrated for the carousing spirit aboard.

Then I called upon the Lieutenant Chevalier Johnstone; and was told he had gone trout fishing somewhere beyond the Miré, with his mistress.

I then started all over again, put on my best buckskin shirt and leggins, and, cap in hand, waited upon the Governor of Louisbourg, the Chevalier de Drucour.

He begged to be excused, turning me over to the Commandant, a Chevalier of St. Louis named Lahouillière, who passed me on to Denis de Bonaventure, Chevalier de St. Louis, "Lieutenant de Roy à Louisbourg"—or that is what he signed himself—begging me politely to take myself and my business to another Chevalier of St. Louis, a Major named Rousseau de Villejouin, whose aid or "Ayde Major," sent me to the acting Town Major, Joubert; * who would have none of me, personally, but took my "pieces of identification"—carefully forged in Albany and supplemented by genuine papers furnished by General Sir William Johnson before I departed.

A fascinating boy, sub-lieutenant of the Grenadiers of

* Afterward Governor of Marie Galante.

the Artois Regiment, sent me to Du Vivier * who sent
me to Captain d'Or Fontaine.†

"Look here," said he in his gruff, good-humoured way,
"there's no use sending you from pillar to post, Monsieur
le Capitain de Cardress! Why don't they tell you very
frankly that there's no room for you?"

"No room, Monsieur?"

"None, except as a gentleman volunteer in the ranks of
the Foreign Regiment, without commission."

He added, consolingly: "When I point out to you,
Monsieur, that the Chevalier Johnstone, who was premier
captain in Prince Charles Edward's army, could only ob-
tain the rank of ensign, and, lately, that of lieutenant,
you will more readily understand why there are no commissions available for even"—he bowed to me with a
charming smile, "—the most gallant and meritorious of
Scottish officers. . . . Believe me, sir, I regret it, and I
trust that social recognition will in part compensate for
your military disappointment, and that, in time of peril,
we shall find you fighting as a volunteer, shoulder to
shoulder with your Scottish countrymen, Major Follis
and the Chevalier Johnstone."

We bowed to each other a number of times with every
ceremony. At my request he recommended me to a
tailor and a haberdasher. Oh, yes, there were haber-
dashers in Louisbourg, with the most fashionable stock
of goods outside of Paris. And when I tell you how gay
was this same fortress-city, and that in a single year
nearly eight thousand pairs of women's ball-slippers were
imported from France; and more than a hundred and

* Died at sea, 1761.
† Killed at Louisbourg, July 9th of the following year, 1758.

sixty quintals of haberdashery, also, you may believe me that even Montreal and Quebec were not as gay as was Louisbourg in the days of the last and greatest war of all——

But I go too swiftly as I often do, desiring to get forward to an end, yet shall not be very glad when at last my journal reaches its proper end. . . .

Oh, Lord, what an amusing city, it seemed to me in those days, and how feverishly gay! Heigho!—when I think of it! And my very first waking impression, after my first night ashore, was of clear, musical voices,— of young girls' laughter; singing, gossiping, greeting, and calling back and forth across streets and between open windows. A glimpse of pretty women at windows, whose voices had the liquid, golden, melodious lilt of woodland birds a-courting.

Then I got up out of my warm bed and looked out into the sunny, stony street; and two or three women, seeing my sleepy-looking head and general dishabille, laughed at me in friendly fashion—oh, Lord, they were very charming and seductive, the little ladies of Louisbourg!

Then, of a sudden—bang! clash-toot-toot! Ding-a-ling and rub-a-dub-dub!— And down the rue de Canada and along the rue d'Orléans into the rue St. Louis came the band of the Regiment Artois, drums, fifes, clarions, cymbals, playing a lively march. The long, wavering lines of white coats faced with brilliant colour, under a torrent of flashing bayonets, wheeled into the rue Toulouse, heading for the King's Bastion, officers mounted and riding magnificent horses, and the Colonel's flag and the bewildering folds of the numerous other gaudy flags and guidons made a gorgeous riot of colour in the narrow streets of silvery grey stone.

In the rue Royale I could see long waiting columns of field artillery, evidently just in from a practice march beyond the Miré river-road, and now blocked at the rue Toulouse by the Regiment Artois. Very soon, however, I saw their officers' naked swords flash upward, sparkle, then slash out forward; and the trample of gun-teams and the clash and rumble of flying artillery filled the stony streets of Louisbourg.

Leaning from my window to look down into the busy and swarming ways of this almost fabulous city, I could see Black Robes and nuns of the Louisbourg Convent, walking two and two; and Frères de la Charité from the Hospital, and Récollect Brothers—quiet monks of a kindly order—who did not get on very well with those of St. Sulpice, it was said.

Everywhere there were wooden shoes clattering under saucy short skirts and well made legs, or slim ankles in chaussons, or slimmer feet in high heels and silk stockings under rose silk and lace-trimmed hood and cloak.

Oh, the odours and smells and stinks of Louisbourg! Odour of fresh baked rolls and roasting coffee! Smells of hair-powder, of cosmetics and perfumes! Stinks from latrines, from the fish-docks and the markets! And everywhere a spice aroma from West Indiamen, from dock and warehouse, from sugar casks at the wharves. But I think the stench of cod prevailed—as it does in the seaward towns of those fish-faced, fishy-eyed Puritans who so dote on cod that they pray to a wooden one in their damned hall of justice when they do a witch to death.

My landlady's servant, a little rosy maid from Annapolis Royal, and part Irish, fetched me hot shaving water as well as a bowl and a jug; but I asked for a wash-tub, and got it, and scrubbed my chilled body until it glowed.

It became my custom, after my breakfast of a roll and a bowl of chocolate or dish of coffee, to stroll about, usually beginning at the Dauphin Gate—the most important and main entrance to the city—and thence by the grand mansion of Mezy and the Rodrigue house to the rue de l'Hôpital and the Espérance place on which Verrier's little house stood, and near where De La Forest's fine house once stood before the Dauphin Bastion had been built.

I liked to wander near to the school where the Sisters of the Congregation taught daughters of officers and of gentlemen of rank in the Government.

In the pleasant streets and alleys one often saw boys playing, but I never could discover that they had a school or were taught elsewhere than at home, yet they were well mannered and spoke and wrote their native tongue as well as any American schoolboy in the Colonies.

That day I went to see my tailor who had been recommended to me, and my haberdasher. I also went to one of the fashionable dressmakers—one Marie Paris—who sent me to a Madame Radoub to procure blond lace for my stocks and wrist-bands, and queue ribbons of fashionable military cut.

While my clothing was a-making, I often used to sit

238

a-sunning on mild days when there was no fog or rain—
which now was seldom the case—and look out to sea
where nothing except grey waters surged between me and
the southern and eternal polar ice.

And it made me shiver to think on it, and it was warm-
ing to see sunshine on the blue-grey ocean, and to hear
St. Louis, St. John, and St. Anthoine-Marie making mellow music in the sky—which were three bells christened
by these names, and belonged in the Citadel chapel. Also
the bells in the Récollet church were lovely to hear, and
pleasanter than the fiddle which Simon Rondel scraped,
a-teaching fashionable folk to dance in his chambers
across the rue de la Grave.

Behind the Lorembecs the Fathers of Charity had their
monastery and hospital, and a small office, too, near the
Place d'Armes.

It was a happy city, as I say, despite a vile climate of
fog and gales and sleet—yet, perhaps the better part of
the time it was pleasant weather—a gay, light-hearted
city, contented and prosperous, and joyous despite the rot-
tenness of the Intendant whose villainies and lusts and
robberies were known to all; and all save him and his
creatures already beheld and understood the writing on
the wall, where Quebec and Montreal were already swaying upon their cracking foundations.

And behind all, across the grey Atlantic, leered the
Pompadour—Jane Fish—smirking at America with sickly
yellow lips plastered with scarlet paint.

Yes, Louisbourg was gay; and, in the hearts of its
people, invincible.

There was gilded gaiety and noble glamour in the very
names and titles of its inhabitants—my neighbours—the

De La Tours of Acadie, the De La Vallières, Du Chambon of the Midi, De Rouville of Isle Royale, De Gannes —Falaise, the Daugeacs, Fierrots, Souvignis, Du Viviers —Lord!—even Baron de l'Espérence and Bois Berthelot who married one of the demoiselles de Goutins breathed an atmosphere of courts and crusades and the brave adventures of missionary and voyageur carrying ever forward the Cross and the Lys d'Or, and facing the God, that failed them, with laughter and a dying jest.

Brave men upon whom I had come to spy! Men of heart and courage whom I had come to undo! Wise, clear thinking men who had made the Pax Gallica! And I was here to poison its sources if I could, and turn every mission into a yellow-jacket's nest!

More than that—and less, God pardon me—I was here to see that the Scottish rebels who officered the Foreign Legion should not escape the noose of George II, King of England, when at last the red-faced, red-fisted, sweating regulars of that dumpy little German had taken this beautiful French city by siege or storm!

A dirty mission, my lords and gentlemen!

CHAPTER XIX

THE DUCHESS SLAYS

IN the Street of the Little Birds sunshine fell on the roadway. Across it, shadows of sae-gulls swept, always gliding southward. But always, also, the gossiping, bird-like voices of women filled the street, calling musically from high windows or chirping on wet side-paths and in open doorways.

I had commanded sufficient clothing to make myself acceptable among gentle folk. I had a suit of mauve silk with blond lace at cuffs and a primrose waistcoat, the long pocket-flaps of which were embroidered with roses.

I had a suit of black silk for solemn occasion, with plenty of lace for cuff and stock, and even for a jabot if I chose, but that had become unfashionable.

I had a pearl coloured waist and breeches to wear under a beautiful vermillion coloured coat of finest cloth.

I had stockings of silk, of thread, of wool; shoes suitable, good linen for every day, fine linen for fêtes, a black cloak edged with otter; a blue cloak heavily edged, lined and collared with beaver, and a black cloak like an abbé's, with no fur at all and silver clasps.

Against need, also, I had a Micmac woman make for me a hunting shirt, breeches, leggins, and moccasins of good deer-skin well cured and worked with deers' brains to a softness incredible.

The Souriquois, men and women, are noted for their fondness for thrums; and this forest dress of mine had

them plentiful so that when I put it on and walked
I was a tossing cascade of long yellow, undyed fringes
from shoulder to ankle, and had a cap of silver fox with
its black and white tipped tail a-dangling upon my back.

I will say that I found the Louisbourg inhabitants—
both citizens and military—polite. Those upon whom I
waited returned my visit and promptly invited me to dine,
or to English tea, or to a concert or a dance. The renegade Scots were favourably thought of in Louisbourg,
and I, of course, was supposed to be one.

I had no desire to pretend politeness, much less friendship for men I had been commissioned to keep under surveillance and, ultimately, to deliver to the King of England's deputy hangman. It was too much like betrayal—
too Judas-like. So I avoided Charles Follis altogether,
and merely left a card for the Chevalier Johnstone.

But the next day I found at my lodgings his card, de-
livered in person, and my flustered maid-of-all-work stam-
mered out that my caller was no other than "Monsieur le
Lieutenant du Roi et Chevalier Jacques Johnstone de
Moffat, de l'ordre de St. Louis, héritier de la Maison de
Johnstone, Marquis d'Annandale, Paire d'Ecosse!"

I didn't wish to see my fellow Scot, and had not attempted any further civility when he strolled in one morning while I was shaving, in friendly, unconventional style,
carrying a trout-rod of Edinburgh make, and a few artifi-
cial flies fastened to the breast of an old red jacket.

"Well," said he, shaking hands—I feeling like a very
Judas—"the world seems to be full o' Scots, Captain
Cardress—even after Culloden."

We chatted pleasantly for a few minutes. He spoke
of my request for a commission in the Foreign Volun-

teers. "There's not a chance of it, Captain," said he. "Look at me, a lieutenant, who was Senior Captain for our Bonnie Prince, and my commission dated September 21, 1845! Think of that, sir!

"We have 38 officers and 526 men—full complement, and every officer savagely jealous for promotion. After all, sir, you must concede that Major Follis has a hard job with his battalion."

I admitted it. I was polite but restless, never having played the spy before, and now feeling soiled and Judas-like in my friendly politeness to this gentleman whom I was under orders to betray.

He told me that he had the rank, also, of King's Interpreter, which gave him better than a captain's pay, otherwise, he would be unable to exist. He was frank, friendly, and kind. By God, I did not like it, and felt my liver souring within me.

He asked me if I cared for trout and salmon angling, but I pretended not to care, so averse was I to enter into such easy camaraderie with this friendly and outlawed Scot whom I had liked instantly at first view.

Everybody upon whom I had called in pretended quest of a commission was polite enough to make me personally welcome in Louisbourg; and I dined and wined and danced and flirted with wives and daughters of the garrison officers: with the Du Vivier de Vannes, with the Vallées—the artillery Captain, his wife, and Josette Vallée, his charming daughter—with the Tournays, the Dupont Duchambons, Dupont de Gourvilles, the Leneuf de La Vallières, all that amiable company, all poor, all proud, all determined to laugh and to have the best of times in this world of trouble and Labrador mists.

The gaiety, glitter, extravagance and corruption of Montreal and Quebec under the Marquis de Vaudreuil and the infamous Bigot with his attendant pimps had no real counterpart in this great walled City of Mists here upon the Isle Royale—partly because its Governor, Drucour, was serious, brave, and honest, and possessed of a brave and lovely wife; partly because of the poverty rife among all these civilian nobles and noble officers.

Yet, there was constant gaiety in the city, particularly now that the last menace of an English attack had vanished with the skulking English transports, and the storm which had fairly hurled the Scottish Vice Admiral out of the northeast seas.

I had not been long in Louisbourg before I had plans of the enceinte with every bastion, demi-bastion, curtain, redoubt, battery—all the guns listed and numbered, all the fortifications on the islands and across the bay described and sketched.

Every week I made a tabulated schedule as follows:

Garrison, Oct. 15, 1756

	Officers	Men Fit for Duty	Sick and Wounded	Total
24 Companies and 2 of Artillery and Scouts	76	746	195	1,017
2nd Battalion Regiment Artois.....	32	407	27	
2nd Battalion Regiment Bourgogne	30	353	31	
2nd Battalion Regiment Cambis	38	466	104	608
Foreign Legion	38	402	86	526
Total Garrison	214	2,374	443	3,031
Marine Officers and Sailors	135	1,124	1,347	2,606
GRAND TOTAL	349	3,498	1,790	5,637

Well, it was dirty business, but somebody had to do it or the French would own North America in a year or two more.

My total report of shot and shell was enormous,—round shot, grape, bar, case, shells for 36, 24, 18, 12, 8, and 4 pounders; shells for brass and iron mortars up to 12½ inches calibre; there were a hundred thousand musket cartridges on hand and eighty thousand making; there were 1,500 barrels of gunpowder alone!

A warm, cottony fog possessed the city. I had a pretty good horse named Cocu, which I rode—though why Cocu I never knew, the animal being a gelding and immune to marital worry.

I went out of the city, my horse gently feeling his way, but presently the fog grew a little thinner and Cocu broke into a harmless amble, taking the river-road which was broad enough for two carriages to drive abreast.

But there were no gilded coaches, calèches, or carriages of any description on the highway—only a few wayfarers —fishermen, log-cutters, a dawdling trapper or two, silent Indians going about their business in the soft and cottony fog.

Near the river I dismounted and took Cocu by the head, leading him off the road down a fragrant ferny trail where frost already had killed the brake and turned blueberry bushes to mounds of crimson.

Where an icy trout brook ran under writhing mists and clots of thick foam I caught a glimpse of a Souriquois village, and presently saw an old witch doctor I knew, called White Muskrat.

We spoke politely; he sponged on me for brandy, and,

not getting any, accepted tobacco with a gleaming grin.

To my inquiry he told me that Santu was a good girl and industrious, having learned sewing and other useful arts at the Mission.

The only trouble, he remarked, was that she loitered about Louisbourg too much and had the name of being sweetheart to the Regiment Artois—which he said was a lie, because she had plenty of opportunity to amass a competency that way and refused to do so, greatly to the grief of her adopted parents, Old Buck and his wife.

"Is she your girl?" he added naïvely.

"No. Where is she?"

He told me; and after a while I discovered her down stream, weaving a fish weir out of willows.

"Kuai!" I called out gaily.

She clapped her slender, brown hands, came dancing over, and was inclined to play the twining vine to my tree, so I gave her a few hearty caresses and asked her what she had done about employing messengers for me.

She had, with great caution, found two runners whom I might trust to carry my reports to Halifax. They wanted their pay in Spanish milled dollars at Halifax; and I already had arranged for that contingency with my Lord Loudon before I left New York.

"You know," said I to Santu, "if they betray me I shall hang over yonder from the lighthouse under the marine telegraph."

I pointed to the distant semaphore. She nodded.

"Yes," said she, "you will hang, your messengers will die very, very painfully under the skinning-knife and by fire; and my people will take me to the cliffs and cut me, slowly, into little pieces, and drop these pieces into shallow water so that all may see the Canso crabs seize them and swim away with them backwards!"

I smiled faintly: "Very well, then, if you are so sure of the loyalty of your runners."

"They are Young-Man-Who-Paints-the-Sky, and the Green Eel. They are faithful—" she grinned slightly —"for love of me! Tok! What I beg you to take they would give me all Louisbourg to possess."

"E?"

"O'hou! Kalaato!—" Her arms were around my neck again, but I suddenly picked her up from the ground and set her in the forks of a cherry birch over my shoulder.

"Toni ait?" said I, "—where is your messenger, then?"

"He is yonder in his lodge. Do you desire to speak with him?"

"O'da! It is better that I do not."

I gave her the packet in its little covering of soft buckskin. She put it into the neck of her beaded tunic, between her breasts.

"How long will it take?" I asked; "nisinska?— twenty?"

"Nsinska, thirty—to go and return. . . . Is the paper here"—she tapped her breast—"which tells them in Halifax to give to him his Spanish dollars?"

"O'hou."

"Then all is properly done, my dear and elder brother."

"But—will you take nothing, Santu?"

"For serving my witch-captain? O'da!"

She disengaged her lithe body from the forks of the cherry birch, slid to her moccasined feet, caught my hand and led me to the stream to examine and praise her fish weir.

We gossiped for nearly an hour, then I had to go;
she kissed me with reasonable moderation, patted my
horse, and stood looking after me on the wet river sands
as I rode away through the clinging mist.

"O kuai!" she cried out.

"O'hou, Santu—sis!"

"Yes," she called after me, "you can give me something
if you wish to, my white witch-captain Bouyn!"

"What is that, little sister?" I shouted back; and saw
her frame her mouth with both palms to carry her laughing voice to me:

"A baby for Santu the Osayana! A love-baby for
poor little Sis-Santu. Ouliouni nijia! God loveth a
cheerful giver, O Bouyn!"

"Tan, Santu?"

"Saba!"

I shouted back, laughing: "Tach, Santu?"

She was already but a vague grey spot in the fog. Her
voice came clearly still: "As many as you will, Nidokan,
—or as many as shall please your White Sorcerer, Kchi
Sazos!"

As I say, I had commanded clothing proper for a
gentleman of my condition, who was supposed to have
been one of Prince Charles Edward's unfortunate partizans.

Pre-winter gaiety already had begun in the city by a
grand dinner and ball offered by Monsieur de Drucour,
Governor of Louisbourg, and his noble wife, to the
quality of the entire military district, including those from
the outlying villages, forts, fishing stations and seigniories
such as Petit Lorembecq, St. Esprit, Ile Madame l'Ar-

doise—all the little settlements and considerable places along Gabarus, and even from distant Gaspé and the Bras d'Or.

Louisbourg was en fête; flags and lanterns decorated the rue du Quay, rue du Pont, Royal Street, Orléans, France, Scatary, Toulouse, St. Louis streets.

The rue de l'Etang, rue Le Fort, rue de l'Hôpital, rue du Remparé, and rue d'Estrées were decorated with evergreens and gorgeous festoons of brilliant scarfs, curtains, and other fabrics.

Bowers of hemlock and fir-balsam set with the scarlet berries of the black alder made of it all an appearance more like an English Christmas than a French fête.

It was a kind of carnival; in part a celebration of victory at Fort William Henry, partly a rejoicing at the retreat of the Flying Scotchman, Holburne, and my Lord Loudon.

The band of the Regiment Bourgogne played at the Place d'Armes in the centre of a frolicking crowd of men, women, and children.

The band of the Regiment Artois played opposite the Château.

There was a fanfare and chœur de chasse by the music of the native light infantry—badly done because of horseplay and drunkenness among those undisciplined Colonials.

Everywhere there was dancing in the streets, on the quays and rampart promenades. What charmed me was to see so many children everywhere—and I think I never saw prettier and sturdier young ones—peasantry, or habitants, as well as children of the bourgeoisie and of the quality—such graceful, well-mannered, gay little things, aprons and skirts held up daintily, and little feet dancing to the noise of fanfare, the crash of military bands, or the perpetual scraping of fiddles.

Fiddles! There seemed to be thousands in Louisbourg, and every one being scraped and picked by excited fiddlers. Canada was—and is—the land of fiddles; and the twang and shriek of catgut the Canadian expression of emotion.

Fireworks were rising from the Citadel and from every one of the bastions when, wearing my best of silk, lace, powder, patch, and pomade, I made my way to the Governor's apartment under lighted lanterns and evergreen boughs, through streets choked with noisy and happy people, and between long lines of soldiers to the Château St. Louis.

Here was a crush of coaches and sedan-chairs full of perfumed beauty muffled in silks and furs; and, as coach and chair disgorged them, they scurried through the corridor guarded by artillerymen with naked sabres, and, meeting their escorts, filled the stairway with colour and vivacity.

The gay chatter of voices, swish of rustling silk and tap of jewelled heel filled the palace, stair, gallery, and reception hall where Drucour, wearing the star and ribbon of St. Louis, and his good and noble wife received their invited, military and civilian, amid the dazzling radiance of unnumbered candles.

Lord! It was like some magic scene—as I pictured it, at Versailles or the Louvre—where I never had been except in imagination. The jewelled coats and uniforms of the men, the beautiful embroidered gowns of the women, formed a most entrancing spectacle that excited me who had seen only the English way of doing such things, which was both gaudier and clumsier.

It was the fashion at the moment for women to wear their hair closely dressed and powdered—a mode which was charmingly suited to such as had shapely heads—and it gave a roundness to cheeks and a full value to a pretty neck and bosom, which a later and more towering coiffeur did not.

That slut at Versailles had set such a fashion for vivid cosmetics, on account of her own chlorosis, that lily-white, cupid's blush, lip-salve of Olympus, and other extravagant lotions had transformed all these pretty young things— and the old ones, too—into a lovely throng of painted and animated dolls all looking more or less alike.

Well, I could hear hautbois, horns, and kettle-drums, and the picked strings of harps in minuet measure, as I went up stairs, nearly choked by warm waves of cloying perfume and clouds of scented powder.

The aphrodisiacs of scent, of propinquity, of dance-rhythm and contact, of food, drink, glitter, do not agreeably excite me. Odours now plugged my nostrils, noise dinned in my ears; I felt too warm; I did not like to be crowded, either.

A handsome lad wearing the uniform of Béarn—one of Drucour's aids-de-camp—announced me.

I kissed Madame's hand; I bowed to the level-eyed Governor of Louisbourg who looked worn and ill and harassed—secret knowledge of La Friponne, of Vaudreuil, and of Bigot, no doubt; and of much mischief and evil in Quebec and Montreal.

Well, God save us all—there was evil of that sort in New York and Albany, too, I fancy.

I made my bow. Madame was kind enough to say that Scots were always welcome. Monsieur the Governor was distressed that no commission was available, but applauded my suggestion of Gentleman Cadet without pay.

Johnstone came sauntering to take me to Charles Follis.

He was surrounded by pretty women—a handsome fellow, straight and youngish, and brilliant in his white uniform faced with turquoise-blue and gold.

"Well, I'm damned," said he in his genial, boyish way, "—more Scots? They sprout out o' nothing in this country, Captain Cardress—come up among rocks and woods and glens like ferns and whinns and brakes at home!"

He gave me a hearty hand—for which I was sorry—I hating to shake hands like a very Judas with those whom I was ordered to watch to their destruction.

I saw a battery of bright eyes regarding me—a demi-circle of flower-like faces all a-row and a-gog.

Charles Follis named me to each damsel in turn, while my part was all hand-kissing and bows, with gloved fingers spread across my heart and a court sword point sticking up toward the ceiling like the quill on a sparring cockerel.

Mademoiselle Josette Vallée—she was the first!—a little animated beauty whose painted fan spread as wide as her skirts when she curtsied; and there was Mademoiselle Cecile Lanoy, all golden and powder frosted hair, and ice-blue of eye; and then I kissed the hands of Mademoiselle Fitzgerald, a dark Irish girl, Madame Betty Leslie, red-head Scot; and a bouquet of laughing French and Canadian ladies—Mesdemoiselles Magdelaine Loppinot, Jannette de Caux, Nanon, Emilie, and Jannette Benoist, Anne and Marie de Gourville, and Mesdames du Portail, De Pommeroy, and Du Vivier de Vanne.

Oh, Lord, enough to turn my head and drive a dod-

dering St. Antoine crazy; and I was still happily bewildered when, like a sword, the voice of Charles Follis
cut the joyous tumult around me.

I heard him naming me to some lady just arrived—
his cousin, I thought he said—and, bowing a preliminary
bow, was recovering myself to perform another with a
ceremonious touch of lips to finger-tips at the third bow
and advance. . . .

When, lifting my head with the formal smile on my
lips which urbanity requires, I found myself looking into
two familiar eyes.

The dark-fringed brown eyes widened in sudden amazement, then in wild alarm, while my disturbed, agitated,
and blundering gaze strove to fix itself with self-possession and penetrate with intelligence the most exquisite
apparition that ever graced a dream.

Then, far within my brain, I felt a soft crash of my
senses.

I was looking into the eyes of Sandi.

I heard the voice of Charles Follis continuing the
formal introduction: "My cousin, Gayette Alessandine
d'Auvray, Duchess de Boïens, but a good Follis, too, and
as good a Whinnloch as there is in all the Northland!
Are you not, my little crazy one?" he added in a mischievously affectionate voice, but with the carriage, de-
meanour, and grace of a peer of Scotland.

"Yes, by God," said Johnstone to me aside, "there is
this advantage in France, at least, that where terms of
the patent so run, a young girl may be a duchess in her
own right, nor await espousal or widowhood from some
sly Silenus or doddering old ducal Bacchus!"

He laughed uproariously; I heard him as in a dream,

and his mirth sounded a deadened tattoo on my ears, like goblin thunder.

For I was looking into the eyes of a woman who had just slain me with these same heavenly dark weapons; and I knew I was dead o' my wound, and that my soul knelt captive to hers.

CHAPTER XX

PAX GALLICA

THE Duchess de Boïens! Gayette d'Auvray! Alessandine! . . . *Sandi!*

The terrible surprise in her eyes at sight of me in Louisbourg had been noticed, I hoped, by me alone; for immediately her very deep court-curtsey and her lowered head responded to my profound—if bewildered—bow.

Bended low, left hand on ivory hilt, right spread over heart, nevertheless my eyes lifted as I bowed and never took their intense gaze from her, striving to reconcile this exquisite, brown-eyed young thing of silks and jewels and powdered hair with the ragged lad in smock and breeches and wooden shoon, or the camp-drudge in her humble garb, trudging at the heels of a weary regiment to the mechanical tap-tap-tap of a drum.

There was neither time nor opportunity for more than the prescribed formalities.

Her eyes were still wide with fear and she seemed ill, so white her pallor under the rouge.

"Monsieur is a recent arrival in Louisbourg?" she inquired in a voice so faint I could scarce hear it.

"Yes, Madame."

"Some day," said Charles Follis, "the Duchess should relate to you her astonishing adventures and the perils she encountered in arriving here. No novel or history or other romance can compare with my kinswoman's experience—"

A loud clash of quadrille music, strings, horns, cymbals, harps, and kettle-drums drowned all voices.

Charles Follis, a figure of courtly and experienced grace, led out Madame de Drucour; the Chevalier Governor gave his hand to the little Duchess; the Chevalier Johnstone took out Jannette de Coux, and Major de la Vallière was cavalier to Nanon Benoist.

That was a gay, pretty figure with twelve ladies and twelve gentlemen—of which I made one—in waiting to exchange favours with those dancing.

Nanon fell to my lot, then Madame de Drucour, and, in the last quartette of the triple quadrille, I felt my gloved hand trembling where Sandi's little white-gloved fingers rested upon it as coolly and lightly as five snowflakes.

Trumpets, then, signalled the end of that dance, and a feathery roll of kettle-drums the beginning of the next.

The arm of the little Duchess remained within mine, scarce touching my sleeve at all; her attitude one of silent hesitation and inquiry.

The violins began the air of the ever popular old dance with Lulli's lovely music, called *En Ballet,* which the Roi Soleil so loved to figure in.

The Duchess de Boïens looked at me as though she had no power to utter a word. I made her a profound bow which started her sinking down into a Versailles curtsey; from which, doubled up myself, I managed to lift her by that narrow hand of hers, and touch her glove with my lips.

Between thumb and forefinger, now, she took hold of her skirt with her left hand and spread the delicate fabric of primrose, ivory, orange, and gold, holding it high in impulsive and pretty effrontery as though, of a sudden, self-confidence had returned.

No feet, no ankles, no legs in their sheer, pale yellow silk, could compare with these so gracefully revealed as the little Duchess danced Lulli's *En Ballet* to the gay thump of kettle-drums and the golden jangle of picked harp and fiddle strings.

Sixteen couples danced it; then, retiring, ceded the floor to sixteen more.

Sweeping her flushed cheeks rhythmically with air-waves from her great fan, and barely touching my supporting arm, the Duchess de Boïens moved leisurely beside me from the floor.

"A glass of something cold," she murmured, "—no, don't fetch it, Monsieur; let us go in quest of it together—"

"Gayette!" called out Major Follis, as we passed by, "pray don't completely ignore the Chevalier and myself!"

Her only reply was a smile and a flourish of her fan held on high for an instant, to telegraph, "Au revoir!"

We discovered champagne in the supper-room, and she drank a frosted glass of it in silence.

The evening had turned warm; the palace, over-heated, became oppressive, yet, that morning, there was a thin skim of ice over the swamps beyond the city walls.

"Shall we stroll on the ramparts?" she asked, politely.

"Let me carry a cloak for you then—"

"No; I'm too warm—"

But I sent a maid to the cloak-room for her silver fox cloak and my own black cloak with silver clasps and chain; and, when we reached the city wall, I laid her wrap around her naked neck and shoulders, and flung my cloak over my own.

From the fort on the Isle de l'Entrée they were firing rockets and Roman candles, and it made a handsome spectacle to see all the sky afire and the waves reflecting it, while everywhere, in canoes and bateaux, in skiffs and fishing-craft, folk were drifting about and fiddling and singing those charming songs of the voyageurs, which all in New France know so well.

Under us, their frail, rocking boat almost scraping the barnacles and seaweed from the rampart wall where it plunged into the sea, sat two—a young girl and her beau, hand in hand, watching the fireworks, and singing, "I had a lover—" that familiar air—

> *"I had a lover!*
> *All on Isle Royale knew him,*
> *The Souriquois slew him,*
> *Where shall I find another*
> *So hardy and brave,*
> *On land or wave?*
> *The green mosses cover*
> *His woodland grave!"*

Many ladies and gentlemen were promenading the ramparts to take the air. We paced the massive battlements, passing slowly along crenellated walls where sentries stood; through armed redoubts dominated by watch towers, along bastions and demi-bastions behind the shadowy carriages and beds of ponderous cannon the vast, shadowy breeches of which our elbows brushed en passant.

Those warmed with dancing or with wine we very soon left behind, and presently, excepting a sentry here and there, the walk we moved along was silent and deserted.

For the first time, then, my young companion's lips unclosed in a tremulous whisper:

"My God, sir, I never dreamed you could penetrate this place!"

"Nor did I suppose you were bound hither," said I, "nor dream who you really are—"

"For heaven's sake, sir, be careful we are not overheard!" She let go my arm and backed into the shadow of an embrasure where a long eighteen stood, its muzzle gaping at Gabarus.

"You know," said I, "it is almost incredible—this romantic drama in which you play heroine. And, for that matter, I was warned in New York that a female of Charles Follis' family was supposed to be on her way to Louisbourg—a French Duchess—"

"Who told you that, sir?"

"Why, no other than our peppery Scot, my Lord Loudon. All vessels were warned against you; all ports, forts, posts; all troops in garrison and in the field were under orders to be on watch for you and to stop you and seize you wherever found. And I—good Lord!—I had to be the jackass to encounter you and be fooled and deceived by you."

There was a bitter silence; she drew her cloak of silver fox around her. In the gun's shadow I could just see her dark young eyes watching me.

"I *had* to deceive you," she said huskily.

"My compliments, Madame; you made a very ass of me."

"No. . . . You couldn't know. I am a good actress.

The King knows. I have performed at Court in ballets and comedies and spectacles."

"I cannot understand it," said I desperately, "—how you, so tenderly nurtured and sheltered, could take ship as a boy in the service of your country."

"Oh, no, sir. . . . If you will have truth, and not a glamorous and gilded lie, I had no choice in the matter."

"I don't understand."

"Well, to speak plainly, the Pompadour was the cause. I refused her offer of a place as one of her wardrobe maids of honour. Can you imagine a Follis paying a Pompadour for a tabouret?"

"No, I can't," said I.

"Very well, the rest is simple enough. The Marquise hated me for it. She hated everybody who slighted her. She heard I had laughed at what the King of Prussia said about her. There are tale-bearers in every court in a proportion of 99½ per cent. One o' these ran to her.

"She asked me if I laughed and I said yes. She almost screamed in her rage and ran to the King for a lettre-de-cachet.

"He gave me a solemn lecture—he and Chamilly—and when I asked whether the rumour was true that the English King meant to hang my kinsman Charles and the Chevalier Johnstone as soon as Lord Loudon took Louisbourg, he pretended not to have heard of it.

" 'Sire!' I cried in a white rage, utterly regardless of where I was and to whom speaking, '—is it possible that your Majesty would permit the King of England to hang a gentleman of my own family, and heir to the Duke of Whinnloch!'

"He said he couldn't prevent George II from doing

what he chose to do to rebel Scotchmen taken in arms against him.

" 'Sire,' cried I in a passion, 'these Scottish gentlemen who are serving your Majesty and shedding their blood for France ought to be warned what fate to expect if made captive by this German King of England!'

" 'Madame,' said he, 'do you pretend to instruct me in my duty?'

"That scared me; and I saw little Chamilly, plump and unctuous, shaking his foxy head behind the King's back.

"I don't know what I said or how I tried to make amends, or how I ever got out of the King's cabinet whither I had run in a great rage when summoned by Chamilly.

"I went to my apartments where very soon I had a message from Chamilly who may have been a fop but also was a brave man and good soldier.

"One of the slimy familiars from the Parc aux Cerfs carried the oral warning that Pompadour would surely have her way with the King and that a lettre-de-cachet must shortly send me to a cell if I did not flee Paris.

"Then it was that I made a promise to God's gentle, suffering Mother, the Queen of Heaven, to go myself into the western wilderness of New France and seek out Charles Follis and warn him of this frightful disgrace which threatened our family if Louisbourg were stormed, and he and the Chevalier taken prisoner and delivered to the King's hangman in London town!"

After a long pause: "And this you have done, Madame, in the face of indescribable perils, humiliations, and hardships."

"Yes." She lifted her dark eyes to me: "Why are *you* here, sir?"

I was silent.

"I know," said she. "You came here to send news to Pitt and the English King. You are here to watch my kinsman Major Follis, and Lieutenant the Chevalier Johnstone, to see that they don't escape the hangman when this city surrenders to the English."

"What are you going to do about it, Madame?" I asked, "deliver me to a French hangman?"

"Sir," said she, "will you be pleased to leave Louisbourg by the very next vessel?"

"And if I do not?"

"What is that you say, sir?"

"I say, 'and if I refuse to leave Louisbourg, what then?'"

"Well, do you think I shall remain silent while you haunt these two gentlemen like the shadow of Death itself, to procure for them a disgraceful and cruel end upon a gallows?"

"My orders are to arrest them and I mean to do it when this city is taken. If you drive me out of Louisbourg," said I, "and if I then send word to the ruler of France, whose name is Jane Fish, that the Duchess of Boïens is in Louisbourg, then the next ship carries a warrant for you which Vaudreuil and Bigot will have executed. And it will be you, Madame, who leave Louisbourg in your turn, for an apartment in that pretty château they call the Bastille. And if I can judge Jane Fish by what she already has done to those who offend her, you are most likely to remain her guest for life!"

After a moment: "I did not think you were that kind of man, Captain Cardress."

"I am not. I loathe what I am ordered to do."

"Oh. . . . A martyr to duty?" she said mockingly.

"I am going to carry out my orders unless you prevent me."

"By betraying you?"

"That is the only way you can stop me from carrying out my orders, Madame."

"I'm no hangman's helper, if you are," said she angrily. "It is unthinkable that I should betray anything—even a dog! But neither shall you remain here to deliver these two gentlemen to your brutal English justice! You must leave this city immediately!"

"If I do, then the Marquise de Pompadour learns where you are."

"What!" she exclaimed in a stifled voice, "you dare interfere in such a matter which is no business of yours!"

"If I hold any weapon of defense I shall use it, and that's flat, Madame! I can't help your having me hanged. But I can prevent your driving me out of the city by threatening you with your Pompadour, who will not only do for you, but for your Scottish friends, as well!"

"What!"

"Certainly. She will, if paid, oblige Pitt! If that's a secret you are welcome to it!"

"Do you—do you threaten me with this vile woman!" she demanded passionately. "Do you dare menace me with blackmail?

"Damnation, sir," she cried, stamping her little foot, "I am not to be warned and bullied and frightened by any man, I'll have you understand!"

"Good God, Sandi," I burst out from an overwhelmed and tortured heart, "I love you better than life, but not better than honour! I won't betray my King, my country, my orders! I won't betray posterity. This is a holy war. Either England rules on this Continent or France rules.

"It isn't a question of living kings and queens and regents and royal mistresses; it is a question of human liberty and happiness for all future time!"

"If England's flag goes down in these forests and on these seas, then Tyranny triumphs and all mankind go about in the heavy shackles of soul slavery!

"For the wars of the world are being fought out here in this hemisphere; and will be continued and fought to a finish *here*, and not in Europe!

"So, though the Lord knows I am a plain, healthy man who has no desire for martyrdom, but wishes with all his heart to live, I have no other choice than to remain here, try to execute orders, and abide my fate——"

I came nearer to her and looked into her shadowy eyes:

"I love you, Sandi! I love you, Madame la Duchesse. I would not cause you or yours any sorrow or shame or harm.

"Yet, I must abide here as long as you let me remain alive, and try to execute my orders when the hour arrives. Because I am a soldier and neither traitor nor poltroon."

I could see her shudder. There ensued a terrible silence. Then:

"Lend me your arm, sir," she said in a choking voice, "——this place is deathly cold——"

I sprang to her side, for she was swaying a trifle, and drew her arm through mine.

She said: "How have you the wickedness and effrontery to boast of your English civilization and insult our French, —when your army is afraid of your own Indians, and—" She halted and flung wide both arms in the foggy moonlight, embracing in one gesture all of the northland called New France: "Look!" she sobbed, "—everywhere is peace, security, happiness and plenty—save for your ferocious armies—your butcher-soldiery—your pirate ships!

"You tell me that unless this land becomes wholly English the world shall crouch hereafter in spiritual shackles!

"My God, sir, how can you say that when you see a world of Indians of myriad nations living in brotherly contentment under our white banner sewn with the golden fleur-de-lys!

"Look, sir! Here is the Pax Gallica! Here is a peace woven by wisdom, kindness, toleration, and truth! Here is a peace made by France!—the Pax Gallica!

"And—oh, God!—you tell us we are Popish idolaters, bigots, tyrants!—and you threaten—threaten me with— blackmail—"

She hid her face in her silvery black furs.

We walked slowly toward the Château St. Louis.

CHAPTER XXI

THE MAGPIE'S NEST

IT was vain for me to attempt to take the situation jauntily, or even coolly.

I did not wish to hang. Few do. I knew that these Frenchmen would not hesitate an instant to string me up and swing me to the icy winds off the lighthouse or from the Dauphin's Bastion or, off Grand Anse, from the yard-arm of a tall ship while their drums beat gaily from the quarter-deck.

Who could blame them? Who could blame a Duchess of Boïens if she sacrificed me to protect a kinsman from the disgrace of the British gallows?

Now, following Rampart Street, we came in view of the great stone-paved esplanade of the Château. Here, in the ruddy torchlight, a merry, noisy company were gathering to escape the heat and din of a crowded ballroom, and enjoy the mild sea-winds and moonlight of Rampart Street.

All about, in their powder, patches, and silks, strolled the gay ladies of Louisbourg. Some seated themselves upon the polished breeches of the cannon, some found perches aloft along crenellated battlements or ensconced themselves, with their pomaded gallants, within some magpie's nest under the marine telegraph, the gallows-like arm of which stretched out suggestively in the moonlight overhead, affording me disagreeable sensations.

266

Out of her silvery furs, at my elbow, came Sandi's voice, pitched scarcely above a whisper: "'Sieur John."

"Yes, Madame."

"I am sorry I cursed you in my heart."

"I am sorry we quarreled, Madame."

"I, also. . . . My Captain?—"

"Yes, Madame?"

"You will leave the city, will you not?"

"After all," said I, sullenly, "it's the Bastille for you against a ship's yard-arm for me. We can discuss terms if you wish. A modus vivendi is possible."

She said angrily: "There need be no Bastille for me, and no shame to my family, if I point you out to that sentry yonder!"

"Do it, then."

"You know I won't," said she hotly. "You know I'll not expose you except in the dire necessity of self-protection. You are not the least bit alarmed for fear of betrayal by me, and you know it!" she added, her indignation rendering her voice unsteady.

"Nor are you afraid that I'll turn you over to the Bastille," said I. "But if Versailles sends word to Quebec, and Quebec sends a guard for you here, then it will be time for alarm and for giving me up to the Governor of this fortress."

"Very well," said she huskily, "let us make terms for a modus vivendi, then. But I warn you that no kin of mine ever shall suffer on Tower Hill or Tyburn, and no heads of my kinsmen ever shall be set all a-row and a-grinning upon Temple Bar, through any mistaken sense of duty on *your* part, John Cardress, or any notion of mercy upon *mine!*"

We had turned our steps away from the crowded esplanade and lights. Above, reached by narrow, winding steps of stone, was the pulpit of a watch tower, just under the tall stone lantern of the bastion.

We went up, and found ourselves in the dark starlight, high above the torch glow and coloured lanterns below.

Far out across the water, golden rain from the last rocket drifted eastward and faded out above the Isle de l'Entrée. Underneath, a few lamps burned dimly in the depths of some dark street. The beat and measure of the dance came up to us distantly from the Château—the throb of painted drum and the fiddled rhythm of a country dance.

She stepped into the narrow Magpie's Nest, in her scented furs and rustling silks. It was constructed for only a single watchman.

"Are you coming in?" said she, making for me what room she could. But in the Magpie's Nest was scant space for two, and the little stone tournelle crowded us almost into each other's arms, who already had been at each other's throats.

"Look," says she, "at the tall war-ships riding the Grand Anse, and all strung with a million coloured lights. . . . See the beacon, too! . . . And I can make out L'Isle Verte, the Tour de la Lanterne, and bonfires on the Marais beyond Grand Laurembec. . . . There is," said she, "a vast conflagration to the westward. I think it is the beacon afire on the Devil's Mountain. . . . For heaven's sake, sir, are we so crowded that you must pass your sword-arm around my body?"

My right arm slipped up from her waist to her shoulders and then around her neck where the warm, perfumed fur fell away, disclosing a flawless, innocent, scarce-formed bosom.

"How shall I send you to Jane Fish's jail in Paris?" said I, "who am so passionately concerned with you that I can not sleep for heartache?"

"God forgive us," said she, and gave me one of her lovely blind looks as my arm tightened about her neck and drew back her head so that our mouths were nearly touching.

"And I," she said, "how shall I send you to your mortal end, John Cardress, who have had of me scarcely less than a husband takes of a willing wife!—and who, for all I know, may even yet take more of me—"

"More?"

"A lover takes more, they say—"

"Will you have me for yours then, Sandi?"

"I can't seem to avoid it—" She reached up both arms and took my head, pulling it forward, and whispering so close that her lips fluttered against mine: "If you're thinking of marriage, put it out of your darling head, my Captain, for they'd kill you for the very thought of it!"

"You *will* not, Sandi?"

"Aye—if it were *my* will that wills such things. But it's the French King's. And, after him, it's all the Boïens, and the Follisses and Whinnlochs—and the devil take them a', King and Duke and every peer both French and Scottish!" she cried in a passion.

"Sandi!"

"Th'ould Nick's in it," says she, "to make a scarlet woman o' me ere I step fairly across the bounds," says she, "out o' childhood and into harlotry!"

"You *shall* marry with me, Sandi—"

"Not I in a million, million years then, my darling lad —my darling, darling lad—"

"Is it cowardice or lack o' love—"

"Oh, Lord! Ah, mon Dieu! Listen to my Captain whom I loved in rags—and why should my curled hair and pearl-powder and jewels and silks stifle passion or cool the body they clothe? I'm telling you, Jock o' my heart, that all rebel Scotland would bury their dirks and skene-dhus in you, and the French Court and peerage would cut you to slithereens with their little court-swords if you ever dared talk of marrying a Duchess of Boïens!"

"Well, damn them, will they do less if I love a Boïens *par amour?*"

"My poor child," said she, "don't you know it? And what are the adventures and amours of a Duchess de Boïens as long as the King of France disposes of her hand and her person, her dot and her duchy, to any suitable and privileged gentleman of a peerage which passionately screams 'privilege!' in the very face of the King of France himself?"

"I'll not do it!" said I in a rage.

"Ye'll nae do it, John? An' why not, if I love?"

"By God," said I, "the French nobility shall never spit upon my tartan, then, or count a Cardress as less than a man! D'ye ken our slogan, Sandi lass?"

"Nae."

" 'All or Nothing!' 'Tis the Cardress motto."

"Vous ne m'aimerais plus alors?"

"Si! Mais je ne t'aimerais jamais à la dérobée et comme amant coupable!"

"Coupable? *Toi?* Am I not the scarlet one, then?

And who forbids a young man to seek his good fortune where Chance and Fate welcome him, my Captain?"

"I could have used you like any camp-woman, there at Fort Edward. And did not. . . . And will not, even if you were a Queen of France!"

"Mary Blessed," she wailed, "it was for your pleasure, then, and because I love you and can give you nothing better!" A very fury seemed to seize her and she took hold of my shoulders and fairly shook me with her slender arms.

"It was for *you!*" she cried in a voice strangled with tears. "What is it to me, then, who never yet have had a lover and know nothing concerning such matters save only that men go mad if mocked and denied? I love you, too much to mock or deny you!"

"But not enough to be my wife?"

"If I marry you there'll be only a corpse stickit full o' daggers, and a widow to bewail you within the week, John Cardress!"

After a silence our lips joined in a long, deep embrace. Breathless, inarticulate, she rested her burning cheek against mine. Then: "Is this your 'modus vivendi'?" she asked.

"Does it suit you, Sandi?"

"Yes—until another English fleet and army arrive to insult these walls of stone."

"And then?"

"Then," said she, "I may turn Bethulian."

"And what may that be?"

"I may turn into another Judith if you ever attempt to play at Holofernes, John."

"And slay me, Sandi?"

"And then myself. Some doors must be unlocked that way."

"Yours?"

"Ah, no; not the door of love, my Captain. Only—only the dark door of Honour. For heaven's sake, sir, let us leave this dread door locked until a day dawns when we must unlock it! There, I offer you a modus vivendi. Do you take it?"

"Yes."

"Very well, then, I advise you to lay siege to and carry by storm my heart before the English lay siege to this city and end forever all tenderness that ever was between you and me!"

"Then—I begin," said I. "I love you, madame, and offer you marriage."

"Denied, sir, with vain regret. . . . Proceed further, if it pleases you."

"Then—I love you, Sandi."

"Oh. . . . And I, you, sir."

"I will not," said I, "love the Duchess of Boïens *par amour,* if I am not good enough to love her as her husband! Tell that to your damned dukes!"

"But," said she, "you will not be too proud to love poor Sandi, the little mousse, as perfectly as it pleases you—will you, my Captain?"

"You lovely little Jesuit!" said I, under my breath, "I'll teach you that a Cardress is not to be trifled with or summoned by any French Duchess in this manner!"

"What do you mean to do to me, sir—"

"You'll live to learn," said I, taking her so completely into my arms that she said something in a frightened voice that ended in a swift and wordless sigh.

All the night around had turned crimson where they were burning red fire upon the battlements along Rampart Street. And, stirring in my arms where she nestled, high above the bastion, she rested her flushed face against mine and looked down into Convent Street where the nuns were singing in honour of Our Lady of Louisbourg and her victory over the heretic English at Fort William Henry.

Very, very far away beyond the Marais we could hear the wolf-like yelping of the Souriquois dancing their scalp-dance in honour of their own Manito, too, where the ceremony of the Red Roll-Call was in solemn and pathetic progress, picturing the history of the world from the beginning until the coming of the god-like Whites!

CHAPTER XXII

LETTRE-DE-CACHET

IN November the snow flew and all the northern world was shrouded in crystal-beaded cerements of white. Shoreward, grey waters raced dashing and clashing over brittle skins of ice and burst into a million cutting crystals among the shadowy, sagging foliage of black pines.

Seaward, icy vapours writhed, brooded, or drenched the pale and sickly sun till he languished and died in a smothering deluge of flowing fog. And, through it, spectral shapes of icebergs sailed out of grey and empty space into pallid depths, to vanish in a hushed and silvery dusk.

The winter in the fortress-city of Louisbourg was a gay one; and that it was gay, cheerful, and confident was due to the Governor, the Chevalier de Drucour, and his high-minded wife. Brave, honest, devoted, a splendid example of French naval officer, Drucour saw himself tricked and cheated by Bigot in Canada, abandoned and betrayed at home by a courtesan without talent even in her own profession, yet into whose scented hands had slipped the fate of France.

Jane Fish, called the Marquise de Pompadour, was far more worried by the sardonic laughter of Frederick the Great than by the plight of New France, now trembling upon its foundations from Montreal to Louisbourg, before the mighty menace of England.

Now that it is over and I can look back upon that year in Louisbourg, so fraught with approaching peril, so threatened with final disaster, I can appreciate and honour the sturdy, cheery, unshaken courage of the Chevalier Augustin de Drucour, forty years in the King's service, who let the people believe that there was two years' supply of provisions in Louisbourg and ammunition a-plenty with which to endure any siege. But he knew that Bigot and his corrupt politicians had stolen nearly everything which made defense possible; and that the yellow-lipped Versailles harlot never would send him the ships and men required to face the terrific power of Pitt.

Well, none o' this did the gay folk of Louisbourg know, nor did I suspect; yet, knowing England, I knew that the British Lion never would let go his claw-grip on North America; and that meant that France must release her frantic clutch some day. But I knew that the Gallic Cock would go down to death fighting till the end of all.

I had several pretty notes from the Governor's wife, signed Courserac de Drucour, asking me to various entertainments at the Palace—dances, dinners, and, above all, cards—for everybody was forever playing cards in Louisbourg that winter, and that was one of the evils which ruined many—that and the great number of duels fought between officers of different regiments—between officers of Sourlaville's * status, for example, and those who were aristocrats on both sides. It was an ugly business.

There was rivalry and jealousy between the *Gens de l'epée* and the *Gens de la plume;* between army and navy, between naval officers afloat and those serving on shore.

* Le Courtois de Sourlaville was an aristocrat on his mother's side only. He left Louisbourg, 1754.

Regulars and Colonials could not agree, officers from Beauséjour fought duels with Louisbourg officers.

Two Canadian officers named Langis murdered a regular officer, Du Caubet.

All wanted to exchange shots with Prévost, our Commissaire-Ordonnateur, but the Governor trusted him; and his pretty young wife, who had been Marie Carrerot, got him more toleration than did his own manners and behaviour. Father Alexis made a madrigal about him, beginning:

> *"A la paix toujours tranquille,*
> *Prévost donne un sûre asile—"*

But the prevalence of gambling in society was already shaking the morale of the place. It bored me who did not play cards, for I found gaming tables in every parlour and drawing room.

The Chevalier Johnstone felt as I did; often we met while paying our respects to some pretty hostess, and remained only as long as civility required, politely watching the gamblers, male and female, before we took an elaborate leave. Only a dance or dinner or supper, or some healthy outdoor frolic, made those who did not play cards welcome in the gay, amiable, and somewhat dissipated circles and salons which composed society in this strange, walled, fortified, medieval city of Louisbourg.

Meanwhile, my sinister activities remained perfectly unsuspected, and I sent out a weekly report in cipher, which a Souriquois runner, procured for me by Santu, carried to Canso, or, God knows how, relayed to Halifax in all that watery world of tempest and fog and icy gale and sunless weeks of freezing fog.

LETTRE-DE-CACHET

I paid a few Spanish dollars for services that all the millions of the British Crown could not hire me to perform; and how those Souriquois ever succeeded I can not understand, when even a sea-gull could scarce live in those freezing hurricanes out of Labrador, or face the Polar ice grinding and groaning from the Gut of Canso to the Grand Banks.

But, somehow, my reports got through to New York and, thence, to London and to Pitt: information like the following, for example, which, if intercepted, meant a swift and savage death for me:

Take notice! Garrison now here!

Regiment Artois	520	men
Regiment Bourgogne	520	"
Regiment Cambis	680	"
Foreign Legion	680	"
Detached battalions	1,000	"
(Colonial)		
Artillery	120	"
	3,520	"

Also

At Maurepas Gate, West Gate, Princess Bastion, Brouillan Bastion—

Grenadiers	200
Militia	300
Colonials	400
Marine	150
Isle Royale population	5,845
Ballaine	54
Petit Lorembec	289
Scatary	81

Gabarus 37
L'Indienne 48
St. Esprit 123
Port Toulouse 282
Isle Michaux 28
Gabarus 37

From the Gut of Canso to Louisbourg—

3,400 fishermen
500 fishing vessels
60 brigs, schooners

Total Fishermen at Isle Royale fisheries, 5,260.

Gaspé .... 6 ships 360 men
Quadre .... 6 "   360 "
Port au Basque .... 6 "   360 "
Trois Isles .... 3 "   180 "

Morice Vert (Out of France)

554 ships }
27,500 men } Yearly

Artillery still here—

18 mortars
221 cannon

Particulars already sent:

It is suggested that our ships shall fire at the barracks near the Queen's Bastion, which are very combustible.

Officers' quarters and chapel in the King's Bastion should be shelled. Easy to set on fire.

Take notice!

A partizan officer is organizing the Acadians, Canadians,

and Souriquois as Scalping Scouts. About 400 have enlisted.
Take notice!

A raging surf, thick fog, and a gale are to be expected on
this coast at any moment, summer or winter.

There are four places for landing troops:

Fresh Water, four miles west from Louisbourg
Flat Point, two miles west from Louisbourg
White Point, 1 mile west from Louisbourg

Gun emplacements, redoubts, trenches defend these; to be
armed and garrisoned by irregulars and Indians.
Take notice!

There is no possible doubt that Louisbourg is the strongest
fortress in North America. Frost is the great destroyer.
Walls and gates near the King's Dauphin's Bastion have
cracked and scaled off. Great blocks of stone have fallen
into the moat. Fire at such places. The city walls are a
mile and a half in length. The strongest buildings in it, and
which may be armed and defended, are the Chapel, Government House, Convent, Hospital, and the King's Storehouses.

There is a new battery on the crags of Black Point—18
pounders.

Light House Point is now fortified, but poorly, with two
12 pounders and 2 eights.

Ocean, rock, swamp, moorland, and the endless black forests of the Northland form a vast abattis around this huge
citadel called Louisbourg.

Few warships are here, now, but many expected to defend
Gabarus Bay and the waters of Isle Royale.

I hear you say: "Sir, it was a dirty business you did
in Louisbourg in 1758." You are right, madame, it was
dirty. But always in all wars there is dirty business to
do, which *somebody* must perform.

I am sorry I was chosen to do it. I was sorry to deceive kind, friendly people—venerable ladies like Madame de la Perelle and Madame Costebelle; gentlemen like the Marquis Charry des Gouttes, like that hardy Colonial, La Ronde Denys, Chevalier of St. Louis, one of the bravest men I ever knew.

It *had* to be done. It was I who turned up the fatal card; and fear bade me play my hand for every penny it was worth, in hope that I might save my neck.

But most of all I hated to compromise and betray those Camerons and M'Donalds and those other Scots who had supported Bonnie Prince Charlie and were nearly annihilated at Culloden.

Hither these had come to escape hanging in Scotland and England—Cameron men, M'Donalds, the terrible Claymore men who had rushed upon the English with frightful and Gaelic yells and had fallen in countless numbers under British musketry.

Outlawed, imprisoned, hanged, hunted, exiled, such as escaped British vengeance fled to the New World and settled here and in the adjacent islands and mainlands.

Even Flora M'Donald got away and reached the Carolinas to the southward. Here, now, alas, I had to deceive a cousin of that brave Dr. Cameron who had fled Scotland, had been physician in Ogilvie's regiment, and who died at Tyburn in '53.

Charles Follis, Major in the Foreign Legion, and the Chevalier Johnstone I had to cheat and deceive.

My military oath made it my duty to watch these two fine gentlemen so closely that, if the city were besieged and taken, they could not escape British vengeance and a nasty death at Tyburn.

280

But Sandi had put a stop to anything of that sort. There was no slightest chance she would suffer a Follis to hang, even if it meant the death of the man she loved. And I shuddered slightly as I recollected what she had said about self-destruction in the event of being obliged to denounce me. And I did not for one instant doubt this young woman capable of doing both.

Nevertheless, as in duty bound, all that terrific winter in Louisbourg I was planning to deliver the city, as instructed, as soon as a British army appeared; and I watched the changing aspects of the town, daily—its shifting hospital lists, its walls weakened a little here and there by frost and flood, its dwindling stores, the condition of its magazines, the morale of the garrison and of the inhabitants.

And all these statistics went to Pitt by fur-swathed Souriquois runners who were bribed by Santu for a few dollars, to sell out the French, whom they liked, to the English of whom they knew nothing.

But I had made up my mind that official corruption was killing New France and would ultimately do the tragic business that British cannon could merely hasten.

A harlot in Europe had France by the throat; and her yellow vampire lips sucked the very life from the nation.

In the Western World an equally sinister figure had New France by the throat. His name was François Bigot; he was Royal Intendant; he lived in the old brewery on the St. Charles, and he watched the Governor of Canada, the Marquis Vaudreuil, out of one eye, and the wife of Major Péan out of the other.

Always ailing in health, yet always tireless in business

and pleasure, generous, good-natured, he was a born thief and gambler.

He shared twelve millions loot at one stroke.

Péan's wife, his mistress, became the Pompadour of the brilliant little court at Quebec and Montreal, and her husband took for his mistress his partner's wife, a handsome woman who presently was taken from Péan by the fascinating Chevalier de Lévis.

A dissolute knavery ran through civilian life, through official and colonial-military life—but the regulars were not involved. Robbery, bribery, frightful financial corruption centred around Bigot the Intendant, his mistress who had been the beautiful Canadienne, Mademoiselle Desméloizes before she married Major Péan; and Cadet, the thieving Commissary General who made millions by falsifying accounts.

Bigot lost 204,000 francs gambling; and shrugged his shoulders. He and his friends—Varin, Naval Commissary, Maurin, and Martel, the Royal Storekeeper, knew how to replenish empty purses.

Bigot had forty guests to dinner every day for a week. He travelled with his mistress and with a chief steward, chef, under chefs, servants, valets, grooms, half a dozen military officers, and often as many friends, both ladies and gentlemen, for whom he furnished everything.

Others of his creatures made money everywhere—like Marin and Rigaud, brother of the Governor, at Green Bay, who took a thieving profit of nearly half a million at the expense of some starving Indians from whom always at least two-thirds of their allowance was stolen by the cripple Maurin, by the rascal Corporon, by Le Verrier, and by Varin of the Marine Bureau.

All these matters I learned about and reported in my weekly budgets of news because Pitt, with his thousands of paid spies in France, would be certain to make use of such information to the ultimate destruction of the power and glory of France in the Western World where now were kindled the embers of a vaster war which must very soon leap an ocean and engulf all Europe in its flames.

And, all this time, I was wildly enamoured of the little Duchesse de Boïens, and was becoming more desperately in love with her every day.

Not that I saw her every day. Oh, lord, no! I saw her at dances, at dinners, at various frolics where ladies and gentlemen of quality and consequence gathered. I even sat through enervating evenings with a polite smirk on my features, watching her play cards, merely for the sake of being in the same room with her.

But, except for these occasions, and when driving or walking, I never saw the little Duchess any more—never alone except for a few moments at some ball—once at a masquerade where I had her to myself for nearly half an hour—but there was no more opportunity for the liberty which we had enjoyed—and perhaps abused—no chance for conversation unobserved, and none at all for endearments or disputes, or embraces, or quarrels—no, all that was ended very definitely.

For Madame la Duchesse—with a couple of healthy young peasant girls as retainers and a few assorted and loutish habitants to cook, wait on table, and attend her Grace as footman or coachman on occasions where a promenade afoot or in a sleigh was to vary the monotony of social life in Louisbourg—was in residence where the Governor and his lady also dwelt in official pomp and circumstance.

That is to say, that where the new officers' quarters and barracks had been built by the New England soldiery in '48, a new stone wing of Government House extended along the rue de la Flotte, or Fleet Street—which also was a new street in the city, formed out of the alley or mews of the Château by the Yankees when they held the city under Admiral Sir Peter Warren, polite Sir W. Pepperrell, and peevish Shirley.

Here was the little Duchess in residence, having an apartment facing the small square, and flanked by her kinsman's quarters, Major the Honourable Charles Follis on one side, and by the palace of the Governor on the other.

Well, being violently in love, the conditions and restrictions were repugnant to me; for, as the young Duchess so sensibly observed, if I showed the least pretensions of paying serious court to this young lady the Scots in Louisbourg would carve me with their dirks, claymores, and skene-dhus; and the French nobility and colonial gentry, as she remarked, were very likely to cut me into slithereens with their nasty little court swords.

A perfectly maddening prospect to a man extravagantly in love.

I could see her only at such places as, for example, the dinner for forty, given by Charles Follis, where I scarce had a chance to brush her hand with mine; or at the King's Chapel vespers where, at the close, a Te Deum was sung in celebration of the English retreat from

Halifax; on the Esplanade by the Maurepas Gate where there was a bonfire and salute and barbecue.

The Governor's house, with its large gate, had windows looking on the rue Royale and rue de Toulouse, but it was not large enough to accommodate all the distinguished people in town at one time, so Monsieur de Drucour had the army at one dinner, the navy at another, then the clergy, then during the week others who had not yet been bidden to official feasting and good cheer.

It was at such places that I had my only opportunities to see Sandi, to touch her hand with my lips, and to look into her bonnie brown eyes so full of tenderness one minute, so shot with devilry the next.

Now, I don't know how the rumour reached Isle Royale that the Pompadour, learning of the Duchesse de Boïens' flight from Paris, had not only attempted to have her intercepted and fetched back for discipline, but now was despatching an officer of the Crown to hunt her up wherever she might be in New France, and, by virtue of a lettre-de-cachet, fetch her back summarily to reflect upon her enormities in the Bastille.

One never can trace the origin of such rumours, or how they are carried like vapours out across a freezing ocean, over a freezing bay, and into a frozen city when, apparently, no ships and no men are stirring in all this snowy waste of moorland and forest and endless leagues of steel-grey, wind-lashed ocean torn into livid strips of ice and foam.

I was walking along the Street of the Little Birds— in fact, was thinking of Sandi with the raging and amorous impatience of any lover, when, passing me, a little servant maid in starched white bonnet-à-cornet and fluted collarette, gently thrust into my gloved hand a small three-cornered bit of paper.

Back in my lodgings and burning with curiosity, I read the billet from Sandi—

My poor Lover:

Here is a pretty pickle in which I am like to swim, and out of which brine I hope you'll fish me before, in fact, I fall into it at all! Which sounds Irish but is Scottish-French!

Alas, darling, troubles come thick and fast upon me. Travelling in disguise, and very sure that my friend, Jane Fish, meant to stop me and send me as her guest to that fat, four-towered castle of hers in Paris if she could catch me, nevertheless I reached New York—you know *how!*—and, ultimately, Louisbourg, dressed like a camp-wench.

God alone knows how Pompadour has learned of my presence here, but she has and means to display all her cruelty and power by seizing me here and sending me aboard a King's ship to France.

I can neither deny the symmetry of Jane Fish's arm nor its length nor its terrible power, for she can, if she chooses, thrust this same arm across an ocean and make me prisoner here in this freezing fortress of the Northern Seas.

This news was fetched into Louisbourg by some partizans and officers of the Indian Department, who came in with the Micmac and Abenaqui scouts and Acadians last week.

They heard it from the captain of one of Monsieur de Drucour's scout sloops off Halifax, who got it from our spies down from Quebec—*that* Pompadour has a lettre-de-cachet of the King to take me wherever encountered, and fetch me to France aboard one of our ships—either Vauquelin's *Arétheuse* or some ship of the line under some of Des

Goutte's contemptible sea-officers—either Beaussier de l'Isle on the *Entreprenant,* or Marolles on the *Célèbre.*

Now, my poor, adored one, I have just learned that this lettre-de-cachet is on its way here *now!*—some wretched officer of the King's Red Guards or of the Gendarmerie—how the devil should *I* know, darling?—but he's coming with Le Loutre's Indians—Boishébert's Abenaquis and Mission Savages, and the Souriquois.

Darling, I know you have bought some of our Souriquois. Be generous then and use them to stop this terrible Gendarme sent by Pompadour.

For if he comes into Louisbourg nobody can help me any longer, and I must go aboard the first King's ship that sails.

My friend John, you have me at your mercy. I can be of no aid to Charles Follis if this Red Gendarme comes tramping into the presence of our Governor with a sack full of warrants!

Will you interpret your orders generously and stop this marplot out of Paris and give me a chance to fight you loyally for the honour and safety of my kinsman?

Or, will you choose to take a pedant's view—the narrow interpretation of a martinet—and leave me to look after myself, my honour, and my kinsman?

SANDI.

This reply I sent back to her by her little maid who loitered at my threshold:

Anything that has to do with police or gendarmes or with hangmen is utterly disgusting to me. And, as for Jane Fish's gendarme, I have taken a dislike to him and shall see to it that neither he nor his documents annoy anybody in Louisbourg.

For heaven's sake, is there *no* way I can see you alone even for a moment?

To which I had this:

My iron balcony sags dangerously. Masons have a ladder there to repair the stones forced out by frost.
Does that convey any idea to you, my friend?

CHAPTER XXIII

FIRELIGHT

LEARNING first of all that a scout was going out, I, in order to avert all suspicion, went straight to Gautier, the coureur-de-bois, and volunteered to accompany him and help to destroy the new buildings in Halifax if he and his Indians really could get that far. He laughed and said that he was going only to scout out toward that port and Canso and Lunenburg, with some Souriquois trackers who were looking for English Indians to scalp for the bounty.

So, on snow-shoes, I and three Souriquois went out with Gautier and his own Indians. And the second day left them; and, being joined by Santu, proceeded until we ran across the northern party we had heard about, and its escort, moving slowly overland from Quebec to Isle Royale.

I had with me three young rapscallions—all full blood Souriquois—whom Santu had bought for me, soul and body, and who were wholly in my service. With me, in her caribou cape, came Santu herself.

When we caught a glimpse of the men composing the escort, who were nothing more than a dozen honest farmers picked up in Acadie by this emissary of Pompadour, we all laughed very heartily as we unslung our rifles.

They exchanged a long-range shot or two with me and my Souriquois, then ran for their lives, leaving the nearly exhausted gentleman from Versailles all alone on the snowy plain, and so petrified with terror that he had no power to run after them. Besides, he was very fat, and never before had been on snow-shoes or seen an Indian.

I kept my pointed fur hood well down over my face as I came up to him; and I demanded his name and business in a disguised growl that seemed to frighten him terribly, which I did not intend to do.

All he could stammer and babble and repeat, while that little imp, Santu, and her Souriquois beaux, were turning his clothing inside out to search him, was to stammer incessantly like a parrot, "—De par le Roi! De par le Roi! Pour l'amour de dieu, Messieurs les Peaux Rouges, ne m'enleve pas mes pauvre cheveux—"

"Stop your silly noise," said I, taking the papers, warrants, documents with seals, and the Royal harlot's lettre-de-cachet from the poor trembling sbire, "—nobody is going to scalp you if you conduct like a gentleman. What is your name, if you please?"

In his terror he forgot his own name and quality for a while, but finally remembered it in a flood of tears.

I read the documents he carried, gave back all except the lettre-de-cachet and a few other papers bearing upon Sandi's case.

I said in the Souriquois dialect to Santu: "Get this cowardly fellow to the coast; signal the first English fisherman out of Canso, and send this gentleman and his papers a prisoner to the English commander at Halifax."

"Will they cut his throat there?" inquired the girl, smilingly.

"No, they'll treat him well."

"Won't they take his scalp at all?" she demanded in dismay.

"No, you little devil of a savage. Come, then; take him to the coast under guard of your young friends here, and when you return I shall have your Spanish milled dollars all ready for you."

"Tok!" said the girl with a shrug; "I do it for you and not for your Spanish dollars, my pretty witch-captain!"

She came up to me like a young bear in her furs, pulled our hoods together, kissed me passionately under their cover, then, laughing, stooped and made a snow-ball and hurled it at me, crying:

"Vlan! Attrap, donc!"

In another instant the three Souriquois, Santu, and I were indulging in a lively snow-ball battle while the Red Gendarme, his eyes fairly starting out of his apoplectic face, gazed wildly, incredulously, upon what, no doubt, he considered to be the behaviour of five lunatics out of hell's own depths.

"Allons, donc!" cried Santu to him, "we, also, are good fellows, Monsieur le Gendarme Rouge! All the agreeable people don't live in France, you know! Come! Cheer up! A little good will, now! Come, make a snow-ball and throw it at me!"

He had no heart for it. The girl, in all the beauty of her disordered hair, fluttering with furs and brilliant thrums, danced about in the snow, her mittens on her hips, out of sheer joy of health and youth.

As she danced she smiled cordially upon the prisoner,

and began to sing a barrack song disrespectful to King
Louis XV, and sometimes heard in Louisbourg:

> *"Our King a-fishing went in vain,*
> *He caught no fish with hook or seine,*
> *And drove home in a dudgeon;*
> *But when the fish fished for the King,*
> *He bit the bait like anything,*
> *And Jane Fish caught a gudgeon!"*

The moon came up and for all the world it seemed as
though the dead white expanse we travelled was the burnt
out barrens of the moon itself, so ghastly, deadly blank
and glittering and still.

The great silvery wolves' hunting cry broke the sound-
less horror of it all. We saw them far on the plain, leaping like freezing and furry demons around a fighting
caribou.

We ran in on them, knives in hand, disdaining a shot,
and slashed and kicked and bruised them with hatchet
and knife, and with such hearty fury that they cringed
and skulked and slunk away, all flecked with snow and
foam and blood. So we slew the fighting, panting bull
for our own kettle, while starving wolves, gathered from
everywhere, squatted and howled protest to the moon-
witch, Atensi, who plays her tricks upon wolf and Souriquois alike.

Our prisoner, the Red Gendarme officer, or Pompadour's
Pimp, as Santu amiably named him, finding that nobody
tried to tear his scalp off, ventured to lick his thick lips
and sniff earnestly at our smoking kettle, although every
time a wolf howled he blanched and took hold of Santu's
mink-tails or scarlet thrums.

We were warm enough in our brush hut by a huge fire, and I don't know why our prisoner shivered so, for I told him plainly he would come to no harm from us, and that the English had more food than we had in Louisbourg and would treat him kindly.

His name was Gobineau—the Sieur Jessel Gobineau. He had been an under-jailor in the Bastille, a sergeant of Red Gendarmes, and now, he admitted fearfully, he served the King and Chamilly in the Parc-aux-cerfs and betrayed them both to Pompadour, with whose particular and intimate occasions he seemed to be shamefully acquainted.

"And for whom was that lettre-de-cachet?" I demanded.

He gave me a timid yet cunning look and shrugged his fat shoulders.

"The Duchess de Boïens is not in Louisbourg, you know," said I, looking him in his sly, grey eyes.

He said he was sure of that. We both knew that the other was lying.

"Well," said I, "that being agreed upon, what is your budget of news out of France, Monsieur Gobineau?"

Fright made him truthful and very voluble.

He said that a French fleet would sail very soon to aid in the defense of Louisbourg. It seemed to give him satisfaction to tell us this. Naturally he took me and my Souriquois for English partizans, and was even more right than he dreamed of being.

He said, further, that Pitt was furious over the failure of Lord Loudon to take Louisbourg—that our Flying Dutchman of a Scotchman, Holburne, had lost several ships by wind and tide and devil's weather; that Pitt already was gathering a great fleet under an Admiral named Boscawen, to attack Louisbourg in the coming spring, and a great English army under a brand new Major General who had been a Colonel until within a few weeks—one Jeffrey Amherst.

He mentioned particulars; he boldly stated numbers, items, details, dates; named individuals.

This powerful expeditionary force was further to be officered by three brigadiers—Whitemore, Wolf, and Lawrence; and was destined to besiege and storm the fortress-city of Louisbourg.

He was a great glutton, this Monsieur Gobineau, and I think even an Indian could not eat more than did he the next morning.

Santu and I had another snow-ball fight which made the Souriquois roar with laughter; then Santu, in excess of spirits, chased a red fox on her snow-shoes—a game the fox also seemed to enjoy, for he would stop every little while, roll over in the snow, and wait for Santu; then, jumping up and uncurling his big, fluffy brush, he would glide away again over the snow with a cunning glance at the girl behind him, as though to say, "Come on, pretty friend, pluck the three magic hairs out of my beautiful tail, and the world is yours!"

I bade adieu to Monsieur Gobineau, gave Santu her instructions, cautioned my three Souriquois, White Bird, Laughs-at-Night, and Three Legs; and, taking what I needed of the caribou meat, slung my rifle and set out alone toward Louisbourg and in the general direction of some stunted evergreens where I knew deer yarded in winter.

I was glad to learn of the expedition under Colonel

Amherst—or rather, Major General Amherst. I was content to hear of this Admiral Boscawen, too. And, thinking of my poor, peppery General Lord Loudon, I could almost read again the painful letter which he had predicted almost word for word that Pitt would send him—

My Lord,
 I am with concern to acquaint your Lordship that the King has judged proper that your Lordship should return to England—

Fourteen thousand troops—and mostly regulars! The thought excited me. If Pitt does that, then North America never will be French, I thought to myself.

Twenty-three great ships of the line! And Hardy to be second in command!

A vast concentration of arms, provisions, munitions; of soldiers, sailors, and ships at Halifax in March, so that the siege might begin in April!

Good Lord! this energy was very different from the careless sloth that made last year's disasters possible—the ignorance that once had caused the massacre of Braddock, and the many other disgraces since, to both British and Colonial arms.

Now, God willing, a fight to a finish was close at hand; and, French for all time or English forever; America must abide by the result!

Three days later I sauntered into Louisbourg, carrying my rifle and as much venison as I could lug—which sufficiently explained my extra-mural activities to the Gate Guard.

Replying to idle questions concerning the rumoured despatch of any messenger from Versailles, I merely asked with much innocence whether any such had arrived.

No, said everybody in disgust; and added that it must have been only a false rumour. After all, they argued, why should the kindly King or his douce amie, Jane Fish, send any warrants or lettres-de-cachet into his Majesty's brave and loyal and merry fortress-city of Louisbourg?

"Yes, why, indeed?" said I naïvely.

I saw the Duchess de Boïens that same evening. She wore cloth of silver and vermilion, and was playing cards at a grand party given by Madame Laforest. She looked up with a cool smile to receive my compliments when I came to wait upon her. It was then that I began to realize the absolute courage of this young girl.

My eyes told her that all was well. I told her so with my lips, also, when I found a moment to speak without being overheard.

"I have their damned warrant," said I. "It's meant for you, without doubt, and Jane Fish had it executed."

"Bring it," said she, smilingly, "when you come to kiss my hand and receive my grateful thanks."

"What is that you say?" said I, bewildered. "Where am I to come to you, in God's name!"

"The ladder still stands up against the house, where they are fixing my balcony, darling," said she with a seraphic smile—a smile to win straight into Paradise without absolution.

There was music and dancing, also. I danced with Nanon Benoist, and she was a sweet, innocent girl, and so was her little comrade, Josette Vallée, the artillery Captain's daughter, who also had all the loveliness, charm, and spirit of everything that is best in France and Canada.

Madame du Portail, with whom I took wine, talked scandal very wittily; Madame du Vivier de Vanne told me about poor Montalembert's suicide, he being driven crazy by his wife's affair with an officer in the Regiment Bourgogne.

"That is the trouble," said Dupont de Gourville, "she preferred that same officer when Montalembert married her. He should have felt his horns even then pricking through his scalp!"

There was a certain sameness about our banquets in Louisbourg, fish being staple and an endless tune with myriad changes played upon the dishes made from spoils of the sea.

Well, Louisbourg had been built to protect and to secure for France the most valuable fisheries in the world, so why complain if fish usually formed the pièce-de-résistance at all Louisbourg banquets.

However, there was plenty of shell-fish, too; plenty of game—fur and feather both—and, this year, enough flour and dried fruit and vegetables which, last year, had nearly failed, and the want of which had almost caused famine, misery, disease, and death. Also, there was abundance of every kind of wine, liqueur, and spirits; and even Paris was no better supplied than Louisbourg.

So our gaiety was very solidly founded, gastronomically speaking.

There was no moonlight; heavy clouds obscured the night-sky; an icy fog rolled in from the sea and smeared every wall, tower, ledge, and grim façade with glare ice.

Vaguely, paley red in the ghostly smother, the battle lanterns burned on every bastion; torches flickered in their sockets by city gates, barracks, and along the fortress battlements; a few lanterns glimmered high on stone walls fouled with rust.

The rungs of the ladder which led to Sandi's balcony were covered with ice, and I expected to slip and break my neck—and would rather have done so than miss the chance of seeing this young girl—my violent passion for her making me almost ill at times.

On the iron balcony, which now had been firmly triced up, I slid about, groping for something to hold while I ventured to knock upon the dark panes of glass. However, the casement had already begun to open.

There was no light in the chamber excepting a lovely, rosy glow from logs burning in the big fireplace of stone.

The young Duchess still wore her beautiful cloth of silver gown with its sprays of pale green leaves and vermilion buds.

She took my hand and led me to the fireplace where was a chaise longue buried in white furs. Here we were seated presently and in silence, while she, by the firelight, studied the ominous lettre-de-cachet which I had brought to her.

"Oh, fie," said she in her lovely, guarded voice, "how ugly is all this affair! Would you credit it, Monsieur, that because I refused to figure as demoiselle d'atours to anybody named Pompadour, and because I laughed at what the King of Prussia said about her, and at the very indecent verses he wrote, that this very common woman, who has France by the throat, should threaten me with her cursed Bastille—even reach out and attempt to clutch me here—claw me out of the New World back into the Old!—hell-rake me out o' Louisbourg and into Paris and the Bastille!"

"Monarchs," said I, "seem often quite as mean as their mistresses. Look at dumpy German George and his spite which sends me here to keep his hangman busy at Tyburn! Is there anything meaner than a man who can't forgive bravery in his enemy?"

"Oh, Lord," said she, "this is a sorry world and topsy turvy, where a Jane Fish bullies a de Boïens and a vulgar Hanover German would hang the heirs to Annandale and Whinnloch!"

She looked up at me in the firelight, held out the lettre-de-cachet. I took it, and the other papers, and laid them on the coals where they burned black, then a pulsating scarlet, and then fell to pieces in grey-white flakes.

"That ends that business," said I.

"For the present."

I nodded: "And that's the point I mean to discuss with you, Madame—"

"Oui, Monsieur!"

"Very well, Madame—"

"Madame be hanged," said she; "you don't seem to be in love with me any more!"

"You know better—"

"Oh. Then why am I not Sandi any more?"

"Sandi—"

"Yes, my Captain Jean—John—Jock—"

"Will you be serious a moment?"

"God knows. . . . Why did you flirt with Madame du Portail at the dance tonight?"

I ignored the accusation. "I suppose," said I, "that you never could learn to love me enough to send the world to the devil and marry me."

"Holy Virgin," said she, "what do you mean then? People don't marry for *love!*"

"They ought to—"

"But they never do, darling. Love has nothing to do with marriage. Else, how is it that in France and England—and everywhere else, I fancy—married women have lovers and married men mistresses?"

"That is seldom true in our American colonies, Madame."

"What? You tell me people in America—in New York, in Virginia, in Maryland, in Massachusetts Bay, fling prudence, economy, thrift, rank, race, aside and marry just because they love?" She began to laugh.

"I tell you that, Madame la Duchesse," said I stiffly, "and it is almost universally true."

"God save us," said she, "may a prince, then, marry a pretty beggar in your Utopian colonies?"

"There are no princes among us. And, excepting those sent to govern us, we have practically no resident nobility or gentry in the American Colonies of England."

She stared: "Are there then among you no questions of rank, of breeding, of position, of precedence?"

"Plenty, Madame. We lack titles but otherwise seem quite as virulent as any among English or Continental aristocracy. Nevertheless, we do usually marry for love."

"Oh. And so no woman need take a lover and no man a doxy—"

"I don't say that. Both happen. I am not trying to analyze love for you or even identify and classify the passion. I merely have the honour to make a few polite representations to you regarding marriage as it obtains in North America."

"Oh, darling, you speak so jerkily and stiffly—are you offended?"

"No—"

"But, darling, *don't* be! . . . I can't marry you, darling, but you are lord and master of my very tender heart —and that is a risky affair for a girl, but—"

She turned where she was seated beside me, placed her hands on my shoulder, and laid her cheek upon her hands.

"What do you mean to do?" said I, kissing her, "—marry some rickety old peer or some poxed and impotent young prince?"

"Lord," said she, "I hope the King will select a healthy one, at least—"

"Probably," said I, "there aren't any in France—"

"Oh, yes there are," she retorted, laughing, "—and gallant, witty, and handsome, too! . . . It seems strange," she added, "that I could not find it in me to be pleased by one of these, but must go blundering into the arms of my first lover as soon as ever I laid eyes on you—"

She looked up in that blind way of hers, sustaining my ardent gaze, enduring, then welcoming my lips and drawing me toward her with impulsive arms.

"Jock Cardress," says she, "would ye steal the heart out o' my breast and the bird from its very nest?"

"I shan't let you go, Sandi!"

"You mean you won't let go my heart, darling. No, you couldn't even drive it away from you. But, whichever way this war will be turning—and whichever way this coming battle goes, God help us, you and I must say good-bye and part."

"I'll not say it then."

"What! You mean to follow me to France?"

"I do not, by God!—and never shall beg and plead and growl, and never, *never* shall sneak and loiter about to take what your husband leaves—"

"Hang it!" says she, very red, and growing hotter and redder as she spoke, "what does it matter to you when there's no love in a marriage the King of France commands of me! . . . And I'll have you to know that in France marriage is marriage and is accomplished for sensible and substantial reasons; and that love has no part in it at all—"

She caught my hand, gave me a strange, passionate look, and kissed it:

"—Love is love," she said in a husky, breathless voice, "—and all I have of love to give is for you alone if you wish it, John Cardress—"

"You offer everything?"

"Everything."

"And knowing that if you ever marry I shall no longer love you?"

"What's that you tell me?" she cried. "My God, how many times am I to repeat to you that marriage has nothing to do with love and that no matter whom I marry I always, always, everlastingly shall be in love with you, and give you all that love can give—always, always —to you alone!"

After a silence: "Sandi," said I, "if ever—after you were completely mine—any enterprising gentleman of the French peerage attempted to marry with you, I'd take him by his princely nose and lay him by his noble heels!"

She began to cry, silently, the tears glimmering along the curve of her flushed cheeks—seeming to weep in a kind of exasperation because I appeared to be so totally a fool.

"Nevertheless," said I, "that is what will happen to any legitimate spouse of yours if through your stubborn obstinacy you and I merely love par amour!"

She told me with a sob what Charles Follis would do to me. But I'd heard that before.

"I only wish," said I, "that you were somewhere where I could get my hands firmly on you."

"W-where do you mean? V-violence, d-darling?"

"Yes, if I had you in New York, or New England, you'd never get back to your Duchy! You'd go back to the Mohawk with me and take up a great tract of wild land to develop it, alongside the tracts of Sir William Johnson, Sir Peter Warren, and the Duchess of Gordon. I'd not care what your lascivious King had to say about it, or what my own vulgar German-born monarch might say; I'd marry you and we'd love in spite of marriage, and I tell you, Madame, the children born of such a union would more nearly resemble angels than humans! Now, you don't like that, do you, Madame la Duchesse de Boïens!"

She said nothing, but she had stopped weeping, and seemed to be considering the situation and what I had just said.

"That is an impossible thing you propose," said she, sniffing and swabbing her eyes with a laced handkerchief. "Am I to lose my Duchy of Boïens merely to marry you, when I can love you just as well without losing it?"

303

She wept a little more.

"Am I to throw away my heritage of Astarac and my Armagnac property in Gascony? My château of Armançon-sur-Yonne, and my Ardennes forests of Hercynienne?" she demanded in a fresh flood of tears and all flushed with reproachful indignation.

"No," said I angrily, "you may keep your damned Duchy and all your petty wood-lots and back-country settlements, instead of having a hundred thousand acres on the Mohawk. Also, you may marry your nasty, rickety, leering peer of France as soon as you choose and become reconciled to your foolish King and his female friend, Jane Fish—"

"Oh, heaven," she smiled, "he treats me with cruel sarcasms, who love him to distraction—"

"Will you stop your noise!" said I, "or do you want your servants to discover me here so that I shall have to fight Major Follis—"

"Mother of God," she whimpered, "if you kill him then I am utterly done for!"

"What is he to you more than a kinsman?" I demanded. "After all, I begin to believe that you came out here to warn him because you were, and are, in love with him!"

"I came," she retorted furiously, "because your miserable King of England wished to hang a gallant Scottish gentleman who, one day, please God, will be Lord Whinnloch. . . . And who," she added defiantly, "has been chosen by the King of France—*to be my husband!*"

Well, there it was—suddenly—and all of a fury!—the cat out of the bag! A wildcat, too. And now I understood at last why this young girl, le diable au corps, had come out of France, risking everything, to warn Charles Follis, her kinsman, that the King of England meant to hang the man whom the King of France had selected to marry the Duchess de Boïens, and so to join the Whinnloch estates to Boïens and erect out of both a French dukedom linking one of the most important Scottish peerages and estates to the peerage of France forever!

"So that is why you came," I repeated in a cold rage.

"Yes, sir; that is why. My King desires this marriage. Pompadour wishes to mate me to the half-witted Duc de Somport—Canfranc. It was she who bargained with Pitt and a vindictive German King to have my kinsman hanged! That is the real reason she desires to shut me up in her cursed Bastille—so she can get at Charles Follis and force me into Somport's arms! But I have made up my mind that no man of my race ever shall be hanged like a thief at Tyburn; and I have sworn to marry the Whinnloch dukedom to my own Duchy of Boïens, in spite of Jane Fish and of all the lettres-de-cachet on earth! And I'm going to do it!"

Her dark eyes were blazing and so were her cheeks. She sprang to her feet in the firelight, menacing me with outstretched finger:

"If you won't love me, Jock Cardress, and be my lover and my true-love forever," said she, "then amen, and suit yourself! But there's one thing you'll never make me do, and that is add a hangman's slip-knot to the Whinnloch coat of arms! And so I say to you in all kindness—stay here and welcome while you do no harm! But if the English come and the city falls, *then* I shall speak! And it will be your life for the life of Charles

Follis and for the life of Lord Annandale's son, and it's a flag for them or the gallows for you!

"And, by God, sir," she flamed, "if I loved you so that I died of the passion, I'd see you dead at my feet before I'd foul my family's name to save you!"

We stood in silence for a while, confronting each other in the wavering firelight. Then I bowed to her with perfect politeness, turned and opened the icy casement, closed it noiselessly, flung one leg over the iron rail of the balcony, searching for the ladder.

The toe of my boot touched something which I supposed was the icy rung of the ladder, and I set the other foot beside it and let go the balcony.

It was not the ladder; it was an icicle which splintered under me, and I fell heavily down, down into darkness.

CHAPTER XXIV

GYR-FALCON

I WAS still confused in my battered brain when, one day, I awoke conscious, and heard military music—which I believe was the band of the Regiment Bourgogne playing for guard-mount on the plaza at the Dauphin Gate.

They were playing that jolly air so popular in Louisbourg:

> *"Saint Crispin made a pair o' shoes*
> *To fit the Lord Almighty,*
> *Who said they did not suit his views*
> *But pinched his toes too tightly;*
> *'I'll never pay your bill,' says he,*
> *Fiddle-de-dee!*
> *Fiddle-de-dee!*
> *Instead of paying you your price*
> *I'll kick you out of Paradise!'"*

Gaily the cymbals, fifes, and clarions rang out; joyously sounded the horns and drums and hautbois to the lively, galloping tempo.

I opened one eye and saw a glazed window brilliant with sunshine, and, through it, a bit of pale blue sky full of little white clouds sailing eastward, and sea-gulls soaring.

The military music soon wearied me and I fell asleep.

307

The next time I became conscious I heard the bells of Louisbourg ringing.

It was a grey day outside; no wind, and seemed to be quite warm, I thought, because the window was partly open, and on the ledge was a thin bar of melting snow.

Lying motionless, and now fully awake, I took a feeble look about me, and noticed a seated nun reading in her breviary and holding the book up close to her near-sighted eyes in the dull light.

I couldn't tell what the bells were ringing out—certainly not the Angelus—nor could I recognize what particular peal of bells was sounding their mellow golden musical sequences—ding-dang-dong! Ding-dang-dong! Clin-clin-clan! Clinkty-clinclin-clang! Cling-clang-clong! Clong! Clong!

It tired me.

The sun was in my eyes again when again I unclosed them.

I was all bandaged, and my body itched and was hot, but not feverish.

Turning my gaze sideways I could see two nuns measuring and pouring liquids from flasks into cup and tumblers.

From the streets came the familiar sound of movement, clatter and clang of traffic, the voices and bustle and coming and going of humble folk upon their simple occasions; cries of fishermen and rattle of spars and cordage from the basin.

That arrested my attention and gave me a definite idea: the ice and snow must have gone; the water seemed to be open. *Where had I been since last winter?*

Not that day, nor the next, but nearly a week later I learned that it was April. A nun, Sister Rose Aline, told me after the doctor had examined me, taken off some plasters and splints and bandages, and the sisters had washed me.

"Yes, indeed, my Captain," said Sister Rose Aline cheerily, "you have been coasting along the shore of Death for many, many days and weeks. Do you have any recollection of how you came to be in so terrible a plight?"

I had used what brain remained; I could remember being on that iron balcony outside Sandi's window. But that was the last I could recollect. However, it made me cautious.

"It is believed," said the nun, busy with her bandages and lint, "that, in the darkness and freezing fog, you walked under a ladder which fell on you."

"That," said I with an attempt to smile, "is what one deserves who walks under ladders!" And I thought to myself that this same damned ladder must have given way with me when I attempted to descend from the bed-chamber of the little Duchess de Boïens.

"I suppose," said I, with weak humour, "I didn't break my neck?"

"No; you fractured only your left arm, left leg, three ribs and shoulder-blade," said the nun smilingly, "—which," she added, "gave you a pleurisy, a flux, a concussion, a shock, strangulation of both lungs, and a cut on your head which we sewed up with thirteen stitches."

She made me swallow a dose of black stuff, very bitter, which nearly turned my stomach inside out like a purse, and made me angry.

"Hang it! How long is this to go on, Sister?" I gasped.

"What a temper!" said the pretty nun. "Well, then, cheer up and have plenty of courage, my poor Captain, for they say you're merely lazy now, and they are not going to keep you in the Hospital here in idleness and luxury any longer."

So I was in the King's Hospital, then!

"Next week," said she, "they mean to send you to your own lodgings."

"That's better," said I. "And how about those bandages that torment me by making me itch, Sister?"

"Oh, we have removed most of your splints. You may use crutches very soon, now. Have patience a little longer, Monsieur: you have been, so far, very well behaved, even when delirious."

"Delirious?" I repeated in alarm. "What extravagances did I commit when in my frenzy, Sister? What did I do and say, if you please?"

Said she: "You talked continually about a lettre-de-cachet which you desired for an English General called Webb, whom you wished to clap into the Bastille."

"Is—is that all, Sister?"

"All anybody could understand. You talked, otherwise, only in a barbarous tongue which somebody said was the language of the Souriquois. Santu! Santu! Santu! That was the burden of your feverish babble. And if you know what that means it's more than I do."

"What month is it?" I asked fearfully.

"April, of course."

"Is it really and truly the month of April, Sister?" I asked incredulously.

"It is, God be thanked," said she.

"Is the ice and snow quite gone then?"

"Mercy, no! You don't know Isle Royale! Many of the lakes are still frozen. There's snow in the woods and on all northern slopes; and will be into late May. But it's gone from the marais and the coast; and the streams are free and all a-roaring, now, bank-high and full of slush and ice."

I ventured this much more: "Is all well with Louisbourg, Sister?"

"Yes," said she tranquilly, "so far—" she crossed herself—"all gratitude to our Lady of Louisbourg!"

"No enemy ships?"

"None, sir. But some of ours have arrived."

"What news do they fetch us?"

"Oh, a plenty o' that, my poor Captain. To hear the talk in the shops and streets one would believe that the entire army and navy of wicked old England are on the way to blot Louisbourg from the face of the earth!"

I dared not question her further concerning this. Nor could I risk a question at all regarding Sandi. The Duchess de Boïens was not supposed to be anything to me, nor I—a poor volunteer without commission—to her.

That I had been discovered all smashed to pieces under her windows, with a ladder lying across me, evidently had not aroused the slightest concern or suspicion regarding this lovely young Duchess herself, nor seemed to have connected my plight with her at all.

There remained, therefore, nothing for me to do except to continue to lie flat on my back and await some notice from her. But, as I remembered the painful circumstances of our last encounter, and her parting words to me a few seconds before I fell from her balcony, I lost all expectation of ever again being noticed by this violent young lady who had, practically, told me to go to the devil.

When it became known in town that I was convalescent, a number of friends and acquaintances did me the honour to call on me, or send polite messages with some little trifle —usually in the nature of food, or something to read, such as a batch of last year's English newspapers fetched in by recently arrived French warships; one or two copies of the New York *Mercury,* and some French novels and romances.

Friendly people, they were, who came to see me abed and all patched up, or stumping about my chamber on crutches.

Dupont de Gourville came with kind inquiries and an orange—worth its weight in gold in the ice-bound city! Du Vivier de Vanne and his lady and Nanon Benoist; De la Vallière; Madame du Portail with Josette Vallée came bringing gaiety and little gifts and gossip.

Even the careworn Governor and Madame de Drucour came to the hospital for a pleasant word, and to leave a bottle of very old Burgundy for me.

But neither Charles Follis nor the Chevalier Johnstone came, nor sent any message.

Nor did the Duchess de Boïens.

I could understand why Sandi did not come. Even had she been more kindly disposed, she had not dared show enough interest in me to make a hospital visit seem reasonable.

Sister Mary of the Thorns, in recounting to me the names of those who had made inquiries during the days of danger and unconsciousness never mentioned the name of the Duchess de Boïens; and I dared not ask her in case she had forgotten.

As I say, I could, perhaps, understand her silence; but it concerned and alarmed me that neither Major Follis nor the Chevalier had taken any notice of my condition.

Certainly this conduct on their part would seem callous and heartless—even insulting—unless their suspicions in some manner or other had been aroused—either suspicion concerning my being found under Sandi's windows, or suspicion due to some rumour or discovery regarding my true character and the real reason that I had come to Louisbourg.

Sister Rose Aline told me that, during my illness, an Indian had called at the hospital office very frequently to ask news of me, and had fetched caribou meat, out of which he recommended that they make broth for me.

This touched me; and I could not doubt that it was one of my Souriquois spies sent to me by Santu who dared not start gossip by appearing in person.

During an interval of calm blue weather—rare always on Isle Royale and particularly during early spring—I was carried to my own lodgings.

And I must say this for the honesty of the habitants and garrison—not the slightest object had been disturbed in my rooms which my servant had kept clean; my strongbox, in which was my money belt, stood untampered with; everything remained exactly as I had left it when I left my apartment to play Romeo on an icy ladder to an icier

Juliette who had explained that while she liked me enough to be my mistress I really couldn't expect her to love me sufficiently to marry me!

I was trying to recollect the name of the silly, spindle-legged whippet who had been selected for her to marry by that ramshackle, disgusting old bellwether, Louis XV, King of France; and I was standing in my chamber, leaning upon my crutches, while the rare, pale sunshine fell in a broad stripe across me and the bare floor with a faint and delicate warmth, when, chancing to glance around, I noticed that my chamber door was opening very slowly and silently.

Curious to see who was doing it, I fixed my eyes upon the widening aperture, which presently disclosed Santu in her pointed capuchin, and all fluttering in a shower of fringes and twice belted like every Souriquois girl.

Resting on my crutches I ventured to hold out both hands to her a little way, and she gave me a joyous look, came noiselessly on tip-toe, and, coiling about me very tenderly, behaved as passionately as she dared.

"What news?" I whispered, motioning her to close the door.

When she came back I had found a chair and she curled up cross-legged at my feet; and long pent-up words flowed from her in a torrent unrestrained.

It seemed that when she had heard of my accident she had instantly destroyed every slightest evidence which could possibly have involved me or her or my three runners.

As the days passed, and I seemed to grow no better, she had sent word of this to Halifax by White Bird, explaining the situation and saying that the hospital nuns did not believe I could get well.

"Then, my white sorcerer," she whispered, rising lithely to her little moccasined feet, "there came a day when I went to inquire at the hospital, and they told me that the doctors thought you were dying.

"I was very sad," said she, "and covered my face with my hood and went away with my head hanging.

"And while I was walking upon my snow-shoes along the marais where a wild storm lashed the coast, O, my white witch-captain, the sun for an instant suddenly pierced the grey sky and the flying snow, and up there, battling wildly against the gale, I saw a white gyr-falcon from the uttermost icy pole.

"The howling hurricane and sheeted snow were driving him out to sea to die; his powerful, snow-white wings beat back toward shore.

"For a long while I was in doubt; then the great bird, high in the air, won his death-fight against the tempest, and I saw it sheer down into the black spruces and clutch them, panting, exhausted, but safe!

"Then my heart leaped, for it was a sign; the white gyr-falcon was *you!* I knew it! I slept very peacefully. And when next day I came to the hospital a nun told me that you lay drenched in sweat and that your fever at last had broken!"

"Santu," said I, "do you believe that there is any suspicion among any of the people in Louisbourg concerning what I am about in the city?"

She did not think so.

"I wonder," said I, "why Major Follis never has been

to see me or to make any inquiry. Or the Chevalier, either."

She knew nothing about that. She had, she said with a mischievous smile, one or two friends in the Foreign Regiment, and would make cautious inquiries.

"Was there any news of an English fleet and army?"

The whole town was talking about it, but that was all she knew.

Then she took passionate leave of me and danced away on brilliant moccasins—a whirlwind of scarlet thrums and of flashing teeth and beads and hair.

CHAPTER XXV

THE BEGINNING OF THE END

WHILE I was too ill even to get about on crutches, the first of the French warships arrived—*The Prudent*, 64 guns, Captain the Marquis des Gouttes, and I heard her batteries saluting the Citadel, and the nuns informed me what the noise was all about. *The Prudent* had been chased in and her consort taken, it appeared.

On March 28th, Beaussier's squadron arrived amid thunderous demonstrations from the Citadel and from the flagship, *L'Entreprenant*, 74, and a 64 gun ship, *Le Bienfaisant*, Captain Courserac. These two shook the city with their saluting cannon; but the other three ships—*Le Capricieux*, De Tourville's ship; *La Célèbre*, 64, Captain de Marolle; and *La Comète*, 74, commanded by Lorgeril, were *en flute*, which means serving as transports and store-ships; and in these came provisions for the siege that so surely was close at hand. Also a battalion of the Foreign Legion, under Lieutenant Colonel d'Anthonay, arrived aboard the ships. This officer ranked Charles Follis, senior Major, and therefore was now in command of the foreign corps. Which I knew would enrage the Scots.

On the 31st of March the *Magnifique* arrived and became involved in the drift ice off White Cape and was caught there as in a floating trap—a sickly and stricken man-o'-war where more than a hundred sailor men sickened and died of cold and disease aboard her where she

317

swung in the fog, an unclean and cursed thing under piti-
less and freezing skies.

I was well enough, now, to try my crutches. Santu
aided me. The Duchess de Boïens never came near me.

During April the *Apollo* arrived on the 15th and *Le
Chèvre* on the 24th; in May arrived several merchant
vessels and *La Fidèle,* frigate; and the frigates *Bizarre*
and *Aréthuse*—the *Bizarre en flute.*

All these made the city secure as far as provisions were
concerned. But I did not believe their Admiral was very
clever or enterprising.

Always I was getting stronger; and now began to feel
pretty well, being able to use crutches very easily to get
about indoors, but on account of the cold and ice dared
not attempt to go down into the freezing streets or mount
the slippery ramparts, though Santu offered to aid me.

I did not know why Charles Follis continued to ignore
me, but was aware that there must have been some grave
reason, and feared that my being discovered under Sandi's
windows might have aroused his suspicions. For if my
activities as a spy had really been discovered I had long
since been sent to the donjons in the Citadel. Besides,
Santu, as I say, visited me freely; and, had I been under
military suspicion, this Indian girl long ago would have
been arrested.

As for Sandi, not a sign from her.

April is a winter month in Louisbourg; so is the greater
part of May.

In April the Brothers of the Hospital told me that
Sir Charles Hardy, with the *Northumberland,* 74; *Terrible,* 74; *Summerset,* 70; *Orford,* 70; and the *Defense,*

Captain, Kingston, Southerland—all ships of the line—
and one frigate, were cruising off Louisbourg and had
taken several French provision ships and a French frigate,
the *Diana,* loaded with uniforms, arms, and provisions.
Also, they assured me that a British fleet had been seen
by our scouting Indians and Rangers to the eastward of
Halifax Harbour, and was supposed to be Admiral Boscawen with the main British armada.

On the 8th of May we had a terrific snowstorm lasting
thirty-six hours, and making Louisbourg look like mid-
winter again. The floating ice, it seemed, had so troubled
Sir Charles Hardy's ships that none o' them came near
enough Louisbourg to be seen.

Every day, however, the Souriquois and Rangers and
Acadians brought news of more British ships arriving at
Halifax, warships and transports by scores. But that
source of information soon failed me.

Santu came to tell me the latest gossip, that their priest,
the Abbé Maillard, Missionary to the Souriquois of Isle
Royale, had decided to retire to the mainland and take
with him all his Indians.

I couldn't believe it, never dreaming that Drucour would
permit it, but the Abbé got away with his flock, leaving
only Santu and the White Bird, who refused to go; and
Drucour, who was to lose some good scouts among the
loyal Indians who left, could not stop them or persuade
the Abbé to remain. For this priest, having talked with
a fisherman who had seen the vast English fleet at sea off
Cape Sambro, believed that the city was surely lost.

It was a huge fleet—one hundred and eighty sail carrying fourteen thousand seamen and thirteen thousand sol-

diers, all standing for Isle Royale under a light wind, their miles and miles of snowy-clouded sails turning rose and gold in the rays of the setting sun.

To hear it, a little rejoiced my heart, which was very sore, and sickening for the wayward jade I loved.

On Thursday, the first day of June, I ventured to go outdoors on my crutches, feeling strong and well, and desiring to accustom my legs to exercise as soon as might be. Santu helped me.

The sunshine was warm; wild birds twittered and sang; I saw some golden yellow wild flowers in the marais.

On the rampart promenade, limping and stumping along like an old peg-leg soldier, I met an officer of the Regiment Cambis, whom I knew a little. He told me that of the three British brigadiers under Amherst, James Wolf was the one to be most feared.

"A surly devil, and all dead below his brain!" said he; "—a strange, long-legged, chinless fellow, red-headed, with pasty pig-face, and sour tempered from a perpetual bellyache. His is not a generous character; nothing suits him.

"God knows why soldiers like him, but they do. Yet, one of our secret agents heard him tell the Captain of the *Princess Amelia* that the American Ranger battalions are made up of vulgar ruffians, and that Americans in general are the dirtiest, most contemptible, and most cowardly of dogs.

"He said that the Americans deserted by battalions, officers and all. And he speaks quite as roughly of his own British regulars, saying to his officers that he believes no nation ever has paid so many bad soldiers at so high a rate as does England. But he speaks well of the Highlanders."

I didn't believe this story at the time. Yet, it was quite true; and General Wolf did say and write these things—and it showed that the French military intelligence system was pretty good to report it so accurately.

I learned, further, that Wolf landed at Halifax on May 8th; and that on the 28th, a fair wind blowing at night, the Admiral signalled to unmoor at daylight; and by eight o'clock the entire fleet had weighed and sailed, the *Namur* leading, in which both the Admiral and Amherst were—the *Dublin* having fetched in the General from the sea off that new port of Lunenburg.

Well, the city of Louisbourg was fearfully nervous and expectant, now. All day the stony streets echoed with drum and fife and bugle, and the clank of artillery.

Limping along the ramparts on my crutches, I could see and hear the noisy activities where batteries were being erected at White Cape and Point Plate in the west, and near the lighthouse and the Lorembecs to the eastward.

I saw the garrisons of Port Toulouse and Port Dauphin march in on the 7th of May; and, after that, Acadian irregulars and Indians came in nearly every day.

The larger French ships lay on a bowline between the Royal Battery and the Bastion de la Grave, and those, lately *en flute,* were mounting their guns.

And I nearly perished with the desire to laugh when, under the noses of the French ships and the rampart cannon, a saucy English frigate came into Gabarus Bay, sent out her boats, and took soundings, lying the night at anchor two gunshots out of range off Pointe Blanche.

Why no French ship attacked her I don't know to this day. But I tell you it thrilled me—this defiance that Old England flung at New France so flippantly—and though I am a Scot by origin and an American Colonial by birth, I felt a pride that warms me still every time I think of it.

On Friday, June 2nd, about four o'clock in the afternoon, where I was sitting on the ramparts with Santu, the artillerymen in the Citadel fired three alarm shots.

For a few moments every sound in the city ceased and the silence of death itself reigned over all. Then such an uproar arose as I never before had heard, shouting, yells, screams, clatter of carriages and carts, drums and fifes beating to arms in every barracks and on every bastion and redoubt, bells pealing, the marching music of Cambis, the street echoing to the racket of their tread; the marching field-music of Bourgogne, gallop of horses, clatter and rush of light artillery; and the enormous waves of sound from streets and squares and battlements packed with excited people all crowding to some point of vantage.

For the English fleet was in sight at last, sailing slowly into Gabarus Bay under a light wind, and coming to an anchor southwest of Coromandière Cove—and off a lee shore, if I could believe my eyes—the great battleships of England in two lines, *The Prince of Orange, Namur, Bedford, Nottingham, Sutherland,* in the inshore line; the *Princess Frederick, Princess Amelia, York, Burford,* in the second line, and the *Lancaster* astern.

Thousands of people in Louisbourg could see them; and Amherst and the Admiral and thousands of British sailors and soldiers staring across the bay between Flat Point and White Cape could see the slender spires and

322

great walls of Louisbourg to the northeast, all brilliant in the westering sun.

And I for one was terribly afraid to see our ships at anchor on that treacherous lee shore, for with a clever Admiral or Captain to lead them, and the prevailing fogs and east winds to conceal and aid them, the French ships could have run into the bay where the English ships at anchor were crowded not two miles off a lee shore, and destroyed them every one!

A little wind rose, suddenly covering the bay with white-caps, and a haze covered the sea.

Good God, I thought, what is this British Admiral thinking of to so expose his fleet with a French battle-fleet ready, and wind and mist favouring?

The city walls were now crowded where men, women, and children thronged to see the English in Gabarus Bay. The little wind had become heavier; foam fringed cove and cape.

Very soon the French batteries at White Point began to fire, covering themselves with smoke; and we could see the line of English frigates dragging shoreward under a stiffening wind that already was blowing half a gale. But very soon it died out; fog came and hid the English ships. Through it a phantom sun made a pale white spot, and the cannon boomed and boomed with a mournful and muffled rhythm like the erratic thumping of base drums underground.

Through the foggy city the Regiment Artois was marching without music, filling the streets with the shuffling roar of its worn boots.

Making my way to my lodgings by instinct more than by sight, I saw, in the fog, awful demon faces where painted Abenaquis and Micmacs, hideously bedaubed and stinking of rancid oil, were creeping out across the marais after scalps.

The heavy fog lasted. Strange sounds of hammering and sawing came to us on the ramparts where carpenters were busy aboard the British ships. I don't know what they were doing.

Every day I took my crutches and went up onto the ramparts—usually with Santu—but could see nothing for the fog. God only knows why the French did not take advantage and why the English fleet did not suffer the greatest naval disaster in the maritime history of England!

On Sunday, June 4th, at dawn, there was little wind and a thick haze. We could hear and sometimes see the British frigates, *Kennington* and *Halifax,* firing.

At five o'clock the wind freshened and it grew foggy. By eight it was blowing a gale; and, with a glass, I could see our ships getting down their topgallant yards, and, later, striking yards and topmasts.

The batteries ashore were firing; and two of our English frigates, in trouble, were towed into deep water by our ships' boats.

My God, thought I, here is like to be the finish of our English fleet and army, and the end of English power in North America!

But God was kinder than were my thoughts regarding this British Admiral floundering like a beached whale in Gabarus Bay.

The sight of the English fleet was, of course, no surprise to Louisbourg which, long before, had had news of it; and now this entire matter concerning North America, and which people, English or French, should rule it for all time, was coming to a head; and the battle to decide it would surely be fought here in this grey-blue bay surrounded by rocks, surf, shoals, ledges, black woods, and sandy crescent beaches.

Here, where a little trout brook—beloved of Charles Follis—runs into the bay, was the only practical landing place for an invading army. Above it a small watch tower rose.

This was l'Anse à la Coromandière, split by a rocky headland and flanked by lovely sandy beaches.

Here ran the French trenches armed with cannon.

I saw Santu on Sunday, but she said that no canoe could live in that gale and that White Bird could carry no warning to the English ships.

Monday was foggy and calm; and Santu took a letter to White Bird who went off with it. My news was as follows:

Eleven companies of Cambis had arrived at Miré, and the other six were aboard French ships already clear of Port Dauphin.

White Bird could not get into touch with Wolf's outposts, and all of the Regiment Cambis marched safely into Louisbourg unharmed.

With a terrific racket of fifes and drums the Foreign Legion, under Colonel d'Anthony, marched past under my very windows, headed for the trenches at White Cape; Artois marched from Coromandière; Bourgogne for Flat

Cape. The thunder of drums were deafening in the narrow, stony streets—three thousand men, counting irregulars, scouts, and Indians.

It was quite evident to me that Amherst meant to attack all these places where his frigates could slip in very close to cover the landing with a terrific fire—Whitmore's regiments to attack White Cape, then swerve toward Lawrence's regiments and the Grenadiers under Wolf, who were ordered to take the intrenchments in Fresh Water Cove near a trout brook which runs into the sea near Flat Point.

I was much excited over the prospect. I rose very early on Tuesday, took my crutches, and hobbled out to the ramparts. A southwest wind, calm sea, and fog, turned to heavy rain, wind, and great swelling seas; and I knew that no boats could land troops in such weather.

On Wednesday, the 7th, the weather was clear but the surges too rough. A ship threatened the lighthouse but it was only a feint. She was the *Juno,* frigate, and some transports carrying Bragg's regiment.

I could scarcely eat or sleep for my excitement. All day and all night we could hear the thudding of the French guns five miles to the southwest of Louisbourg, where the coast artillery and eight inch mortar were firing on the English troop-ships and frigates.

On Thursday, the 8th of June, the surf was less heavy.

Before dawn, in my dark bed I heard our frigates firing on the French shore batteries.

As day broke, from the crowded ramparts of the city I saw some four hundred boats pulling between the British ships and headed shoreward.

It had come at last! A deep groan went up from the

city walls loaded with humanity. Thousands of frightened eyes were fastened on those boats all rowing straight for Coromandière where husbands, sons, sweethearts of these poor women were intrenched.

There came a terrible flash, a sheet of fire, a deep thunder, the reverberations continuing like the detonations of a tumbling surf, shaking the bedded rocks of the great fortress.

Another flare and fiery glare from the French batteries at White Cape.

Then we saw those boats full of English and Provincial soldiers and Highlanders drive into the surf; saw the red-coats leap overboard and wade shoreward, led by their officers.

In my mind and heart I knew that it was the beginning of the end of France in North America.

CHAPTER XXVI

HONOUR

THAT night, as I sat all alone in my lodgings, eating a crust and drinking a glass of claret—the only food I had been able to swallow in my excitement—my mind continually reverted to that terrific little battle there on the coast.

Once again, in my mind's eye, I saw the red-coats, wearing their knapsacks and carrying their muskets, thrashing ashore waist deep in the surging, boiling surf, some falling under shot and shell, others crushed to death between the tossing boats, others, still, knocked over by heavy waves and drowned among the weed and rocks; yet, the masses of them still pushing on doggedly, like the John Bulls they were, driving Marin's men into the city and forcing the troops of St. Jullien to scatter and run like rabbits—Indians, Canadians, Acadians, all breaking into wild, disorderly flight toward the sheltering walls of Louisbourg beyond.

And I saw the Foreign Legion which had held White Point until ordered into town, march sullenly and in good order, through the Dauphin Gate, their mounted officers scowling down at the throngs of anxious, frightened people in the squares and streets.

While I was eating, the good-looking young Carrerot, *Ensigne en second,* came in to show me a list of the British regiments which had landed, and he accepted a glass of wine while I read the stirring record. They were:

The 1st, Royals (2nd battalion)
The 15th, Amherst's
The 17th, Forbes'
The 22nd, Whitmore's
The 28th, Bragg's
The 35th, Otway's
The 40th, Hopson's
The 45th, Warburton's
The 47th, Lascelle's
The 48th, Webb's
The 58th, Anstruther's
The 60th, Monckton's (2nd battalion)
The 60th, Lawrence's (2nd battalion)
The 78th, Frazer's (2nd battalion)

With them landed 500 of those same American Rangers upon whose characters Wolf had voided his spittle, which, with the artillery, and men of other corps, made a total of more than 13,000 fighting men now on land and possessed of the French batteries and emplacements outside and to the southwest of Louisbourg.

Already they were laying out their intrenched camp; three block houses and redans on the west, one to the north, one on the Miré Road, protected the camp from French Indians and irregulars; three more on the other side—instantly marked out and begun—were ominous of future siege batteries.

For Louisbourg could be attacked both by land and by sea. But the latter attack could not be pushed until both the French fleet and the formidable Island Battery were destroyed.

I talked a little with the handsome young Ensign, but dared not even make the most guarded inquiry concerning

Sandi, although I was miserable at not hearing from her and deeply worried as to the reason. All that I could hope and pray for was that my visit to her apartments by ladder had not been discovered by anybody who could make trouble for her.

Well, my young and dissipated Ensign went gaily away—having first borrowed some money to pay gambling obligations, which really was why he had favoured me with a visit—and I, not being disposed to sleep, sat down by the empty fireplace, my crutches beside me, listening to the noises in the turbulent streets where a tremendous excitement still reigned and where now they were bringing in the wretched wounded and forlorn dead from the foggy moorland to the westward behind White Point.

I heard women talking on the landing outside my door, and heard them say that the British had caught, killed, and scalped a sachem of the Abenaquis, and that all the Algonquin Indians on Isle Royale were preparing to condole and mourn his death.

Then a woman in the street below screamed; a babel of voices filled the hallway; the women outside ran downstairs, and I heard one of them say: "It's her only son!"

I hoped that Santu would come in and tell me about it; and, even as I thought of her, somebody knocked very cautiously at my door; and, in a low voice, I bade whoever knocked to enter.

Sandi came in. The little Duchess wore a great grey cloak with a hood to it; and I did not know her until she stripped back the hood with desperate white hands and came and knelt down beside me with a great sob, burying her face upon my knees.

I did not know what to say. She sobbed and sobbed, violently but in almost utter silence, each spasm and access of dumb grief merely wracking and tormenting her body while she clutched my knees the closer.

When, at length, she was somewhat more composed and had regained her voice and could control it, she rose up on her knees and laid her wet cheek against mine, whimpering like a hurt bird.

"John Cardress—John Cardress," she wailed under her breath, "you'll never know what terror was mine because of you—what grief and dread—"

"Was my visit to your chamber discovered?"

"Oh, my God, yes! Oh, darling, you left a portfolio full of papers and a handkerchief; and, oh, heaven!—your anger so blinded you that you went away leaving your gloves and your hat!"

"How greatly have I damaged you, Sandi?" I asked quietly.

"Darling—I heard your fall, and near died where I stood, knowing what must have happened. Then I ran downstairs—and there you lay—oh, John!—your body all twisted and broken, and the ladder lying across you—" She choked.

"Yes; tell me, Sandi!"

"I called out for help; and when people came from Major Follis's apartment which, you know, is next to mine, they found me struggling to lift the heavy red ladder from your body—"

"Yes. What then, dearest?"

"Oh, I didn't know that there were any evidences of you remaining in my chamber, and when the Brothers of the Hospital took you away on a stretcher I ran upstairs to put on furs so that I could go with Major Follis to the hospital and learn what the doctors had to say.

"Then it was that Charles Follis found every evidence of your having been with me in my chamber. . . . Had you been out of danger of a kinsman's anger I would not have denied it. No! I would have avowed it. Yes! I would have told Charles Follis that I loved you and was glad I did love you!"

She pressed her body closer to me and put up both arms, resting her head against her linked hands on my shoulder:

"But I lied. I denied it. I hoped you were not dead or dying and that my family's anger would not pursue you after your recovery. Do you understand, now?"

"Yes."

"Well, it was useless to deny that we had been together and that you had fallen from my balcony when leaving me.

"So I, being driven into a corner, I said yes, I did love you; and if I chose to love you it was nobody's business but yours and mine.

"And, John, my poor friend, at that they kept me in my own apartment, and they went to Drucour and raised heaven and earth, clamoring for a ship to send me somewhere into the nearest Spanish possessions at St. Augustine in Florida, where neither you nor Pompadour nor the King of England could get at me."

"Who wished to do that?" I demanded.

"Charles Follis! Can you believe it? I stormed and raged to no purpose, demanding that he keep his barbarous hands off this affair and asking him how he found enough impudence to presume to manage the business of a Duchess and peeress of France!

"It did no good, darling. He and the Chevalier have kept me practically a prisoner ever since—for of course no ship could get out of this port; and the Governor had other use for his ships, anyway, as he drily but politely informed Major Follis.

"I could not bribe anybody to carry a word to you— or even get near enough to anybody to bribe 'em. Only when in society, at cards or tea or supping at the Château, or elsewhere, could I learn that you were still alive and likely to recover of that frightful fall—"

She pressed my body between her arms, making pitying and crooning sounds, as women do to reassure a hurt or frightened child.

"Oh, oh," she said, "I came because the Foreign Regiment went out to fight, and, for the first time, I find myself unguarded by these damned kinsmen of mine—"

"Really," interrupted a bantering voice from the threshold where the door suddenly swung wide open, "—really, Duchess, your damned kinsmen must be very remiss in their duties to allow you access to your Yankee paramour."

Sandi's arms were around me where she was kneeling beside my chair; and now, looking up in amazement, we saw Charles Follis standing there in the candle light, his graceful, muscular figure framed by the doorway, and his right hand buried in the basket-hilt of a naked claymore which he clutched, and the broad blade all stained with blackish blood.

He said, "I ought to kill you *now,* Captain Cardress! I ought to throw this young rake of a Duchess aside and go over and slit your throat for the treacherous seducer that you are. But I'll do no murder on you, Cardress!"

333

His uniform was all torn and stained by the stress of battle; there were two bullet-holes in his gilt-edged cocked hat which he took off, now, and, taking a few steps forward, bowed to his kinswoman, the little Duchess de Boïens.

"Madame," said he, "if you do not come with me instantly, and take your guilty arms from this young man's neck and free you of his embrace, I swear to you, Madame, as God's Mother hears me say it, I will take this shameless lover of yours by the collar and run him through the body with my claymore!"

Sandi, her eyes dark with fear—not for herself—sprang to her feet and went toward him.

"What are you talking about in your wanton wickedness and cruelty, my cousin?" said she. "Here is no matter of seduction—"

"Madame," he interrupted violently, "I shall not discuss the matter here! Will you be pleased to draw on your hood and clasp your cloak and take the arm I lend you as far as your lodgings!"

Sandi gave me a terror-stricken look.

"Will you be good enough to hasten, Madame?" cried Follis, almost beside himself with rage.

"No," said she, "I'll take my time." And, turning to me: "Duchess or no Duchess, and whatever I may be, I love you, John Cardress, who loved me when you thought me only a ragged slut and maybe a soldier's wench!

"But though it was love you would not have married me. I can not marry you, even if I would. And with me, also, it is love. Therefore, let this end everything between us. . . . And may"—she dissolved into bitter

334

tears, "—may God have mercy on our souls," she sobbed, "for the spirit dies a thousand times where the body dies but once—"

So infuriated was I that I caught up my crutches and, hobbling to the table, took up one of my pistols. It was primed and loaded, and now I cocked it and glared at Charles Follis who gave me a look of hatred and contempt and shrugged his shoulders.

He was right. Such murder was impossible for me to perpetrate. I said, "Sandi, go with your kinsman, and let him return to discuss this matter with me, soberly, if he be a gentleman. There is far more to be said between him and me than what already has been said and done so rashly. . . . Major Follis, may I have the honour to expect your return, sir?"

His eye gleamed with an understanding which my request had not aroused in Sandi.

"Yes, sir," said Major Follis, "you have a right to expect a further and sober explanation which, you very rightly point out, is proper between two gentlemen of quality and sense who have differed."

I bowed. Sandi gave me a bewildered but hopeful look; then she and Charles Follis went out. And I sat down by the empty hearth to await what could not be avoided.

I think I had been seated there about half an hour when I heard spurs and boot-heels resounding on the stairs; and, after knocking, the Chevalier Johnstone stepped into the room, giving me a sharp look, then bowed very aloofly, his gold-banded officer's hat in his gloved hand.

"Sir," said he, seating himself upon a bench which I had indicated, "there seems to be some confusion in the mind of Major Follis concerning which of you is the aggrieved party in this unfortunate misunderstanding—"

"I care not a tinker's damn—or his slut, either—" said I, "how you choose to arrange it. All I know is that I'm on crutches and can't fight with rapier or claymore. That must have been evident to Major Follis."

"Major Follis," said the Chevalier coldly, "waives formality and begs to leave the choice to you, sir."

"I'll not have it!" said I angrily. "I'll not accept. Let Major Follis choose! And," I added in rising passion, "if he really must have claymore play, then he shall have it while I can stand on one crutch!"

"No, sir," said the Chevalier gloomily, "my principal chooses dragoon pistols and thirty paces—if your courtesy permits him this choice. . . . Have you a friend to whom you can refer me—"

"I have not! Formality does not interest me, sir. I am persuaded that Major Follis and his friends do not wish to play me foul. Very well, then; find your medical gentleman, your seconds, your witnesses, and in God's name hasten and let us finish this affair before the English batteries finish us in the morning."

"Have you a choice of place, Captain Cardress?"

"None. The Miré Road is safe from interruption, I suppose."

There had, already, been three duels this week between quarrelsome officers on the edge of the Miré.

The Chevalier Johnstone rose: "Sir," said he, "you are, I understand, a son of a gentleman of Loch Cardress in Cardresshire, the late Colonel Cardress; and, further, you are nephew to my Lord Scaur, of that same family, whose seat, Quilting Castle, is in Cardresshire?"

"Yes," said I, "I am all that—if it be any comfort to the Honourable Charles Follis and the Lairds o' Loch Whinnloch, and all that moss-trooping, ragged-tailed company which ran at Culloden!"

The Chevalier turned pale with rage.

"Sir," said he, "if Major Follis misses you, I pray God that I shall not."

"Pray away, sir. If you hit me you'll hit an American and no ragged rump of the Scottish nobility or landed gentry! And if any of your breek-less friends want a shot at me, why, sir, it is a pleasant way to pass a dull hour or so. And my only regret, Chevalier, is that I may not take a shot at the heartless gentleman who ran like a rabbit and left Flora M'Donald to shift for hersel'!"

White with passion, the Chevalier Johnstone strove to speak; but what I said to him about Bonnie Prince Charlie left him inarticulate.

He contrived to bow; so did I. Then he went away, his claymore and spurs clashing and clanking at every step.

As for me, I realized I had better prepare a document or two before daylight, for I might have all the Argyle Campbells and Lochiel Camerons on my back if Charles Follis and the Chevalier missed me.

So, mending a pen, I seated myself at my table, drew a sheet of paper toward me, and wrote:

In case I fall, I leave everything of which I die possessed to Gayette Alessandine d'Auvray, Duchess de Boïens, because I have no immediate family, and because my kinsmen in Scotland are sufficiently well to do already.

I have 25,000 acres of land in the Sacandaga Patent and on that River; some of it cleared and very fertile along the flats; the rest wild forest of oak, beech, hemlock, hickory, and white pine.

I have a nice house of logs beyond Fish House, Sir William Johnson's shooting lodge under Maxon Hill.

I have, with my Albany bankers, about £1,000 hard cash, and as much more invested. My bankers are Van Steenwyck and Cornelius.

My Solicitor is Arent van Ruyven.

My evidence is the Van Courtlandt Patroon and Colonel Philip Schuyler. I want no damned New England Puritan to whine a burial service over me. Get it done briefly and make an end!

My hand and seal,

JOHN CARDRESS.

I sent for my physician, Doctor Sevier, and for two Brothers of the Hospital, to witness my signature and append their own, with a little wax.

It did not astonish them. Many folk were making their wills in Louisbourg that foggy night, and within sinister sound of the English pick-axes and shovels where the British engineers continued busy with preliminary steps of the siege of Louisbourg.

CHAPTER XXVII

ARROWS

THE bombardment awoke me in my bed. My servant fetched bread and milk. I commanded a chair and bearers for sunrise.

I was some little time shaving, bathing, and dressing; being lame on the left; but managed finally.

Enough light now came from the east, so I snuffed my candle and sat down in the sickly grey light to await events.

Presently comes a pretty gentleman to me, one Duplessis, Ensign, who smiled delightedly, and was not averse, apparently, to help the barbarous Scots exterminate one another.

Followed him one de Villeray, Ensign, very fussy and a stickler for form and circumstance. It made no difference to me, and I left the business to him.

I asked their pardon for travelling by chair when they were a-horse, but they understood, of course.

When we came in view of the Miré I saw the Chevalier, some other scowling Scots, and Charles Follis, waiting.

God knows how many times everybody bowed to everybody else. I did not look at Follis after the first salute to him, nor at anybody in particular.

The ground was covered with violets and some butterflies, pure white in colour, fluttered in the grasses.

Birds sang in spite of the bang of English cannon from two frigates close in shore.

339

Well, as there were no words to withdraw—for the offense was not capable of such settlement, our seconds wasted no time in trying—or in pretending to try—to patch up matters.

Those horse-pistols looked huge to me. A ball from one was like to disembowel.

As I stood on my two crutches, waiting, I noticed a hooded figure come out of the woods just to my right. As this young person wore a war-belt with a hatchet, and as there was no other girdle under the breasts, I took the intruder for a Souriquois adolescent in his fluttering fringes and capote.

Then the young Indian came quickly toward me, pulling aside the caribou hood; and I saw it was Santu.

"What do you do, my white Captain?" she said. "Is this to be another of those strange games where one and often both perish at the one-two-three?"

"Send that Indian girl away!" cried Duplessis, crossly; but I told him I had use for her who should witness this business and make proper report in a certain quarter.

As nobody seemed averse—and as the affair already was irregular enough, considering the type and bore of pistols to be employed, I had my way; and I motioned Santu to stand back and be very careful not to interfere or display any excitement which might destroy the equanimity and aim of the gentlemen involved.

My second, Duplessis, said to me in French, as he handed me my pistol: "He means to kill you, my Captain. Try to be the first to fire."

Then, for the first time since saluting him, I looked upon Charles Follis, and he upon me. There was death in his gaze.

Duplessis took my right crutch from under my arm, leaving me standing and leaning upon the left crutch, my pistol hanging in my right fist.

While we were being properly instructed, I glanced sideways at Santu and smiled faintly.

Then, being warned, the counting began; and, at the word, I lifted my weapon and took a careful squint at the left knee-cap of my adversary.

Before I could fire, bang! and down I went, my left crutch cut in two, and my own pistol exploding in mid-air.

I was hurt a little, my broken left leg having doubled under me; but it was not again broken. However, I was as mad as a dogged lynx in a tree, where I lay sprawling on my broken crutch which Charles Follis had shot in two.

"Give me that other crutch to lean on," said I to my seconds, "and I'll try to be a little quicker next time."

"I'll not fire again at a cripple," said Follis. "Wait till the gentleman is able to stand on his own legs."

I was becoming excited. I desired to lame this man but not to kill him, having, as I have said, other orders concerning him.

I told Duplessis that I insisted on another shot; Follis petulantly refused, but took fire when I told him aloud what a contempt I had for the marksmanship of a man who aimed at my heart and hit my crutch.

"Very well," said he passionately, "if this insolent Colonial gentleman wishes me to blow his head off, I'll accommodate him!"

There was some disputing; pistols were examined, loaded again with every ceremony.

I said to myself: "I'll hit him under the knee, which will keep him quiet until Mr. Amherst catches him."

For I had that in mind, to let General Amherst do the King of England's dirty work on Charles Follis while I gave him and the Chevalier a harmless quietus apiece. It was behaving less like Hanover's hangman, anyway.

I heard the usual admonition being given; the counting began; I saw my adversary's pistol lifted. Then, before I could fire and cripple him, and before he could murder me, I saw his pistol jerk up, fly out of his hand— saw that hand squirt out bright blood where a scarlet-feathered arrow had transfixed it.

"God-damn it!" shouted Charles Follis, "some cursed Indian has plumped an arrow through my pistol-hand!"

We looked around us, stupefied. Nothing stirred in the encircling woods; there was no sound excepting the river's mellow voice and a White-throat fluting on a distant balsam tip.

"Where is that Indian girl of yours?" demanded the Chevalier, striding over to me. I looked around me.

Santu had disappeared.

"That teaches me!" shouted Charles Follis in a fury. "That's what comes of letting one's Indian mistress hang around when serious business is going on! . . . Here— break off that arrow and pull it through! Break off nock and feathers and the barbed head, I tell you!"

While they were doing this, he streaming with blood, and the doctor, horrified. trying to stanch the vivid hemorrhage which was spattering Mr. Follis and his friends and the grass, I said to Duplessis: "Pray ask this gentleman whether he has any slightest suspicion that I was a party to such an outrage."

He went over and spoke to Follis who roared a reply, in pain and anger, to the effect that he had no reason to suspect me, but that, as soon as they had dressed and bandaged his hand, he'd exchange shots with me again.

"No," said I, "you can't aim with your hand bandaged. Besides, you're a poor enough shot without such a handicap."

He gave me a raging look: "I'll use my left hand, then!" he insisted.

"No," said I, "it isn't fair. But if the Chevalier would like to take up the matter—"

"Sir," said Johnstone, "you both honour and pleasure me, Captain Cardress. I am entirely and politely at your service."

With that I bade Duplessis arrange for an exchange of shots between the Chevalier Johnstone and myself; and, having finally succeeded in doing so, and our pistols having been handed to us, the Chevalier took a long aim at me, and I at him; and the next instant a red-feathered arrow hit his trigger-finger and nearly tore it off, and his weapon exploded, the big bullet blowing a hole in the brim and crown of my cocked hat.

I *could* have fired and killed him. I would have been within my rights since he had fired upon me.

But I was so shocked at what Santu had done, lying hid in the thickets somewhere across the river, that I flung my pistol on the grass with a gesture of disgust and despair.

"I don't know what devil out of hell possesses that Indian girl," said I. "I never dreamed of any such outrage when she came out of the forest across the Miré.

Gentlemen, I hope you all hold me quite guiltless of this business."

Johnstone was in great pain, yet he managed to laugh, too.

"Good heavens, Cardress," said he, "you seem to have inspired a very reckless passion in young ladies when they fill your adversaries full of arrows."

I told him I was very, very sorry. I placed myself at his disposal and at that of Major Follis.

"Well," said Dr. Sevier, "neither of you gentlemen will be able to do yourselves justice with a pistol or a rapier for several weeks to come."

He, not knowing what was my quarrel with Follis, asked, en bon enfant, if there could be no accommodation and a jolly handshake à l'Anglais; and very soon saw by the glare which Follis turned on him that no reconciliation was possible.

Well, there was nothing more to do about it at present. No use trying to chase Santu out of the thickets of the Miré; no use doing anything more. And, although I offered to exchange shots with the seconds of both Major Follis and the Chevalier, these young gentlemen refused with grimaces, saying that a man on one crutch was no fair game, and that, if he was, all they'd get would be an arrow for their pains.

Duplessis aiding me, I got into my chair; somebody whistled for the bearers who came looking rather wildly about as though expecting to see a holocaust.

So, with the boom-boom of cannon from the British frigates shaking the Miré, this strange party took up its way toward Louisbourg. And, though we could see our Indians and coureurs-de-bois between us and the coast, nevertheless, I deem the entire episode a crazy one, and am still amazed that the rangers and Indians of Mr. Jeffrey Amherst did not catch, tomahawk, and scalp us every one, on the Miré that misty morning in June, 1758.

CHAPTER XXVIII

FALLING WALLS

I STUCK to the ramparts, partly because I had hurt my left leg when Charles Follis shot the crutch in two upon which I was leaning, partly because I hoped to encounter the little Duchess de Boïens there and have at least one last word with her. For I had an idea that she might be sent by Follis aboard some one of the ships in Louisbourg harbour, which were awaiting an opportunity to slip out of the port and stand for the open sea in hopes of escape.

As for Charles Follis and the Chevalier, they had no way of getting at me to shoot me legally until their wounded hands were sufficiently healed to hold pistols.

I saw them going glumly about their business in the barracks of the Foreign Regiment which presently took the field again under its Colonel d'Anthonay and its two sulky Scots with their bandaged hands. I use the expression "take the field," but the field over which the Foreign Regiment was to make the summer campaign of 1758 was extremely limited in area. The Foreign Regiment merely marched out with its music playing proudly, and took solemn possession of some slight and feeble works on the Miré Road, facing Mr. Wolf's command. Which made that cadaverous young man with the preposterous and pasty profile show his teeth in a nasty laugh; and his light guns went into action almost immediately.

346

The Lighthouse battery replied.

Through a good glass I saw and recognized two old acquaintances, McKellar and Bastide, the English engineers. Then I saw Williamson, the bland Chief of Artillery, ride out toward the Citadel, the large guns of which were slowly and majestically firing upon Wolf; and I thought to myself that the bull-dog jaws of Britain already were closing upon this great, splendid fortress-city of stone; and I wondered whether bull-dog teeth or granite walls would last the longest.

One night there came to my room Requin, a Sergeant in the Foreign Regiment—I don't know what was his nationality, but think he was an Eurasian and came from Pondicherry.

At any rate, he was one of the treacherous fellows in my pay.

I was just going to bed when he came up to my landing and knocked; and when I admitted him he told me he had decided to desert and take as many men as he could.

"Do you wish to go with us, Captain?" he inquired.

"I can't," I said.

He then told me that the morale of some of the French battalions already had begun to crack, and asked me if I knew what had happened south of the Miré.

I hadn't heard.

"Well," said he, "the Grand Battery has been deserted by the French and the Lighthouse Battery has been destroyed by Wolf's gunners."

I didn't believe him. But it proved to be true; and a terrible mistake for the French to make, the abandonment of the Grand Battery.

As for Requin, the dirty lemon-coloured scoundrel, he kept his word and took four men with him on the 10th to Wolf's lines.

He was a real wolf, that Wolf with his bellyache and face of a drowned pig: he marched instantly, a regiment of Rangers acting as advance guard, followed by his grenadiers and light troops from Otway's, Warburton's, Lascelles', and Hopson's commands; and he pounced upon the Grand Battery and the Lighthouse, shoved aside the spiked guns, ran his own into the embrasures, and cannonaded the Island Battery when it opened on him next morning.

I heard the devilish din in my bed, and hobbled to the window to see vast tornadoes of smoke whirling up to the northeast and the fog aflame where the hidden Island Battery thundered its rage at sight of red-coats below the Lighthouse.

All that day the cannonade continued and all Louisbourg was looking on from the walls where they could see the shells bursting in General Wolf's intrenchments. But the sly, fierce wolf-beast couldn't be routed out. He was there to stay, and merely snarled and dug himself in the deeper, showing a double row of teeth to Louisbourg.

Now, lying in bed after having bathed my leg with a strong embrocation, and rubbed it, I could see out of my eastern window the red glare of bursting bombs where Wolf still crouched and showed his fangs to the French ships in Louisbourg harbour.

At five o'clock next morning, limping along the fortified way adjoining the Governor's house, I saw a young officer of Cambis, whom I knew, and who had been slightly wounded. He told me that a council was then being held in the Governor's house, consisting of all the high officers of the garrison, the ships, and the forts; and that Des Gouttes, the Commodore, was demanding of Drucour permission to take his ships out of the port before Wolf's guns knocked them to splinters or the British Admiral sailed into the harbour and destroyed him.

I looked across at the sombre house which, in the grey and dripping fog of morning, was all lighted up behind its mist-smeared windows where the shadowy silhouettes of officers passed and repassed.

As I stood there I saw the massive doors swing open, and d'Anthonay come striding out, gesticulating, evidently very angry.

When he saw me he was too excited to notice my salute, and he seized me by the arm and began to shout at me.

"Imagine, sir," said he; "they say this fortress can't be defended. I told them I'd teach 'em how to defend it. 'No,' said they, 'Louisbourg is doomed!' 'By God,' said I, 'then we're all damned, and might as well die fighting as whining!' "

"Colonel," said I, amazed, "is Drucour talking of surrender?"

"Oh, no," said the Commander of the Foreign Legion, "he is merely telling us that in his opinion Des Gouttes might just as well sail out of the harbour before Wolf blows him out at the muzzles of his 24's!"

"Yes," said I, "but what is the French Commodore and his great ships of the line doing all this time?"

"Ah," shouted the Colonel of the Foreign Regiment,

349

"he does nothing except to beg of our Governor permission to run for the open sea!

"If Des Gouttes is not a fool or a coward he will sail out and give battle to these English ships. Look at Vauquelin in his little *Aréthuse,* where he takes his frigate inshore and drives Wolf's gunners from every emplacement that might bother us! What we need are fewer Commodores and more Vauquelins; and I said so in council; but that God damned French Chef-d'escadron swallowed the insult whole!"

He went away fuming. I had to leave the ramparts presently, so heavy the bombardment was becoming— an unbroken thunder from the English guns.

I went to my lodgings to eat a crust and drink a glass of wine. People in the street were saying that the French ships were being hit.

The steady thunder of the bombardment shook the solid walls of the city but no shells fell inside the outer walls.

My landlady told me that the American battalion of artificers had taken the smallpox and that their Colonel and his son were both dead of it already, which was why the English had been so long investing the city and why the walls were not tumbling about our ears.

She laughed when she said it, seeming not at all concerned. In fact, the women of Louisbourg were gay and lighthearted and not at all afraid; and I saw them helping the troops everywhere, both on the walls and in the hospitals.

I learned, now, where the young Duchess of Boïens was. She and Madame de Drucour had organized the ladies of Louisbourg into committees to look after hospi-

tal work, to help the ammunition vaults, to care for the
homeless, to guard children, to encourage the soldiery,
to regulate rations, to install soup-kitchens—in fact, to
attend to everything that required attention in a be-
leaguered, bombarded, disturbed city which was becoming
a disconcerted city on the verge of distraction.

There was plenty to eat in Louisbourg. Famine did
not menace us. Neither hunger nor thirst were evils to
be dreaded; but, in the outer works beyond the city walls,
disease had begun to seize and decimate the battalions
facing the English sappers and miners and their gunners
in the new parallels.

British stubbornness refused to employ hurdles and
fascines for road-making, which caused an amazing delay
in operations. This I learned from our engineers, Poilly
particularly finding reason for amusement in the slow-
ness of the British advance.

Summer possessed Isle Royale and the city of Louisbourg now; and the weather, for the most part, was
fine when the first storm of shot and shell burst directly
upon the city.

There was no panic, only a terrible surprise as the first
shell fell in the courtyard of the Citadel and blew up.
Instantly another struck the ditch, plastering everything
with mud and slime.

I was on my way to call upon the Frères de la Charité,
to offer my services for any work within my power, and
was swinging along on my crutches toward the Hospital
gateway, when a big shell came screaming through the
sunset glory, pierced the slates, and exploded in the
crowded hospital.

A horrible silence followed; then I saw a Brother of the Hospital reel out of the door. His arm was torn off; blood was spouting like water jerked from a pump. The next moment he fell dead in the courtyard.

As I say, there was no panic, only a frightful surprise.

A nun appeared, all spattered with blood. Seeing me, she asked where the Governor of the City could be found. I offered to find him.

"If you please," said she, "say to our Governor that a shell has exploded and killed two Hospital Brothers and the Surgeon of the Foreign Regiment, and that the place is full of dead and wounded!"

As I went toward the Dauphin Gate where I knew Drucour was to be found, the heavy shells fell fast on the Hospital, the Château, and the barracks—in fact, it was perfectly evident that the English gunners afloat and ashore were aiming at the spires of the city.

The noise of the cannonade and the racket of exploding shells and of falling masonry in the city was terrific.

Dead soldiers were being fetched into the smoke-filled square and borne along the narrow ways; dead men, women, children lay in the streets, looking like filthy piles of clothing wet with blood, and all blown into strange, crippled shapes, lying in dismembered and atrocious attitudes. Dogs, horses, sheep, cattle, wounded or dead, filled the Place d'Armes where a battalion of the city volunteers was mustering.

I saw Madame de Drucour walking calmly among them, encouraging the frightened men who seemed stupefied by the first storm of shot and shell.

"Messieurs," said she, very coolly, "a besieged city must expect to be bombarded. It is part of this gallant

game of war at which brave men play. There is nothing
to discourage one in the situation. Therefore, be of
heart and courage, gentlemen, and, when you have formed
your ranks, march with confidence into the new southwest battery and serve the guns as faithfully as you
serve God."

Noticing me, she smiled as she returned my respectful
salute.

"There must be some mistake, Captain Cardress," said
she: "the English are shelling the Hospital. General
Amherst is a gallant man and can not know where his
shells are falling."

"Madame," said I, "the shells are bursting among the
helpless wounded, and I am on my way to notify Monsieur the Governor."

"I pray that you will do so," said she, cheerily. Then
this brave lady called to an Ensign of Cambis: "Monsieur! Would you be kind enough to take this battalion
of city volunteers to the new southwest battery? . . .
Thank you so much—"

A shell burst in the square; the dust and smoke hid
Madame de Drucour from sight. When it drifted clear
the battalion was in confusion and I saw her calmly
kneeling beside a screaming soldier who had been hit.
Nuns came from the hospital to help.

I went out across Rampart Street where I could see
how terribly the Island Battery had suffered. The roar
of the guns was now tremendous; shells swept over the
King's Bastion into the rue St. Louis where four or five
thousand terrified citizens, men, women, children, sick,
wounded, soldiers off duty, were huddled to take shelter
from the shrieking iron storm.

The naval barracks to the west of the rue de la Grave was a spouting heap of flame and black smoke; between the rue Royale and the rue Toulouse—where the latter crosses—many dead lay, and exploding shells tossed and blew them about the streets. Shells arriving, as I say, by way of the Bastion du Roi, were falling as far in the city as the rue de Condé and rue de Scutari, and even reached the convent. But I saw the French batteries at Black Cape flaming away and spouting shells and smoke as dauntlessly as though the Wolf were not already at the city's throat and biting deep.

I found Drucour, calm, polite, desolated to learn of the bloody business at the Hospital. He sent a staff officer with a flag to Amherst, and we stood on the battlements and watched him march forward with a drummer and his white rag on a lance-head. And presently he came back with a letter from Amherst, still damp from the pen, saying that, as there seemed to be no place in the city for women and children and sick and wounded, the Governor had better send his sick aboard a ship and anchor her out of danger in the upper harbour, and that the women and children might go to the Island Battery.

I saw Drucour frown as he read this. It was, of course, impossible, as the Island Battery was in ruins and afire.

He shook his head, shrugged, motioned the officer and drummer to retire. There was nothing to be done, then; the sick, wounded, dying; the women and children must remain in the city where two hundred shot and shell had already fallen on roofs and in the streets.

I began to feel very nervous concerning the young Duchess de Boïens who, wherever she was, must be quite alone, as Madame de Drucour was at the Governor's side and exposed to every hazard on the ramparts and in the shell-swept streets; and her kinsman, Major Follis, with the Chevalier, second in command, with a battalion of the Foreign Regiment, were intrenched along the flank of the Devil's Mountain and the Miré Road.

One evening, after the bombardment had ceased for the day, I came down into the street to go out by some gate and get a breath of fresh air if possible.

On my way I saw Lieutenant Colonel Marin, of the Regiment Bourgogne, who told me that he had been ordered to take his regiment out that night for a sortie, but that the men had been drinking very heavily and he did not know how it might turn out.

I went with him to the barracks where the Governor was; and about midnight the regiment, with unloaded muskets and fixed bayonets, left the city and advanced along the coast.

Afterward I learned what a horrid surprise was Amherst's when the French regulars came upon his men asleep; and I think, still, that it was a wretched bit of neglect on the part of the English; and that if the Regiment Bourgogne had not been drunk, almost to a man, the English army had been ruined that dark and foggy night in July when Lord Dundonald fell among his Grenadiers of Forbes's Regiment, so disgracefully surprised.

Well, the French infantry was too drunk to accomplish the ruin of the English army.

On the fifteenth, at night, the saucy *Aréthuse,* Vauquelin's frigate, slipped out past the lighthouse which saw and fired on her; and Hardy's cruisers chased her; but in vain.

Wolf had a mean streak in him and sneered at this brave man's brave attempt to carry news to France.

And now, day after day, it was plain to me that the garrison of Louisbourg was becoming weaker. The city was full of sick, dead, and wounded citizens and soldiers; shot and shell swept it all day and every day; the pig-faced Wolf, labouring incessantly, was slowly and surely encircling the harbour and city with a ring of batteries which belched fire and smoke and shell and shot all day and every day.

A vast and stinking fog of cannon smoke possessed the city, its environs, outer defenses, and the Marais. Through it filtered a sickly mist from the sea, stinking of fish.

In this, like a gigantic candle-flame, the sun burned redly.

On the 16th the French pickets at the Barachois Bridge were driven in. The ramparts opened fire in vain; the English seized and held the bridge, and intrenched themselves within a few hundred yards of the Dauphin Gate. I could see the British dead lying there, officers in scarlet coats and gold-laced hats, men in black spatterdashes and worn shoes.

All day and night a ceaseless blast from the cannon at the Port Dauphin swept the British lines; guns thundered from the French ships, from *The Cavalier* on the spur beyond the Dauphin Gate. The discharges of the British

cannon rocked the city; big shells rained on the Queen's
Bastion and on the Citadel.

I could see red-coat soldiers falling when a rush of
British infantry attempted the outer works on the Marais.
A colony officer beside me, watching them serve the great
siege guns on the demi-bastion, told me that forty of the
Regiment Artois had fallen since the beginning of this
business, sixty of Bourgogne, and a hundred or more of
the Foreign Regiment and Colony troops.

A steady pounding from the Barachois continued where
Wolf's sixteen guns and two mortars flashed redly and
their iron shot and shell beat upon the walls curtaining the
Queen's Bastion, detaching huge masses of masonry and
stone which fell crashing into the moat below. I saw a
great section of crenellated barbette slowly part company with the curtain on the south side of the Citadel
and fall outward with all the inflexible grandeur of a giant
tree.

I recollect, one day, hearing an officer of Cambis cursing the French ships because their grape shot were falling
among his own regiment, so bad was the aim.

As he went off, still cursing, the racket of the drums
of the Regiment Etranger filled the esplanade, and I saw
the Chevalier Johnstone at the head of a battalion, marching out of the City Gate into a very hell of musketry.

Everywhere in the smoky, shell-swept streets of the city
the people were cheering the Foreign Regiment.

From the Cavalier overhead I could see these troops
attempting to carry an English trench. A few of them
did seize an outpost, but the others were hurled back into
Louisbourg.

The bombardment was always heaviest between the

hours of eleven in the morning and two in the afternoon, when it was concentrated on the Citadel.

On the 21st of July a sortie of two thousand regulars, colony troops, volunteers, and Indians was planned; and the stupid French Commodore ordered the *Bienfaisant* to open fire.

The town militia under Daccarette who had been scouting as far as the Miré River with Acadian irregulars and Indians, came back ingloriously, having caught and scalped only one or two English sailors and set fire to a few hogsheads of tobacco of which the French privateers had taken enough to make a breastwork against Wolf's riflemen in No. 2 Battery.

This No. 2 Battery, firing over the silent and disgraced Battery Royal, annoyed the stupid Commodore's ships.

They were ranged on spring cables along the Barachois in this order: nearest to shore the *Bienfaisant;* next, to the south'ard, the *Prudent;* next the *Entreprenant;* then the *Célèbre;* and last, just northwest of the battery on Rochefort Point, the *Capricieux.*

These splendid French warships were being peppered from Wolf's batteries at Lighthouse Point, and the No. 2 Redoubt erected June 21st; as well as by American riflemen at Careening Point.

Hogsheads of American tobacco were used to protect the ice house and lime kilns outside the eastern walls, and were manned by French coureurs-du-bois—as good riflemen as came from New York, and better than the New Englanders.

The splendid French ships fired continually upon Wolf's redoubts—the *Célèbre* alone hurling 3,500 shot. Then that ass of a French Commodore sent his battalion of sailors ashore, leaving but scant crews aboard the great ships.

There was no sortie on the 21st. De Gouttes refused.

That afternoon, about two o'clock, standing on the demi-bastion, I saw a shot strike the *Célèbre,* which exploded some of her ammunition. The flames leaped to her mizzen. Sparks flew in torrents, lodging aboard the nearest ship, the *Entreprenant,* which caught aft and very soon was a raging furnace in spite of the desperate efforts of her crew.

The walls of the city became jammed with soldiers and citizens, horrified to behold their fleet afire.

In fifteen minutes this magnificent ship was ablaze from stem to stern and had set fire to the *Capricieux.*

It was becoming a scene of horror; the cannonading was deafening; smoke and flame filled the harbour and blew into the city, choking everybody with hot smoke.

I saw the *Prudent,* which was to windward, slip her cables and beat out toward blue water. The blazing *Bienfaisant,* swinging on her cable, saved herself.

All Wolf's batteries now concentrated upon the burning ships and the boats plying between them and the city, and the spectacle became shocking.

The horror of the scene was accentuated by a column of smoke from the English hospital, set afire by accident, where the British wounded were burning to death. Also, a ghastly sight was afforded by the shotted guns of the burning French battleships which, becoming red-hot, began to explode, hurling shot into other ships and into Louisbourg.

All night long the great ships blazed, drifting in to the Barachois shore where they stranded and lay all caved in, still afire, their guns and cartridges still bursting at intervals in the white-hot ruins of their hulls.

I saw the brave and gentle wife of the Governor on the ramparts. She told me very quietly that the sortie had been abandoned.

"I am sorry," she said, "that our navy seems to have become discouraged; but, believe me, Monsieur Cardress, there is not the slightest thought of surrender in the hearts of the Governor and his wife."

I took off my hat to her in a profound salute.

"Madame," said I, "it is the batteries of Monsieur Wolf that are doing the serious damage, I believe."

"Yes, sir—he has three great batteries of 32 and 24 pounders, and three other smaller batteries. The 13 inch and 8 inch mortars send the most frightful projectiles into our city. Then all these, with the coehorns and royals, and the musketry and rifle fire, have made havoc with our soldiery. But I am worried only about one matter."

"What is that, Madame?"

"Major Follis and the Chevalier cause me deep anxiety. If, by any chance, they are taken prisoner, how will it go with them? Because, sir, the German King of England is a mean man, and very barbarously inclined toward ex-rebels."

"Madame," said I, "it would be a foul business if these gentlemen should ever die at Tyburn. I did not, until recently, realize how foul a matter it would be if any such evil happened to these very gallant Scottish gentlemen merely because they fought as rebels at Culloden against the Crown of England.

"Now, Madame, I also have concluded that this dumpy little King of England is a more disgusting savage than any in North America. And, I hope and trust that Major Follis and the Chevalier will escape in case matters go very wrong in Louisbourg."

"Sir," said she dauntlessly, "there is, then, as you see, an added reason for us to defend this fortress-city. Because I do not believe that these Scottish gentlemen could get away if Louisbourg is carried by assault, or if it capitulates at the last moment before sinking into fiery ruin."

I kissed this charming woman's hand in the whirling smoke and by the red light of the battle-lanterns on the ramparts.

She moved away as lightly and gracefully as a young girl; and I saw her laughingly accept a linstock from a gunner under the magpie's nest and, one after another, fire the three guns in battery there, just to encourage the artillerymen, who cheered her as she laughed and hastened on through the flowing sparks and smoke.

"Yes," said I to myself, staring after her, "I'll be damned if I play hangman's dog to Pitt or to this mis-begotten Hanover King, and go a-sniffing at the heels of these gallant gentlemen to track them to their deaths."

That terrible night all Louisbourg was as bright as day under the prodigious blaze from the burning ships. One could see very plainly their high, castellated sterns with their gilded and painted galleries set with windows, and the carved taffrails afire on poop and quarter-deck.

Such superb, tall ships! It was sad.

But worse was at hand; for the storm of shot, shell, and flame that had blown into Louisbourg day after day now became a frightful tempest, increasing as the hours of the night wore on to a horrible, howling, hell-born hurricane.

At seven o'clock in the morning a huge shell exploded in the barracks north of the belfry which barred, on the town side, the parade ground of the Citadel. This now took fire.

Soldiers from the Regiment Cambis, ships' carpenters, and other workmen ran to put it out, carrying ladders and buckets; but very soon the Citadel was all on fire; and the English, seeing the smoke, turned all their nearer batteries upon it.

I seized my crutch and hobbled down stairs. The street was in an uproar. A woman began to scream and sob, saying that the wounded in the casemates would be burned to death.

I went to the Citadel where, in the casemates, were shut in the ladies of the garrison as well as many other women, and a number of wounded soldiers, waited on by Récollete Nuns.

Here were hogsheads of tobacco and flimsy wooden barricades; and it was certain that if the fire reached this barrier the wind would blow the smoke and flames into the casemates and stifle everybody.

As I reached the parade, many women, and a vast company of little children, ran out of the burning Citadel and, being terrified and bewildered, wandered about in the bombardment where great shells were exploding all over the parade and fortifications.

I saw monks, nuns, and soldiers bringing out wounded officers on stretchers.

The entire city, now, seemed to be wrapped in smoke

and flame. Three times the Queen's Bastion caught fire, and three times the flames were extinguished.

Shells charged with Greek fire began to fall in the city. The crash of musketry from the trenches and the covered way, the abominable noise of the bombardment never ceased.

CHAPTER XXIX

THE DUCHESS WEEPS

ALL night and all the next day the thick smoke in the streets made it seem like a lurid pit where frantic shadows rushed about amid the tremendous diapason of the guns.

The barracks, now entirely afire, burned and burned and vomited a horrible greenish smoke. Soldiers of the engineers were pulling down wooden huts to prevent the spread of the flames in the city.

On the 24th there was no abatement; the city fairly rocked in the smoke under the roar and thunder and earth-shaking shocks of the cannon. The Dauphin Gate was a wreck; the French gunners were driven from the Citadel. It was plain to me that the English artillery had been ordered to ruin the city first and make a breach later; for the terrible fire swept this way and that like the wind-blown spray of waves, and everywhere and in every square and street and plaza and place the great 13 inch English shells were bursting in a glare of scarlet that rained hot metal over everything.

It made me bitterly ashamed to observe that the English artillery fire now was concentrated once more on the Hospital and neighbouring houses where the helpless wounded lay. It was a damned outrage and put me in a fury to think that Wolf planned this—this pig-faced man who had spoken of the Americans so insultingly!

Great pieces of the walls of Louisbourg were falling

into the ditch and moat; there was not a house in the city undamaged; only five heavy guns were now replying to the English fire; but two riddled battleships still fired on Wolf's batteries from the harbour.

That thick, flame-shot night the English fire-ship *Etna,* under Captain Balfour, and the *Hunter,* Captain Laforey, led a line of armed barges, pinnaces, and ships' boats from Sir Charles Hardy's station, and from Gabarus, into the harbour; and there they fell upon the two doomed French warships, carried them by the board, and set one of them afire and towed the other to the head of the harbour where she lay helpless in the mud under the British guns.

The cannon firing from the city walls awoke me in my bed. I dressed, took my crutch and limped down stairs where a frenzied throng was shouting that the English were storming the city and were bayoneting women and children.

I managed to quiet this panic; and while I was doing so I saw Major Follis ride up. When he noticed me and what I was about he came toward me and offered me a cold salute which I returned.

"Sir," said he, "you had better send these poor people into the casemates or there is like to be a slaughter of the innocents in these streets which will make the Herod affair seem as nothing."

"Sir," said I to him, as soon as the crowd began to run toward the Citadel, "may I have a word with you?"

He got off his horse and walked up to where I stood leaning on my crutch.

"Major Follis," said I, "whatever we think of each other we can scarcely doubt each other's courage."

"No," said he, "I don't doubt yours."

"Nor I yours. And I do not care to see a brave gentleman made the victim of a common, vulgar and mean fellow, who chances to be a King."

"What do you mean?" said he, astonished.

So I told him very plainly that Pitt and German George had marked him and the Chevalier for a disgraceful death; and that I had this on the best possible authority which nobody ought to doubt.

"Major," said I, "these walls are about to fall. You know it, sir, as well as I do. Let me beg of you, and of the Chevalier, to go before Louisbourg is carried by assault."

"Sir," said he, "this is a very strange thing for a gentleman who is my enemy to say to me."

"Well," said I violently, "may God damn me if I do you a harm to please Mr. Pitt or George II!"

"You are a strange enemy," he repeated.

"Enemy or not," said I, "the part played by the King of England disgusts me, and I'm cursed if I remain silent while a brave man goes—and all unknowingly—to a felon's death at Tyburn, merely because he once faced the English fury at Culloden!"

Charles Follis took off his gold-bound military hat to me.

"Captain Cardress," said he, "the Chevalier and I are under obligation to you. I do not know exactly how to thank you except to say, for God's sake hurry and get well, sir, so that you and I may exchange a few more shots to satisfy honour. . . . For, sir, I render you the homage of a man who loves honour as much as you do, and who is very certain that he could make you no pleasanter thanks than to offer to satisfy the honour of so gallant a gentleman as is Captain Cardress!"

We bowed to each other in the lurid flare of all that hellish tumult. I remember a shot hit a chimney in the rue Royale and sent the bricks in every direction.

"God go with you, Charles Follis of Loch Whinnloch!" said I in a loud voice. "I wish you well and a safe escape!"

"May God preserve you, John Cardress of Loch Cardress," said he gravely.

"Get you gone, sir," I repeated, smilingly; "and may German George hang in his own slip noose!"

"Amen, sir," said Charles Follis, "and I wish to God you were of rank to mate with the young Duchess of Boïens, John Cardress, for if you were you should have her!"

"My rank suits me in America," said I coldly. "Let the Duchess of Boïens see to it that *her* rank doesn't leave her the guest of Jane Fish for life!"

"By heaven," said he, "that is a miserable matter, too. I can't go into France as fiancé of the Duchess of Boïens. If I do the King will chase me over the frontier. And I can't go to England. If I do they'll hang me. As for this marrying—"

He gave me an embarrassed look and I saw him scowl in the dull light of the battle lamps.

"John Cardress," said he, "why are you not my equal in station?"

"In my own pride," said I, "we are equals. I care not a tinker's slut what the Whinnlochs think about it, but to be a Cardress at all is better than any other in all Scotland, as far as I'm concerned."

"Hell's goblins!" said he, taking offense, "ye'll not expect a Follis to agree to that, then!"

"What do I care whether a Follis agrees with it?" said I. "Or an Annandale, either!"

"By heaven," said he, "you shall eat that!" He pulled his claymore free, and I tried to get out my officer's sword, but, being on the left side, my crutch was in the way and I caught my sword on it and stumbled and fell on one knee.

The next instant Charles Follis was lifting me tenderly to my feet and steadying me with one arm around me.

"The devil's in us," said he, "who ought to love each other but are ever reaching for dagger, sword, and pistol. And the arrow-wound scarce healed in my hand!" He held it aloft to display the red scar; then he laid one arm around my shoulder.

"John Cardress," said he, "I can't marry my cousin of Boïens. There are two Kings to reckon with and a poisonous snake of a woman. And Pitt!"

"My God, sir," said I, "does the lady know your sentiments and mind?"

"No, sir. But I shall tell her my mind—though not my sentiments—for, God help me, sir, I'm in love with a Canadienne of Quebec, and that's the terrible truth, John Cardress; and if Canada falls to England I'll have to run for the Spanish Grants. So I might as well marry my Canadienne and be done with all worry and ambition,— and to hell with a title that never yet has brought either happiness or riches to any laird o' Whinnloch!"

"What will Annandale—I mean the Chevalier Johnstone—say to that?" I asked, scarcely believing my ears.

368

"I don't care what he says. And if he doesn't leave the city and save his head he'll not be able to say anything—"

He moved aside as the French midshipmen and bluejackets who had escaped from the burning ships came marching out of the marine barracks.

When they had passed: "There, sir," said I, "goes the last dying flicker of French sea-power in North America! Major Follis, the city will fall tomorrow. I beg you will notify the Chevalier and take proper measures to save yourselves—and old England from staining herself with your murder."

"Good-bye, Cardress!" said he earnestly, and took me by both hands.

"Where," said I, "is the Duchess de Boïens?"

"She has been very ill of fever in the Citadel casemates, sir. Better—indeed, nearly convalescent now. Had the Citadel burned completely she must have perished among all the others."

"Was *she* in that perilous place!"

"Yes, Captain. Will you come with me while I make my mind known to her?"

He lent me his arm and I hobbled swiftly along beside him.

On the way, near the Princess Bastion, we encountered a strange scene of revolt in the Regiment Cambis where their Colonel and d'Anthonay and Du Vivier were talking in loud, excited voices and the soldiers were shouting: "We are betrayed! The Marines have betrayed Louisbourg! Pitt pays Des Gouttes to abandon us!"

And we could see them in their barrack square, weeping with rage and breaking their muskets and burning their colours in a big bonfire made of benches, shutters and doors.

At the Brouillan Bastion a vast crowd of people had gathered, shouting for the Governor and demanding to know whether it was true that he had sent a flag to the English asking the best terms.

Officers on horseback kept waving their arms frantically and shouting: "No! No! No! The city is not to be surrendered! Go home to your houses and go to bed!"

I saw and recognized the unpopular Prévost lurking near the Palace, in conversation with Loppinot.

Charles Follis called across to them inquiring for the best news from Gabarus. Neither of them answered him.

"Yes," said he to me, "you are quite right, John Cardress; it is high time that Johnstone and I 'took the key to the fields'!"

"I think so. Do you want a guide to the Miré?"

"Who?"

"Santu. . . . That same Indian girl who drove an arrow through your hand, sir."

"Would she take Johnstone and me?"

"Safely, Major."

"Where is she?"

I drew him down toward the water front where was the Convent and Chapel of the Récollettes and some houses belonging to the civil staff. Here, near the lot which belonged to De Beaucours, was a fire; and near it, between the rue d'Estrées and the rue de l'Hôpital, behind Verrier's house, and close to the Dauphin Bastion where the house of the Admiralty Procureur had been demolished, was an Indian lodge.

"Santu!" I called loudly.

"I am here," came her voice, fresh from slumberland, and as sweet and gay as a bird's.

"Santu, look upon my friend, Major Follis," said I when she came out of the lodge, slim, lovely, and quite naked save for the two belts.

The girl laughed when she saw Charles Follis and heard me speak of him as my friend. And, thinking of the arrow she had shot into his right hand, she laughed again.

"Santu," said I, "Major Follis and the Chevalier Johnstone do not desire to be taken by the English when this city surrenders."

"Oh," cried the girl, "is Louisbourg going to surrender?"

"Probably tomorrow," said I. "So I wish that you would take this Scottish gentleman and his friend, the Chevalier, into Canada to the outposts of Montcalm, where they will be safe. Take White Bird, also. Is it understood?"

The girl looked demurely at Charles Follis. He was good to look upon.

"Very well, my Captain," said Santu, calmly, "but is this a wise thing you do?"

"Wise?"

"Yes, wise! Because, my white gyr-falcon, this Scottish Major is even prettier than you of whom I am very fond. And, maybe, I might become fonder of my new Major than of my beloved witch-captain John!"

She reached into the hut, coolly drew a doe-skin hunting shirt over her naked body, then she came up close to Major Follis.

"Trust a Souriquois girl to break your heart," said she, laughing, and taking him by the hand.

I said to her: "Find the Chevalier; leave the city at once; and start from the Miré as soon as the first gun is fired from the English trenches in the morning."

She nodded absently, much preoccupied with the charms of Charles Follis who seemed a little embarrassed.

"You'd better stay here," said I. "I will take your message to the Duchess de Boïens."

"Well," said he, "you know what to tell her, John Cardress."

"What you told me?"

"You might as well," said he, smiling slightly at Santu.

Neither noticed it when I left.

There was a vast quantity of thick smoke and fog in the streets of the city when at last I came to the casemates and saw the Récollette Nuns moving about in the courtyard.

The city was very quiet; a strange silence possessed land and sea. Overhead a few stars looked down through a thin mist. Night birds twittered from the marais; and the churn and clash of the tide echoed along the rocky, mist-bound coast.

I said to a Récollette Nun: "Sister, where is the Duchesse de Boïens? For I must see her instantly."

"In bed, pardie," said she, surprised. "Is the matter urgent, sir?"

"Very. Is Madame la Duchesse convalescent?"

"Oh, yes, sir."

"She walks about?"

"Well, no, sir. She sits in a chair and listens to the cannonade. We all were nearly burned to death the other day."

"Yes, I know it, Sister. . . . Go you in and awake Madame la Duchesse, and say that Captain Cardress comes with a message from Major Charles Follis."

The young Récollette looked searchingly at me: "Sir, is the situation desperate in Louisbourg?" she asked quietly.

"Sister, the Regiment Cambis cries treason, and are burning their colours."

"Oh, Holy Mother, then it is ended!"

"It is ending, Sister—"

A terrible explosion shook the casemates. It was the first gun from the English trenches in the dark o' dawn.

The Récollette went away and presently returned to conduct me into the casemates where, seated upon a chair, I encountered the dark eyes of her I had learned to love better than anything in all the world.

"John Cardress," said she, "you abandoned me very shamefully."

I went to kiss her thin hand which closed nervously on mine.

"Have you been very ill, Sandi?" I asked.

"No, darling."

"The nuns say so."

"Oh, I have been a little feverish and flighty. . . . What of you, darling?"

"Quite recovered."

She glanced derisively at my crutch, then, leaning her pale cheek against my shoulder: "How is it that you and Charles Follis have become reconciled?"

Very briefly I told her, waiting at times until the increasing thunder of the bombardment slackened sufficiently for her to hear my voice.

She leaned her head closer, resting one little ear nearly against my lips.

"Drucour," said I, "can not hold out another day. Charles Follis and the Chevalier have gone with Souriquois guides into Canada."

She looked at me intently.

"Well," said she, "what else did this man, to whom I am to be affianced, tell you?"

So I told her, gently, to spare her pride. But I knew she was not in love with him.

"Oh," said she coolly, "so this lax, colonial life has made of Charles Follis another example of degenerate nobility!"

"If you call it degenerate, I am, also."

"I suppose you'd like to have me, also, sufficiently degenerate to overlook my pride and my rank, and become a frontier Duchess on the Mohawk—like that Gordon Duchess who married Staats Morris. . . . Would you, John? . . . Well, I *won't!*"

I said nothing.

About sunrise a most frightful bombardment opened, deluging the city with fire.

I sat beside Sandi, her frail hand of a convalescent in mine, my crutch across my knees, ready for instant action in case I was called on to help Sandi escape from a hospital on fire.

From time to time a nun came calmly into the casemates to report what was happening in the city.

"Louisbourg is in extremities," she said. "Our Governor has sent Loppinot to the English General with a flag."

374

Another time, amid a terrible din of exploding shells:
"The English demand that we surrender at discretion.
Our Governor, horrified at such harsh terms, has sent
d'Anthonay to say that Louisbourg prefers to submit to
assault rather than surrender upon such terms."

A little later she came again:

"Prévost has had his way," said the pale, calm nun;
"Louisbourg surrenders."

Sandi rested her pallid cheek against my shoulder.
Her tears fell slowly.

The cannonade had ceased.

I left her about dusk and went out for news. Vast
crowds, silent, frightened, roamed the ruined streets
where torches burned.

The Regiment Cambis had renewed their rioting but
stuck to their own parade. Workmen by lantern light
were repairing the Dauphin Gate through which the
British were to enter. Its vaulted roof echoed with their
hammer blows.

I saw d'Anthonay. He told me in confidence that the
English had meant to seize and execute Charles Follis
and the Chevalier Johnstone, but that both had escaped
from the city and were now safe.

I pretended surprise.

I had a bowl of broth, a bit of bread, and a glass of
wine in my lodgings.

After dark I went to the casemate hospital. Sandi
lay deep in her chair, her dark eyes gazing on me intently
as I advanced and kissed her hand.

I told her how sorry I was for Drucour and his brave
lady. High minded, generous, fair, these two had most
nobly defended the city with what they had of men, which

was not nearly enough even if the navy had done its duty.

The silence in the city after those weeks of bombardment made us very nervous; and I could feel Sandi's slim hand clench and unclench inside mine.

She slept some. So did I.

About sunrise a tremendous outburst of British fifes and drums awoke us. Sandi rose and, leaning on me and I leaning on my crutch, we made our way to the embrasure.

The British Grenadiers from three regiments were marching into the city by the Dauphin Gate with a tremendous drumming and fifing and clash of brazen cymbals.

We stood a moment, watching the end of France in the Western World which was to become English for all time.

Then the little Duchess laid her face in her hands and wept bitterly.

I led her back to her chair. I drew her fingers from her wet cheeks and kissed her mouth.

"Darling," she said, "I might as well go with you and become a Mohawk River Duchess. There is no place in Scotland for me; none in England; and only Jane Fish and a prison cell in France."

"Yes, dearest," said I, "a hundred thousand acres on the Mohawk or along the Sacandaga, and a warm welcome and a glass of wine at Sir William Johnson's is better than a lettre-de-cachet and Jane Fish and the Bastille. Isn't it?"

"Yes, John Cardress," said the loveliest and wisest woman in the world—my future wife.

THE DUCHESS WEEPS

Rub-a-dub-dub! Bang! Clang!

The British Grenadiers were striding up the shattered street which echoed to their brazen music and the rippling roar of horses' hoof and heavy boots.

"Oh-h, darling—"

The Duchess of Sacandaga wept upon my shoulder.

Pig-face did it all. After all is said and done, pig-face is a great soldier if not a great man. And a soldier is what England needed—what—your pardon, gentlemen!—the *World* needed—in that terrible month of July, 1758.

England got North America; the World got Freedom!

As for me, I got my Duchess of Sacandaga. For whom I still thank God.

Amen.

(2)

THE END

BOOKS BY ROBERT W. CHAMBERS

THE PAINTED MINX

A gay historical romance concerning the New York of Revolutionary days and presenting the bewitching actress, Marie Guest, as heroine. $2.50.

THE HAPPY PARROT

A gallant tale of pirate ships, slave-runners, a fair heroine, and a valiant hero, set against a historical background of authenticity and bright color. $2.50.

THE ROGUE'S MOON

A stunning tale of piracy written with all the dash and scarlet color of the period. Its pages are made vivid by picturesque personalities, are alive with great sea fights and are softened by a charming love story. $2.00.

THE SUN HAWK

With the pomp and majesty of great romance is unrolled this tale of Count Frontenac, the heroic pioneers of New France and the love of a valiant young Englishman for a French noblewoman. $2.00.

THE DRUMS OF AULONE

From the gay court of Louis, the Fourteenth, "the Sun King of France," to the mighty wilderness of the New World moves this romance that is a vivid recreation of one of the most illustrious periods of history. $2.00.

THE MAN THEY HANGED

A historical romance in which Captain Kidd is shown, as proved by authentic documents, never to have been a pirate. $2.50.

D. APPLETON AND COMPANY

NEW YORK   LONDON